SPIRIT HOUSE

MARK DAPIN

Atlantic Books
London

First published in Australia in 2011 by Pan Macmillan Australia.

First published in Great Britain in 2013 by Tuskar Rock Press,
an imprint of Atlantic Books Ltd.

This paperback edition published in Great Britain in 2014
by Atlantic Books.

10 9 8 7 6 5 4 3 2 1

A CIP catalogue record for this book is available from the British Library.

Paperback ISBN: 978 1 78239 088 6
EBook ISBN: 978 1 78239 110 4

Printed in Great Britain by CPI Group (UK) Ltd, Croydon, CR0 4YY

Atlantic Books
An imprint of Atlantic Books Ltd
Ormond House
26–27 Boswell Street
London
WC1N 3JZ

www.atlantic-books.co.uk

To Jimmy and Frida Benjamin
ava ashalom

SIAM DIARY

MAY 1944

There are ways of escape without tunnels or disguises, boatmen or barges, partisans or guns. On torpid afternoons, when the work is slow and futile, and our guards lie in the webbed shade of trees – sleeping children with flat mustard faces, rifles propped against their thighs like toys in the nursery – the spirits of the heat haze dance in puddles in the air, beckoning me up the hill.

They only sing when the path is safe and I can pad past the Koreans into the jungle, grappling the vines and arching through the undergrowth, my soles and toes hardened to jagged rocks and thorns. I keep my own private name for the mountain – I hide a secret word for everything – and the various stages where I rest on my way to the peak. I have lost the energy of the days before the war. This squat hill is my Everest, but also my Olympus. I never understood Norman Lindsay back home in Sydney, among the paperbarks and gums. To me, he was a pornographer and worse. But here I can almost see the country through his heathen eyes. There are souls in the soil, older than man, and they spell out the names of God in the petals of hibiscus and the shadows of the sun.

Beneath the brow of the cliff face is the mouth of a cave. Its palate is cool and dry, watched over by a painted idol carved from hardwood. I visit the Buddha to remind myself that man can put his imagination to some other purpose than war. Beyond the lips of the cave, and behind its gums, sits a craftsman's shrine, a timber house on legs of knotted bamboo. Its roof follows the curves of the temples we saw from the rice trains that carried us from Singapore. Inside the shrine sits a tiny altar planted with incense and decked with gifts to placate the spirits of the cave. There are no Siamese in the camp, and the peasants in the native village are starving, but somebody climbs here before dawn each day to freshen the offerings, to leave the ghosts a segment of jackfruit, the stub of a coarse cigarette, a thimble of green tea. And although my stomach, a beehive, begs for food, and my bamboo fingers tremble for tobacco, I never disturb the setting because the cave is my escape. When I'm here with the Buddha, I'm no longer in jail. It is the only time I think of women.

The first girl I bedded had fallen fair hair, like the model for Lindsay's *Desire*, and her breath tasted of hot milk. She grasped my hand tightly, crushed it against her own magpie bones. I loved her for her generosity, her carelessness. The others I remember for their grace or their carriage, their breasts or their drinking, their laughter or their thighs.

I recall old schoolfriends, and the kind of love I once felt for boys with downy lips and crackling voices, young muscles tautened by sport, strong wills hardened by the strap. And I wonder how many of them are dead.

This afternoon there was no *gunso* to supervise the Korean guards. He left at lunch, when we had thirty minutes crouched like coolies to eat half a pint of rice. His men were at first wary, then they began to relax. They like to sleep, to dream of their grandfathers' fields, of bull carts and oxen and a good year's harvest. They don't care if we never build anything in this jungle.

It doesn't matter to them who wins the war, as long as they get back to the farmyard shacks where they were born, to torture their pigs and behead their chickens and beat their wives like dogs and mount their dogs like women.

I heard the call of the spirits – one day, when I get back to my studio, I'd like to paint their song – and they led me in safety past the brutish swain, through the garden of bush graves and up the pathway to my cave. I knelt before the Buddha in his garland of flowering jasmine, and prostrated myself like a Mohammedan then crossed my legs, peered up past his rounded chin and gazed on his nigger smile.

The mountains crumbled, the jungle canopy collapsed, Siam slipped back into the sea and the Japs and Koreans drowned screaming, and all that was left were we prisoners – free men now – floating on the Horae's clouds, watching whirlpools suck away the land.

Pagan legend holds that the Buddha lived for weeks without food or sleep. I have seen statues of the fasting Bodhisattva: his knees, like mine, the heads of hammers, his ribs a corset of chopsticks. I could look at my body and see only abrasions, wounds and scars, but I contemplated instead the grandeur in the contours of our cave, the arabesques cut by oceans into the walls. I breathed low and deep, bloating my lungs with air to slow my pulse, closed my eyes and melted away.

I felt filled with God. His glow was inside me and radiating like sunshine from my tortured skin. I walked lightly, unburdened, down the track back to the worksite. I stood for a moment on a lower ridge, saw butterflies quake in the air, a sky by Botticelli, a sun by Turner, a heaven by Fra Angelico. I looked down on the Koreans and felt a kind of love for them because they, like everything else, were a part of this perfect world. I saw the *gunso* – the one they called 'Lucy', for Lucifer – parading up from the camp, followed by two uniformed men and another in rags, walking taller than the rest. The big man was joking with the soldiers; I could tell by the loose, friendly way he moved. He seemed relaxed, untroubled, a sportsman out for his afternoon stroll. I imagined him exercising a greyhound, whistling a popular song.

When the men laying the foundations noticed the *gunso*, they began lifting rocks that need not have been moved and carrying them to places where they would serve no purpose. The Koreans barked and growled. The brute with the drooping eye, the closest man to a beast, lashed out with his cane and felled a blameless prisoner with a blow to the spine. The enemy have a theory that the way to make a man work harder is to beat him until he can work no longer.

I crouched behind a bush, close enough to hear the Japs. My command of Japanese is limited – it is limited to commands – but I understood when the *gunso* called for volunteers, and the Korean beast stepped forward with two of his attendants, and then other damned souls abandoned their sentry duties to whisper and plot and slap their bamboo canes against their palms.

The tall man stood apart from it all and smiled. I saw his hands were tied behind his back. Another Australian approached him and tried to pass over a gift from the world of the living, but a Korean batted him aside. I did not know it was supposed to happen now. They never told me it would be today.

The *gunso* motioned the tall man to his knees, and the tall man laughed and shook his head. He would not bow, he would not kneel. They would have to take his legs from under him. I started to pray.

The *gunso* marched behind the tall man and kicked him with his split-toed boot in the back of the knee. The prisoner buckled but held. The *gunso* struck him again, and the tall man grunted, only grunted, then dropped. Now his head was level with the weapons of his guards. His eyes were aligned with their canes. His lips were moving furiously. I wondered if he, too, were praying, then I understood he was swearing.

He was cursing them, shaming them, goading them.

The *gunso* beat him first, smashing him across the back of the neck, then Lucy stepped back and kicked him in the face, a drop punt, aimed to meet the head as it came down.

There was only one victim, so each executioner had to take his turn. The valley was silent but for the sounds of the beating, deliberate and ordered, like the labour of a team on the hammer and tap, lining up to drive in the stakes. The tall man shook and sometimes jerked. He shied from blows when he saw them coming, tried to roll with kicks when he could, but he would not call out. Blood oozed from his mouth, from his ears, from his eyes. His body went into spasms, as if he were possessed. His movements, even bound, became unpredictable, and they had to hold him to hit him. One man grabbed his hair to pull him back and part of the scalp came away in his hand. The Koreans laughed, because they had never before seen a piece of skin and hair peel from a head. The others wanted to tear him too, so they could boast around their campfire, tell the story about how they had each played their part. But the *gunso* thought this a distraction. He screamed they should knock out the tall man's teeth, leave them scattered like pebbles.

The *gunso* commanded the prisoners to watch, and they did, at first, with courage and strength, but they began to feel complicit, as if their witness implied consent, and one by one they turned their backs. The *gunso* yelled at them to face the punishment squad, but instead they stared up at the trees, away into the hills, through the clouds in the sky, searching for a way of escape without compasses or scythes, hideouts or bribes, or longtail boats navigated by night.

BONDI

WEDNESDAY 18 APRIL 1990

A glass bead curtain hung like frozen rainfall from the front door of my grandmother's house in Bondi. I sat on the doorstep in the cold sunshine, waiting for Jimmy to stumble back from the RSL, watching the *frummers* hurry to the yeshiva and Maori women glide by with bags of pork bones and potatoes.

Grandma called me into the kitchen and told me about the Christmas Day in 1949 when Jimmy had not come home from the Club. The house was dark because my grandparents didn't like to use electricity. Their mantelpiece and sideboard were crowded with Kiddush cups and candlesticks, and photographs of children and grandchildren, birthdays and weddings. I felt like I belonged here, in the weatherboard cottage where Mum and her three sisters had grown up after the war, when men wore suits and hats and the world was black and white.

Grandma peeled potatoes over the big iron sink. The chicken for tomorrow's baked dinner floated in a bucket of saltwater, to draw out the blood. Grandma was small and round with a flattened nose. She had dark and beautiful eyes that peered at me through spectacles smeared with grease.

'Your mother phoned this morning,' she said. 'She wants you to stay the whole week.'

I shrugged.

'She told me to give you five dollars,' said Grandma, 'from her.'

My eyes followed the patterns on the lino.

'Five dollars is five dollars,' said Grandma. 'It's nothing to be sneezed at.'

'I'm not sneezing,' I told her.

I was crying.

Day after day, Mum chose the Dark Man over me.

The glass beads jingled as Jimmy tumbled into the living room, flooding the house with the smells of beer and smoke. He wore a cream shirt and white shorts, and a white cap to keep off the sun. He smiled false teeth at me, and banged his knee into the sideboard. Photographs of my aunties' weddings shuddered.

'Well,' said Grandma, 'look what the Club threw out.'

Jimmy danced across the room and into the kitchen, took her in his arms and pushed his purple nose into her ear.

'Daisy, Daisy,' sang Jimmy, 'give me your answer, do . . .'

He waltzed over the lino, with Grandma hanging from his arm like a dishcloth.

'Let me go,' she said. 'I'll burn your dinner.'

Jimmy was hungry. He rubbed his belly.

'Have we got any challah?' he asked.

'Have you got any eyes?' asked Grandma. 'Look for yourself.'

He stumbled around, opening boxes, lids and cupboard doors.

'Why is there matzo in the bread bin,' asked Jimmy, 'but no bread?'

'Why is there hair in your ears,' snapped Grandma, 'but none on your head?'

Jimmy lifted his cap and patted his scalp.

'There's younger men than me with a damn sight less hair,' he said.

'And a damn sight more brains,' said Grandma.

'Pesach is out,' said Jimmy. 'We can have *chametz* in the house again.'

Grandma showed him her sharp yellow teeth.

'I bought a challah from Stark's,' she said. 'Last night, you buried it in the yard, like a dog hides his bone.'

Jimmy hunched his shoulders and withdrew to his armchair in the living room. Jimmy had been a cabinet maker at work and an infantryman in the war. He did not know what to do with his retirement. He studied the newspaper, read history, drank beer for lunch and dinner, and buried things in holes in the yard. He had always worked with wood and had begun to look like a tree, with deep lines and twisted branches, and a feeling of age and sadness. I could see now that he wouldn't always be here, smiling and swearing and banging on machinery with the side of his fist.

I'd always called him 'Jimmy'. He hated rank, and any title – even 'grandad' – reminded him of captains and kings.

He picked up the *Daily Telegraph* and folded it open at the racing pages, but in a moment he was snoring like a leaf blower.

Grandma looked over her shoulder at him, then creaked to her knees. She coaxed the challah out of its hiding place under the sink, where it sat, safe from Jimmy, with the scouring pads and bleaches.

Grandma had a small fridge with a rounded door and a freezer compartment the size of a shoebox. She reached in and pulled out a bag of flathead fillets, then beat an egg in a bowl to make batter.

'The Jews invented fish and chips,' she told me.

'Nobody invented fish,' I said.

'The Jews invented frying it,' said Grandma.

She rolled a white fillet in salted flour and dipped it into the egg mix.

'Jimmy doesn't like my fish any more,' said Grandma, 'but he eats fish at the Club, and it's rectangular. What kind of fish is rectangular?'

'A hammerhead shark,' I said.

Grandma fried the fish in one pan of waxy dripping, and the chips in another, while I set the table with fish knifes and forks, around doilies for placemats. Jimmy had built the furniture in his workshop and Grandma had knitted the doilies for Brievermann's House of Lace, which was now a Chinese gambling club. Many of the things they had in their home, my grandparents had made for themselves.

Grandma carried the plates into the living room on a tray painted with roses. She stroked Jimmy's arm and whispered, 'Wake up, you drunken sod.'

He looked around carefully, then climbed out of his armchair and groped along the TV cabinet to his seat.

'Food, glorious food,' he said. 'A yiddisher fella wrote that song.'

Jimmy showered his lunch in malt vinegar and ate it methodically, starting at the top of the plate and working his way down. When he'd finished all the fish, he wrapped the leftover chips in slices of challah and ate it as a sandwich.

'You've left your peas,' he said to me.

I gave him my plate. He speared each pea with his fork and popped it into his mouth like a lolly.

Jimmy went to the bathroom and didn't come back. I found him standing outside the door.

'He's in there again,' said Jimmy. 'He's always got to get the jump on everyone else.'

I tried to push past and turn the door handle. Jimmy gripped my shoulder.

'They say he'll be out by Christmas,' he said, and laughed.

'I have to pee,' I told Jimmy.

'Go on the vegetable patch,' he said.

'You haven't got one,' I said.

I squeezed my legs together.

'Have you heard any furphies?' asked Jimmy.

'I don't know what they are,' I said.

He looked down at me, as I held onto my pants.

'Rice balls,' he said, and he scratched himself.

I hopped out of the house and emptied myself against the back fence.

*

At five o'clock Jimmy and I went to the RSL to meet Solomon the tailor, Myer the optician, and Katz, who was once a war artist. When I was very young, I used to think the three were one person, Sollykatzanmyer. Solomon, big and red, like a fat plastic tomato, gave him the belly. Katz, a sad *Shabbes* candle with his features melted down his face, lent his long, bony nose. Myer, small and neat, with slicked-back hair and yellow teeth, provided the eyebrows and the hedges in his ears.

Grandma called Jimmy's friends 'the Three Stooges' or, when she talked about the Christmas Day in 1953, 'that Pack of Drunken Bums'.

Mum once said they were 'the Three Wise Monkeys'.

'The Three Prize Flunkeys, more like,' said Jimmy. '"Earn No Money", "Save No Money" and "Spend No Money".'

'And which are you?' asked Mum.

'Just "No Money",' said Jimmy.

I loved the RSL, its bingo and keno and glass cabinet filled with regimental plaques and samurai swords. Jimmy signed me in and we walked into the bar like men. I was only thirteen, but I was allowed to sit near the bistro, where Jimmy sometimes bought his rectangular fish. Behind us were the banks of singing poker machines, but we took a table with our mates because we came for the conversation, not the gambling. Katz ('Earn No Money') slipped a packet of lollies into my hand. Myer ('Save No Money') tweaked my ear. Solomon ('Spend No Money') lifted his empty glass.

'Are you familiar with the "shouts" or "rounds" system of drinks procurement?' Katz asked Solomon. 'Otherwise known as the "rotating purchase method"?'

'I'll rotate you,' said Solomon, 'if you don't watch it.'

'It's an ancient arrangement,' said Katz, 'and nobody knows when it was first adopted, but archaeologists and historians agree that it emerged in an attempt to stop tight-arsed *trombeniks* bludging off their more generously inclined peers.'

'What's he on about?' Solomon asked.

'I knew it,' said Katz. 'He's never even heard of it.'

Katz pulled his spectacles down his nose and looked up at Solomon like a kindly teacher.

'According to the conventions of the shouts or rounds system,' he explained, 'when one member of the circle or "school" finishes his middy, another member purchases a further drink for every person at the table.'

Solomon relented, disappeared for a moment and returned with a jug of Old.

'Tonight is the night that jugs are cheap,' said Solomon. 'They call it "Cheap Jug Night".'

'I wonder who came up with that name,' said Katz.

'The same bloke who writes this,' said Myer, peeling the Club newsletter from the table. It was called *Newsletter*.

'Who's deceased?' asked Solomon.

'*The Last Post*,' read Myer. '*Life member Fred Linderman passed away in the war vets' hospital in Narrabeen.*'

'I don't remember him,' said Solomon.

'He was the unknown soldier,' said Jimmy.

The men took off their hats, poured black beer from the jug and raised their glasses to Fred Linderman.

'Rest in peace, dig,' said Solomon.

'By the going down of the sun, we won't remember him,' said Myer.

I smelled soft lavender through the old men's aftershave and hair cream as a woman a little older than Mum showed Sollykatzanmyer a book of cloakroom tickets. She had hazel eyes and bare brown arms.

'Can I interest you gentlemen in the meat raffle?' she asked, and she pushed back her hair with her hand.

'I've got enough meat for any man,' said Solomon.

She pretended he hadn't spoken.

'It's for the Ladies' Auxiliary,' she said.

'It is indeed,' agreed Solomon, and pulled out his wallet.

'*Ach du lieber Gott!*' said Myer.

'What on earth is that?' asked Katz. 'It looks like a relic from some bygone age.'

Solomon took out ten dollars and bought five tickets.

'Who's that on his banknote?' asked Myer.

'It's Edward the Seventh!' said Katz.

As the woman hurried politely away, the men watched her buttocks wobble in her blue crocheted dress. Her perfume hung in the air like potpourri. The sight of her thighs reminded Solomon of girls he'd known during the war, and Myer of the handjob he'd got from a blonde *shiksa* at the National Association of Jewish Ex-Servicemen's Anzac Day march in 1951.

'It's coming up again,' said Myer.

'You're kidding yourself, mate,' said Katz.

'Not this bloody deserter,' said Myer, prodding his crotch. 'Anzac Day.'

Myer pointed to an announcement on the back of *Newsletter*: minibuses were leaving the Club for the war memorial in Martin Place at 3.30 am on 25 April.

'I'll be on the march,' said Solomon.

'He didn't march enough in the army,' said Jimmy.

Katz said he was never in the army, so he would stay at home and think about his mates who'd died. Solomon punched him on the arm.

'This one never used to miss a chance to march,' Solomon told me. 'He marched against the bomb, against the Vietnam War, against Apartheid in South Africa, against Aboriginal rights.'

'That was *for* Aboriginal rights,' said Katz.

'Whatever,' said Solomon. 'If the commos ever needed somebody to walk from one place to another, they could rely on Ernie Katz, the hiking kike.'

'I stood up for what I believe in,' said Katz.

'You stood up, and you walked a bit, and then you stood somewhere else,' said Solomon. 'Nobody can take that away from you.'

Solomon hooked his thumbs into the lapels of his pinstriped jacket.

'Who will join me on the march?' he asked.

Jimmy looked into his glass. Myer tapped his bad leg.

I liked war, all the guns and tanks and uniforms – especially the helmets – and boots and knives and mines. I loved to look at pictures of my dad when he was a nasho, lined up with his mates, with the tallest standing at the back, like they were posing for a class photo. Dad never went to Vietnam, but I knew Jimmy had shipped out to fight the Japs in 1941.

'I'll go,' I said.

Solomon grinned and patted my head.

'Listen to the little soldier,' he said.

'Listen to the fat idiot,' said Jimmy.

But nobody listed to anyone.

'He wants a handjob,' said Myer.

'Let the boy come with me,' said Solomon. 'We can march together.'

Jimmy shrugged.

'The boy can do what he likes,' he said.

'The grandkids are allowed to wear your medals,' said Solomon.

'He's welcome to,' said Jimmy, 'if he can find them.'

'They're in the drawer under the TV,' I said.

'I know where they bloody are,' said Jimmy.

There was a silence at the table while the old men searched for something else to fight about. Solomon pulled on Katz's sleeve to expose the paperback in his liver-spotted hand.

Katz always carried a book to read on the train between Bondi Junction and Kings Cross. Tonight, it was *Herodotus: The Histories*.

Solomon snatched it from him and held it in the air.

'Ernie Katz,' said Solomon, 'is a cultured man, an artist, a tortured soul. He is like our *haimisher* Vincent Van Gogh, in that he has sold no paintings and remained unrecognised during his lifetime. Am I right, Ernie?'

Katz looked at Solomon with brutal pity.

'The day he is right,' he said to me, 'this man, Solomon Solomons – or, to give him his full title, "Solomon Solomons of Solomon Solomons & Sons, continental tailors to the wealthy and discerning citizens of Darlinghurst Road, such as various drug addicts, pimps, hoons, child molesters and pornographers, including Mr Sin, the King of the Cross, Jake 'The Take' Mendoza himself" – the day he is right, I will eat my kippah wrapped in bacon, rolled in pork and topped with cheese.'

'What kind of cheese?' asked Solomon.

'The cock cheese of the uncircumcised,' said Katz.

Jimmy thumped the table.

'Watch your language,' he said. 'He's only a boy.'

'Bullshit,' said Solomon, patting my head. 'I went to his bar mitzvah nearly one year ago. It was a wondrous, moving event, marred solely by the drunken, lecherous behaviour of his maternal grandfather, who would've been knocked down by every husband in the Hakoah Club had he, of course, been able to stand up in the first place.'

'He's my grandson,' said Jimmy. 'I drink because I am proud. He can read Hebrew. He sings like a songbird. The *shiksas* will flock to him like homeless people with the need to urinate flock to Solomon's awnings in the early hours of the morning.'

'He has a voice that would charm the birds out of the bees,' said Myer.

Solomon tried to silence the others by spreading his arms.

'The point I am trying to make,' he said, 'is that Katz is an artist. He *studied* art, while the rest of us went out to work to give something back to the parents who'd raised us. He is well versed in the *history* of art, and God knows that's exactly what you need when you're seventy years old and spend every day in the RSL. Yes, Katz may be an artist, but I've never seen him with a pencil or a sketchbook, let alone paints or an easel.'

Katz yawned, throwing back his head and opening his mouth like a bird waiting for a worm, and looked from side to side, as if trying to find someone more interesting to listen to in the pokies lounge or in Myer's ear.

Solomon flicked through the coffee-stained pages of *The Histories*, searching for evidence against his friend.

'Ernie Katz,' he declared eventually, 'is a classicist. He has the inside word on events that occurred in both ancient Greece and ancient Rome, and often notes parallels between these occurrences and apparently similar happenings in modern times. He is able to do this because he was schooled at Fort Street High, a selective school that was not, nonetheless, sufficiently selective to screen out the *Yidden*. At Fort Street, Ernie Katz learned of the lives of emperors, the strategies of generals, and the myths and legends of the great goyim who invented civilisation. This set him in good stead for his later life, when he became a signwriter of some local renown, responsible for both the design and typography of such famous artistic landmarks as the for-sale sign used throughout the 1950s by Gilbert Levy Real Estate, and the no-entry sign at the bottom of the Hakoah Club steps.'

Katz lightly lifted the tail of Solomon's wide maroon tie, and gently rubbed it in a small puddle of spilt beer on the table. When Solomon didn't notice, Katz dipped the dampened, darkened tip into the ashtray.

'Ernie Katz is an aesthete,' Solomon carried on regardless. 'This means he doesn't believe in God.'

'You're thinking of an anaesthetist,' said Myer.

'Ernie Katz is anathema,' said Solomon, 'to polite society. When he trained as a painter, a painter was a rogue who only got into the game to get into the life models. Women like an aesthete, because they believe he is a poof, so they allow him to watch them undress, a process which took a lot longer in those days than it does today, I might add. It is a sad thing for a tailor that the youth have largely abandoned wearing clothes – but a good thing for an old perv.

'Ernie Katz chose to be a figurative painter in the days of abstraction. He would have you believe this was a political decision, brought on by his commitment to social realism, but I would point out that an abstract painter has no need for models, whereas a realist must spend his mornings gazing at a young woman's breasts in order to secure his inspiration.'

'You know what?' said Katz. 'Fuck you.'

He stalked off to the bathroom on his drainpipe legs.

'What did I say?' asked Solomon, turning his palms to God.

'You called him an amateur,' said Jimmy.

'Perhaps he's just an agnostic,' said Solomon.

Jimmy raised his eyebrows, put a finger across his upper lip and twisted his mouth as if he were chewing a cigar.

'What do you get when you cross an insomniac, an agnostic and a dyslexic?' he asked.

Myer shook his head.

'Someone who stays up all night wondering if there is a dog,' said Jimmy.

He pronounced dog as 'doig', because he was imitating Groucho Marx.

'During the war,' Myer told me, 'we used to call Jimmy "the Man of a Thousand Voices". Even though he only had three.'

Jimmy liked to impersonate the Marx Brothers, the Three Stooges and Al Jolson. I had no idea who any of them were.

'We were always making something out of nothing in those days,' said Myer.

When Katz returned, he pulled his book out of Solomon's hands.

'Katz knows his history,' said Myer.

'Katz's nose is history,' said Solomon, leaning over to grab it. Katz pushed him aside.

'Look,' said Solomon, 'that bright, meandering vein on the north face of his schnozzle maps the wanderings of the children of Israel through the desert – where they invented, among other things, fish and chips – and onwards to the Promised Land.'

'I thought his nose was the Great Pyramid,' said Myer.

'From one nostril alone hang the gardens of Babylon,' said Solomon. 'Yes, Katz is a historian, but the question remains: what mark will Katz himself leave on history? If he had stuck with his vocation, he could've been a minor Australian painter, spoken of today in the same breath as Herbert McClintock and Rod Shaw, who are never spoken of today. But in the absence of an oeuvre, will he be remembered for his pants, which he always wore an inch too short, giving the unusual impression of an adult male who had somehow grown taller in his dotage?'

'Will he be remembered for his shirt?' asked Myer.

'An item which, I believe, I sold to him in 1973,' said Solomon, 'at cost price, when such generous collars were highly fashionable and cheesecloth was *la fabrique du jour* – modelled by the stars of stage and screen – as opposed to today, when the few surviving examples of cheesecloth shirts can only been seen on homeless people and the mentally ill, or purchased from the WIZO thrift shop on Bondi Road.'

Jimmy rose from his seat.

'A tailor is a *faygeleh*,' he said. 'An artist is a *faygeleh*. A man who comments on another man's shirt is a *faygeleh*.'

He clapped his hands over my ears and picked me up by my head.

' "A Jew", as they say in France,' said Jimmy to his mates.

*

Jimmy and I walked home through Bondi Junction. It was the only time I spent in the adult world at night, where people smoked and laughed and careened across the pavement, and I wished I was older and taller and stronger. I wanted to grow up to be like the surfers with their fringes in their eyes, and the women who swayed and stumbled and caught their high heels in the cracks in the pavement. But I worried I wasn't tough enough, that my parents hadn't taught me what I needed to know to survive. At school I was sometimes baffled by the slang and the swearing, and always surprised at the jabs and slaps that came from nowhere, the wrestling holds suddenly fixed on me by the boys on the back seat of the bus. There had been nothing like this in my life, no violence to learn from, only hot tears and Yiddish and a sticky kind of love.

BONDI

THURSDAY 19 APRIL 1990

My grandmother's house was falling down around her ears she said, but I thought it was cracking up under her feet. The floorboards rasped and groaned, as if Jimmy kept a monster chained under the house. But everything else was wrong as well. Pastel-blue paint had peeled from the kitchen walls, leaving holes the shape of faces with long trailing tongues. The door handles hung loosely in their mountings. The lounge had lost a wheel and the wardrobe in the spare room was missing a door.

Jimmy had added a third bedroom to the house when Deborah Who Lives in Israel turned twenty and refused to share a room with her younger sisters. He built the extension out of timber, not fibro, and tacked in onto the back wall. Deborah Who Lives in Israel's room had a small deck that looked out onto the paved backyard, but to reach it from inside the house you had to walk through the bathroom. As soon as it was finished, Deborah Who Lives in Israel moved to Haifa. It was the last piece of work Jimmy did on the house, in 1969. He had been driven to finish the job by the space race, because Grandma said they'd land a man on the moon before Jimmy made his daughter a room of her own. A month later, Neil Armstrong and Buzz Aldrin planted an American flag in the Sea of Tranquillity.

The bead curtain jangled as Jimmy came in from the narrow strip of lawn between the front wall and the fence, where he'd been keeping an eye on the neighbours.

'I don't know why you bother going outside,' said Grandma. 'There's cracks in the door you could see an elephant through.'

Jimmy crouched behind the closed door and pressed his eye against the splintering timber.

'There's no elephants,' he said. 'They mustn't be working. It's a *yasumi* day for the mahouts.'

'Either that or there's no elephants in Bondi,' said Grandma.

'They need elephants to clear the tree stumps,' said Jimmy. 'This place is inaccessible by road.'

'No, it isn't,' said Grandma. 'Unless you've dug up the tarmac again. *Lieber Gott*, you haven't, have you?'

She pushed him aside, got down on all fours and peered through the crack.

'Okay, the road is smooth and flat,' she said, 'but the bath is full of water.'

'And the sky is full of clouds,' said Jimmy. 'Who knew?'

'But it was you that filled the bath,' said Grandma.

'No,' said Jimmy, 'it was *him*.'

'It's not me,' I said. 'I don't even have baths.'

'I'm getting tired of this *mishegas*,' said Grandma. 'Why don't you just empty the bath after you've filled it and not got into it?'

'Because I didn't fill it,' said Jimmy.

*

The *frummers* were standing outside their home, where Jimmy hadn't seen an elephant. There were eight religious students living in one cottage opposite my grandmother's house. Their front window was broken but they had patched it over with a poster that said, *Moshiach now!*

The *frummers* dressed in black coats and black pants, with white shirts and black hats. They looked like the bad guys from a Western, who had disguised themselves with stick-on beards so as not to be identified from their wanted posters. Like cowboys, most of the *frummers* were American, but there was one Australian, whose teeth were all different sizes. His name was Barry Dick, and he was the son of Sid Dick from Dad's poker game. Barry had run away from home to become a Buddhist, then shaved his head and joined the Hare Krishnas, but now he was a Jew again.

'And what are you doing this morning, Mr Rubens?' asked the *frummer*.

'We're going to the Club,' said Jimmy. 'And what're you doing? Waiting for *Moshiach*?'

'That's right,' said Barry Dick, pleased.

Jimmy shook his head and walked into the shade of the crumbling electrical substation next door to my grandmother's house. Barry Dick followed us, trying to persuade us to put on *teffilin*, which was the main thing he did while waiting for *Moshiach* to return. The *frummers* believed *Moshiach* would come more quickly if all Jewish men strapped little black boxes to their heads.

We arrived at the Club earlier than usual, and Jimmy and I were the only people we knew. I sucked my drink through a straw, then blew the bubbles back into the glass, imagining a head of lava on my lemon squash.

When Jimmy had finished his whisky, he palmed the glass under the table, where he refilled it from his hipflask. For the rest of the day he would buy middies of Old from the bar, but chase them with shots of Bells from his drinks cabinet.

Sollykatzanmyer came in together.

'Whose round?' asked Katz.

'Who's round?' asked Myer, slapping Solomon's belly.

But Jimmy had already shuffled to the bar. While he was gone, the old men asked me how was everything with my mum.

'I hear he boarded up her room at home,' said Solomon.

'No he didn't,' I said. 'He just turned a picture around.'

'I can't believe he got his tools out,' said Solomon.

'He didn't,' I said.

'And he's covered all the mirrors,' said Myer.

'He hasn't,' I said.

Jimmy handed Solomon a middy of Old, which Solomon held up high and close to his chest.

'It's times like this,' said Solomon, 'a man needs a table.' He looked down in despair.

'You've got a bloody table under your big red nose,' said Jimmy, who had made all the furniture in the bar.

Solomon planted his glass with a shudder. Dark dribble spilled over the lip. He grabbed the tabletop and shook it, spilling more.

'Call this a table?' he asked, angry hair sprouting like bush grass from his nose.

'What would you call it?' asked Jimmy.

'I'd call it "Lucky",' he said, 'after the three-legged dog.'

Jimmy took a sip of his whisky and a gulp of his beer.

'A table is a raised platform with several supports of equal height,' said Myer. 'Using that definition, this is not, in fact, a table.'

'What kind of *gonif* would make a table like this,' asked Solomon, 'then sell it to a shikkered old clublican to taunt members and guests?'

Katz leaned his elbows on the table.

'Watch it,' warned Solomon. 'One nudge'll bring the whole lot down.'

He slapped the wet surface. Cigarette butts jumped around in the ashtray.

'This table would have been better off if it had stayed a tree,' said Solomon. 'A tree is a thing of beauty, a work of God.'

Katz asked me about school. I told him I was getting better at football.

'You should study hard,' said Myer, 'and pay attention to your teachers. Otherwise, you might end up a carpenter.'

'Jesus was a carpenter,' said Solomon. 'Carpentry is for goys.'

'Jesus was a yiddisher fella,' said Katz.

'Would you let him marry your daughter?' asked Solomon, his eyebrows shooting upwards, crushing his forehead into worms.

'Too late,' said Myer, 'he's already run off with Jimmy's.'

Jimmy's face showed no change.

Solomon folded a coaster and passed it to me.

'Shove this under the stump, will you?' he said.

I ducked beneath the tabletop and made my way between the old men's feet. As I scrambled among the boots and shoes to find the shortest table leg, I heard the old men hissing over my head. When I came back up, they were talking about the hand-job Myer got from a blonde *shiksa* at the National Association of Jewish Ex-Servicemen's Anzac Day march in 1951.

'She was a real professional,' said Myer. 'I think she must've worked on a dairy farm.'

'She must've worked in the Pussycat Bordello,' said Solomon. He turned to Katz. 'Remember the party the night that place opened?' he asked.

'No,' said Katz.

Solomon sighed.

'Ernie Katz,' he said, 'is a septuagenarian. This means, as my mother *ava ashalom* would say, he is as old as his tongue and few years older than his teeth. In the case of Katz, however, my *mamen* would have been only half-right – which, truth to tell, is considerably superior to her lifetime average. After the war Katz had his few remaining teeth pulled, as was the fashion in those days, replacing them with a notably unconvincing set of dentures. The idea was that dentures would require less maintenance than natural teeth, be free of decay and cause the wearer to suffer only occasional phantom pangs of toothache, in the manner that – so we are told – amputees are wont to feel a twinge in their missing limb, wherever the hell *that* may be.'

Katz bared his teeth at Solomon. They were all the same size, like a mouthguard. He pretended to bite at Solomon's pink cabbage ear.

'Yes, Katz, like all of us, is in his seventies, and he has seen a lot but done very little. Perhaps the most surprising thing about Katz is his lifelong association with Jake Mendoza, the King of the Cross, one of the few genuine yiddisher *gunsels* in the milieu. Katz was born in Balmain and went to school with Mendoza (then known as Rosenblatt) and his partners in crime, Maurice "the Little Fish" Bass (then Baser) and Big Stan Callahan (whose real name is lost to history, which is no loss at all). Katz came from a poor family and, in order to earn an income in his early teens, he turned his right hand to pornography. With the aid and encouragement of Jake Mendoza, he produced a portfolio of drawings of men with cocks like cucumbers making love to women with the breasts of watermelons. (It should be noted here that Katz's father, Isaac, was the local greengrocer.) Katz and Mendoza manufactured and distributed pornography that was extremely well liked – loved, even – by its consumers. Katz's gimmick was that he would draw the customer together with the movie star, stage actor, neighbour or schoolgirl of his choice, in a position nominated by the client. Although Jimmy and I were educated – if you can call it that – in Bondi, even we had heard of this yiddisher Norman Lindsay, this modern master of the female form. Indeed, I myself owned an illustration of the young Solomon Solomons (drawn from a photograph) passionately embracing the younger Gertie Steinberg, doggy style.

'At the height of his fame and commercial success, Katz was producing three or four commissioned artworks a day, and up to two dozen in a week, but the whole operation came to an end when Katz won entry to Fort Street selective school. Free of the supposedly baleful influence of Jake Mendoza, he never once equalled the output of those heady years at Balmain High, and when an artist in his seventies looks back on his life to discover that he reached his creative peak at the age of twelve, he must surely feel a phantom twinge of regret, in the place where his talent used to be.'

'Don't you ever get tired of repeating yourself?' asked Katz.

'Don't you ever get tired of *being* yourself?' asked Solomon. 'They were the good old days.'

'Bullshit,' said Katz.

'When Mendoza ran the rackets,' said Solomon, 'crims didn't shit in their own nests.'

I imagined convicts as birds, carrying worms in their beaks.

'They rolled in their own shit,' said Jimmy.

Solomon thought Jewish crims kept you safe from *goyish gunsels*, but Jimmy said the only crooks you had to look out for were people like Mendoza, who knew where you lived. Solomon said Mendoza understood how to dress, which was an important thing.

'He is a mensch, underneath it all,' agreed Myer.

'He was always a gentleman when he came to have his suit fitted,' said Solomon. 'He recognised a good piece of cloth, and was prepared to pay the price. Not like some.'

Katz smiled and patted Solomon on the head, as if he were retarded.

'Jake and his boys never mugged old ladies,' said Myer.

'Listen to him,' said Jimmy, '"Jake". I'll bet he calls you Pincus, too.'

'It's my name,' said Myer. 'It would be nice if somebody used it. Even if it was a gangster.'

Jimmy shook his head like a pony.

'Gangster!' he said. 'You call Mendoza a gangster? The Kray twins in London – now they were gangsters.'

He made gun barrels out of his fingers and fired off two silent shots at Solomon and Katz.

'Their *zayde* was Jewish,' said Katz, 'and he was a fighter. They say he tried to knock out a horse.'

Katz threw a left hook at an imaginary animal.

'Your breath could knock out a horse,' said Jimmy.

Katz panted on him, heavily and deliberately.

'With the twins in the East End,' said Myer, who had been to London, 'you knew you were safe.'

'Your *tochis* wasn't safe,' said Katz.

'Twins?' said Solomon. 'He calls them twins? The Schiller twins – now they were twins.'

He danced around in his seat, thrusting his hips at the table.

'Whoo-hoo!' said Myer. 'Were they ever.'

He bent his right arm at the elbow and wobbled his fist.

'I could've had them both,' said Solomon.

'But you had neither,' said Katz.

'I got tit off Elsie,' said Solomon, squeezing the air like a ball between his fingers.

'He got tit when he was fourteen,' said Katz, 'and he's still taking about it today.'

'Listen to you,' said Solomon. 'What did you get when you were fourteen? The clap?'

'What's the clap?' I asked.

Solomon clapped his hands.

'It's what girls do,' he said, 'when they see a tiny weenie. They think if they clap, they can make it bigger.'

I was horrified, but I enjoyed thinking about it.

The old men's speech shared a rhythm and tone. After a while, their voices blended into a chorus and I couldn't separate their words. I thought about Mum and Dad and the Dark Man and the Woman in White. If Mum hadn't left Dad, he would never have met the Woman in White, who worked as a dental nurse because she liked to strap people to chairs and torture them. Mum must have known Dad would have to find someone new, since he couldn't even make toast, and that he would cling to the first Jewish woman he met just to keep from dying of starvation, but she hadn't thought what that might mean for me. For the first few months, when he was lonely and single, I had Dad all to myself. We had to go to the zoo a lot, which was boring, but we also talked about the holidays we would take and the presents he was going to buy me and the pocket money he was going to give me when I stayed at his house, which used to be our house, and which was now their house because the Woman in White had moved in, even though she had her own two-bedroom unit in Bellevue Hill.

She had drafted a new set of rules for life in their house, including taking off your shoes at the door; keeping the front room for best; washing behind your ears; asking to leave the table; and not listening to the Walkman in bed. This last was the cruellest since, when I went to sleep over for the weekend, after a day of walking in bare feet around the back room with a spotless head, I had to listen to her and Dad bouncing, giggling and squelching on their queen-size bed. At the unit where I was now supposed to live with Mum in Redfern, she and the Dark Man were quieter and more serious in their bedroom, but they went on for longer. At least at my grandmother's house I could get a good night's sleep.

We'd been in the Club since before lunch and it was now nearly time for dinner. Jimmy walked home carefully, sometimes pausing to lean on my shoulder. When we reached the end of his street, he stopped and looked down the empty road.

'Where've the elephants gone?' he asked.

'There weren't any elephants,' I said.

He bit down on his jaw, then tapped his fingers against his thigh, as if his patience were slipping away.

'Digger,' he said, 'where-are-the-fucking-elephants?'

His eyes were burning. He clenched his fists.

'It's *yasumi* day for the mahouts,' I told him.

Jimmy let his hands relax.

'Ah yes,' he said. 'That'd be it.'

BONDI

FRIDAY 20 APRIL 1990

Grandma grilled a mound of toast for breakfast, slices of white bread as thick as books, soaked in salted butter. She passed Jimmy a mug of sweet tea, which he took with both hands. His fingers were shaking.

'One morning I shot an elephant in my pyjamas,' he said in his Groucho Marx voice. 'How he got in my pyjamas, I don't know.'

Jimmy winked and I knew he was all right again.

Mum rang, because she was feeling guilty. I answered the phone and Jimmy left the room, because he was pretending she was dead. I asked Mum how she was and she said, 'Oh, he's fine. He's just on his way to work.'

'Who is?' I asked, although obviously I knew.

'Yes,' she said, 'I'll tell him.'

Our conversation clattered. Mum spoke quickly and clearly, as if she were reading from a set of instructions. I tried to trip her with the truth to make her human again.

She told me the Dark Man had been decorating. 'He's very good like that,' she said, because she knew my dad wasn't. She asked how were Grandma and Jimmy. I said they'd been arguing about elephants.

I told Mum I was going on the Anzac Day march with Solomon.

'Solomon Solomons?' she said. 'I'm surprised he can still walk.'

I wished Jimmy would come with us.

'He'll never go,' said Mum. 'He hates the army.'

She said she had heard from my brother Daniel in Lyon, and he had a new girlfriend.

'He's just showing off,' I said. 'I bet he's never had any girlfriends.'

'Why are you going on the march anyway?' asked Mum.

'Because I like war,' I said.

(The Rats of Tobruk were my favourite part of the Second World War, although I also enjoyed the Kokoda Track, the atomic bomb and the Holocaust.)

'I'm not sure that's what Anzac Day's really about,' said Mum.

She told me to wrap up warm because the weather forecaster had said it would be cold, and to take care when I crossed the road. She warned me not listen to everything Jimmy said, especially when he was in his cups. She asked me to tell Grandma she'd phoned and ask her to call her back when Jimmy was out of the house. She told me again that the Dark Man was fine, and blew a kiss down the receiver. As soon as Jimmy heard me hang up, he came back in from the yard.

'That was Mum,' I told him.

'Another wrong number,' he said.

Grandma brought more tea.

'The bath is full again,' she said. 'It's such a waste.'

'Having a bath?' I asked.

'No,' said Grandma. 'Not having a bath.'

'It'd use less water than having a bath,' I said.

'Not if you don't get in,' said Grandma.

'You're talking about nothing,' said Jimmy.

'I'm talking about you,' said Grandma, 'you water pirate.'

'All pirates are water pirates,' said Jimmy.

'Can't you talk sense just for once?' asked Grandma. 'Why the hell do you keep running the bath?'

Jimmy wiped the air to brush her away.

'And you dug another hole last night,' she said.

'I did not,' said Jimmy.

She took his hand and led him outside.

'What's that then?' she asked, pointing to a burrow near the front step.

'A wombat hole,' said Jimmy.

'You're the only bloody wombat around here,' said Grandma.

She plunged her arm into the hole.

'Watch it, love,' said Jimmy. 'They bite.'

Grandma pulled out a tin of shortbread.

'What's this?' she asked.

'It's a type of unleavened biscuit,' said Jimmy.

'For God's sake, Jimmy,' said Grandma, '*why did you put it there*?'

'Storage,' said Jimmy.

'It was already in storage in the larder,' said Grandma.

'It wasn't safe there,' said Jimmy.

'Safe from what?' asked Grandma. 'Bloody wombats?'

'Thieves,' said Jimmy eventually. 'Some of the men, they're so hungry they can't help themselves.'

'Which men, Jimmy?' Grandma asked. 'Dead men? What is going on in your bald bloody head?'

She thundered off to put the shortbread back in the pantry, but I heard her sit down at the kitchen table and sob. Jimmy heard it too. He hung his head and pressed his lips together tightly, and his shoulders trembled like his fingers.

'Bastard,' he whispered to himself. 'You bastard.'

He wiped his eyes.

'Go to her,' he hissed, 'you bastard.'

He bent beside Grandma in the kitchen, and spoke into her ear.

'I'm sorry, love,' he said. 'I'll fix everything.'

She batted him away.

*

There was a muffled knock at the front door, like a mallet hitting meat. Grandma peered through the gap in the wood.

'My brother is here,' she said, 'with your sister-in-law.'

Uncle Maurice's wife Sylvia was my least favourite auntie, although they all got worse as they grew older. She wore horn-rimmed glasses and her hair in a bun, and her husband was a pharmacist, who waddled around with spectacles balanced on his head.

'Hasn't Daniel grown,' said Sylvia.

'I'm not Daniel,' I said, 'I'm David.'

She took me by the shoulders and held me at arm's length.

'Let me look at you,' she said. 'Aren't you tall.'

'I'm the seventh shortest in my class,' I said.

I had moved up from sixth shortest in February, although opinion at school was divided as to whether I had grown a centimetre or Little Jack Binder (widely known as 'Horner') had shrunk.

'And what is your academic position?' Maurice asked me.

'I'm sixth from bottom at English,' I said.

Maurice looked at my shoes, then at my forehead.

'But what is your best subject?' he asked.

'English,' I said.

I had lost interest in lessons and fallen below the average height for a boy of my age, and yet I seemed to be growing a moustache.

Maurice clicked his tongue against the roof of his mouth. Jimmy examined his hands.

'So, how's retirement, mate?' asked Maurice. 'Finding enough to keep you busy?'

'I'm happy,' said Jimmy. 'How's the pharmaceutical trade?'

'Pharmacy is a profession,' said Sylvia.

There was a silence filled with shuffling and snorting and knuckle cracking.

'Let's go into the yard,' Sylvia said to Jimmy. 'I'd like to see what you've done with it.'

'I've paved it over,' said Jimmy.

'Show me anyway,' said Sylvia.

'It's just flagstone,' said Jimmy. 'There's nothing to see.'

But Sylvia took Jimmy by the elbow and marched him out the back door.

Through the kitchen window I could hear Sylvia telling Jimmy it was time he started to think about what was best for Frida. They were both growing old. He wasn't looking after the house. Everything leaked or sagged or smelled. ('Like me,' said Jimmy.) They needed a caretaker, a handyman. They should have a nurse on call. And Jimmy's chest sounded bad. Had he even spoken to a doctor? Their house wasn't a home for old people. It was a builder's project. The land was worth more than the cottage. They could sell the place to a developer, and have enough money to stay in sheltered accommodation for the rest of their lives.

Jimmy spat on the flagstone. It made a sound like a pebble hitting a wall, as if he had coughed up a fragment of rib.

*

It was midafternoon before Jimmy got to his shed to collect a hammer and nails. He carried his tool bag into my bedroom, which Mum and the others had shared with Deborah Who Lives in Israel before Jimmy had built her the extension and Deborah had gone to Israel, and sat on the blanket box looking at the wardrobe. As his bony buttocks met the weak wood, dampened by decades under an open window in warm Bondi rain, the lid of the chest collapsed under his weight. His knees jackknifed to his chin, and his body folded into the box, like a child in a nightmare, trapped in a toilet bowl. I rushed to pull him out but, as his thighs cleared the box, he tore his pants on a rotten plank.

Swearing something about wood lice, he changed into a pair of paint-splattered King Gee stubbies and announced, 'Smoko.'

We sat on the front step, where Jimmy wet his yellow thumb and coaxed a cigarette paper from a packet of Tally-Hos. He dropped in three pinches of tobacco then massaged them into one fat worm, and rolled the paper around it in two tight twists. He pulled out stray flakes of White Ox like he was plucking hairs from his nose, then tapped his rollie against a box of Redhead matches to settle the tobacco. He took the cigarette in his mouth, lit a match, touched the flame to the tip, closed his eyes and breathed in. He held the smoke in his lungs for a moment, then let it out slowly, and smiled as he watched the genie vanish in the air. It made me wish I could smoke.

He coughed softly and laughed, then he coughed harder. His throat began to rake and roar. He choked like the brakes on a bus, he spat green and black and red, then suddenly he stopped.

He glanced at the blobs of blood and phlegm.

'Better out than in,' he said, and persevered with his smoke.

Barry Dick the *frummer* wished us 'good *Shabbes*' and said he hoped we weren't planning on working today. 'Commandment number four,' he said. 'Remember the Sabbath and keep it holy.'

Jimmy nodded.

'Would you like to lay *teffilin*?' asked Barry Dick.

'No, thanks,' said Jimmy, 'but I'd like to buy one of those vegetarian recipe books you used to sell on George Street.'

Barry Dick ignored him.

'Would *you* like to lay *teffilin*?' he asked me.

'What's the point?' I asked.

'It is a commandment,' said Barry Dick.

'What number is it?' I asked.

'There are more than ten commandments,' said Barry Dick. 'In fact, there are six hundred and thirteen. But on *Shabbes* we must rest, because in six days He created the heavens and the earth and everything in it, and on the seventh day He rested.'

I had been wondering about this.

'So, did God create dinosaurs and people at the same time?' I asked.

'He did,' said Barry Dick.

'So why aren't there any dinosaurs in the Torah?'

'The Torah,' said Barry Dick, 'is a holy book. It is not a book about dinosaurs.'

'How come Tyrannosaurus rex didn't eat Adam and Eve?' I asked.

'Perhaps he was a vegetarian,' said Barry Dick.

'No,' I said, 'Tyrannosaurus rex was a meat eater. Brontosaurus was a vegetarian.'

'Brontosaurus wasn't even a dinosaur,' said Barry Dick. 'It was a misclassification of the apatosaurus.'

'So you *do* know about dinosaurs,' I said.

'I've read a book about dinosaurs,' said Barry Dick, 'but it wasn't the Torah.'

'Was it the Bhagavad-gita?' asked Jimmy.

'Good *Shabbes*,' said Barry Dick, and went off not to turn on any lights or drive his car, plant trees, till soil, bind sheaves or reap or thresh corn.

Jimmy decided to try to fix the wardrobe again, and now he had to repair the blanket box too. I waited in the kitchen with Grandma, who was rinsing chicken livers and sprinkling them with salt. She asked who my friends were and which games we played, and if I'd ever smoked a cigarette or kissed a girl. She had started to remember her schooldays more clearly as they drew further away. She sang a skipping rhyme and told me about a boy who had taken her into the bushes and shown her his thing. She said she was always grateful to Jimmy because once they married she didn't have to work at Brievermann's House of Lace.

She was dozing off in the living room when Jimmy screamed, and the skin on my arms raised like a forest. I ran to my bedroom, where Jimmy was crying and throwing his arms about, and I could see he was blind and mad and I had to dodge his fists and his feet, as he crashed his head against the wardrobe door, which splintered and split and worked at the deep cut in his forehead sending blood flowing behind his glasses and into his eyes.

He was an old man screaming like a baby then whimpering like a dog. His body was shaking, from his feet to his forehead. White spit gathered like beer foam in the corners of his lips.

'No!' he yelled. 'No!'

Grandma came into the room slowly, looked around at the smashed timber and the mirror that lay broken on the floor, and at Jimmy, who hugged his elbows while he bounced on his toes.

Across the rail in the wardrobe hung a thin black tie.

'He's there!' he cried, jumping and pointing. 'Take him down! Take him down!'

*

There was more screaming at night, and calls for help, a cry like a man falling. I woke and slept to the pulse of Jimmy's dreams.

Sometimes he howled out names. I heard him thrash around in bed, thumping and banging against the mattress, rocking the headboard into the wall.

The next morning, I rang Mum and told her I wanted to come home.

'He's fine,' said Mum.

'I don't like it here,' I said. 'I think Jimmy's going mad.'

'He's just on his way out now,' said Mum, 'but I'll tell him. Thanks for asking.'

I waited until I heard the Dark Man kiss her lips – ugh! – and push his stupid bike out of the front door and into the corridor.

'Why won't you just let me come home?' I asked.

'Christian and I are going through a delicate time,' she said. 'We need our space. It hasn't been easy, the past year, you know. Christian gets tired of having to be on his guard.'

'I'm not going to attack him, am I?' I said. 'He's about three years older than me.'

'Christian is *twelve* years older than you,' said Mum. 'And it's your comments that upset him.'

Jimmy walked past and glowered at the phone. He didn't really like anything that wasn't made of wood.

'If you're so worried,' said Mum, 'why don't you go and stay with your father?'

'You know Dad's got to work,' I said.

I heard her take a deep breath.

'So he can't look after his son for one week in the year?' asked Mum.

'He probably wants to,' I said, 'but *she* won't let him.'

Normally Mum would say, 'Who's she? The cat's mother?' But not when I was talking about the Woman in White.

'Look,' said Mum, 'we just need a little more time. Can't you just stay another week? Please?'

It was a long, sweet 'please', the kind that comes with a gift attached.

'It'd be a lot easier,' I said, 'if I had a Nintendo.'

'If you can make it until next Friday, you can have a Nintendo,' she said.

I could see there might be a catch.

'Not as part of my birthday present?' I asked.

'No, you'll get a totally different birthday present,' she promised.

'Will that present cost the same as it would've cost if you hadn't bought me a Nintendo?'

'It'll come out of a different budget,' she promised. 'I'll use the money I've put aside for palliative care in my old age.'

BONDI

SUNDAY 22 APRIL 1990

Jimmy asked if I wanted to go to the beach.

'The beach?' I said.

'Big crescent of sand at the bottom of Bondi Road,' he said. 'You'll recognise it once you see it.'

He never went to the beach.

'What's at the beach?' I asked, suspecting a bar.

I was happy to go out, but I didn't want to walk. Old people loved walking. They didn't seem to see that it was a waste of time and energy, and probably the main reason they were tired all the time.

Jimmy kissed Grandma goodbye as we left the house, which was something I'd never seen him do before.

We passed under the shadow of the electricity substation. I lingered at the bus stop, but Jimmy kept on marching, past the kosher supermarket and the WIZO charity shop, all the way down to the beach.

I was a swimmer, a body-boarder and a wave jumper, but that morning the water was too cold for anyone but the surfers. The wind chewed my cheeks and Jimmy held onto his cap as we walked towards Bondi Pavilion, a Roman temple looking out over the flags. The face of the pavilion was a troop of arches, and I imagined them guarded by a centurion and legionnaires. In the cloister, at a row of squat concrete tables, Jimmy found Myer sitting with a chess set, facing a fat man wearing a pork-pie hat.

The old fellas liked to come here on warm days, to talk and play cards in the fresh air. Myer used to say he was a chess champion when he was younger, although I suspected he was only champion of the PCYC 'D' team or something, since he could never win a game without cheating.

'It's Slim Jim,' said the fat man.

'G'day,' said Jimmy, 'Slow Eddie.'

I thought of waves flowing lazily past half-submerged rocks.

'They don't call me that any more,' said Slow Eddie. 'Not since Fast Eddie died.'

Slow Eddie took a box of cigarettes from his shirt pocket and a lighter from his hatband.

While Slow Eddie fiddled with the flame, Myer pocketed his rook. When Slow Eddie looked back to the board, he moved a pawn forward and left his queen undefended. Myer chased her with a knight and cornered her with a bishop, and Slow Eddie tapped his king on the crown, knocked it onto its side and resigned.

Slow Eddie's scowl made Myer smile like a sphinx.

'I've got deals to make and hearts to break,' said Slow Eddie, standing up and brushing dust from his pants. 'G'day.'

'G'day, Slow Eddie,' said Jimmy.

'G'day, Slow Eddie,' said Myer.

'G'day, Slow Eddie,' I said.

'Youse're a hatful of bastards,' muttered Slow Eddie, and he hiked across the grass to the car park.

'Have you ever tried to make one of these?' asked Jimmy, pointing to the chess set.

'Surprisingly, no,' said Myer, 'being as I'm an optometrist.'

'They're a bugger to get right,' said Jimmy.

'I dare say,' said Myer. 'It's just as well you can buy them in the shops.'

A cloud passed over the sun.

Myer opened his newspaper while Jimmy and I went into the pavilion to look at a frieze of photographs of Bondi in the black-and-white days, when the esplanade was clogged with touring cars. Bow-lipped beach girls watched beefy lifeguards flex their biceps like circus strongmen under an inky sky.

'Look at them,' said Jimmy. 'Between the wars.'

Jimmy had three stories about growing up in Bondi. There was the one about boxing in the street, when he got knocked out by a girl; another where he shot the coalman; and a third in which he tried to swim to New Zealand but ended up in Botany. His parents, the *Bobbe* and the *Zayde*, were poor – but, said Jimmy, everyone you knew was poor in those days so it didn't matter. The *Bobbe* worked in a cigar factory. The *Zayde* was a returned soldier who couldn't settle down. Sometimes he sold *shmattes* from door to door, or waited on tables at a restaurant. After Jimmy shot the coalman, the *Zayde* delivered coal.

My grandparents kept one photograph of the *Zayde*, looming tall and stern over the *Bobbe*, who wore a dress laced up to her throat. He had a moustache shaped like a magnet, and dull, frozen eyes.

Jimmy was only comfortable talking if he was drinking, working or walking, and I could tell he wanted to say something because he kept shuffling backwards and forwards in front of the frieze.

'What was it like in those days?' I asked.

It looked boring.

'It was harder,' he said.

I wondered what he meant by hard.

'Did you used to get into fights?' I asked.

'Everyone did,' he said. 'People were tougher then. We had the Great Depression, we had the memory of the war. We didn't expect to live forever. The *Zayde* served under Monash with the 3rd Division in France. He had his ear shot off. Did you know that? The *Zayde* had only one ear.'

He cupped his own intricate ear with one hand.

'You used to see returned men begging in the streets,' said Jimmy, 'with no legs, with no hands, with scorched tissue where their eyes used to be. I wanted to get shot too, to take a bullet, to joke about it with my mates. I felt jealous of the *Zayde* for only having one ear.'

I wouldn't've minded being shot either, provided I didn't die. There was a kid at school who'd been run over by a ute and it had made him twice as popular.

'The *Zayde* used to march on Anzac Day,' said Jimmy, 'behind a banner and flag, with his medals all in a row. We had the day off school to watch them, all the fathers and grandfathers, strutting and limping to the war memorial and back. When it was over, the old men went drinking and we ran down to the beach to play in the sea. So I thought war would be a holiday too.'

Jimmy wasn't looking at me. He was speaking to the photograph, to the women in bathing caps and the lifeguards in hooped costumes, the sunbakers from the days before everything.

'All the *Zayde*'s friends were from the army,' he said. 'He still played poker with the blokes who'd fought with him in Flanders, and he laughed louder with them than with anyone, because they'd shared something that set them apart. Because they were laughing, I thought it must be something good.'

I wanted an ice cream, even though it was cold.

'But you couldn't ask the *Zayde* about the war,' said Jimmy.

'He was good with horses. That's all he had left from the army. And he kept a rifle under his bed. Sometimes he'd take me out to shoot rabbits. One night when he was drinking with the diggers, I stole his gun, and the next morning I shot the coalman. I did it because I thought he was a thieving gypsy, and when the *Zayde* found out, he belted seven shades of *gonif* out of me.

'The next day,' said Jimmy, 'the *Zayde* apprenticed me to a cabinet maker named Aaronson. He was missing a finger, but that was because he had sawn it off trying to make a table. He'd never been to war, and I thought less of him for it and I think the *Zayde* did too.'

I imagined the *Zayde*, ancient or ageless, his moustache trembling with fury.

'I didn't much like being a cabinet maker's boy,' said Jimmy. 'I fancied myself as a singer, or a boxer. Then I got knocked out by Rebecca McGilligan – I think I've told you about that – and decided to swim to New Zealand and start my life again. But the Tasman Sea's a big bugger, as I might've known if the *Zayde*'d let me finish school. There didn't seem any point in starting a new life in Botany, so I caught a bus and a tram home, and the *Zayde* walloped me into next week.'

I wondered if he had brought me to the beach to tell me this.

'I came down here because I wanted to look at the ocean,' said Jimmy, 'because the ocean's where it all started. We left by sea, and we came back the same way.'

Jimmy gazed at the water then suddenly lurched forward and pointed.

'Do you see that?' he asked.

I couldn't see anything but waves.

'A swimmer,' he said, 'way out there.'

There was nothing.

'It's him!' shouted Jimmy, and pushed me aside. He ran onto the beach, dropping his cap, splattering sand up his legs. He sprinted to the water's edge, shouting words I couldn't understand. I chased after him then, when I realised he was going to run into the ocean. I tried to cut in front of him. He crashed into me, tripped, but kept on running, like a forward pressing towards the line. When he reached the sea, he kicked off his shoes and waded in, waving his arms above his head and calling out, 'Stop! Stop! Stop!'

He was shin-deep in surf when a lifesaver, who'd been watching from thc flags, grabbed him from behind. Jimmy struggled and pushed, tried to wriggle out of the lifesaver's grip, but his strength quickly faded and he allowed himself to be dragged back to the beach, panting and soaking.

'What were you doing out there?' they asked.

'I saw a man drowning,' he said.

'That was you, old fella.'

Jimmy was still wet like a dog when we got back home.

'What the hell happened to you?' asked Grandma as she towelled him down in front of the fire.

'He was out there,' said Jimmy, 'drowning.'

Grandma breathed deeply and quickly.

'Don't do this to me,' she said. 'You bloody bastard.'

She threw down the towel, stormed out of the house and slammed the door.

Jimmy opened a can of beer at the living room table.

'Why don't you ever talk about the war?' I asked him.

'Because the war's over,' said Jimmy.

'Myer's handjob's over, but you still talk about that.'

'That was over before it started,' said Jimmy.

There was something I'd been meaning to ask.

'What's a handjob?'

'Manual work,' said Jimmy. 'Something Myer would know bugger all about.'

'But what was the war like?' I asked.

'It wasn't like anything,' he said.

Jimmy dragged the ashtray around the table. He lifted one finger then dropped it. He started the same sentence twice, then gave up.

'I want you to understand some things, David,' he said. 'I want you to understand that there're some things I don't want you to understand.'

'I understand,' I said.

'The past is called "the past" because it's passed. It's gone. The *Zayde* was right. There's no point in thinking about it. There's nothing good to learn from it, nothing that'll make your life happier. I don't want you to know it.'

'But I *want* to know,' I said.

He closed his eyes and was silent for a long time. I thought he might've fallen sleep.

'I'm starving,' I said.

'Starving, are you?' asked Jimmy.

I nodded.

Jimmy took lunch out of the oven and cut his pie into six small pieces. He stripped one slice of its pastry and prodded it with his knife.

'See that?' he said. 'That was a week's ration of meat on the line. That was all the Japs gave us. Can you imagine what it's like to live on so little food? No, you can't. Because you think "starving" is when you've waited ten minutes for a meat pie. I might as well talk to you in Japanese.'

Then, alarmingly, Jimmy started speaking Japanese, very quickly and loudly, while slamming his fork on his plate.

'Did you understand that?' Jimmy asked me, his fingers flecked with gravy. 'It means, "This war will last one hundred years, and you will die building this railway."'

'We did Japanese for a year at school,' I said.

'But you didn't understand,' said Jimmy slowly. 'Did you?' He bared his teeth, his eyes narrowed.

'You told me what it meant,' I reminded him.

'But you didn't understand.'

'I don't really speak Japanese.'

He growled at me like a dog.

'Well, maybe you'll fucking understand this!' he roared, and he punched me in the head so hard that I flew backwards off my chair. It felt like I'd been hit by cricket bat. I put my hands to my face and blood ran between my fingers.

By the time Grandma came home, we had managed to stop the bleeding, but I was sitting with a cotton bud stuck up each nostril and tears in my eyes.

Jimmy was saying, 'Sorry, son, sorry, I'm so, so sorry.'

I told him it didn't matter, but really I was scared of him and I wanted to go home to my mum.

'We should call a doctor,' said Grandma.

'The boy's all right,' said Jimmy.

'Not for him,' said Grandma. 'For you.'

Jimmy reached out and gripped Grandma's shoulder.

'Don't tell the others,' he said. 'Please. Don't tell Solly.'

That night, Jimmy got arrested for digging up the memorial gardens.

*

I was asleep when the police knocked. Grandma ran to the door in her salmon dressing-gown, with curlers in her hair. I followed, suddenly frightened again. It was four o'clock in the morning. Two officers, a man and woman, escorted Jimmy into the house. Angry and confused, he kept trying to shake the policewoman from his arm.

Grandma lit the gas fire and offered everyone a cup of tea. Jimmy said he'd take whisky, but the policeman told him he'd had enough.

'Has he ever done this before?' the policeman asked Grandma.

'Well, he always was a dirty stop-out,' she said, 'but he usually comes home when the pubs close.'

'Desecrate a war memorial, I mean,' said the policeman.

Grandma made a pot of tea and opened a tin of biscuits. The policeman said they had been called to the scene when a driver had noticed somebody digging a trench around the Anzac statue in the memorial gardens.

'We believe he might've been trying to steal it,' said the policeman.

Jimmy laughed.

'What would I do with a bloody statue?' he asked. 'It's the size of a house.'

'You tell us,' said the policeman.

Jimmy shut his mouth, to show he would never tell them anything. When they didn't ask him anything, he opened it again.

'Am I under arrest?' he demanded. 'What're the charges?'

The policeman was big and gentle, with a slow, deep voice.

'We're here to help you,' he said.

Jimmy shook his head.

'If you're here to help me, pick up a shovel,' he said. 'You jacks are the idlest bastards in the army.'

'Watch your language, sir,' said the policeman.

'I'm not your "sir",' said Jimmy. 'And you're not mine.'

The policeman made a note in his book.

'My husband is a returned serviceman,' said Grandma, 'and sometimes he forgets he ever came back.'

Jimmy crossed his hands on his lap, covering patches of dirt and grass.

'What were you doing out there, sir?' the policewoman asked him.

Jimmy rubbed his thighs.

'There's a digger standing in the field,' he said. 'A tall man, bigger than life, with a heart the size of a fucking lion –'

'May I remind you, sir –' said the policeman.

'You remind me of the guards at Changi,' said Jimmy.

Jimmy stood up like a sentry and stuck out his chin and chest.

'All piss and wind,' he said. 'All mouth and trousers. All spit and polish. All cock and bull.'

'Stand at ease,' said the policeman, and Jimmy relaxed.

Everybody took a bite of biscuit.

'We found these in the hole,' said the policeman, and showed Grandma a tin of corned beef, a can of tuna and the shortbreads.

'He's always burying the shortbreads,' said Grandma. 'I'm not going to buy them any more.'

Jimmy rolled his fist in his palm.

'The Japs've had that poor bastard standing out there for days,' said Jimmy, 'with bugger all to eat or drink. I brought him some tucker.'

'So, you were feeding the statue?' asked the policeman.

'Fuck you,' said Jimmy.

The policeman flushed.

'If you continue to speak to me like that, I'll have to take you to the station, sir,' he said.

'Do I look like a bloody Abo?' asked Jimmy.

While the policeman stared at him, Jimmy bent his elbows to scratch his armpits, and made monkey noises.

Grandma slapped him on the head.

'My husband was at the Battle of Singapore,' she said. 'He was sent to Changi. He worked on the Burma Railway.'

'Choo-choo!' sad Jimmy. 'Chuggety-chug, chuggety-chug, chuggety-chug!'

'I see,' said the policeman.

Grandma stabbed Jimmy in the arm with her finger and hissed at him to hush.

'He is an active member of the local RSL,' she said.

The policeman nodded and played with his shirt buttons.

'And we're Jewish,' said Grandma, pointing to the Star of David on the mantelpiece.

The policeman wrote that down.

'So he's not likely to go desecrating war memorials,' said Grandma, 'is he?'

The sun came up behind the television, casting a glow on Jimmy and lighting the downy hairs on the policewoman's arm. The policeman looked at his watch.

'What're you doing here anyway?' Jimmy asked him. 'Haven't you got thieves to catch?'

The policeman closed his notebook.

'How about he goes back and fills in his hole, and we don't say anything more about it,' offered the policeman.

'How about *you* fill in the hole,' said Jimmy. 'You cunt.'

BONDI

TUESDAY 24 APRIL 1990

Jimmy was arrested and spent the morning at the police station. He would only give the police his name, rank and army number. He called the desk sergeant '*gunso*' and insisted on speaking to him in Japanese.

'Hurt me and you'll hang,' he shouted when they brought him a cup of tea and a sandwich.

They let him out at lunchtime, and I got the feeling he had enjoyed himself.

'They thought they could break me,' said Jimmy, 'with their cheese and tomato sangers, but I'd never betray my mates. Although I gave them Solomon's name, obviously.'

Grandma hugged him.

'You're a mad old bugger,' she said, 'and you've got to see someone.'

Jimmy shook his head and looked away.

Grandma said Mrs Ethelberger's son, Arielberger, was a psychologist.

'Not clever enough to be a doctor, eh?' said Jimmy.

He had a practice in Macquarie Street, specialising in post-traumatic stress.

'Making money out of the diggers,' said Jimmy.

Mrs Ethelberger thought he could help.

'And Mrs Ethelberger's qualifications are what?' asked Jimmy. 'Apart from a *tochis* like a bear?'

Jimmy rolled and lit a cigarette.

'I'm not going back on meds,' he said.

'You don't have to,' said Grandma. 'Mrs Ethelberger says there're other ways of dealing with it.'

*

Every Tuesday night, Sollykatzanmyer ate at the Thai Dee Town restaurant on Bondi Road. If any of them missed a dinner, he was shunned by the others for days – if he hadn't already been black-banned for buying a soft drink; driving a Japanese car; leaving food on a plate; leaving drink in a glass; disputing a known fact about the war – such as the superior fighting spirit of the Aussies, the uncanny mechanical skills of the Kiwis, the generally cold and treacherous nature of the Dutch, the big-noting showboating of the Yanks, and the methodical but justified savagery of the Red Army; saying something complimentary about the pianist Arnold Zwaybil, the *gonif* Slow Eddie Finkel or the crooked artists' manager Izzy Berger; or failing to share the sausages when they won the meat raffle. There were at least six hundred and thirteen commandments in the lives of Sollykatzanmyer, all of them unwritten but handed down by God.

Jimmy put on his special fawn pants, matched with a brown cardigan with buttons as deep as biscuits. Katz and Myer wore jumpers, as it was a cool evening, and Solomon was dressed in a suit. The restaurant was empty, but the waitress, Dee, eyed the old men unhappily.

I thought she was beautiful, with black hair down to her shoulders and lips that were red and fat, as if swollen by kissing.

'Good evening, Miss Suzie Wong,' said Myer, taking off his invisible cap.

'You ready to order?' she asked.

'You haven't brought us the menu, darling,' said Solomon.

'You always have the same thing,' she said.

'But we like to look at the menu,' said Katz.

'You like to look at my arse,' said the waitress, as she walked back to pick up the menus.

The walls of the restaurant were decorated with posters of elephants and temples, beaches and boats. The waitress's dress mirrored the colours of sand and sea.

She collected the menus, bound in boards, and held them to her chest.

'This one's banquet,' she said, 'and this one's standard.'

It looked as though she was talking about her breasts.

'Which one's bigger?' asked Solomon.

She glowered at him.

'There are three entrees, four mains and two desserts on the banquet menu,' she said. 'And one hundred and three dishes available à la carte.'

Solomon tried to count to one hundred and three on his fingers.

'What does "à la carte" mean?' asked Myer.

'It's French for "at great cost",' said Solomon.

'Listen to the polygon,' said Katz.

Solomon spread his hands, then grabbed Katz's book, Simone de Beauvoir's *The Blood of Others*.

Katz fought him for it, half-heartedly. When he lost the battle of pushing and pulling hands, he took hold of Solomon's earlobe and twisted it like a knob. Solomon backhanded him, and almost knocked him from his chair.

'Ernie Katz,' said Solomon, 'is a Francophile, a long-term ardent admirer of French culture, couture and cuisine. In his youth he dreamed of dining at Claude's, and ordering *cuisses* and escargot. Although Katz never reached these heights of sophistication, fate was to deal him the chance to eat frogs and snails under other, less comfortable circumstances.'

Katz made another attack at Solomon's earlobe. The tailor defended blindly, pushing him away with his palm turned back.

'After the war, Katz modelled a black beret, a red scarf and a long grey raincoat. He was a disciple of Sartre and the leading local spruiker of French popular song. But at the heart of his admiration for all things Gallic was, of course, the extraordinary French feeling for painting. What other nation in the world could have given us both Monet and Manet, David and Coubert, Degas – often incorrectly pronounced "de-gas" after the flatulence medication – and Pissarro (who was, incidentally, a yiddisher fella)?

'And yet one thing that might strike you as strange about Katz's Francophilia is this: the French were not at all Katzophiles. When the Germans overran *la patria* in 1940, the Vichy government called its refugee Jews "rubbish", then rounded them up and handed them to the Nazis.

'These days, of course, the French say that they didn't know where the Germans were taking the Jews. But although I've never asked where the garbos cart my rubbish, I'm ninety-nine per cent certain they either bury it or burn it.

'Which is why we are eating tonight in a Thai restaurant, rather than a French one.'

'This is a Thai-Chinese restaurant,' said the waitress.

'And where are you from, love?' asked Solomon.

'Auburn,' said the waitress.

'And although we affectionately call you "Dee",' said Solomon, 'after the humorous sign over your door, I don't believe we have ever asked your real name.'

'You haven't,' said the waitress.

'Do you have one?' asked Solomon.

'I do,' said the waitress.

'And may we have the pleasure of learning that sweet appellation?'

'She's no Appalachian,' said Katz.

'She's a sweet-apple Asian,' said Myer.

'My name is Dominique,' she said. 'As in, "Dominique tells you to piss off."'

Solomon tapped my knee.

'She's flirting with me,' he whispered loudly.

Jimmy was getting impatient.

'Are you finished?' he asked. 'What shall we have?'

'You'll have fishcakes, chicken satay and curry puffs,' said Dee, 'massaman beef, red curry chicken, pad Thai, whole snapper, beef with basil, choo chee vegetables and fried rice. Anything for the boy?'

'Do you do hot chips?' I asked.

'No chips!' she said, scowling, then leaned over and pinched my cheek. 'Except for handsome young men.'

Sollykatzanmyer muttered and nudged.

'You're in there,' said Solomon.

'Urine there,' said Myer, pointing to the bathroom.

Dee brought over a plate of prawn crackers like frozen snaps of cloud.

'I don't eat prawn,' said Solomon.

'You're crackers,' said Katz.

The old men began a long, irritable argument about the importance of keeping kashrut. They each believed they were religious to precisely the right degree: anyone who was more observant was a maniac, and anyone less *frum* was a goy. Katz, by general agreement, was an atheist, an aesthete and anathema.

Dee delivered an entrée plate and the old men squabbled over three curry puffs. Dee had given us five satay sticks, but Solomon said he didn't eat satay and Myer said he didn't eat sticks. Jimmy bit into a curry puff, and Solomon accused him of eating a poof. Myer advised him to spit before he swallowed, and Katz said Myer was a homophone.

Dee glided out of the kitchen with a silver bucket of rice and ladled a scoop into Solomon's bowl. As she served him, she leaned away. When she filled my bowl, she pressed a breast against my elbow, and I held onto that feeling for the next two years.

'Why are there so many Thai restaurants,' I asked Jimmy, 'when there aren't any Jewish restaurants?'

'What's Jewish food?' asked Solomon.

'It's what Jewish people eat,' said Myer.

'I ate Arab food in Africa,' said Solomon.

'And for that he got a medal,' said Myer.

Dee returned with more dishes.

'Is this Jewish food?' Solomon asked her.

'One massaman beef,' she said. 'One beef with basil.'

'But Solomon wants to know what religion was the cow,' said Katz.

'Animals have no religion,' said Dee.

'Lionel Kirtz had a Jewish dog,' said Myer.

'Lionel Kirtz was *meshuganneh*,' said Dee. 'Like you.'

'What we know as "Jewish" food,' said Solomon, 'salt beef, gefilte fish, chicken soup etc, is actually Ashkenazi food.'

'Listen to the gastropod,' said Katz. 'He thinks he knows everything about food.'

'A gastropod is a mollusc,' said Solomon, 'like a fat slug. The word you were looking for was gastronome.'

'No, it wasn't,' said Katz.

Solomon picked all the potatoes out of the massaman curry and piled them in his bowl.

'The Thais,' said Solomon, 'claim to be the only nation in Asia not to be conquered and colonised. They achieved this, as far as I can see, by allowing the Japanese to overrun them without a fight, thus sparing them the indignity of losing.'

Dee glared at him.

'There was fighting at Chumpon,' said Katz, 'and Pattani and Nakhon Si Thammarat and Prachuap Khiri Khan and Surat Thai and Songkhla.'

'I'll have them all with sweet chilli sauce,' said Solomon.

'You really are an imbecile,' said Katz.

Myer swapped Solomon's chopsticks for two drinking straws.

'Ernie Katz,' said Solomon, 'is an Orientalist. In the case of some of the finest painters of the nineteenth century – men such as Horace Vernet, Gustave Doret and Eugene Delacroix – this meant artists who trekked bravely through mountains and deserts, to tug away the veil from the odalisque, to stand before the pyramids in awe, to catch glimpses of life as she was lived in the days when Abraham, Isaac and Jacob walked the earth, and capture them in the bright, swirling colours of Persian rugs, Ottoman robes and Moorish script.

'In the case of Katz, however, it signifies simply that he has buck teeth and a small cock. Am I right, Ernie?'

When his rice was finished, Katz turned over his bowl, looked at Jimmy and said, '*Leggi?*'

The old men wiped up the last smear of sauce with the last piece of meat and scooped the final grain of rice from every bowl. At the end of the meal all that was left were the sticks from the satay. Jimmy slipped them into his pocket.

Sollykatzanmyer asked for Irish coffee to sober themselves up. Jimmy said hold the coffee, he'd just take the Irish. He went to the bathroom and didn't come back.

I found him in the corner of the restaurant, staring at a model villa the size of a bar fridge, with a peak like a steeple. Its walls were red and its roof deep green and trimmed with gold, as if a dragon had wrapped himself around the guttering. Two sweet joss sticks smoked in a cauldron on the decking. Around the altar stood the figures of an old man and woman.

Dee pushed Jimmy aside and laid petals around the incense burner.

'A gift for the guardian,' she said.

A flower in her fingers was the loveliest thing I had ever seen.

Jimmy's eyes clouded. 'I remember these in Siam,' he said. 'In the war.'

'Every Thai home has one,' said Dee. 'It's for the spirits. It keeps them from making mischief.'

Jimmy rubbed his chin.

I watched Dee's arms, her back, her neck.

'I need to buy a spirit house,' said Jimmy.

Dee smiled sweetly.

'This is a restaurant,' she said, 'not a fucking junk shop.'

Jimmy winced, because he didn't like to hear a woman swear. (I found it exciting.)

'So where can I buy one?' he asked her.

'Thailand,' said Dee. 'Are you ready for the bill, or would you like to eat the plates?'

'I'm serious,' said Jimmy.

She gave him her sad and hostile stare.

'Last month, you stole a spoon,' she said. 'You think we don't count them, but we do.'

Jimmy cringed.

'Can I buy your spirit house?' he asked, and took out his wallet.

'No,' she said.

'Why not?' asked Jimmy.

He counted notes into his hand.

'Because you are old and drunk and mad,' said Dee.

Jimmy dropped his eyes and shuffled his feet.

'I thought you people were supposed to respect your elders,' he said.

'I thought *you people* were supposed to be sober,' said Dee. 'Go back to your seat, old man, and get your hipflask out from under the table. It's time for the Last Post.'

Dee locked the restaurant door, and turned the Closed sign to face the street.

'Five minutes,' she warned them.

Solomon stood up, clicked his heels and made a toast.

'To absent friends,' he said.

Jimmy rose too.

'To fallen comrades,' he said.

Katz and Myer joined them and, in one low, quiet voice, the old men began to sing 'We'll Meet Again'.

SYDNEY DIARY

DECEMBER 1941

I spent the morning lost in painting and memory, because painting is memory. Even when you are working with a model's body, you are remembering every other body you have known. I was drawing from life, a silent woman who sat in my studio scowling, killing time before the boys came back from their training camps in Bathurst and Tamworth. The William Street girls are eager to pick up extra pin money in the slow summer afternoons, but Matilda wordlessly made it clear that she would rather be lying on her back beneath a schoolboy soldier than posing modestly on a table with an arm across her breasts and a hand between her thighs.

She wrapped herself in a blanket and smoked a cigarette while I took a break to listen to the radio upstairs. The Imperial Japanese Navy had sunk the American fleet in Pearl Harbor, in the islands of Hawaii. The United States had joined the war, but without the battleships *California*, *Arizona* and *Nevada*. I listened, excited and dismayed, as the world stepped closer to destruction or salvation.

At the same time as her navy had quashed America's armour in the Pacific, the Japan's Twenty-Fifth Army had invaded Malaya from Indochina.

Matilda received the news with the expressionless equanimity characteristic of her profession. Her red lips were tight, her brown eyes blank. She could have been wondering what effect the fighting would have on her income, or if her burden might be lighter under Japanese occupation.

I have kept careful watch on the rise of the new thinking across the globe, and the Japanese plan is clear to anybody who has been studying the strategy and diplomacy of the imperial court. Japan was opened up to trade by force, by the gunboats of Commodore Perry in 1853, after two hundred years of isolation. From that time on, the Japanese have struggled with Western ideas – from democracy through to communism – and sought ways to either incorporate or annihilate them. They learned from us how to organise a modern army, and immediately set it to work savaging the Russians in the Baltic, tearing Korea from the tzar and seizing Manchuria. They saw the great empires of the European powers and lusted after colonies of their own, to feed their industries and spread their influence. Just as the white man brought Christian enlightenment to the savages, the Japanese seek to deliver an oriental peace to Asia.

Their experiment with political parties failed. The people were taught to respect only the Emperor and the military. A nation led by its army will inevitably go to war, and the Japanese chose to march first into China. The whole world knows what the Imperial Japanese Army did to the innocents of Nanking, the tens of thousands of murders, the rapes and mutilations they inflicted on an unarmed populus, and we have looked to these atrocities for clues to the Japanese character and concluded they are nothing but blood-crazed pirates. Yet they are what we made them. They reflect what they see in us. Today, they most admire the Nazis. In Germany, they see a nation where authority has triumphed and order is respected; a country which, like Japan, was humiliated into accepting uneven treaties and now wreaks vengeance on its neighbours in the name of uniting them under a single flag of prosperity.

When the IJA invaded French Indochina, to secure supply routes into China, America placed an embargo on oil sales to Japan, and a wider war became inevitable to anyone whose round eyes were not blinded by blinkers of hope. Without fuel, Japan could not continue to fight the conflict in China, on which rested the fulcrum of her ambitions and the prestige of her army.

Now they must expand south, to plunder oil from the Dutch East Indies, but who is to say that Japan is not, in fact, the natural colonial master of the region? Why should Javanese petroleum go to the Netherlands rather than Tokyo?

I explained this to Matilda, as best I could. Suddenly time was more precious than ever. Every moment might never be repeated. By this day next year, we may both be dead. She looked at me as if this were happy news indeed.

'Are you going to paint me first?' she asked.

'First?' I said.

She knew where my hands would travel before I realised myself. They sought her skin and stroked it, from her ankles to her thighs. She made a sound she had heard through plaster walls, or perhaps imitated a noise she'd once made in passion, and drew me to her, unbuttoning my smock.

I let my face fall into her breasts and I told her, 'I love your smell.'

'I smell of soldiers,' she said, and it was almost poetry.

I had already made love to her body with my eyes, followed every youthful curve, explored each cheapened mystery. I told myself I was attracted by her mixture of innocence and guile, or girlishness and steel, but in truth she could have been any woman. I needed some warmth before the frost to come.

Afterwards we smoked, passing the one cigarette back and forth between our lips. I called a cab to carry her back to William Street, then filled my pipe with tobacco and walked to the stationers to buy a diary.

I spent the afternoon lost in writing and war.

BONDI

WEDNESDAY 25 APRIL 1990

I was shivering in bed, half-awake, when Jimmy brought in a mug of tea. I pressed it against my lips, but it was too hot to drink: my grandparents used powdered milk because they thought it was more hygienic. The house was dark, with only a lamp lit in the corner of the living room. The clock on the mantelpiece said 3 am. I felt like I was walking through a blizzard. I flopped onto an armchair and smelled the toast before Jimmy carried it to me on a plate. The bread was burned. Like my dad, Jimmy scorched everything he cooked. He coughed softly and gave me two medals. I pinned them onto my shirt. He straightened them, turned down my collar and fastened my top button.

Before I left the house, he kissed me on the forehead.

Solomon's Volvo was waiting in the street. Solomon saluted Jimmy on the porch, and held open the car door. Jimmy shook his head and waved us off. We drove into town through empty streets, down corridors of lights. Solomon whistled softly, as his fingers marched on the steering wheel cover.

Thousands of old men were huddled together in blackness in Martin Place, some smoking cigarettes, others watching the steam of their breath. Solomon kept me close to his stomach, one veined hand on my shoulder. He found his regiment quickly. They shone torches under his chin and squinted to recognise him through spectacles as thick as windows.

'G'day, dig,' they said, and asked after friends.

Solomon had been to the funeral of his sergeant. Another man, Alfie, had buried two mates in Queensland. Solomon said he would have flow up if he'd known. Alfie took his phone number, for the next time.

They paraded in lines, in their berets, toupees and blazers, with their walking sticks and hearing aids. They bowed their heads as the bugler sounded the Last Post, then looked up as he played the Reveille and the sun rose over the post office and banks.

There were minibuses waiting on George Street to take the old men to breakfast. Solomon's regiment had booked a hotel looking over Hyde Park. The tables were laid with silverware, but Solomon ate standing. He fished sausages out of the bain-marie and rolled them into hotdogs with slices of white bread.

'He's lost his appetite,' said a stiff-backed man. 'Fifty years ago he'd've finished the lot by now.'

Solomon ate half a hotdog in a single bite.

'This is Henry,' said Solomon, patting the old soldier's arm. 'Harry to his friends. So I call him Henry.'

A waiter in whites offered rum for the men's coffee.

Solomon and Henry kept touching each other, on the wrist, the elbow, the back of the hand. Once, I saw Solomon's fingers rise to Henry's face, but he let them drop before they brushed his cheek.

'This one here,' said Henry to me, prodding Solomon's chest, 'this one here was a right one, he was.'

They both laughed.

'Anything that moved,' said Henry, making a rifle out of the air, closing one eye and pulling the trigger. 'Bang! Bang! Couldn't shoot straight, but. Couldn't hit a bloody barn door.'

'It's a good thing we weren't fighting barn doors,' said Solomon.

He finished one hotdog and made himself the next.

Alfie the Queenslander had found a bottle of beer. The men passed it around, each taking a swig.

'Couldn't hit a barn door, this fella,' Alfie said to me.

'There was never any need to,' said Solomon.

Alfie feinted a punch at his head.

'Is it true what I hear,' Henry asked Solomon, 'that a mate of yours got a handjob off a blonde sheila after the march in 1951?'

The men were happy telling stories about buglers and AWOLs and the things they got up to in Cairo on leave. They made jokes about Arabs and camels and women, and the difference between shit and falafel. They made the war sound like a school trip, where only your mates were invited and you spent the whole time hiding from the teachers and running off with girls.

Outside, the first line of wheelchairs, the bewildered survivors of the Somme, moved off, steered by their nurses. There were pipe bands and brass bands, and families waving flags. Solomon mustered with his regiment, and we marched alongside Alfie and Henry under the banner that named the battles of Litani River, Jezzine, Damour and Beirut.

'Why doesn't Jimmy march?' I asked Solomon.

'He hates the army,' said Solomon. 'He hates talking about the war.'

'Why don't you hate the army?'

'I do,' said Solomon. 'I just like marching.'

As we passed a group of women, he straightened his shoulders and filled his chest with breath.

I kept in step with the old soldiers, marching like a man. We tramped past one pub and then another. We could hear the noise of drinking over the cheers of the crowd.

'Fuck this for a game of soldiers,' said Solomon. 'Let's go and get a beer.'

He bullied his way into the Coronation Hotel on Park Street, through circles of tottering airmen with small white moustaches, and looming Vietnam veterans wearing sprigs of rosemary.

'Do *you* like to talk about the war?' I asked Solomon as he bought me a lemon squash.

He blinked.

'It's different for me,' he said. 'You wouldn't know it, but I was a madman when I was young. I loved to fight. I lost mates, but I made mates too. I had some of the best nights of my life in the army. I rooted brown sheilas. I drank petrol. I wouldn't've missed it for quids.'

'Did you enjoy the battles?' I asked him.

'I don't know,' he said. 'The waiting was the worst part, the boredom and the training. In battle, at least we were doing something. But they . . . it . . . I . . .' He hesitated. 'The battles aren't the things I think about. If I did enjoy them, I don't want to know why.'

He shook his head and sat silently in the bar.

'What was Jimmy like before the war?' I asked him.

Solomon grinned.

'He was a bit of a larrikin,' he said, 'always after the ladies. He used to get into trouble and I had to pull him out. He wasn't happy at home. The *Zayde* was a stern man, like my father. They didn't know how to bring up kids, those blokes. It was all the belt and the strap and "I'll knock some sense into you". You can't knock sense into a boy, you can only bash it out of them.

'But Jimmy had that American kind of walk, as if he was leaning backwards into the wind, and he could dance, which goes a long way for an ugly fella. He was quick with the jokes and impersonations, his Groucho Marx thing and all the rest, and he dressed well on a Saturday night. He used to go out on the prowl with Frida's brother Moishe *ava ashalom*. Two grinning skinny fellas, Mick and Jimmy were. Peas in a pod.'

Solomon sipped at his drink.

'That poor bastard Mick,' he said, shaking his head. 'He was another one with more balls than brawn, always in a scrape. I don't know what happened to blokes like that. They don't seem to make them any more. Maybe it's evolution – they just don't last. Jimmy and Mick, with their black hair and Mick's green eyes: everyone thought they were Paddies, although they didn't drink, not in those days.

'I remember Jimmy was always at Mick's house. Little Frida must've been around too, but he never talked about her. She was too young for him to notice, even though girls grew up fast back then. Most of them were married by twenty. That was until the war, of course, when it got harder to find a husband. Mick had one brother and three sisters – your Uncle Maurice, your Auntie Sally *ava shalom* and your Auntie Hettie the Mad One. Mick and Jimmy used to sit in the boys' room and play swing records on the gramophone, and practise dancing together like a couple of *faygelehs*. Frida might have helped them along, I don't know. She was quite a dancer in her time, too.'

Solomon remembered Frida softly, but I could hear he found it hard to say Mick's name.

'Frida's father and mother were like parents to Jimmy,' said Solomon. 'Maurice was much younger than Mick, and they all treated Jimmy as another brother.'

Solomon finished his beer.

'How did we get to talking about that?' he asked.

He looked into his empty glass.

'Nobody ever mentions Mick,' he said, 'and that makes it harder. Especially as you grow older and you start to see things the way they really were, instead of how they looked to people at the time. Mick should be with us now, eh? He should be drinking with me in this pub. It should be his fucking round.'

Solomon's eyes were fat with tears.

'He'd've been proud of you,' he said. 'He would've been your "Mad Uncle Mick". He'd've told you all the stories, tapped out the songs on his tobacco tin. I don't know what he'd've thought about Jimmy marrying his sister, but. I don't think any of us would've wanted that.'

He examined the bubbles that clung to the walls of his glass.

'Let's have another beer for Mick,' he said, and bought me a middy of Old by mistake.

'Mick Zimmer,' said Solomon, licking his plump lips. 'Mick fucking Zimmer.' He raised his glass to the window. 'Today, we remember you, Moishe, with your oily hair and your silly bloody dancing shoes, and the fag hanging out of the side of your mouth.'

I clinked glasses with Solomon and drank the beer. It tasted old.

'Frida was a rose that bloomed in wartime,' said Solomon. 'When I got back from overseas I didn't even recognise her. She'd grown big round boobs and . . . I don't suppose you want to think about your grandmother like that, eh?'

I liked it better when we were talking about the war, but that never seemed to last very long.

*

We picked up the car and drove back to Bondi Junction to meet the others at their usual table. When Jimmy saw me, he shook my hand.

The Club doorway was draped in union jacks, and a man like a small general walked between them, nodding to either side, as if the flags had been hung for him. He wore a short ribbon of service medals across the breast pocket of his blazer and was followed by a much bigger man who wore none.

'Well, take me up the Patton with a sergeant major's baton,' said Myer. 'It's the King of the Cross.'

Jake Mendoza put a hand on Katz's shoulder.

'You're looking well, Ernie,' he said. 'How's your love life?'

'Happy Anzac Day, Jake,' said Myer.

Mendoza stared hard at him, as if he were trying to make him vanish.

'Who's this?' he asked Katz.

'Pincus Myer,' said Katz. 'He used be thinner with more hair, and his nose was more nose coloured.'

'A *faygeleh*?' he asked. 'Did he used to dress up as a woman?'

'Oh no, your kingship,' said Myer. 'You're thinking of Solomon.'

Jake Mendoza nodded at Jimmy.

'What are you doing here, Jake?' asked Jimmy.

'On Anzac Day, I like to be with my fellow returned servicemen,' said Mendoza.

'What I don't understand,' said Jimmy, 'is where it was that you're supposed to have returned from.'

'I served my country,' said Mendoza.

'They also serve,' said Jimmy, 'who only rob their mates.'

'Now, now,' said Mendoza, smiling, 'let's not fight amongst ourselves. Let's remember, instead, our victories against common enemies – the Japs, the Nazis and the Maltese.'

Mendoza caught me looking at his Star of David signet ring.

'And who's this little fella, then?' he asked. 'Don't tell me it's Leah's boy.'

Jimmy didn't answer, so I nodded for him.

'Your brother Daniel was at school with my grandson Martin,' said Mendoza. 'We often asked him to our home, but he was always busy. He lived a very full life for an eleven year old.'

'He's in France now,' I said.

'Well, tell him to drop by when he comes home,' said Mendoza.

'He's still busy,' said Jimmy.

Mendoza lowered himself into a chair and sat on it like a throne.

'We go back a long way, eh, boys?' said Mendoza. 'Do you remember the Patton? Aphrodite's? I've still got that wardrobe you made for the girls' dressing-room, Jimmy. What a lovely piece of furniture.'

'You never paid us, Jake, you snake,' said Jimmy.

'Ah,' said Mendoza, waving away his words, 'you were under my protection.'

'*Your* protection?' said Jimmy. 'Other blokes did your fighting for you in the Cross, and other blokes did your fighting for you in the war.'

Mendoza smiled at his knuckles and fondled his ring.

'There wasn't a lot of fighting in the POW camps,' he said, 'as far as I know.'

Jimmy arched his back like he was about to jump.

'You know fuck-all,' said Jimmy.

'I know the difference between you and me,' said Mendoza. 'I've never surrendered.'

Jimmy clenched his fists. Mendoza raised an eyebrow. I wished I could raise an eyebrow. His bodyguard came to attention behind him. Jimmy sat forward in his chair. Mendoza leaned back, as if he were lying on a big, soft bed.

'It's funny,' said Mendoza, 'but I don't remember you as a tough guy. You must have hardened with your arteries.' He sucked the salt off a peanut. 'Instead of softening with your cock.'

The bodyguard's hand held Jimmy down as Mendoza snatched a glass out of Myer's fist, rested one foot on Myer's thigh and climbed onto the table. He pushed aside the ashtray with his foot. A nest of cigarette butts spilled like slaters into Myer's lap. Mendoza finished Myer's beer in one gulp, pulled a silver pen from his breast pocket and banged it against the empty glass.

'Diggers!' he shouted. 'Cobbers! Heroes! Cooo-eee!'

'Get off that table, you short-arsed cunt!' someone shouted.

'Jake Mendoza!' said Mendoza.

'He's not here!' called an old sailor.

'He's AWOL!' yelled another.

'He's in the fucking nick!'

Mendoza laughed with them. His grin seemed to glow. When the joshing and whistling had stopped, he addressed the crowd.

'Jake *Corporal* Mendoza!' he cried. 'Number N213136! Reporting for duty! And it is my duty, as a returned serviceman, to buy a beer for every man in the house! And a whisky!' The men cheered, Mendoza beamed. 'And another beer!' he cried. 'And another! The fucking bar's on me, boys, from now until the Last Post!'

'We've already had the Last Post!' shouted the sailor.

'Until the last man standing then!' called Mendoza.

I had to trot to catch up with Jimmy, who was trying to push his way out the Club doors. I pulled them open for him and he almost toppled into the street.

'I've had enough of this bullshit,' he said. 'Anzac Day, regimental fucking blazers, everyone in their units. Another couple of drinks and those senile old fuckers'll be dancing on the tables with Jake Mendoza.'

He stopped to steady himself against a fence.

'Give me a fucking cigarette,' he said.

'I don't smoke,' I told him. 'I'm only thirteen.'

'Lot of fucking use you are,' he said.

'I could go back and get you one,' I said.

Jimmy laughed blindly. A man in a suit tried to slide past him, but Jimmy bent his knees and cupped his palms.

'Smoko for an old soldier, sir?' he begged. 'Penny for a fool?'

The man patted his pockets. 'Steady on, digger,' he said.

'Steady on,' agreed Jimmy. 'If you can keep your head while all about you are losing theirs, then you'll spend the whole rest of your fucking life wondering why you're still walking around with a head on your neck and they're all lying six feet under in Kanfuckingburi.'

'You should take him home, son,' the man said to me.

I cupped Jimmy's elbow and steered him along the street, past white-haired officers drinking on the pavement. Jimmy set his head so he wouldn't see them, thundering forward.

'They say you should remember,' said Jimmy. 'Mick Zimmer, Bathurst Billy, Townsville Jack . . . Boys dressed up as fucking soldiers. Do you think they want to be remembered like that? That wasn't who they were.'

He wiped sweat across his forehead with a grey handkerchief.

'I remember them,' he said. 'I remember every word they said.'

Jimmy slowed as we came closer to my grandmother's house, and stopped by the electrical substation. He lingered in the street, as if he wasn't going home.

'What're you staring at?' asked Jimmy. 'You silly-looking cunt.'

'It's not my fault,' I said. 'I didn't do anything.'

'No,' said Jimmy. 'You didn't do anything, you don't know anything, and you've got everything.'

BONDI

THURSDAY 26 APRIL 1990

While Grandma was stirring porridge, Jimmy folded open a sketchpad at the table and took a pencil from behind his ear.

'What're you doing?' I asked.

'I'm busy,' he said.

I was tired of him going off at me, and I was starting to feel like it wasn't worth staying at my grandmother's house, even for a Nintendo. I was sad, because he had always been such a good grandad and now he had turned sour, just like Mum and Dad.

'How can you be busy?' I asked. 'You're retired.'

'He's off with the fairies,' said Grandma.

'Go and play in the yard,' said Jimmy.

'I will *not*!' said Grandma.

'I was talking to the boy,' said Jimmy.

'It's freezing out there,' I said.

'Freezing, is it?' said Jimmy.

'What're you drawing?' I asked him.

'A pension,' said Jimmy.

I tugged at the corner of his sketchbook. He rapped my knuckles with a ruler.

'Keep your hands to yourself,' he said.

Jimmy went to the shed, came back and laid his tools on the table. He chose a hammer, a screwdriver and a chisel for his belt, and he gave me a bag of nails.

'We're going to make everything right,' he said to Grandma.

She cleared a space among his tools for his breakfast.

I ate my oats slowly, waiting for one of them to say something about it being a school day, but neither did, so I just took the nails and waited.

Jimmy waved me to follow him outside, and together we looked at the narrow strip of lawn between the front of the house and the fence.

'We're going to build it here,' he said, as if he were planning a city in the desert.

He unveiled his diagram. Two boys my age came walking up the road, so I pretended to be interested in the sketch, which looked like a picture of a doll's house on a pole. I guessed it must be some kind of complicated bird table.

'I'm sorry about last night,' said Jimmy. 'If you've got questions, ask me now. I'll talk to you while I'm working.'

'It's all right,' I said. 'I don't care any more.'

Jimmy scrubbed away at his drawing with an eraser.

'Don't sulk like a sheila,' he said. 'What do you want to know?'

Two other boys passed in their blazers and ties.

'Where did you meet Sollykatzanmyer?' I asked Jimmy quickly.

'I knew Solomon before the war,' said Jimmy, still staring at his sketch. 'He lived with his father in Bondi and worked in the shop on Darlinghurst Road. I'd heard of Myer. He was older. His family used to have a tobacconists in the city with a bright orange sign. Katz was my age, but he was from Balmain, so I'd never met him. But we were all at the same dances, chasing the same girls.'

'What about Jake?' I asked.

'Who's Jake?'

'Jake Mendoza.'

Jimmy squinted into the pale sun.

'I had nothing to do with him. He was a *gonif*, even then. You'd hear about him selling stolen car radios, but you had to look for him to find him, and I had other things to do. Cabinet making was hard work, but then there was the dancing . . .'

Jimmy looked down at his motionless feet.

'Solly wasn't good with the girls,' said Jimmy. 'They were afraid of him because he was so big. They thought he'd crush them, but he was as gentle as a lamb with any sheila who'd go near him. He was handy in a blue, but. You wouldn't think it, but he could cop a flogging and come up smiling. I suppose it was all the padding he had. But Solly was different from the other Jewish lads. He was always looking for some kind of adventure. And he had that *goyishe* spirit in him: he liked to smash things up.

'I used to wonder if Solly would have lasted on the line. Sometimes it was the big ones that gave up first.'

'Did you all join the army together?' I asked.

Jimmy shook his head.

'Solly signed up pretty much the day the war began,' he said. 'His father was angry. He thought fighting was for goys, that Jewish boys should be tailors. Me and Mick waved him off at the docks, and I never saw him again until 1945. I enlisted in June 1940.'

'Weren't you scared?' I asked.

Jimmy rubbed his chin, pushing back bristles as if he were pressing through long grass.

'Scared? No,' he said. 'I joined up so I could be like the *Zayde*. In those days people were religious and they were patriotic. I was

British first and Jewish second, because the *Zayde* had a problem with rabbis. He had a problem with everyone, although I didn't understand that then. But I was proud of the *Zayde*, and proud of the Anzacs, and proud that they'd fought under Monash, because he was an Aussie and a Jew. I wanted to have what they had, and so did Mick. Moishe was my age, and he knew all the newest dances. Frida was his baby sister, six years younger, all curls and freckles. Me and Mick were best mates. They said we were inseparable, but it turned out we weren't.'

It was hard for Jimmy to talk about Mick, too.

'The *Zayde* told me not to go, but then he always told me not to do everything. Back then, people cared a lot more about what other people thought. In the Jewish community it wasn't respectable to go off and be a soldier – not in 1940, at least. There were a lot of . . . weak men. There were boys who'd run away from other wars, old fellas who'd served thirty years in the tzar's army. And the English Jews who'd been here the longest, they were too good to be cannon fodder. I was the son of an Anzac, but the *Zayde* hoped for better for me. I didn't know it then, though. I thought he felt I wasn't up to it.

'There were so few Jewish blokes signing on at the start that they didn't even have an Old Testament for me and Mick to swear on. They had to send out a runner to pick up a proper bible. "Five-bob-a-day murderers" the conchies called us. We got one pound and four shillings a week and three square meals a day, and for some blokes who'd been on and off the swag since 1929, it was like they won the Melbourne Cup every week. Or at least a chook raffle.

'The funny thing was, I ended up working for ten cents a bloody day and three cups of rice. I'd've been better off starving in the bush, or locked up in the Bay with the real murderers.'

Jimmy coughed and opened his handkerchief to catch the spit, but his throat was dry.

'Me and Mick joined the infantry, thinking we'd go to Africa and fight the Germans. The Japs weren't even in the war then. We trained for desert warfare, the sand dunes and the wide open spaces, and they sent me to the jungles of Malaya. It was like learning to play cricket for a footie comp.'

He thumped his chest to unclog his lungs.

'We were with a training battalion, then the AIF, under Lieutenant Colonel Jack Callaghan. "Callaghan's Greyhounds", they called us. Well, we were greyhounds soon enough: blue-skinned and bone-thin and cowering like whipped dogs.

'But when we joined Callaghan, we were fit and hard. We were young blokes who'd just come out of months of bloody drill training, ready to defend our country or anything else, but Callaghan took a look at us and told us we weren't soldiers. Soldiering, to Callaghan, wasn't about fighting. It was about being in an army, being subject to discipline, being hard in a way that wasn't about what you could give out but how much you could take. He wanted to make us into a group that followed orders without question, because that was how you won a war. He started to train us again, the Callaghan way.

'He was a career soldier. He'd been in uniform all his life. What type of bloke stays in the army when there isn't a war, marching around like a madman, cleaning old guns? But Callaghan loved the military. His head was full of army regulations and King's Regulations and clothing regulations and every other bit of bullshit. He needed those rules to live by, every bloody one of them, like the *meshugannehs* who read the Talmud to tell them which way they should wipe their arses. Mick hated him.

'Callaghan was made of muscle and pomade. He stood straight as a bloody steeple, as if somebody had slipped a drainpipe up his arse. He liked to shout and strut and say you weren't a soldier. Sometimes I think he thought he was the only real soldier in the world. Apart from the Japs.

'I wouldn't've got through it without Mick. We watched out for each other. It wasn't always easy to be Jewish in the army, even for two fellas with Irish names – Moishe joined as Mick Ryan; I kept Rubens, which was lucky, in the end, because Callaghan liked everything done alphabetically, and Rubens and Ryan were usually put together, along with our little mate Bathurst Billy Rutherford, the third bloke on our team.

'Me and Mick were the rough end of the Jewish community because we worked with our hands, but we weren't hard men. We kept quiet about the Jewish thing, never used Yiddish words and didn't take the holidays. At first we tried to keep away from bacon, but after a month's hard training we'd eat anything just to keep our strength up.

'We gave anything to anyone, threw our money around to show we weren't Jews like *that*. And we talked like bloody Queensland cockies: fair dinkum, my oath, mate, mate, mate.

'Mate, mate, mate,' said Jimmy. 'Mate, mate, mate. Fancy a durrie? Buy you a schooey? Bet you a Teddy? Mate, mate, mate.'

The way he said it, it sounded more like 'might'. Jimmy wiped spittle from the corners of his mouth.

'Callaghan told anyone who paraded sick to get out of his unit, anyone who wanted to take it easy to get out of his unit. He gave us all a thousand chances to get out of his unit, and I've cursed myself a thousand times for not taking them. But the last time Callaghan opened the door, Moishe picked up his kit-bag and walked through it. He'd had enough of all the infantry bullshit, and he'd got this idea that he was going to be a commando. I knew I wasn't good enough to join him, so I stayed behind with Bathurst Billy. The funny thing is, all of us made the wrong decision – and how do you explain that?'

It was strange to hear Jimmy talk for so long, without jokes or gee-ups, and without even a drink in his hand. It was like he was reciting a book he had learned by heart. Sometimes he had to close his eyes to imagine the words on the page, but for the next half-hour he held the same steady, marching pace.

'We finished our training in Bathurst, where we had to get up at half past four in the morning to have our tents ready for inspection. You had to make your bloody bed like a housemaid if you were one of Callaghan's puppies. It's funny, really, when you think we ended up sleeping on bamboo platforms, that they spent weeks teaching us how to keep the corners of our blankets square. We'd've been better off learning how to yodel.

'Bathurst Billy had lied about his age to get into the army. He was the smallest bloke in the unit – you could carry him around in your kitbag – but he was a vicious little scrapper. We learned how to polish our boots, to shine them until we could see our faces on the toes. "I'd like to see Callaghan's face on my toes," said Bathurst Billy, but we stuck with it because we knew we were turning into soldiers and that's what we'd signed up for.

' "Polish your fucking boots," ' said Jimmy. 'We spent three years of the war in bare feet.'

He looked down at his slippers.

'Finally they reckoned we were good enough soldiers to die,' he said, 'and we got our orders to ship out. We came down from Bathurst on a troop train marked *Berlin or Bust*. It was bloody bust all right. I didn't see a single German the whole war.

'At the docks we were told we had to embark like perfect soldiers. Any man who smoked, or drank, or even fell out of bloody line, wouldn't be allowed to leave. We could've saved ourselves with a cigarette, most of us.

'But the band played "There'll Always be an England", and we climbed aboard the transport ship with our kitbags and our slouch hats, and bits of useless baggage like greatcoats and officers – all ready to chase Fritz around the pyramids. After a few days at sea they told us we were steaming for Singapore and Malaya. I was twenty years old, and I didn't even know where Malaya was.

Bathurst Billy found it on a map. He said, "If I were the Nips, I'd come down from the north." But the army got the good griff that they'd land in Singapore and fight their way up, which was a bit of luck, since Singapore was an impregnable fortress. When the Japs came knocking at the door, they'd get the shock of their lives. The Royal Navy had total command of the sea. And the Japs weren't a sea-faring race, Blind Freddy could see that. They didn't know their arse from their elbow. They couldn't tell up from down.

'There was a lot of excitement about race in those days. The Anglo-Saxon race was supposed to be good at some things – sport, war and heroism, for instance – the Asiatics had their own talents, like brothel keeping, swindling and shirking; and the boongs were good at nothing.

'When we got to Singapore our officers told us everything we needed to know about the Japanese race. They were five feet tall, half-blind with slitty eyes and great big teeth. They couldn't fly planes, were too small to be any use in a blue, couldn't see in the dark, and couldn't aim a rifle because they couldn't close one eye.

'Someone said they sounded like Bathurst Billy, and Bathurst Billy backhanded him so hard that he fell onto a steel rail and knocked himself out. It was true, though; the Japs were an army of bloody Bathurst Billys.

'The officers said they were a surly, savage style of mob, who'd been flogging the Chinese in Manchuria on and off since the nineteenth century. If anything, the Chinks were even lower than the Nips, commos to a man. But the rub was, Singapore was chockers with Chinese and we would have to defend them along with all the good stuff – rubber planters, buildings and loyal Malays and Indians. I learned a lot from the officers, but not one bloody word of it was any bloody use.

'We got settled into our camps in Singapore and went around the place having a bit of drink – not that I used to drink in those days – while we waited for the war to find us. None of the Sydney boys had ever felt that kind tropical jungle heat, or smelled ginger in the air, and rotten fruit and Chinese cabbage and roasting pork under clouds of bloody jasmine. There were Chinamen pulling rickshaws over bridges like beasts. The coolies used to squat by the kerb, in their straw hats and ponytails, picking rice out of their bowls with chopsticks. The first time I saw them, I thought they were sheilas doing their knitting.

'Me and Bathurst Billy decided to take a captain cook at the Raffles Hotel. Even the blokes who'd never been out of Sydney had heard of the Raffles. We stood outside and watched the rubber planters and officers file in for tiffin. We weren't allowed in. The planters treated us like boongs. I had to check in the mirror sometimes to make sure I was still a white man. We were like some new kind of servant for them, and they didn't like to see us out of barracks.

'I met a lot of planters in the war, David, and I wouldn't care if I never met another one. Some of them were tough blokes, some were weak as piss, but not one of them ever planted a single bloody thing. They were slavedrivers, really, but they fancied themselves as thinkers. They had theories about the boongs, theories about the Chinks, theories about the poor bloody Tamils. Their theory about the Japs was that they'd never dare to attack Singapore.

'One afternoon me and Bathurst Billy were supposed to be delivering some papers to an officer who was having drinks at the cricket club. There didn't seem to be much of a hurry, so we stopped to watch girls in a tea house when a Chinese funeral passed by, with a carved coffin on a horse and cart and the Chinese wailing and burning incense and banging cymbals, and I thought to myself, *We're in a different kind of place now. This is where I'll grow up.*

'I felt like a man for the first time, sitting there in my slouch hat, with my little mate across the table and my rifle at my side.'

I tried to imagine Jimmy as a young bloke, to take off his glasses, scribble hair across his head and smooth out the deep lines around his nose and mouth. We had the same mint-cream eyes, flat cheeks, pointed chin and sandy skin. He could've been me, all those years ago. What would I have done with a rifle? Shot off my toes, probably, or sat on it and broke it. I wished I had a mate called Billy who I could trust with my life, instead of a friend named Ari who had stolen my pencil case in Year Four.

Jimmy looked at his heavy watch.

'I've got to go for my tests,' he said.

*

As he grew older, Jimmy coughed harder and slept less. There were things broken in his body that had never been mended after the war, so he was always having tests. I thought of rows of multiple-choice questions, where he had to circle a letter between A and D. Jimmy had used the same doctor since 1947, Emmanuel Feingold of Potts Point, who was also known for playing 'Hava Nagila' on the spoons at WIZO charity nights. Manny the Spoons had big rotten yellow teeth, a doctor without a dentist. I had known him since he'd made me have my tonsils out when I was five years old, and I hated waiting in his surgery with the women's magazines and the clean-toilet smell.

'There's no need to sit outside,' said Jimmy. 'You can go and keep Katz company. He's got no mates.'

On the way to the railway station Jimmy stopped to speak to a man with a white stick and a lemon dog. They talked about how it used to be drier in April. The blind man thought the weather had got worse since the Beatles.

'He used to drink at the Club,' Jimmy told me.

Jimmy knew the kind of people you didn't notice, men who sat in booths and kiosks, or rollered the oval or ticketed cars. He bought me a Coke from a convenience store. The owner asked after Frida. ('He used to drink in the Tea Gardens,' said Jimmy.) At the ticket office at Bondi Junction, where Jimmy showed his pension card, the railwayman asked if he had any tips for Randwick.

As we waited on the platform, Jimmy chatted to an Aborigine in a Akubra carrying a didgeridoo wrapped in tape. ('He used to drink in the street,' said Jimmy.) The train arrived and we breathed the sweat of its brakes. The carriage was warm but not crowded. I never knew where to look on trains. I didn't like to stare at people because I didn't want them to think I was weird, but I didn't want them imagining I was scared either. I usually focused on their necks or their knees. All the kids were plugged into their Walkmans, while adults read the back pages of their neighbour's newspaper. Only the old fellas tried to catch each other's eye, to start a yarn about the days when the sun always shone.

A Fijian giant inspected our tickets at the barrier at Kings Cross.

'Can I see your pension card, sir,' he said to Jimmy.

'Are you blind as well as black?' asked Jimmy.

The Fijian laughed.

'Go through, you bald bastard,' he said, 'and keep your hands off the hookers or you'll give yourself a heartie.'

('He used to work the door at the Beach Hotel.')

Up until a few years before, Jimmy had drank with friends all over the Eastern Suburbs, but now he didn't like to pay hotel prices. He hated the Hakoah because no one ever ordered a beer, and he said he didn't want to be surrounded by Jews, although he always was. His night-time world was the Club, which grew emptier every year, like a milk bar that never restocked because it was always about to close down.

Jimmy was late for his appointment with Manny the Spoons, so he pressed the buzzer on the tall iron gates of Katz's apartment block then hurried down to Victoria Street. Katz lived on Darlinghurst Road, in a building with high windows and a locked courtyard, across the street from the El Alamein Fountain. He opened his door wearing a long Chinese robe, like the waitress at the Thai Dee. Jimmy had warned me that all artists were *faygelem*.

Katz always looked paler outside the Club, before his cheeks were flushed by beer and the dancing lights of the pokies. In his living room were shelves of books and LPs, a guitar, a saxophone and a flute, a typewriter and a stack of closely typed papers, but no easel or paints.

'They're in a cupboard somewhere,' said Katz. 'I more or less gave up painting when I came back from Singapore. Once you've been a war artist, you've already painted everything.'

'What is a war artist?' I asked him.

'A liability,' said Katz. 'A dead weight. A mouth to feed. A bludger.'

'How do you get to be one?'

He laughed.

'I was appointed by the art committee of the Australian War Memorial,' he said. 'They liked me because I'd won the Archibald Prize for my first proper portrait, and I was a realist painter, who described the world as *they* saw it – not one of these commo modernists. They were strange men, looking for a role in the war, and I guess I was too.'

'Did you have a rank?' I asked him.

'I had an honorary commission as a captain,' said Katz, 'but no military training and no gun. I used to wear my tunic with a red cravat, and a beret instead of a slouch hat. We had funny ideas about what an artist should look like in those days. You didn't get to see many of them in Balmain.'

Katz pulled open a drawer and showed me a painting of a head shaped like a balloon, with dark eyes and no front teeth. It was sharp and detailed, like a photograph.

'That's my father,' said Katz. 'The fruit man. He saw me off to war with a bag of oranges.'

A notebook lay open on Katz's table, next to a cup full of pens and pencils and brushes.

'I'm writing my diary,' he said.

'Can I read it?' I asked.

'No,' said Katz, closing the cover.

He nodded to himself, then cleared the table for the checkers board. We played six games in silence. He beat me four-two. Either I'd got a lot worse at checkers, or he'd let me win when I was younger.

Jimmy returned from the doctor.

'How were your tests?' asked Katz.

'I must've done well,' said Jimmy. 'They've invited me back next week.'

*

'Let's walk,' Jimmy said to me. 'I need to get my circulation going again.'

We got as far as the Kings Cross Hotel, on the corner of William Street.

'Do you want a drink?' he asked.

'I'm only thirteen,' I said.

'I was apprenticed at thirteen,' said Jimmy.

We popped into the bar for a schooner of Old and a middy of lemonade.

'What did the doctor really say?' I asked.

'"Hava na-bloody-gila,"' said Jimmy. 'What do you bloody think?'

'You were telling me about the war,' I said.

'Was I?' asked Jimmy.

'You were in Singapore,' I reminded him. 'Sitting in a café with your gun.'

Jimmy looked over the lip of his glass and out onto Darlinghurst Road, as if he might see something on the strip that would remind him of those days.

'We weren't usually allowed to take our guns into the city,' he said eventually, 'in case it upset the planters with the idea there might be a war coming, but we had to carry them that day because we were on duty.'

He took a sip from his beer.

'You never know,' he said, 'when you're going to wake up to the day that changes your life. A rickshaw coolie came running up to Bathurst Billy and me, his little legs going fifty to the dozen, and said, "You want jig-a-jig, Tommy?"

'He was barefoot, wearing blue shorts and a ragged shirt like all the other coolies, but he looked different from the rest because he had a kelpie-chewed Akubra instead of a straw hat. He asked where we were from. We told him we were Aussies. He said all the girls in Singapore loved the Aussies, and rickshaw men knew all the most beautiful girls.

' "Are you from Townsville?" he asked. "Townsville is the capital city of Australia."

' "First I've heard of it," I said.

' "The men of Townsville are kings," he said. "You want jig-a-jig? *Chandu?* Have you ever had a Chinese girl? They do whatever you want. They never answer back."

'I always liked a sheila who answered back, but I could see Bathurst Billy was ready to go. "How about it, Jimmy?" he asked. "Want to show these sheilas what a real Aussie's made of?" So we climbed into the cab.

' "My name's Frank," said the rickshaw man. "Pleased to meet you."

' "Are there many Chinamen called Frank?" I asked.

' "I am the only one," he said.

' "You speak good English, Frank," I said.

'"I taught myself," he said. "I made myself up."

'"He means he's a self-made man," said Bathurst Billy, laughing, but that wasn't what Chinese Frank meant at all.'

When Jimmy told his story, he was like a troupe of actors reading a play. Bathurst Billy had a high, lilting voice; Chinese Frank spoke quickly, but stumbled over his words. Jimmy gave his characters bodies too. He could shrink himself for Bathurst Billy and grow tall and stiff for Callaghan. He would even do climates, squinting in imaginary sunshine to show a hot day in Singapore. When Tamworth was cold, he hugged himself to keep warm. Fear widened his eyes, confidence strengthened his jaw, parades straightened his back. He bent at the waist to show Chinese Frank dragging his cart.

'The rickshaw man pulled off,' said Jimmy, 'and straightaway I knew something was wrong.

'"Lavender Street's the other direction," I said, but Chinese Frank had suddenly forgotten how to speak English.

'He galloped off the main road and into a side street that led to an alley that ran by a drain that went under a bridge.

'"Lavender Street no good," said Chinese Frank. "I know a better place. Young girls fresh from China."

'"That's what we want," said Bathurst Billy.

'The street where he took us was crowded with rickshaws and rickshaw men. Their laundry hung on poles from their windows. He led us into a three-storey shophouse that smelled of sweat and rubber, cabbage and congee. We walked through a stonemason's workshop, where a Chinaman with huge arms was carving an inscription onto a tombstone, and another rickshaw man was mending a tyre in the doorway. I remember two bony coolies sleeping in a huddle on the steps, rib to rib like the teeth of a hairgrip. Details like that, they stick in your mind. We came to a door on the second floor and Chinese Frank tapped once and then twice. The door opened slowly, as another coolie man answered. We were surrounded by rickshaw men.

'"What's going on?" asked Bathurst Billy. "Where are the girls?"

'"Girls coming soon," said Chinese Frank. "You want *chandu*?"

'A thin, brown-skinned rickshaw man smeared in oil passed Bathurst Billy a pipe, and we smoked opium together, lying on a mat on the floor. There was bugger all in the room bar an opium lamp, a cracked tea pot, a nest of yellow cups and a huddle of red blankets.

'"It's a queer style of cathouse that doesn't have any beds," said Bathurst Billy.

'The *chandu* made me feel loose and happy and free. I knew we were in a rickshaw men's house. I knew they were going to try to roll us. I saw Chinese Frank didn't take the pipe. But we were twice their size – well, I was anyway – and we had the guns. This was the kind of adventure we'd come to Singapore to find, the kind you couldn't have in Sydney – not until your little mate Jake Mendoza took over the Cross, anyway.

'The door opened again and these two Chinese sheilas came in. I was quite surprised because I wasn't expecting we'd see any girls. Chinese Frank introduced them as Mei-Li and Lim and said they didn't speak any English, which was why they couldn't answer back.

'The rickshaw men left the room and Mei-Li lay down beside me on the floor and we started to kiss. I pushed at her clothes, but she wouldn't take them off. I looked over at Bathurst Billy and Lim, and they weren't even touching. It was like neither of them knew what to do.

'Mei-Li snuffed out the opium lamp. She let my hands go further in the dark, but not by much. Lim climbed on top of Bathurst Billy, and I heard the door creak. It only opened a couple of inches, but I was waiting for it, and I watched Chinese Frank slide in on his belly and slither towards Bathurst Billy like a yellow-bellied black snake.

'Bathurst Billy had left his rifle by his side. As Chinese Frank reached for the stock, I pushed Mei-Li away, jumped up and stamped on his hand. Chinese Frank looked up at me down the barrel of my gun. It was the first time I had pointed it at another human being.

'The rest of the rickshaw men came rushing in, but backed off when they saw the gun. Mei-Li and Lim stood up slowly and walked to the door.

'"What's the joke, Frank?" I asked him. "Were you going to butcher us, or just steal our money?"

'Bathurst Billy was up by now, too, poking his rifle at every man and his shadow.

'"We need your guns," said Chinese Frank, "to fight the Japanese."

'I laughed.

'"We're here to batter the Nips for you," I said. "And anyway, they're not coming."

'"We have begged the government for arms," said Chinese Frank, "but the Chinese are not even permitted to join the militia. We have nothing but kitchen knives and clubs. But we will cave in their skulls with rickshaw shafts. We will gouge out their eyes with soup spoons."

'"Who are you, Frank?" I asked him.

'"I am the organiser of the All Chinese Union of Rickshaw Men," he said. "This is our headquarters."

'"He's a commo," said Bathurst Billy. "Shoot him."

'I wasn't going to shoot him – at the time I didn't reckon I'd ever shoot anybody, I didn't think I had it in me – but I wasn't about to let him go either. It was no bloody joke trying to crawl off with a digger's weapon. We were supposed to guard them with our lives, not hand them over to the first boong sheila who turned the bloody lights out. All the bloody Japs would have to do was parachute in a regiment of Tokyo Roses and we'd all be disarmed and dead by morning.

'And even if Chinese Frank hadn't planned to knock us – and, in fairness, I reckon he was just going to knock us over the head with a big stick and drag us out into an alley – we would have been chucked in the bloody boob for losing our guns. They'd've locked us up in Changi and thrown away the key, ha-bloody-ha-ha."

Jimmy paused.

'In history, that's called "an irony", David,' he said.

I nodded, as if ironies happened to me all the time.

'Anyway,' said Jimmy, 'once you've got a weapon in your hands, you've got to do something with it, otherwise you feel like a right bloody galah. If you don't actually fire the thing, you can at least wave it around a bit to make other blokes do what you want. So we used ours to herd Chinese Frank and the rickshaw men away from the sheilas and down the stairs. We were going to give them up to the wallopers and see how they liked it, but Chinese Frank was babbling on about how Mei-Li was his sister and they'd both escaped from Nanking after the Japs had cut the head off their old man and raped their mother to death while they'd watched from under a woodpile, and the only thing they wanted to do was die fighting the Japs but the Poms wouldn't trust them with the keys to bloody shithouse. He kept offering more and more money for the bloody guns, until I asked him how many members he had in his organisation, which must've been richer than the Transport Workers Union in Australia.

' "You have met them all," said Chinese Frank. "It is a difficult industry to organise. Hengwah unite only with Hengwah, and Hokien with Hokien. The *towkay* are ruthless and many *singkeh* smoke *chandu*. When we strike, people say, 'It's a good thing.

Get those cockroaches off the roads.' But we will all die soon anyway. Do you have grenades? Could you give us grenades?"

'"Let's take him to the jacks,'" said Bathurst Billy. "They can shove a grenade up his Chinese arse."

'Chinese Frank stared at him, not angry or frightened, just caught.

'Now I was a union man, the *Zayde* was a union man, all the cabinet makers were union men, but I've never known any blokes who needed a union worse than the poor bloody rickshaw pullers. And you can't give up a bloke for trying to pinch a shooter to knock the bastards who killed his mother.

'"Why don't we all have a smoko," I said, "and I'm not talking about bloody *chandu*."

'So we made a durry each and calmed down a bit, and everyone started speaking more slowly and Bathurst Billy stopped shouting, and Chinese Frank said we were all on the same side, and he knew he'd done the wrong thing, and Mei-Li and Lim came downstairs and looked at us with their sad brown eyes, and Bathurst Billy said, "Ah, let's just piss off and forget it, but if we hear of any digger getting robbed of his rifle, we'll smash up every bloody rickshaw and rickshaw man from here to Sago Lane."

'We weren't too far from Sago Lane but it tickled Bathurst Billy that there was a road by that name in Singapore, so he said it whenever he got the chance.'

*

Mrs Ethelberger was a mysterious figure. Although I'd been told I had met her, I didn't remember her at all. When I heard her name, it made me think of an overcooked beef pattie in a stale roll, sprinkled with potpourri and topped with a pickled herring. Grandma had been playing pinochle with Mrs Ethelberger and had come home to mix matzo meal with eggs to make *knaidlach*.

She asked Jimmy about his tests. He said he'd been passed as fit for overseas service.

'I'm off to North Africa,' said Jimmy.

'Over my dead body,' said Grandma.

'There'll be plenty of those,' said Jimmy. 'Blood up to my boots.'

'*Nisht!*' said Grandma. 'Enough.'

Grandma squinted at me.

'I saw plenty of boys in school uniform today,' she said.

I ran my finger over a pattern in the wallpaper.

'Short pants and straw hats,' she said.

'That'd be the private schools,' I told her. 'They went back early.'

'And the yeshiva boys,' said Grandma.

'The yeshiva's a private school too,' I told her.

'When do you go back to school?' she asked.

'After the break,' I said.

'You don't need an education to carry a rifle,' said Jimmy. 'There's plenty of professors in the boneyard.'

'I don't suppose he got you any lunch,' said Grandma.

'No, he didn't,' said Jimmy.

'Shut up,' said Grandma, 'you silly old fool.'

Grandma gave us bagels with cream cheese and gherkins.

'Beats bully beef,' said Jimmy, smearing cheese over the bristles around his mouth.

'Oh, shut up,' said Grandma. 'And you should shave more.'

'I've got no more to shave,' said Jimmy.

Grandma brought us tea in a pot.

'Mrs Ethelberger says you were with that *gonif* Mendoza on Anzac Day,' said Grandma.

'Well, Mrs Ethelberger must've been there too,' said Jimmy.

'I hate that *mamzer*,' said Grandma. 'He gives us all a bad name.'

'Yes,' said Jimmy. 'The Jews were very popular with everyone until Mendoza came along.'

Grandma kissed her teeth.

'You don't care,' she said. 'It doesn't bother you that a man's a murderer, as long as he buys his round. I don't know how I managed to find a yiddisher husband who's a shikker.'

Grandma waited for Jimmy to finish his bagel, then asked, 'So what did the doctor say about your heart?'

Jimmy wiped his whiskers with his handkerchief.

'He couldn't find it, love,' he said. 'You stole it away, years ago.'

Jimmy stood up at the table, pressed his hand to his chest and, in a deep, soaring voice, sang all three verses of 'The Rose of Tralee'.

'What's that got to do with the price of fish?' asked Grandma.

She went to hang the washing on the hoist, and Jimmy poured himself a second mug of tea.

'When did the real war start?' I asked him.

'The real war?' said Jimmy. 'Soon enough. We made Chinese Frank our personal rickshaw man, although I never felt right about riding the poor bugger like an animal. He pulled us all around Singapore, showed us the sights of the city. The seat was narrow for two normal-sized blokes, but Bathurst Billy squeezed in next to me like a Siamese twin. All the time Chinese Frank kept asking us for arms and ammo, but we hardly had any ourselves. He tried his trick on a couple of Tommies, but they got the joke too. It was the bed that gave him away. You just can't have a knocking shop without one.

'Chinese Frank used to pull us to the taxi dances at the New World amusement park, under the flame of the forest trees on the esplanade, where there'd be girls wrapped up like Christmas presents with red ribbons in their hair. You could buy a book of five tickets for a dollar and use them to pay for a dance. Bathurst

Billy said the sheilas there were like taxis because they'd always take you on the longest root for your dollar, but he never went with one himself. We'd been told ninety-nine per cent of the local women had VD. Bathurst Billy was a betting man, but he said only a mug would put a quid on those odds, although he might be tempted to drop a shilling each way, just in case it came in. He never would've gone with Lim, he said. He knew it was a joke, just like I did. Anyway, he'd heard Chinese sheilas had slanted holes. I think he'd just lost his nerve, to be honest.

'When Chinese Frank wasn't trying to persuade us to steal a field gun from the armoury, he'd tell us about the life of a rick-shaw puller, how they suffered in their feet and in their belly, and their own hearts attacked them. They were robbed by other Chinese, or stabbed for not running fast enough. *Tuam* and *mem* fought them over their fares, peons harassed them, *samseng* beat them, the Sikh police arrested them, motor cars ploughed into them. They measured their lives in pipes. People said they were lazy, opium-addicted fan-tan gamblers and hoons, but they worked like dogs at a pace they called "dog-trot", and no one but another puller could understand.

'After the last strike, he said, many of the men packed their boxes and boarded steamers back to China, to fight the Japanese. The Party – although he never used that word – had ordered him to stay behind and organise.

'"He's just trying to convert us to commo-ism," said Bathurst Billy, but he always gave Chinese Frank the spare change in his pocket, and told him to buy *maa mee* or satay for Lim.

'I asked Chinese Frank if Mei-Li was working. He said she cooked porridge for the congee hawker, and baked mooncakes for the cake seller. She also cleaned the lodging house, where forty coolies slept on shelves in the wall or mats on the floor. At university she had studied to be a doctor but now, like the others, she was waiting to die.

'"And kill," said Chinese Frank. "Mei-Li is ready to kill."

'I remembered her soft hands, so light against my chest.

'"If you like her," said Chinese Frank, "you could give her your pistol."

'But we just laughed at Chinese Frank. We felt like we were missing the war. We knew the Japanese could never take Singapore, because it was guarded by sixteen-inch guns that could destroy a warship twenty miles into the ocean. But the only warships in the ocean were the Royal Navy's unsinkable force, which the Japanese air force bloody sank the same day they tore into the Pacific fleet in Pearl Harbor.

'Once they'd sunk the unsinkable, they came down the peninsula to preg the impregnable, and it was on for big and small.

'It turned out to be us that didn't know up from down. The Nips landed in the south of Thailand and the north of Malaya. We went up there to meet them, and we blued with them a couple of times, and I thought we did all right. I'd never been to war before, but it looked to me like we held our own.

'But the Japs did know how to fight after all. They'd never bloody lost a war. The whole of Nippon was run by the army. It was their show.

'We thought they'd come by sea, not by jungle and river. They cycled down the Malay Peninsula. Can you imagine that? They bloody cycled, like it was a weekend in the country. You'd never've thought you could cycle against tanks and planes, but then we didn't have any: we were told tanks'd be no use in Malaya, and Stalin needed all our planes for Russia.

'When the Japs ran out of road, they dumped their bikes and slipped into the jungle, dismantled their field guns and carried them in pieces. When they came out the other side, they just stole more bikes. They went around us and suddenly they were behind us. They circled us, cut our supply lines, and we had to fight our way backwards just to keep on retreating.

'But we retreated and retreated, over the causeway and back to Singapore. The city was on fire, the Japs were bombing it to buggery, and our air force never arrived. There was a blood storm in the air like dust. The streets were crowded with reffos from Malaya, living in tents and under trees, as if they'd all rounded themselves up in the same place to die.

'We blew up the causeway so the Japs couldn't cross from the mainland, but they just jumped into their little boats and came in from the sea after all. So we were trapped on an island. We were told we'd have to fight to the last man, but suddenly we were ordered to stand down. Nobody could believe it. We weren't allowed to die.

'It wasn't like we wanted to give up our lives for the planters or the boongs, and most of the blokes couldn't give a rat's arse for the Chinese, but we were supposed to be fighting to buy time for Australia to prepare herself for the Nips to swarm down the Dutch East Indies to Darwin. We weren't defending Singapore and the Raffles bloody Hotel, we were fighting for our mothers and fathers and wives and children in Sydney. That's why we would've never surrendered. Everyone in our unit wanted to fight on. But the only blokes who did were men like Chinese Frank.'

'What was it like being in a battle?' I asked.

Jimmy looked out of the window and across the road to the tatty house where the *frummers* lived and stared into the cornered eyes of their *Moshiach*. 'We were the first Aussie infantry battalion to fight the Nips. We ambushed the bastards at Gemencheh Bridge in Malaya, on 14 January 1942. There were hundreds of them, off to conquer the world on their bloody bicycles. We were hiding in the bush at the edge of the road, watching them laughing and singing and pedalling along like performing monkeys. And once the bridge and the road in front were both full of Japs, we blew the bastards back to their ancestors. Everything – trees, rocks, bridge, Japs, bikes – went up into the air and landed in the river like it had fallen from a plane. The noise was like the end of the world, an explosion, then fire, and crowds of men screaming: barbecued men, cooked men, filleted, wrapped and roasted men. We made a dinner for the devil, David, and I'll never forget the smell.

'We broke cover firing, me and Bathurst Billy on the Tommy guns, the artillery on the Brens, bowling hand grenades like cricket balls. We blew them to pieces, literally pieces: arms and legs and feet and heads, and other pieces I'd never seen before, like hearts and intestines and brains and lungs. We didn't stop firing, and they barely started. They just lay there wriggling and struggling, and then they died.

'The heat of the explosion welded them to the frames of their bikes. It was like they were half-man, half-bicycle, bodies with wheels, rickshaw men. And I was shooting and shooting and shooting, and in my mind I was yelling, "Fuck, I'm alive! I'm alive! I'm alive! I'm so fucking alive! And he's dead! Look! He's fucking dead! His head's come off! He's dead and I'm alive! Fucking look at the cunt! He can't even fucking walk! He's got no legs! Oh wow wow wow wow wow! Those bombs are so beautiful! Like fireworks full of feet!" '

'Bang! Bang! Bang!' he cried. 'I'm aliiiiiiiiiiiiiive!' he screamed. 'I'm aliiiiiiiiiiiiiiiive!'

His teeth were grinding and his mouth was twisted and his eyes were crying, as Grandma came hobbling in from the backyard. She grabbed Jimmy from behind and threw her arms around him, wrestling him until he was still.

'It's all right, love,' she said. '*Alles gute*. It's finished. You're alive.'

*

The carriage clock chimed the hour.

'I've got to go for a stretch,' said Jimmy.

'Stretch' was one of the words he used when he meant 'drink', so I got dressed for the RSL, but when we reached Bondi Road Jimmy headed downhill, away from the Club.

'When Singapore fell, it was bloody chaos,' he said. 'Some men ran for the harbour and stormed the boats. The worse types went wild in the city, looting the godowns, raping the boongs, shooting out windows. But the lowest of them all was General Gordon bloody Bennett, the commander of the 8th Division, who ordered us blokes to march into camps with the Japs, while he and couple of fucking officer mates slipped out of the country, once we'd signed the surrender.

'After the ceasefire, there was silence. It was like the bombing and screaming had been the weather, and now the season had changed. The air smelled of wet wounds and dried sweat and burned flesh and lost blood.

'Eighty-five thousand of our troops – three less when you take out Bennett and his cronies – handed over their arms to thirty-five thousand Japanese. And, at first, it looked like we'd been beaten by about six of the buggers, because you hardly even saw a Jap in Singapore.

'The next thousand days, I don't think about,' said Jimmy. 'Not on bloody Anzac Day, not ever. But the day we surrendered comes back to me every morning of my life. We were fit and healthy and armed. We could've disappeared into a cellar. We could've been night scavengers, shadows, ghosts. We could've found a tunnel or a cave, lived under the Chinese, waited for calm weather then crossed the straits with a fisherman. I had a Tommy gun. We were fighting troops. We could've shot our way out. I'm not talking about everyone – maybe just me and Bathurst Billy. I'm not saying we should've fought to the last man. I'm not even saying we should've bloody fought at all.

It's just that everyone had to make their own decision. But all of us gormless bloody Greyhounds made the same one. We all surrendered.'

He saluted an invisible general.

'Sometimes I hear blokes talking about the Holocaust,' said Jimmy. 'They say, "How could the Jews have just marched to their deaths like that? Why didn't they put up a fight?" The Jews were tailors and peasants. What could they fight with? Hatpins and pitchforks? How could they organise? We were in regiments. We had guns and we had training. How could *we* have marched to our deaths? That's what I want to know. Why the hell did we do that?

'Even the Japs didn't expect it. They'd come to fight too. They'd come to die. When we surrendered, it was like we'd cheated death, and you can't do that. You can't stand up in a war and say, "I'm not going to be killed!"

'War's not a boxing match. You don't go twelve rounds trying to knock the other man out, then hug each other and walk away. You haven't broken a bloke's nose when you've shot him, you've pissed on his life. You've made his wife a widow. You've put a hole in his mother's heart. It's not Marquess of Queensberry. It's not a boys' game. Can you see that, David?'

Jimmy took me by the shoulders, but when I stiffened he relaxed his grip.

'I met up with Bathurst Billy outside the Raffles Hotel,' he said. 'It was the closest we ever came to being inside the place. There were twisted cars and shattered trucks and bits of bodies in the bomb craters in the road, and a fog of burning fuel in the air. We had to step through the tangle of telephone wires that had fallen when the telegraph poles came down.'

Jimmy coughed, as if he were still breathing clouds of fire. It started as a rasp, but grew into a growl. It shook his shoulders and forced his eyes closed. He grabbed his chest, leaned away from the pavement and spluttered into the road a black blob flecked with blood.

'We were filthy and exhausted,' he said. 'We'd been fighting for seventy days. We weren't frightened, exactly, because frightened people need something to be scared of, and we just didn't know what to expect. But I'd seen Jap blood run like soup. I'd seen men take souvenirs from their bodies. I don't just mean watches and rings, I mean ears and noses. I mean fingers and cocks. We didn't think of them as human, see. They wore boots with split toes, cloven hooves, as if they were kosher. That was the joke: they had cow's feet but, eighteen months later, we were the ones eating grass. We'd thought they were little buck-teethed devils who couldn't fight or fuck, but they fucked us up good and proper. I can promise you that.

'We marched from the city to Selarang Barracks in Changi, with our watches strapped to our ankles so the Japs wouldn't loot them, past Malays and Indians waving Japanese flags, and coolies perched on their rickshaw shafts, spitting betel juice. Every few hundred yards a Chinese would give us a smile or v-sign or a cup of water, but it still felt the way the Japanese wanted it to feel: like the people we'd been sent over to protect were celebrating that we'd failed.

'Normally our blokes would've been able to finish a march like that with no bloody worries. It wasn't as tough as the exercises we'd done in Tamworth, stomping from the showground to the lookout and back, but we were tired and that made us weaker, and it was hot as buggery and that made us weaker, and were beaten and that made us weaker.

'Also, most of the men had taken everything they could carry, because we knew there wasn't going to be anything waiting for us at the other end. Some of the old soldiers, the retreads, were humping enough tucker to last a month. Other blokes were hanging on to stuff that was about as useful as pants on a dog.

One fella was carrying two bicycle wheels, another tried to get into camp with a great big bloody floor lamp. God knows why he thought he might need that.

'The best of them stuffed their packs with books and records. Without them, the next years would've been impossible. You can't survive without art. I didn't know that before. It's something I learned. You need stories to keep you going. You need pictures of another world. You need music.'

Jimmy coughed.

'But what you don't bloody need is bagpipes. We'd been marching about two hours when some kilted bloody jock started blowing into his ball bag and making every bloody minute ten times worse.

'The straps of our bags cut into our shoulders, and blokes started throwing away bits of kit and clothes they couldn't carry. The boongs scooped them up and ran off. One or two fellas even abandoned their tucker, but others grabbed it and it all got shared out in the end, so I suppose it didn't matter much. A few blokes collapsed and had to be carried the last miles. That was something we had to get used to. That was what we should've trained for at Tamworth.

'I had two dozen tins of bully beef on my back, because you never know when you might next get a good feed – although in a million years I wouldn't've thought it would be in 1945. We heard the war was going to last another six months at most. We heard it from the same blokes who told us the Japs were dead set to attack from the sea.'

Jimmy nodded to himself.

'They also told us the Japs wouldn't accept surrender, because they didn't surrender themselves, so there we were in a situation that couldn't possibly bloody happen. We'd been flogged by a bunch of half-blind midgets who couldn't fight, and bombed silly by bastards who couldn't fly, and now we were prisoners of a race who didn't take prisoners. Up close, the Japs weren't even bloody yellow. They were more brown, like the boongs.

'At the end of the march, we were in Changi. Actually, we weren't in bloody Changi. We were in Selarang, a British Army barracks near Changi Jail. Changi was built by the Brits to lock up short-arse commos like Chinese Frank. Not many soldiers ever saw the inside of Changi Jail, but every man and his dog says they were there. I don't know why.'

We had reached the beach. The wind rattled the flags on the pavilion as Jimmy made a path through rollerbladers to lean his elbows on the rails overlooking the ocean. A salty gust blew in from the sea, and he pushed his cap further down onto his head.

'Frida wants me to go and see Arielberger,' said Jimmy. 'Arielberger is twenty-eight years old. What the hell can he understand? My generation killed other men. And died. And expected to die in return. Our minds work differently to yours. When we came home from the war, we went back into ordinary jobs. So you'd know, when you went to see your bank manager, that he might have bayoneted a man to death. He's talking to you about your bloody mortgage but he's seeing his little mate lying on the ground with his legs on the other side of the road. The bus driver could have driven a tank over women's bodies cut to pieces; that might be what's going on in his head when he rolls into bed with his wife. He might've learned to drive in the army – you can tell because they don't use their bloody gears.

'Nowadays,' said Jimmy, 'death is only for old people, for returned men. It's not the same for you. You take life for granted.'

I felt sorry that I hadn't been in a war, but they didn't seem to have big ones, where everybody joined in, any more.

'I had a Chinese girl in Singapore,' said Jimmy suddenly.

The wind stung his eyes. He rubbed them dry.

'We smoked Wills cigarettes and watched the sun fall into the straits,' he said.

He drew his hand over his eyes.

'Her skin smelled of sandalwood.' He filled his lungs with sea air. 'Her name was Mei-Li. She had black hair and she brushed it while we sat on my army blanket and watched Chinese fishermen haul in their nets.'

There were Asians taking pictures of each other on Bondi Beach.

'I went back to the rickshaw men's house with Chinese Frank,' said Jimmy. 'I bought them a bottle of Chinese wine and they passed around the pipe. When the men were asleep Mei-Li took my hand.'

Jimmy bent towards the ocean. I noticed other old men, spaced out along the rail, dressed in light suits and sandshoes, searching for their memories in the ocean.

'A lot of the blokes had local women they called girlfriends,' said Jimmy, 'but they paid for them, they coughed up the fare. I could never do that. I couldn't want somebody who didn't want me. I was a romantic, David. For me, it had to be love. Even with a Chinese girl – and, for most blokes, that was like falling in love with a toilet. They were just some place you stuck your shlong.

'And she hardly even spoke English, although she understood more than Chinese Frank made out. Mei-Li was my first. Everything before her had been fumblings outside a dance. She was real – the only real thing about my phoney war. Maybe in my memory I've turned her into something she wasn't, but I don't think so. I was broken-hearted with pity for her – she'd lost everyone to the Japs, she'd seen her family die – and pity's the biggest part of love, David. Everything else is just somewhere to put your shlong.

'You know something,' said Jimmy, 'those were the best days

of my life, sitting out under the stars with Mei-Li. She was small even for a Chinese girl. I felt like I was twice her size.'

The Asians on the beach were trying to set up illusions for their cameras, so it looked as though they were surfing in the sea while they were standing in the sand.

'I needed someone to save, David,' said Jimmy. 'A man always needs a woman to save. I was going to protect Mei-Li from the commos and the fascists, from the war, from the whole bloody world.

'She was beautiful in the Chinese way, with eyes that were nearly as black as her hair. Sometimes I've wondered if any woman would've meant the same as Mei-Li, but then I remember the way I felt back then, the hatred for the people who'd hurt her. Maybe it was the hate that was important, not the love.'

Jimmy began to walk again, past dry showerheads hanging like lampposts, to the quieter end of the beach. Behind us, men wrapped in towels struggled with their wetsuits in the open jaws of station wagons while we watched surfers in the sunshine roll with the waves.

'Best bloody country in the world,' said Jimmy.

'Can I have an ice cream?' I asked.

'It was my first time with a woman,' Jimmy replied. 'When I was with Mei-Li I didn't want to die. But it didn't change anything for her.'

I'd had enough of the soppy stuff.

'What's it like to fire a gun?' I asked him.

'I don't remember,' he said. 'It was a long time ago.'

'Did you ever get shot?'

'Shot? No.'

'Did you use your bayonet?'

'I used it to open tins.'

'And stab Japs in the guts?'

'No.'

'So what are your medals for?' I asked.

'For turning up, I suppose,' he said. 'They sent them to me in the mail. I didn't ask for them.'

'You don't ask for medals,' I told him. 'You're *awarded* them. For heroism.'

'I had a Chinese girl in Singapore,' said Jimmy. 'Her name was Mei-Li.'

This was very disappointing. It seemed Jimmy had spent most of the war surrendering, in prison, or thinking about his girlfriend. No wonder he didn't like to talk about it.

'I've never told anyone about Mei-Li,' said Jimmy. 'Even Frida doesn't know.'

'I won't tell anyone,' I promised.

It would be an easy secret to keep, because it was rubbish: fifty years ago, my grandad liked a Chinese girl with a hairbrush.

We caught the bus home. Jimmy watched the pavement from the window.

Grandma had dinner ready for us – steak and potatoes with fried onions and mushrooms.

'Did you have a nice time?' she asked me as we sat down. 'Did he keep you entertained?'

Jimmy cut into his meat.

'Great steak, love,' he said.

'Is it?' she asked.

'Of course it is,' he said.

'The reason I wondered if David was enjoying himself,' said Grandma, 'is because I didn't think he had come to stay with us to hear stories about your Chinese whore.'

BONDI

FRIDAY 27 APRIL 1990

I told Mum I had forgotten to go to school, and she screamed down the phone that I'd end up a moron like my father. Dad used to say he'd earned his degree from the university of life, but he didn't seem to remember a lot about the lessons, and he sometimes asked questions like, 'Do they still have geography?'

I came to breakfast in my school shirt and pants, with my books in my Billabong bag. Jimmy sat at the table with his drawings, a hammer and a tin of nails. He looked disappointed.

'I thought we'd fix up the spirit house today,' he said.

'You knocked it down twenty years ago,' said Grandma.

'That was the outhouse,' said Jimmy.

'Well, God knows there's enough work for you both to do in this house,' said Grandma. 'So what *are* you going to fix?'

'Everything,' he said.

Grandma squinted at him.

'Well,' she said, 'where are you going to start? The windows. We've got to get the windows done before winter.'

'We will,' promised Jimmy.

Grandma unplugged the television cabinet and wheeled it across the room.

'It'll make it easier for you to get at the front window,' she said.

'I'm not doing that today,' said Jimmy. 'I haven't got the tools.'

'So what're you doing today?' asked Grandma. 'The floor-boards? You can't tell me you haven't got a hammer and nails, because I can see them on the table where I've told you not to put your tools.'

'They need replacing,' said Jimmy, 'the floorboards.'

'I know they bloody do,' said Frida.

'Banging in a nail would just split the timber,' he said.

'Walking on them splits the timber,' said Grandma.

'You need a floor layer,' said Jimmy.

'You've laid on enough floors in your life,' said Grandma. 'You and your shikker mates.'

'I can't fix the floorboards, love,' said Jimmy. 'Not with my back.'

'So what *can* you do?' asked Grandma. 'You're not going to paint the kitchen with a hammer.'

'I'm going to build a spirit house,' said Jimmy, 'so the ghosts move in there and leave us alone.'

Grandma looked at him with kindly old eyes, snatched the hammer out of his hand and swung it at his head. He ducked and it missed, but it almost clipped his ear.

'I'll bloody kill you!' Grandma shouted, and tried to punch him on the nose.

Jimmy weaved in his seat, but she caught him and boxed his ears. Jimmy yelped. I'd never heard a person yelp before.

Grandma rubbed his ears into his skull, to make them sting.

'You useless old bastard,' she cried, and stormed into their bedroom.

Jimmy rested his elbow against the doorjamb as Grandma threw her corsets, stockings and scarves into a suitcase with her cardigans, frocks and blouses. The doorframe shifted slightly and came away from the wall.

'Everything in *my* house is broken,' shouted Grandma, 'and you want to build a house for spirits! You're a menace to society, digging bloody holes and hiding biscuits and chasing ghosts! You're a bloody *meshuganneh*! You're as mad as cut steak! You're shell-shocked! You need a hole drilled in your bloody head! I'm going to stay with Mrs Ethelberger! I'm going to have you bloody sectioned!'

She pulled a bundle of money from her bedside drawer.

'I'm leaving,' she said, 'and I'm taking the shortbreads.'

Every time Jimmy went to put his arm around her she pushed him away, and finally she kicked him in the shins. She was sick of everything, she thought Jimmy would pay her more attention if she were dead, and she kept on shouting at him while she rang a taxi.

'Silver Street, please,' she said, 'you senile old fool,' and the operator put the phone down.

Jimmy started promising things but Grandma put her hands over her ears, pushed aside the bead curtain, dragged her suitcase into the street and stamped off to catch a cab on Bondi Road.

Like everyone else, Grandma had forgotten she was supposed to be looking after me.

Jimmy scratched his chin as he watched her leave. He touched the peak of his cap and rolled a cigarette. I wasn't sure if he knew I was there.

I asked if I really had to go to school. It wasn't a proper week, with Anzac Day on the Wednesday, and we never did much on Fridays. The teachers would only want to know where I'd been yesterday, and I didn't have a note from my mum. I said I thought I could learn more by talking to Jimmy.

He looked at me vaguely, as if he could not quite think who I was.

'You can stay,' he said, 'if you help with the drawings.'

Jimmy planned out a structure of beams for the roof, and told me to sketch the altar and urn, but he didn't give me any paper.

'They say Changi was a holiday camp,' he said as he cross-hatched lines in his sketchpad, 'but it wasn't, it was an army camp. We were divided into "officers" and "men". What were the officers supposed to be, if they weren't men? And some of them weren't, either, because they had no bloody balls.

'Changi could've been anything,' he said. 'It could've been a university or a village or a soviet. It could've been an asylum. But the only thing the officers knew was army bull and King's Regulations and drill and parades. Bloody drill and parades. For some of the boys it was the way they spent their last days on earth, and that was fine by old Jack Callaghan, because at least they died as soldiers.'

Jimmy stroked his cheekbone with his thumb.

'We had CO's parades, kit inspections and fatigues. It was like we had been captured by our own army, like we'd breached regulations by surrendering and we'd all been thrown in the boob.

'But you met all kinds of fellas. There was one boy from Bendigo who walked everywhere on his hands. I don't know what that was about. Another kept hold of his ukulele all through the war. Or maybe he kept building new ones. I don't know.

'You had to have a mate, and Bathurst Billy kept me laughing. He'd had a tough life, but not the way he told it. It was one big joke, growing up with twelve brothers. Each of them used to bash the brother younger than him, and their dad used to bash them all. It was like being in the Nipponese army. War wasn't much different to peace for Bathurst Billy.

'I remember the day I first saw Katz. I thought, *That poor bastard's not going to live out the week*. He was so thin, it looked like he'd already been a prisoner for a year. But the thing about Katz was he didn't seem to care that he'd been captured. His job was to paint the war, and prisoners were a part of that war too. He'd managed to keep hold of his brushes because the Nips couldn't think of any reason to steal them, and he hid his paints inside his mate's fucking ukulele.

'Bathurst Billy recognised him from Balmain. Bathurst Billy should've been called Balmain Billy, because he grew up across the road from the West End Hotel. He hated bloody Bathurst. His family called him "Bath-first" because he always had to be in the tub before his brothers.

'I only realised Katz was a Jew when I went over to have a yarn about girls and found he knew Moishe – I mean Mick – through Frida's sister Sally *ava ashalom*. I'd never been to Balmain. Katz told me about the smell from the soap factory, and a *shiksa* who worked there who'd take you to the storeroom for a shilling.

'He was a funny sort of bloke – poncy but not a horse's hoof. I always remember he gave me a cigarette. We still had tailor-mades then, and fellas still gave them to strangers.'

Jimmy examined each of his fingers, as if it were a cigarette.

'When we first got to Selarang,' he said, 'we had to fix the place up, to build our own jail. The officers had us organised to get the water running and sort out the sewage, which was okay because everyone knew it had to be done. Then they told us to build an officers' mess. Most of the time it was hard to know if the orders were coming from the brass or the Japs, but *Schmegegge* Freddy would've had the sense to know the Japs didn't order the officers to build a separate mess.'

Jimmy bit his lip.

'It was mostly Callaghan's blokes in our hut, but there were also a few who hadn't found their units yet. One of them was a fella they called "Townsville Jack". He arrived two days after everyone else and when any bugger asked where he was from he'd say, "Townsville, Jack," whether their name was Eddie, Pete or Alfonso.

'He was a different style of bloke, Townsville Jack. Everything about him was long. He had long muscles on his arms, and fingers like rail spikes, and a big, open face that sort of fell open from his jaw. He had teeth like a horse, and a thick, black mane of hair that was already creeping back up his forehead, and these long, happy eyes. His smile made you want to like him, but it didn't help you trust him. Until you knew him, you could never tell if he was laughing at you or himself or the farce of it all.

'Another bloke turned up after Townsville Jack, a stocky fella called Quilpie who'd got lost somehow in the retreat. There were, I suppose, six places in the barracks where Quilpie could've bedded down: two on each end of the rows of bunks, and two in the gaps between.

'"I'll give you six-to-one he takes the space at the far end," said Townsville Jack.

'It was the first time he had spoken to me.

'"How much?" asked Townsville Jack.

'"How much what?"

'"How much at six-to-one?"

'"A million quid," I said.

'"I can't cover it," said Townsville Jack. "How about sixpence?"

'Quilpie stepped further into the barracks. He looked in both directions, but he seemed more interested in the side of the room that we called "the West Wing".

'"Fair dinkum,' said Townsville Jack. "Eight-to-one. Sixpence'll get you four bob."

'Quilpie rubbed his jaw. He wasn't the sharpest knife in the block, not by a long shot.

'"I'll take a ha'penny at seven-to-one," said Townsville Jack.

'The new man turned east.

'"A penny at twenty-to-one that he goes west," said Townsville Jack.

'Quilpie took one step forwards, one step sideways, headed down the middle and made his way to the space that Townsville Jack had chosen at the start.

'"You could've won yourself some lunch money," said Townsville Jack.

'"With what?" I asked. "I'm as broke as a boong."

'"I could've lent you your stake," he said, "at five per cent. You'd still've cleared a few bob, and I'd've walked away with my pride intact."

'"I've got no security," I said.

'"But you're not going anywhere," said Townsville Jack. "C'mon, I'll shout you a bit of tucker from the mess. I'll give you ten-thousand-to-one they're serving meat pies, twenty-thousand-to-one on steak and potatoes."

'I let Townsville Jack buy me rice and a vegetable.

'"Delicious, mate," he said, licking his fingers. "You can't beat a Changi meat pie."

'I wondered if he was mad.

'Townsville Jack and Bathurst Billy got on like a bloody warehouse on fire, because Townsville Jack could talk about horses until his teeth fell out, and Bathurst Billy missed the gallops more than he missed his mum's baked dinners. He'd been an apprentice jockey at Randwick before he'd signed up. He was so small.

'We had a sergeant major named Ramsay, who'd been with us since Tamworth. He was Callaghan's right-hand man, a good soldier but a believer, you know. And believers are dangerous because they give their lives to something that isn't there. For Ramsay, it was an idea of the army as the best place for men. In war or peace, in jail or in camp, if a man could be a soldier, he could always be a man.

'So he came into our barracks, strutting like he was still in Tamworth, to choose volunteers to build the officers' mess. Townsville Jack had the digger's trick of disappearing whenever anyone wearing pips or stripes came around a corner, but Ramsay caught him asleep on his bunk after a night under the wire.

'Most of the other lads scarpered but me and Bathurst Billy were slow to get started and Ramsay managed to collar us at the door. Townsville Jack woke up to Ramsay shouting an order in his face, and he tried to swat him away.

'"Why can't the officers make their own mess?" asked Townsville Jack.

'"Yours is not to reason why," said Ramsay, "because you haven't got the bloody brains."

'Townsville Jack didn't like taking orders,' said Jimmy, 'but he didn't mind hard work, even though he didn't exactly look for it. He was the only digger I ever met who enjoyed digging. He even had a face like a bloody shovel. We dug the foundations for the officers' mess while Quilpie scrounged timber and Townsville Jack whistled "Colonel Bogey" through the gap in his teeth.

'Townsville Jack was a friendly enough bloke but he didn't give much away.

'"Where's the rest of your unit?" I asked him.

'"I've applied for a transfer," he said.

'"You can't apply for a transfer," I told him, "you're a prisoner of war. Where do you think you'll get transferred to?"

'"Out," said Townsville Jack.

'I couldn't tell if he was serious. Blokes had some funny ideas in those days. They couldn't get a grip on what had happened. I still didn't realise that Townsville Jack didn't accept it at all.

'He turned back to his shovel.

' "Where'd you learn to dig?" I asked him.

' "Townsville, Jack," he said.

'In those early days there was a lot of talk about what had gone wrong. What I didn't understand was, if they weren't going to defend Singapore, why didn't they evacuate it? Why did they just give us to the Japs? And if we'd fought to the end, how much worse would it have been? Sixteen thousand of us men died as Japanese prisoners of war, for no bloody reason at all. Why didn't they let us fight? You'd think we could've killed someone.

'We were told they wanted to avoid a massacre in Singapore, that if we didn't fight the Japs *too* much, they might not take it out on the civilians, but that was the worst fucking joke of all.

'Fucking joke,' said Jimmy, clenching his fists. 'Fucking joke.'

He thumped the table, jumped up and paced across the living room, swearing at the walls. I got frightened again, but he quickly calmed down.

'Sorry,' he said. 'Sorry, sorry, sorry.'

He linked his fingers.

'It's a long story,' he said. 'It's hard to tell it in the order it happened. The film in my head . . . it flickers. Sometimes it seems like the projector's breaking down.'

I reached to touch him, to comfort him.

'They're all I've got left,' he said, 'these . . . images. Sometimes they're fuzzy and faint, but today they're as sharp as a stake. I can feel the sun on my back, the sweat on my forehead.'

He looked at his hands.

'They ache,' he said, 'like they've been lifting a bloody shovel.'

He curled his fingers, then relaxed.

'Everyone noticed how good Townsville Jack was at making holes,' he said, 'so the officers asked him to dig another one, about ten yards from the parade ground. The rest of us swept paths and paraded without arms, while Townsville Jack made a trench that could've changed the course of history if he'd built it around Belgium in 1914.

'I happened to be on a smoko when a captain came over to inspect it. Townsville Jack was resting on his shovel, looking into the ground.

'"That's quite a hole," said the officer.

'"It's a bloody great hole," said Townsville Jack.

'"It's bigger than I imagined," he said.

'"It ought to be on a map," said Townsville Jack.

'"Well, very good," said the captain.

'They looked at each other.

'"What's it for?" asked Townsville Jack.

'"For storage," said the captain. "Most probably."

'Townsville Jack wiped his big nose with his huge hand.

'"Or drainage," said the officer.

'Townsville Jack knew there was something crook, because you don't just tell a man to dig a hole when you don't know what it's for, unless it's for nothing at all. But Townsville Jack liked his hole so much, he kept on digging anyway. The next day, another officer came around and told him to stop work on the hole.

'"I need you to fill it in," he said.

'"What's wrong with it?" asked Townsville Jack.

'"It's in the wrong place," he said.

'"Your arsehole's in the wrong place," said Townsville Jack.

'"Fill it in, soldier," he said.

'"I'll fill you in," said Townsville Jack.

'"I'll put you on a charge," said the officer.

'"It'll be the last thing you do," said Townsville Jack.'

The carriage clock chimed, and Jimmy stopped talking.

'He was a hard bloke, Townsville Jack,' he said, eventually. 'You'd think nothing could break him.'

'What happened to him?' I asked.

'What happened?' said Jimmy. 'Something broke him.'

*

Jimmy drilled into the ground with the heel of his boot and left a shallow brow in the dry soil.

'We'll build it here,' he said.

We went around the back of the house to the shed, where Jimmy stored balls of string and cable; towers of tobacco tins filled with nails; reels of shoelaces and bands; matchboxes stuffed with keys; two jars of hungry dentures, and thousands and thousands of bottle tops.

Mounted on the wall were drills and saws, pliers and hammers, set squares, T squares, axes, planes and files. A stack of waste wood rested in one corner, like a bonfire that had never been lit. Jimmy threw nothing away. He used to buy crates of oranges for his vitamins, and for my grandma to boil into bitter marmalade. When the crates were empty, he'd prise them apart, stack the timber and straighten out the nails.

Jimmy pushed aside the bones of fruit boxes and hunted through bales of chair legs until he found a broom handle. On his workbench vice he measured and marked it, clamped and cut it, and tossed the shorter end back into the pile.

He chiselled the broom handle to a point, as if he were sharpening a pencil, then handed me the stake and picked up his heavy wooden mallet.

'Front yard,' he said, and I followed him back there.

He planted the broom handle in the pit made by his boot, and I knelt and steadied it while Jimmy knocked it into the ground with the mallet. He lodged a second broom handle next to the first, and it looked as if we'd built a pair of very low goal-posts, or high, wide wickets.

'Smoko,' he said, and we took a tea break on the front step.

Barry Dick the *frummer* came over and asked what we were doing.

'I'm planting wood,' said Jimmy, 'to cut out the middleman.'

'I don't follow you,' said the *frummer*.

'This way, you don't have to bother with trees,' said Jimmy. 'You just drive the sticks into the ground and they take root themselves.'

'It's a miracle,' said the *frummer*. 'You should give thanks to *Hashem*.'

'I will,' said Jimmy, 'if I see him.'

The *frummer* blessed us and left us.

I didn't go to a Jewish day school, so I'd never had much to do with the *frummers*. Jimmy said they'd come from Russia or Poland, and fifty years later they still hadn't noticed the difference in the weather. The *frummers* liked to speak Yiddish, even the ones who'd had to learn it when they were grown up because their parents hadn't been *frum* enough.

It was hard to see what they did, apart from *frummering*. Mum said they were Jewish Mormons, except they: (1) had long hair and long sleeves instead of short hair and short sleeves; (2) drove old cars instead of riding new bicycles; and (3) tried to make Jews more Jewish instead of persuading everyone else to be more Mormon.

So they weren't much like Mormons at all, except that most of them were American. Also, they were boring.

The *frummers* were waiting for the Messiah to come to earth. Many of them believed their rabbi, the *Rebbe*, was *Moshiach*, but he was on earth already and it hadn't changed anything.

Dad said the *frummers* weren't really even Jewish, they were a sort of fancy-dress cult, but at least they kept kashrut and wore hats, which was more than he did.

Nearly all the *frummers* in Sydney seemed to live around Bondi, which was a bit of a waste since they never went to the beach or even wore T-shirts, because God didn't like their arms. Jimmy called them 'the Barmy Army', but that didn't stop him from talking to them in the street.

Jimmy watched Barry Dick walk up to Bondi Road, then turned back to his poles. He gripped one stick in each hand and let them carry his weight.

'I've seen a Chinaman's head on a pole,' he said to me. 'All grey and bloody. His lips were blue. They'd bashed out his teeth.'

Jimmy brushed his fingers across his face, trailing his cheekbones and the line of his chin.

'I remember the rest of Singapore like I'm watching a film,' said Jimmy, 'but the heads're a photograph, a picture on their own.'

He wrapped both his hands around a single pole.

'But I was telling you about Townsville Jack, eh? That great big unmilitary digging fucking machine. Well, Ramsay came to our barracks, and Townsville Jack was on his palliasse, peeling the skin off his blisters. Ramsay sat at the end of Townsville Jack's bunk, like a doctor.

' "Do you understand," asked Ramsay, "that you're still in the army and obliged to obey orders?"

' "Much obliged," said Townsville Jack. "Can I ask you a question, Sergeant Major? Why was I ordered to dig that bloody hole in the first place?"

' "In the first location?" asked the sergeant major.

' "In the first bloody instance," said Townsville Jack, stripping a ribbon of film from his foot.

' "It's part of a program to boost the men's morale," said the sergeant major.

'Townsville Jack nodded like he understood.

' "By giving them holes to look at?" he asked.

' "By giving them something to do," said Ramsay.

' "You mean you made me dig a hole for *my* morale?" asked Townsville Jack.

'Ramsay tugged at his bushy moustache.

' "You enjoyed it, didn't you?" he asked.

' "I enjoyed it because I thought I was doing something useful," he said.

' "Well, you were," said Ramsay. "You were keeping occupied."

'Townsville Jack shook his big, heavy head.

' "I don't need to dig holes to keep occupied," he said. "I could read a book."

' "Oh," said Ramsay. "And what was the last book *you* read?"

' "*Lady Chatterley's Lover*," said Townsville Jack.

' "Bull," said Ramsay. "That's banned."

' "Not here, it isn't," said Townsville Jack, and he pulled out his copy from under his pillow.

'Ramsay took the book and opened it near the middle.

' "You could find some chap to read it to you," said Townsville Jack. "It'd keep him occupied. Be good for his morale."

'Ramsay studied the book as if he hadn't seen one before.

' "Where did you find this?" he asked.

'Townsville Jack showed him the flap on the first page that said it was the property of Singapore Library.

' "Are you trying to tell me," said Ramsay, "that while your mates were blueing and whoring, you went into town and joined the *library*?"

' "The library came here," said Townsville Jack. "The brass talked the Nips into letting us have the books. I've got this too," he said, and passed Ramsay *A Homage to Sappho* by Jack Lindsay.

'Ramsay turned the pages and stopped at an etching of two bare-breasted women.

' "That's art," said Townsville Jack.

' "It's filth," said Ramsay.

' "Filth is dead bodies, mate," said Townsville Jack, "not living ones."

'Ramsay went back to Lady Chatterley, whispering to himself

and nodding. After a while he closed the book and locked his hands behind his back, which meant he was about to make a speech. He was only talking to Townsville Jack, but the whole hut was listening – not because we gave a damn, but because there was bugger all else to do.

'"Normally," he began, "I'd be obliged to confiscate this book from you, as the possession of a book that is banned in Australia is contrary to the King's Regulations, whether you're in Singleton or bloody Singapore."

'"Which regulation?" asked Townsville Jack.

'"All of them," said Ramsay. "There is no regulation that states a soldier has a right or duty to read *Lady Chatterley's Lover*. But in our present circumstances I can't see it's a bad thing. You've got eyes, soldier. You know what's going on with a few of the younger blokes. It's not the Aussie way.

'"Maybe," said Ramsay, "reading *Lady Chatterley's Lover* will take their minds off buggery."'

Jimmy relaxed out of his impersonation of Ramsay. His shoulders fell and his mouth softened.

'It was true,' he said, 'there were a few boys who'd . . . become attached to each other. In my day, you didn't have all this . . . stuff you have now with men. You didn't hear about it, you didn't talk about it, you didn't see it, but you were a bloody fool if you thought it didn't go on.

'I don't like it,' said Jimmy. 'It makes me sick to think about it, but I'll tell you this: some of the boys never had any love in their lives, and if they got it from another bloke, if they *wanted* it from another bloke, then I know sailors who've done a lot worse for a lot less reason. Some of the younger ones, they just needed somebody to touch them, to hold them. Better they spent their last days that way than digging a useless bloody trench. And that doesn't mean I'm in favour of any of this rubbish you see on Oxford Street either. But to Ramsay, buggery was the opposite of morale. It was what blokes did when they had no holes to fill.'

*

It was past time for a drink, which meant we had to make up the minutes by dashing like the Energizer Bunny through Bondi Junction. (The old men didn't like the Energizer Bunny. They preferred the adverts with Jacko Jackson, although they didn't like him either.)

We were the last to arrive at the Club. Myer was already halfway through the story of the blonde *shiksa* who'd given him a handjob after the AJEX march on Anzac Day in 1951.

'I'd've rather had it from a yiddisher woman,' said Myer, 'but there weren't many Jewish girls around in those days.'

'There weren't many around *you*,' said Solomon.

'I have my memories,' said Myer.

'Every dog has its day,' said Katz.

'Yes,' said Myer. 'St Bernards, for instance, have St Bernard's Day, which I believe is the twentieth of August.'

'Every dog has its hair,' said Solomon, lifting his glass.

The old men drank, and chewed their tongues. Katz tapped his copy of Flaubert's *Sentimental Education*.

'So,' he asked me, 'what did you learn at school today?'

'I didn't go,' I said. 'I had to stay at home and help Jimmy.'

The old men gloated sadly.

'Is he still having the problem with his *pisching*?' asked Myer. 'I told him to stick a rod in it.'

'Did you shake it for him afterwards?' asked Solomon.

'You should go to school,' said Katz, 'otherwise you'll end up a cabinet maker.'

'I like cutting wood,' I said.

'So you should become a merchant banker,' said Solomon, 'and cut wood in your spare time.'

'It's a nice hobby,' Myer agreed, 'cabinet-making. Because anyone can do it.'

'All you need is no education,' said Solomon.

'And I suppose you have to go to university to read a tape measure,' said Jimmy.

'Yes,' said Solomon, 'the tailoring process must look impossibly complicated to the outsider, but all it takes is a fine mind, an unerring eye and a cock the size of a security torch.'

'You must've slipped in the back way, then,' said Jimmy. 'Like a *faygeleh*.'

'I was apprenticed to Solomon Solomons the First,' said Solomon, 'often known as "King" Solomon, the true "King of the Cross". My father did not need *gunsels* to guard his reputation, his good name rested on his unparalleled skills with the thimble and shears, and a certain degree of confusion with the British pre-Raphaelite painter Solomon Solomon – a yiddisher fella who was, by the way, a great favourite of that anti-Semitic bastard Norman Lindsay.'

'He invented camouflage,' said Katz.

'My father invented electric light,' agreed Solomon, 'nuclear fission and microsurgery. He cured the common cold.'

'No,' said Katz, 'Solomon the artist. He designed camouflage for tanks.'

'So it is possible for an artist to serve a useful purpose in wartime,' said Solomon. 'I would never have believed it, had the information not come from such a reliable source as Ernest Katz, who once told me that Mrs Ethelberger – then Miss Ethellotz – was no longer a virgin and would offer her favours in exchange for a strawberry milkshake.'

The old men raised eyebrows and thumbed chins. There was the kind of silence that usually came before one of Solomon's detailed attacks on Katz. Katz sensed it coming and spoke first.

'Do you know who I saw?' he said. 'Mrs Ethelberger's brother-in-law, Izzy Berger.'

'That *gonif*,' said Jimmy. 'What's he doing?'

'He was walking down Darlinghurst Road,' said Katz. 'I didn't speak to him.'

'I was assaulted by Mrs Ethelberger,' said Myer. 'She slapped me around the chops.'

'It's a small world,' said Katz.

Solomon stabbed the table with his finger.

'You should write down your insights,' he said. 'Make sure they're not lost to the Jewish people when you're gone.'

'The Jewish people, nothing,' said Myer. 'They're the inheritance of all mankind. What did he say earlier? "Every dog has its day." Brilliant.'

'It belongs in the Torah,' said Solomon.

'He got it from the Torah,' said Myer.

The men pretended to *daven* to Katz.

'This morning,' said Solomon at the end of their prayer, 'I almost crashed my car into the driver in front of me, who came to a sudden stop for no reason except that he needed to answer his phone.'

The old men groaned. They hated the new mobile phones.

'He was, of course, Asian,' said Solomon.

'And you were, of course, Jewish,' said Katz.

'What's your point?' asked Solomon.

'My point is that neither fact has any bearing on the story.'

Solomon sighed like a steaming kettle.

'Ernie Katz,' said Solomon, 'is a multiculturalist. That is to say, he sees a unique value in every creed and lifestyle and believes that if only we made the effort to understand each other, not as "others" but as reflections of ourselves, we would realise that we are all pieces of one big jigsaw people, of the kind that used to be popular in the days when we made our own entertainment in dismal parlours after the six o'clock swill, or gathered around the piano to check that nobody had hidden a bottle of whisky inside the footstool.

'Katz believes we should love our enemies, a sentiment he shares with another great yiddisher turncoat, Jesus Christ. But does he love his friends, this is the question. No doubt Ernie Katz, like Jesus, would allow a prostitute to wash his feet – and whatever transpired after that would be the private business of two consenting adults and no concern to us at all – particularly you, David – but would he even stretch his already unusually elongated legs in service of three yiddisher returned servicemen whom he has known all his shirking life? Would he stand up and be counted and declare to the world, "Jimmy has bought one round! Myer has bought one round! Solomon has bought two rounds (including both the last drink yesterday and the first drink today)! Nobody is keeping a scorecard, but if they were, the numbers would not lie! When it is my shout, I hide in the bathroom, disguised as two flush pipes and a float, and this is to my eternal shame!"'

Solomon came out of character for a moment to wipe his brow.

'No, you will not hear those words from the sealed lips of Katz's piscine mouth,' he continued, 'because he is too concerned with the public image of Chinamen to lift a finger for a friend.'

CHANGI DIARY

MAY 1942

Today I gave a short lecture on Japanese history at Changi University.

The men love the university, although it has no great Gothic halls, no quads or colleges, not even a campus, except in the mind. The Commodore of the Changi Dry Land Yacht Club is talking about establishing a boat race although, of course, we have no rivers and no rivals. But dreams and jokes and grand pointless gestures all lend colour to our surrendered lives.

Many of the men did not finish school. They cannot read or write, and they nurture an exaggerated idea of the quality of the faculty of Changi University. I've heard them say their degree certificates will be accepted by employers after the war. They need to think that something good and useful will result from their captivity, because otherwise these months are just a part of death.

My lecture was entitled 'What the Japanese Believe'. Two priests attended, thinking I was going to speak on Shinto. But I was trying to afford the men a glimpse inside the mind of the enemy. I explained the Japanese thought white colonial rule in Asia was a crime, which had fuelled hatred, resentment and independence movements from the Punjab to Java. They were confident to invade Malaya because they would be greeted as liberators. The Malays and Tamils would turn on us because we took their land, or indentured them on plantations, and used them to produce raw materials that we exported to England, where we turned their rubber into manufactured goods we then sold back to them. Since the planters didn't pay the locals enough to buy, for example, tyres made from their own rubber, most of the goods ended up back in the hands of white men.

It is difficult to present a foreign case without appearing as a devil's advocate. At the lecture was a planter who had served in a local volunteer regiment, and he stood up to object. He said he'd never exploited anybody, he'd looked after his Tamils (he was so angry he could hardly speak, and I thought he'd said 'towels') and they were a damn sight better fed on the Tamil lines than when they were starving in their villages in India, which was why they'd come to Malaya in the first place. He ran a tea plantation, and any damn fool who thought the Tamils were too poor to buy tea (or had any use for a set of Dunlop tyres) had no place in a university.

I explained that I was not passing my own judgement on colonial rule, but trying to illuminate the Japanese case, to explain why we had gone to war in Malaya and, to an extent, why we were now imprisoned in Singapore.

The Greater East Asian Co-Prosperity Sphere wasn't a joke to the Japanese. They thought they could reorganise a whole continent in the way of the European powers, and use Siam, Burma, the Philippines, French Indochina, the Dutch East Indies and Malaya to feed Japanese industry and agriculture. They promised the natives freedom and independence within a region whose security was guaranteed by an enlightened, benevolent

Japan. In the Japanese mind we weren't fighting to defend the natives, we were fighting to keep control of them after the war.

The men do not understand the culture of the Japanese military, and ignorance on both sides can only add to the prevailing atmosphere of hatred and mistrust. In the IJA, discipline is maintained through physical punishment. If they have committed the slightest breach of regulations, and whether or not they are aware of the law they violated, a captain might slap a lieutenant who in turn might punch a sergeant who could kick a corporal who'll thrash a private who'll punch the daylights out of a Korean (who don't seem to have any rank, only a nationality). The Japanese do not resent this, they accept it as the natural order. They believe it toughens them, makes them into more vigorous, physical men – which it probably does, in its way. They don't fear blows. They may not welcome them, but they respect them. A *gunso* doesn't take it personally when he's whacked across the cheeks by his CO, so he finds it difficult to grasp why a prisoner objects to being corrected in the same way.

A Jap might see one of the men work a hammer poorly (and, if there were a cup for the most moronic use of a simple tool, the ferociously uncooperative Australian POWs would carry the trophy back to Fremantle) and yell instructions at him in Japanese. Since the prisoner is unlikely to speak much Japanese beyond *tenko*, *ichi bun* and *yasumi*, and the guard almost certainly knows no English apart from some obscene nonsense the men may have taught him, the *gunso* sees no other way to alert the prisoner to his mistakes than a couple of quick stinging blows to the face. His own men would recognise this as a part of their daily routine, and redouble their efforts to please him. Our boys swear they'll never forget the bastard's name, record the time and date of their beating in spidery marks in the margins of Bibles, and pledge to see the poor man hang.

There is also an issue with bowing. The Japanese bow to one another in the same way as we might shake hands or salute. An Australian who claims he will bow down to no man might believe himself to be Ned Kelly or some similar romantic outlaw, but to the Japanese he is simply ignorant. If the *gunso* bows to the lieutenant, why shouldn't we bow to the *gunso*? Or the private for that matter? We have no status here, we're at the bottom of the heap, fighting men who've given up the fight.

In the act of bowing, the idea is to bring your head lower than the waist of the man in front of you. Unfortunately, for some of our boys this is not possible without the skills of a circus performer or the discipline of a yogi. There seems to be no minimum height for entry to the IJA (many of their men are well under five feet tall) and there is, of course, no upper limit for Australians: there is a surgeon here who is the height of one Jap standing on another's shoulders.

When a prisoner fails to bow, or to bow low or stiff or quickly enough, and a Jap acts to correct him, he is merely maintaining the natural order of things. He doesn't expect to be sued for reparations at some distant tribunal.

The men don't want to hear this. They need to believe the Japs are monsters, driven by the compulsion to rape and murder; to tear unborn children from the womb, skewer them on their bayonets and roast them over campfires; to bury prisoners alive. They want to be told they were faced in the field by demonic fanatics, the bitter spawn of hell. They can't grasp that we were beaten by a more disciplined army, with greater political power. The government of Japan is the army; the government of Australia is John Curtin's Labor Party. The Japanese don't have to worry about checks and balances, the niceties of democracy, the compromises with a loyal opposition. They are free to wage war as they see fit, with the whole nation at their disposal. They were never crippled by appeasers, or paralysed with doubt.

'Get back to Tokyo!' shouted the planter. 'You're a bloody white Nip!'

There is a small communist cell in the camp, and they sent along one of their agitators to make their point, which seemed to be that the primary purpose of the war for the working man was to defend the Soviet Union against fascism.

'Hang on a minute, sport,' said one of the diggers, 'it was you blokes who opposed rearmament, and that's the bloody reason we were undersupplied in the first place. If we'd've been able to build all the planes and tanks we needed, we might've been able to stop the Japs in Gemas, never mind scurry down to Singapore where we didn't have enough ships to fill a bath.'

The communist said all progressive people had been forced to tactically oppose the war to give Stalin time to rearm.

'You're as brainwashed as a sheep's head in a bucket,' called the heckler.

I, of all people, have some time for the communists now. They may be blinkered, but at least they are blinkered realists. Many of the men are simple fantasists, who think they were forced to surrender by cowardly officers. All they have to take pride in is the fact their resistance caused the IJA to slow its advance sufficiently to make time for Australia to prepare her defences, but I suspect they are misguided even in this. Our sacrifice was futile; we inflicted only small casualties on the Japanese, their advance was as swift as could be reasonably expected, and Mr Curtin didn't use his seventy days to erect a wall around Australia.

I suspect the biggest problem we have caused the IJA is the logistical conundrum of what on earth to do with us all.

BONDI

FRIDAY 27 APRIL 1990

The old men usually got drunk on a Friday night. At about eight o'clock they would finish their last glass of Old and begin to order trays of whisky. Their speech would droop and their eyes would slur, and the last word they said wouldn't always be connected with the one before. Solomon would become nostalgic, Myer disdainful, Katz reflective and Jimmy more talkative. I didn't like it much. They were all ruder and harder to understand. Solomon would suddenly do something secretly generous, like slip ten dollars into my pocket, then whisper, 'If you spend it on a stripper, make sure you don't get the clap.'

Myer heard him.

'What do you think he'll get for ten bucks?' he asked. 'It's not like the old days when Jake had Aphrodite's, and you could jump on the stage and dip your donga into Tina while you rubbed her Talking Tits. That's all over now. You're not even allowed to touch them.'

'*Nisht*,' said Jimmy. 'Enough.'

'Not even on the *tochis*,' said Myer.

'The boy doesn't need to know,' said Jimmy.

'And certainly not for ten bucks,' said Myer.

He opened his wallet and counted out the notes.

'Lap dancing, they call it,' he said.

'How would you know?' asked Katz.

'Cock teasing, I call it,' said Myer, putting his wallet away.

'Nobody cares what you call it,' said Jimmy.

Solomon had his own thoughts.

'Do you know what I remember the most about Izzy Berger?' he asked.

'The taste of his *tochis*?' asked Myer.

He stuck out his tongue and licked like a lizard at his upper lip.

'The time he managed that singer, Lucky Jack Gold,' said Solomon.

Myer swatted at the air, as if an invisible Jack Gold was trying to climb his thigh.

'Lucky by name,' said Myer, '*putz* by nature.'

'He was in Vietnam,' said Solomon. 'There weren't many yiddisher fellas in Vietnam.'

'It's a Buddhist country,' said Katz.

Jimmy swirled his glass.

'You know what I remember?' he asked. 'You were going to make a fortune selling tripods.'

'Tricorns,' said Solomon.

His fingers traced three corners around his head.

'Admirals' hats,' said Jimmy. 'Like Lucky Jack wore when he sang "Sail On".'

Solomon smiled glumly.

'I wish I'd written that song,' said Katz.

'You'd've written it for Izzy Berger,' said Jimmy. 'He stole the publishing rights. So now every time there's a sale on at *schmatta* shop, run by a shonky *shnayder* who's tone deaf and – for the sake of this illustration – as fat as the bear on a Bundy bottle, and they play Lucky Jack's "Sail On" over the speakers, it's another quid in Izzy Berger's pocket.'

'I've still got those tricorns,' said Solomon. 'Eight dozen boxes in a warehouse in Surry Hills. I ought to have got Jake to burn it down.'

'Buildings don't just burn down any more,' said Katz. 'Have you noticed that? It used to happen all the time.'

'Everything's changed,' said Solomon, 'and none of it for the better.'

'It's better that buildings don't burn down,' said Katz.

'Not if you've got one that's full of tricorns, it isn't,' said Solomon.

'You had them made specially,' said Jimmy.

'Of course I did,' said Solomon. 'There weren't twenty bloody admirals' hats in Australia. We've only got about twenty bloody admirals.'

'And even they don't wear those hats,' said Jimmy.

'No, they bloody don't,' agreed Solomon.

'No one does,' said Jimmy.

'I'll tell you who does,' said Solomon. 'Lucky Jack Gold. And every year, when he needs a new one, he rings me and I send it to him, wherever he is in the world, which is usually some *Hashem*-forgotten hole like Winton or William Creek. I reckon he'd be about fifty now. If he lives to be one thousand two hundred and twelve, I'll be shot of all them.'

'Methuselah died at nine hundred and sixty-nine,' said Katz.

'I'd still have two hundred and forty-three hats left,' said Solomon.

'Listen to him,' said Katz, 'the human calculator.'

'What makes you say he's human?' asked Myer.

'He shares some characteristics with human beings,' said Katz, 'but has a greater volume and density.'

The men each emptied their whiskies, then all looked at me, as if it was my shout.

'I'm only thirteen,' I reminded them.

'I should've given you a tricorn for your bar mitzvah,' said Solomon.

'Maybe you could sell them to the *frummers*,' suggested Katz. 'When they start a navy.'

'He had a voice, but,' said Myer. 'Lucky Jack.'

'They should have called him "the Voice",' said Katz, 'instead of "Lucky".'

'Then Johnny Farnham could've been called "Lucky",' said Solomon, 'which would've been more appropriate, since that man's made a career out of a voice that could've come out of my *tochis*.'

BONDI

SATURDAY 28 APRIL 1990

The *frummers* walked to *shule* in long, happy families. Although the men wore dark suits, they never looked smart or even tidy. Their beards dribbled like gravy down their white shirts.

Their wives had skirts down to their ankles, and wigs to cover their heads, since God didn't like heads any more than their arms. He also didn't like being called God, which was why they always used *Hashem*, which means 'the name'.

I used to have to go to *shule* with my dad, but once I'd had my bar mitzvah and become a man, it was my choice whether to keep going, so I didn't and Dad didn't either.

Jimmy, who never went to *shule*, was sanding down his posts with wetordry paper when Barry Dick, who was off to worship *Hashem* with his seven housemates, stopped to give the time of day to an elderly Jewish war veteran who had gone soft in the head.

'Not going to the service this morning?' Barry Dick asked Jimmy.

'At the ashram?' asked Jimmy.

'You like a joke, Mr Rubens, eh?' said Barry Dick.

'No,' said Jimmy, and stared at him.

Barry Dick turned to me.

'He likes a joke, doesn't he, Dov?'

'No,' I said, and stared at him.

'Well,' said Barry Dick, 'we can't all stand around joking together like this. The service is about to start. *Good Shabbes*.'

'*Haribol*,' said Jimmy, which is Hare Krishna for *shalom*.

The *frummers* all left in a line, as if they were about to start dancing with their hands on each other's shoulders.

I asked Jimmy what Townsville Jack had done next, and Jimmy went back to rubbing the poles, even though they didn't need rubbing any more.

'Townsville Jack had the same idea as the officers,' said Jimmy. 'He knew the men needed to find something to keep them occupied, but his idea wasn't so much digging holes as two-up, crown and anchor, and pontoon.

'He seemed to know all about it, so I asked him what he did in civilian life.

' "The same as we're doing now," he said.

' "Soldiering?" I asked.

' "No,' said Townsville Jack, "prisonering."

'There were a couple of fellas who tried to stand over blokes in the early days,' said Jimmy. 'They were hard men from the bush, who'd been starved off the land. They blamed the Jews, because they thought Jews owned the banks that'd foreclosed on them. One of them was Quilpie, and he wasn't a bad bloke; the other, Bargo, was a bastard.

'The two of them pushed Katz around a bit, stole his brushes and held them to ransom. They called it "jewing" him.

'He was trying to snatch them back when Townsville Jack strolled up with his big hands in his pockets and asked what the blue was about. "We're all Aussies," he said, "we don't want to fight among ourselves. Save it for the real enemy – the Poms."

'"He's not an Aussie," said Quilpie. "He's a Hebrew. They started this war."

'Townsville Jack put on a stern face, turned it towards Katz and said, "Is that the good griff, sport? Did you start the war?"

'"I didn't," said Katz, which was a bloody miracle, since that contrary bastard would put his hand up for anything.

'"You've got the wrong bloke,'" said Townsville Jack to Quilpie. "Try one of those little yellow fellas in the IJA camp."

'"What's it got to do with you, Townsville Jack?" asked Bargo.

'But Townsville Jack had done a bit in the Old Tin Shed and he knew the only way to finish first was to get in first, so he lifted his hands with his palms turned towards Bargo, as if he were trying to back off, then rolled his right into a fist and knocked the bastard down.

'We both kept an eye on Katz after that. It made us feel good to look out for someone else, like we could still be useful. We were always checking he was okay, and that meant we spent less time thinking about ourselves and how we weren't okay. I'd thought that carrying a *putz* like Katz would make us weaker, but it did the opposite. We were frightened for him and that made us fearless for ourselves.

'But Bargo and Quilpie were wary of us – well, of Townsville Jack, anyway – so they left Katz alone. Besides, we were living off a rice-flour bun and two bowls of rice a day. We needed all our energy for fetching water and chopping wood and going on bloody parade. No bloke was going to wear himself out fighting.

'Bargo and Quilpie moved from standover to the black market, and they recruited Bathurst Billy, who was so short he might've walked under the wire. He could squeeze himself into any hiding place and scurry up a tree like a bloody monkey, and after a couple of months he disappeared from our barracks completely. I don't know where he was sleeping. In a shoebox, probably.

'Most of the POWS had a bit of money left over from their pay,' said Jimmy, 'or a pen or a watch they'd sold to the Japs. Townsville Jack started up a couple of card schools and a regular two-up game, but he reckoned frog racing was going to make his fortune. You see, Townsville Jack never stopped trying to make his fortune.

'Before I realised it, I was partnered up with him. I was his cockatoo, watching out for officers or other kinds of Japs. One day I had to run the poker game myself, because Townsville Jack had volunteered for a working party. Nobody wanted to go out with this gang because it didn't look like there'd be a dog's chance of scrounging a bone. It was our own officers' idea: the blokes were supposed to collect saltwater from Changi Beach, so the salt might make the rice taste like something you ate, instead of something you grouted with, but Townsville Jack didn't give a bugger what the rice tasted like because he wasn't eating it anyway. He got all his tucker on the black market. The only reason he went out was to find some frogs. When he got back, he was dying to show me them. He called them "our" frogs, which made me a bit wary. He kept our frogs under his bunk in a bucket, fed them on bugs and called that "training".

'In Changi you could find somebody who knew something about anything. Townsville Jack had met a gunner they called "Professor Scaly", who'd studied amphibian biology, and he identified Townsville Jack's stable as mangrove frogs. He didn't think much would come of Townsville Jack's plan of marking out a track and having them chase each other to the finish, because he didn't believe mangrove frogs understood competition or the idea of a straight line. He said we'd have to fence off an individual lane for each frog, to encourage them to move forward.

'Townsville Jack wanted to know how he could identify a winning frog. I think at that stage he had a plan to breed them off a stud. Professor Scaly said he didn't think there'd be much variation between them, but the biggest would be the strongest and the strongest would probably finish first, assuming you could get them going at all. Frogs aren't known for much else apart from hopping, but they don't even do a lot of that. Your average mangrove frog likes to sit in the swamp and catch bugs on his tongue. He doesn't harbour bloody sporting ambitions. We ran a couple of trials, and three out of six frogs just sat where they landed.

'Townsville Jack was a bit dark on Professor Scaly's abilities as a frog handicapper, but he kept him on retainer as a steward. We held race meetings every Tuesday and Thursday night on a track that Townsville Jack said was "specially designed by an expert in the field". He meant it was half-a-dozen lanes pegged out over a ten-foot distance, with barriers made from blokes' shirts stretched between bamboo poles.

'Townsville Jack turned up with a white tote bag, which he had carried with him all the way from Australia, through the fighting and on the march to Changi. He was an incredible bloke, really. He didn't let the war get in his way, he just carried on like nothing had changed.

'Each frog had a number painted on its back, and the stable was divided into two year olds and three year olds, according to size. I remember the first real race, before we'd got the rules properly sorted out. Each frog had its own steward whose job was to hold the animal until the start. They all let go at the same time, but none of the frogs hopped more than once. The stewards shouted at them and threw mud and stones, and sometimes the frogs would jump to the side, to get out of the way of the rocks, but there was bugger all anyone could do to persuade them to move forward. Blokes got down on their hands and knees and crawled behind the frogs, slapping the ground, trying to beat them out like game birds.

'We had to outlaw projectiles, use a bit of frog psychology

and put something on the finish line that the frogs would want to reach. So we dug a little dam and filled it with waste water and had them jump towards that. It still wasn't much of a spectacle – some of the races took five minutes – but it wasn't as if we had to compete with the cinema or anything.

'Blokes loved the frog racing, and it was good for morale – if you won, or if you were Townsville Jack. A few fellas used to complain that Townsville Jack was switching frogs but, truth be told, Townsville Jack couldn't tell one frog from another and he didn't give a monkey's arsehole. He was making easy money, and the whole business kept us as occupied as bloody Singapore.

'Meanwhile Sergeant Major Ramsay was always trying to re-enroll Townsville Jack in the war effort. I remember Ramsay asking him, "You think of yourself as a fighting man, don't you, soldier?"

' "No," said Townsville Jack, "I think of myself as a bookmaker."

' "I don't mean fighting in the sense of running around the battlefield in uniform," said Ramsay.

' "You mean fighting in the sense of setting the odds on frog races?" asked Townsville Jack.

' "I mean the old one-two," said Ramsay, and shadowboxed a jab and cross. "A bit of mixing it up, eh? A choke here, a rabbit punch there, a knee to the niagaras . . .'

' "What're you talking about?" asked Townsville Jack.

' "The old man wants to train a few tough blokes in hand-to-hand combat," he said.

' "The blue's over," said Townsville Jack. "We lost. And we gave the Nips our guns."

' "That's precisely why we need to know how to use our bare hands," said Ramsay.

'But Townsville Jack already knew everything he needed to know about fighting the Nips, which was that it's a mug's game without air cover, so he wasn't going to get excited about bear hugs and wristlocks.

'Townsville Jack treated the war as an interruption to business. He had to change his operating methods to get around the obstacle, but there was no reason to shut up shop. It was different for me and most of the other blokes. We felt humiliated, demoralised, resentful. I had black moods. And I was hungry, like every other bugger.

'The fellas started to get beri-beri. It made their breasts swell up like sheilas'. Then their bellies bloated with hunger and they looked like they were up the bloody duff.

'I was fit and healthy, but sick about Mei-Li. It was tough for the blokes who'd left their wives and girlfriends at home, but the worst thing that could happen was they'd end up in bed with a Yank. As far as I knew, Mei-Li was still in Singapore with the Japs.

'I joined a work detail to the docks. We skirted the rickshaw men's house by a couple of streets, and all I saw was Chinese heads on poles. Our guard told us they were looters. "Thieves and communists," he said. Their eyes were still, but they followed me all the way back to bloody Australia.

'The blokes on salt parties had seen bodies washed up on the beach, and we knew the Japs were taking the Chinese out on boats, tying them up and shooting them, then drowning them just to make sure.

'There was a bloke on the docks detail called Snowy White. He was one of the toothless and ruthless, the fat and bloody useless. He'd been to war before and he tried to see the Japs' point of view. He wanted to understand them so he could anticipate them, and deal with them like anyone else.

' "This isn't indiscriminate murder," said Snowy. "They're not cutting babies out of their mothers' wombs. They've learned from their mistakes in Nanking. They know they've got the boongs on side, so they're not going to chop all their heads off, are they? But they also know there's always going to be a few diehard resisters, so they're tracking them down and eliminating them. They're torturing them, yes – nobody's saying they've turned into white men – but they're doing it to send a message to all the other boongs: 'Behave and we'll treat you well, because all us slopes are in this together. Step out of line and we'll chop you into little pieces like we've done these few blokes who were all troublemakers and commos, so don't get any ideas yourselves.'"

'"It's commonsense," said Snowy. "It's not sadism."

'I was training frogs with Townsville Jack – which just meant looking at them, really, and talking about them – when Katz came over to our billet to paint our living conditions. He asked Townsville Jack if he could paint the frogs, but Townsville Jack said they were secret and vital to the war effort (on the morale side of things) but earbashed Katz for half an hour about being an artist. Townsville Jack wasn't sure why the war needed to be painted, but Katz told him he'd been instructed to draw it as well. We were sure to batter the Nips, he said, once they realised we had superior draughtsmanship.

'Townsville Jack was just a bookmaker at heart. He wasn't interested in buying and selling. But he got the griff that a fella called Keneally would give good money for one of his frogs. Townsville Jack couldn't figure out why, because you could just pick them up in the swamps around the beach. But Keneally was willing to trade this one frog for a torch, which Townsville Jack needed to light his way to the dunnies at night.

'Keneally was after frog number eight, which meant bugger all to Townsville Jack, who painted a different number on each animal every time they raced. But Professor Scaly pulled it out of the stable and passed it on to Keneally, who gave Townsville Jack the torch (which, if I remember rightly, ended up being swapped with a Dutchman for a jar of chilli paste).

'Keneally said he was going to put the frog through further training, then race it against Townsville Jack's finest thoroughbreds. Townsville Jack still didn't believe there was anything between frogs, but he could see the betting potential in a grudge match, and started to tell anybody who'd listen that number eight – which was now known as Rivette, after the 1939 Melbourne Cup winner – was a traitor and a defector. Townsville Jack had fed and cared for him like a son, only to find one morning he had jumped ship.

'"He's nothing but a slimy toad," said Townsville Jack.

'In Camp Rivette, Keneally was putting it about that he'd trained frogs back home in Ireland, although blokes who knew him from Deniliquin reckoned he'd never left the town. Also, none of the Paddies in camp could remember much excitement about frog racing in the old country, which had been known to produce fairly useful gallops from time to time.

'We heard Keneally was actually walking his frog on a leash in the mornings, although Townsville Jack couldn't see what good that would do. Keneally said he was developing the frog's overall fitness, and Sheldon the Showie, who used to work with a mouse circus, was trying to teach the frog to bench press his own weight.

'Townsville Jack began to worry that his frogs were going into competition unprepared, and he started letting them out of the bucket to jump around the hut. But he had to have fielders positioned to catch them, and he still lost a couple.

'Townsville Jack hired Sheldon the Showie to spruik for the race. He wasn't exactly P.T. Barnum, but he knew how to spin a yarn. Between them, Sheldon the Showie and Townsville Jack decided the race was the "Amphibious Fixture of the Century". Katz reckoned it should be "amphibians' fixture", because otherwise it sounded like part of the race'd be held under water, but Townsville Jack told him if he wanted to name his own fixtures he could start his own bloody racing code.

'Sheldon the Showie found a drum, which was easy in Changi: you'd think the Japs had captured an orchestra not an army. So Townsville Jack set up his frog-racing marquee made out of bits of old tent, and Sheldon the Showie stood outside, banging his drum and telling the story of the two rival stables who hated each other more than they hated the Japs, and had been at each other's throats from the moment they'd got to Changi. Both men, said Sheldon the Showie, were from famous frog-racing families: Townsville Jack was descended from the Aboriginal frog racers of Rockhampton; Croaker Keneally was the grandson of the tinkers who had brought frog racing to Donegal.

'Cowboy Miller sat on a rock outside the tent bashing his guitar and singing a song he'd written called "Changi Races". A fella named Bluey from Warracknabeal, Victoria, turned up with a ventriloquist's dummy, Little Bluey, and he moved its jaw up and down in time with the song, which was one of the stupidest things I'd ever seen.

'To Townsville Jack, the whole show was bullshit, because frogs were frogs and there was never going to be a great racing frog any more than there was going to be a frog that could play the flute. He expected heavy betting on Rivette and offered good odds, and Keneally's mates backed the frog with banana money, pounds sterling and packets of Bonox.

' "If they win," I said, "we'll need to rob a bloody bank."

' "I already robbed a bloody bank," said Townsville Jack.

'I thought he was joking, but he told me the story with a straight face, which was a bit of a miracle since Townsville Jack found it hard to keep even his face straight. "I was running down Bukit Timah Road," he said, "chasing these local fellas who were peeling off their uniforms, trying to look like civilians, and everyone was screaming and crying – just typical boong chaos – and I saw there was a bank still trading. I thought, *Well, now's the time to make a withdrawal but I don't have my bank book with me*. Then I remembered I had my Tommy gun, and bugger me if the bloke in charge didn't recognise it as an official document.

'"He filled up my kitbag and I jumped into a rickshaw to Lavender Street. I bought two whores and three ounces of opium, two bottles of whisky and a pipe, and died and went to heaven. That's why I was a bit late in getting captured. I couldn't find my way to jail."

'Townsville Jack had notes rolled under his hat, folded into his boots and jammed halfway up his arse. He had Straits dollars stuffed in his palliasse and buried in a tin outside our hut, so I thought we'd be okay. I thought we'd be able to cover the bets if the worst came to the worst.

'On the day, some blokes turned up in hats and frocks, with brollies and bags, as if it was the Melbourne Cup. This was the first time I realised that a few fellas in Changi spent half their time taking up the hemlines on their dresses. And they weren't poofs either. I never understood it. Anyway, five minutes before close of betting, Townsville Jack sent me to the Pommy camp to lay off the bets with Whitechapel Dave, who wouldn't accept Bonox as a stake but gladly took on the rest, because he knew only a fool would bet on a frog.

'While I was counting notes with Whitechapel Dave, Croaker Keneally turned up at the marquee with a wad as fat as a bottle.

'"I can't accept that,' said Townsville Jack. "I'll wipe you out. You and every other Paddy in the camp."

'"That's our business,' said Keneally. "Your business is bookmaking. Now piss or get off the pot."

'Townsville Jack was afraid that if he took all the Irish money, the Paddies would back up and kill him.

'"We'll kill you if you don't," said Croaker Keneally.

'So the bet was laid and the race was on.

'The frog races were usually called by Professor Scaly, but

he couldn't attend due to a conflict of interest, so Sheldon the Showie did the honours. Rivette took his place with all the others, the starter made a noise like a pistol, then Rivette jumped – and when he did, all the men in the marquee knew they were witness to a great moment in sport, because Rivette was the Phar Lap of bloody frogs. He jumped higher, faster and longer than anything else in the field, and he was over the finish line in two hops.

'He jumped off the track, into the water, out of the marquee, over the wire and out of the camp, with blokes chasing him and yelling and throwing their arms in the air and cheering.

'It took Townsville Jack a week to settle all the bets, and he had to call in everything. He knew he'd been suckered. Professor Scaly was in Keneally's camp, and Townsville Jack guessed Rivette must've been some special species of frog that only Professor Scaly could recognise, but he couldn't prove anything since Rivette was never found – and anyway, it was the sport of frog racing, not mangrove-frog racing.

'When he'd counted out the last dollar and divided up the last box of Bonox, Townsville Jack dropped his head into his hands.

'"Paddy took us to the bloody cleaners," he told me. "Now we're broke."'

*

Jimmy smoked and coughed, coughed and smoked. Apparently my dad used to smoke, although I couldn't imagine it. Mum had given up when she was pregnant with Daniel, but she'd started to buy cigarettes again when she left Dad. She enjoyed them in secret now, since the Dark Man was a health freak who rode a bicycle.

'They say cigarettes kill you,' said Jimmy, more or less to his cigarette, 'and maybe they do, but in the old days we used to think they gave you wind when you were puffed out. The army used to dole out a ration of cigarettes – the buggers were determined to finish us off one way or the other. In the camps we smoked hibiscus leaves wrapped in Bible pages. But I gave up smoking in Changi and didn't have another durrie until the war was over and I brought a packet to Townsville Jack.'

He shook his head.

'Everything good is bad for you,' he said. 'They've even got people allergic to peanuts.'

By now the *frummers* were coming home from *shule*. I wondered what my dad was doing with the Woman in White. When he was at home she usually made him clean or tidy things, and he was useless at it so she shouted at him, and he'd go into the yard and pretend to cut the grass, which he couldn't anyway because there was no motor in the lawnmower because I'd taken it out to build a go-kart, which turned out to be quite hard but not as difficult as it was to fit the engine back in the mower once I'd given up. There was elephant grass in the backyard. It was so tall, you could lose a gnome in it.

In fact, it was possible the Woman in White was spending the morning looking for her stupid garden gnome.

The funny thing was, although the Woman in White was horrible, Dad seemed happy.

'He needs a woman,' said Jimmy. 'To cook for him and do his laundry. That's why blokes get married these days. They can get a bit of the other wherever they like.'

But even then I knew Dad wasn't smiling because he'd found someone to fold his shirts.

It was easier to understand Mum and the Dark Man. He was younger than Mum, and quite good-looking, and more interesting than Dad (although he was still boring). He never talked about adhesives and sealants – which Dad did all the time, because it was his business – but he never talked about war either, because he hadn't been in one. When he got tired of

Mum going on at him, he usually went out into the hallway to fix his bike, which was never broken.

I thought that when I grew up and women shouted at me, I'd probably go to the Club like Jimmy, instead of pretending to repair the car or something.

'That's why there's all this buggery around,' said Jimmy. 'Blokes just want to live with someone who'll leave them alone.'

'Well, Grandma's left you alone,' I said.

'It's no good them doing that when you're used to them,' said Jimmy. 'That's a different thing.'

Barry Dick stopped by the fence.

'You missed a good sermon,' he said to Jimmy. 'The Rov was on form.'

'Did he tell you not to eat meat?' asked Jimmy.

'Why would he do that?' asked Barry Dick.

'Or mushrooms, eggs, garlic and onions?' asked Jimmy.

'Ha ha,' said Barry Dick without smiling.

One of the American *frummers*, who was tall and freckled with red hair tucked under his hat, said to Jimmy, 'Jewish people are permitted to eat garlic and onions, sir. And eggs and mushrooms. And meat so long as the animal . . .'

'. . . has feet like the Devil and two bellies like Bert Newton,' said Jimmy. 'I know. But I thought you lot were Hare Krishnas.'

The American rubbed his beard, baffled.

'It's just Mr Ruben's little joke,' said Barry Dick.

Jimmy laughed until he coughed, coughed until he choked, and choked until a thread of blood unravelled down his chin.

*

'It was always easy to go over the wall or under the wire,' said Jimmy slowly. 'In the early days there wasn't even any wire. Blokes would go out to get food, cigarettes and medical supplies, and the bits and pieces we needed to keep the canaries and the camp workshops running. Early in the piece Bargo got caught by the Japs, and they dragged him into the square and battered his face with the butts of their rifles until they caved in his eye sockets, smashed his nose, burst his lips and knocked his teeth into his throat. It couldn't've happened to a nicer fella, really.

'They stamped on his hands and broke his fingers, and jumped on his legs until his kneecaps smashed. Then they dragged him into a cell and left him for three days and nights, to see if he'd die. But Bargo was a tough little nutcase, and he hung on in the hope of getting back to Bargo and swimming in the potholes, which was all he ever talked about and probably all there was to do.

'So they tied him to a pole in the sun until his eyes scorched and his tongue swelled and he screamed for God to take him. Just when you could see his soul about to burst out of his body, the Japs cut him down, gave him a canteen of cold water, a cup of rice and a packet of cigarettes, and let Quilpie carry him to the hospital. You could never tell what the Nips were going to do next, whether they felt mercy or regret, if they thought a bloke had taken his punishment or they just got jack of dishing it out.

'Bargo was babbling and crying and shaking, and he stayed in the hospital for about two months while his bones mended. When he got back on his feet, he didn't believe he was in Changi any more. He thought he was camping with Chinese gold miners in Bendigo.

'So it was taking a chance for a bloke to go into Changi village – which was just a chaos of corrugated-iron shops and attap huts, piled on top of each other like humpies in a boong camp – and only a handful got any further. But one night Bathurst Billy crawled back in with a yarn nobody could believe. The locals'd told him there were no Japs left in Singapore. He'd gone down to the quays to have a gander, and it was fair dinkum. There were a couple of officers strutting up and down like dwarfs on dress-up day, but no bloody men. One of the officers saw Bathurst Billy, and Bathurst Billy thought, *I'm done for here*, but the officer saluted him. *He* saluted Bathurst Billy.

'Bathurst Billy thought we must've won the war. He nearly took a sword as a souvenir and jumped on the first sampan back to Darwin, but a Chinese lady called him over for a bowl of chicken and rice, so he decided to sit tight and eat as much as he could before he woke up from the dream. They brought him food, they brought him beer, and they told him the Nips had all disappeared two days ago. The whole of Singapore was chockers with prisoners of war: Aussies, Pommies, Yanks and Dutch, with their feet up in the tea houses, enjoying the view of Chinese girls, and no digger had to put his hand in his pocket for anything. Even the rickshaw men were giving rides for free.

'Bathurst Billy told me and Townsville Jack to get down to Singapore quick smart, before they shut the pearly gates. We talked about it for a day, trying to figure out whether it was all a trick. That night I went outside the barracks and everywhere you looked you could see diggers schlepping their packs towards the city.

'I thought, *Bugger this, I'm off to escape*.

'"I'm off to rob the bank," said Townsville Jack.

'Townsville Jack was one of half-a-dozen blokes in the camp who still had his gun. He probably still had his old Ford car stashed somewhere too, and his mum to make him a cooked breakfast.

'He dug up his weapon, cleaned it and assembled it. He was going to visit the same branch, he said, because he knew their procedures: you pointed your gun at them, they gave you their money. Townsville Jack didn't want to escape, just to come back to the camp with a stake to set him up in a new racket. For a couple of weeks I'd noticed him trying to coax snails to follow a white line. "Imagine how great it would be," he said, "to hold the slowest races in the world."

'The officers tried to stop us from leaving the camp. They ordered us not to go. What would it look like when the Nips came back and found there was no bugger anywhere, just a bunch of captains playing bridge and making lists of blokes who weren't there? They'd think our sirs weren't up to the job of guarding us. They'd think they'd gone over to our side.

'But I packed a knife and a dixie and a billy and went under the wire that a bloke had stolen to fence off his chook run, and me and Townsville Jack hitched a ride with a truck full of Poms going into town.

'Townsville Jack jumped off with the others when we reached Lavender Street. I asked the driver to take me to the rickshaw men's house to look for Chinese Frank and Mei-Li. Townsville Jack didn't bother with goodbyes. He said I'd get nowhere and we'd meet tomorrow back at the hut, by which time he'd be the richest man in Changi again.

'The All Chinese Union of Rickshaw Men had disappeared. Even the stonemason had gone. The shopfront had been closed up and the shop house looked like it was being used for storage. The doors were all bolted and chained. The driver waited while I kicked at the locks, then I asked if he'd take me to Woodlands, to see if the causeway had been repaired, because I was going to head across the water to Johor.

'The journey north took the whole afternoon. We were picking up and dropping off POWs all the way across the island. The driver made up a fares system as we went along, and started giving twenty per cent off for return tickets. I paid my passage by writing out the stubs on Tally-Hos. The funny thing was, the cigarette papers were worth more than the fares.

'I didn't have much of a plan, but every other bugger in the army had started off with a plan and it'd all gone to shit, so I thought if I just pointed my nose north and headed away from my arse, at least I'd see the Japs before they saw me. Unless they turned up behind me because they finally'd decided to attack from the Straits of Singapore, of course.

'I got about half a mile up the road before I ran straight into a Jap convoy, and *they* saw me first.

'The Japs didn't salute me but they didn't shoot me either. They looked at me like they'd never seen anything like me, and I looked at them like I'd never seen anything like them. Then I turned and ran like fuck.

'All over the island, blokes were doing the same thing, jumping out of cathouse windows, hiding under blankets in the back of rickshaws, or dashing through the bush like bilbies. Even though I had the furthest to travel, I was one of the first back under the wire, because the driver – God bless him – came back for me, and we belted down to Changi faster than Rivette the racing frog. Townsville Jack wasn't in the barracks to meet me, but I didn't think anything had happened to him because I didn't think anything *could* happen to him. Townsville Jack seemed invincible to me and, looking back, I can see I had to believe that. I had to let myself think there was someone nothing could touch, that we weren't all going to be destroyed by prison and defeat and the officers and the Nips. You see, I was prone to low morale, David. I could see things the way they were.

'I spent that night talking to Katz. In Changi, when you started a conversation with somebody, there was no end to it. It just went on until they'd told you everything they knew, and everything that had ever happened in their lives.

'Townsville Jack was smuggled in the next morning, in a tea chest on the back of an oxcart. Most of the other blokes managed to break back into the prison, but the Japs caught a handful outside the perimeter and gave them their usual six-on-one beating. One fella lost both eyes.

'It turned out the Japs were relieving their troops and, in typical Nip army fashion, the old lot had left before the new blokes had arrived. I don't know how they ever beat us in the field. They were the most disorganised rabble in the world.

'For the first couple of hours after he got home, Townsville Jack was as happy as a boong in a bottle-o. I thought the robbery must've gone well, but he was still riding the pipe. When the opium wore off, he said he'd never got out of Lavender Street. He'd found his two whores, and he'd somehow ended up selling them his Tommy gun. When the opium wore off, he felt like he'd let himself down, thrown away his future for drink, drugs and women. But then, when he thought about it, it didn't seem like such a bad deal. That was before he started pissing blood and realised he had the clap.

'I was bored and buggered and spent most of my time dodging work details. I kept going over and over everything in my head. Why didn't we leave the camp as soon as Bathurst Billy got back? I could've made it to Johor, and who knows how much further.

'Every bloke found his own way to use his time. There was a lodge for freemasons, a lepidopterists society for butterfly collectors, and the dry-land yacht club for idiots. The boxers did a lot of skipping, which was good exercise in a POW camp because all it took was a bit of rope and a piece of ground – like necking yourself, which was a craze that came later. I enrolled at the university, where Katz taught a life-drawing class, and Professor Scaly and Croaker Keneally were running a course in bloody frog husbandry.

'But all of us were hungry all the time. You can live on rice. It keeps you alive, but that's about it. If you eat rice three times a day, you spend all your time between meals thinking of food that isn't rice.

'Some of the boys carried pin-ups in their hats. They tried to stick them on the walls of the hut, but nothing would last in the heat. The colour faded and the paper rotted, as if the girls had grown old.'

'In March, every bugger was asking Katz to draw sheilas with big boobs. By July, we were passing around Mrs Beeton's cookery book from the library, reading out recipes to each other, fantasising about roast beef and battered fish, lamb's fry and Sergeant's pies. One joker even had Katz paint a picture of a baked dinner, and he got it out to look at every Sunday. I think he ate it in the end. I think he went mad. We all went a bit mad, from the hunger and from everything else.

'When you're starving, you can't concentrate, you get angry. The smallest thing makes you want to cry, and there were so many big things to cry about in the camp, like the fact that our lives were just slipping away. You start to hallucinate, you get paranoid, you think you're dying. The smell of a campfire reminds you of cooked meat and it melts your guts.

'Nobody was interested in Jack Lindsay's *Sappho* any more. After four months on a rice diet, all they wanted to look at was Norman Lindsay's *Magic* bloody *Pudding*.

'One morning Townsville Jack asked me to take a squiz at his wedding tackle. He dropped his pants and showed me a pair of balls so big they looked like King Edward potatoes. But then, everything looked like potatoes to me.

' "Look at this!" said Townsville Jack. "My nuts have shrunk."

'We thought it was another symptom of the clap, and Townsville Jack went to beg for more penicillin, but the MO said it was just rice balls. We called them "rice balls" because the Japs loved to eat rice balls and we swore they would be eating our balls before long.

' "Your testicles need vitamin B," the MO told Townsville Jack. "Get yourself some Vegemite."

'Townsville Jack sent me out to see if I could find any on the black market. Vegemite was easy to get into camp because the Japs thought it was boot polish.

'The racketeers used to work in a spot we named Change

Alley. I found Bathurst Billy selling bully beef looted from a supply dump, and tinned fish called "modern girl" because it "stinks like sheila", he said.

'"How would you know?" I asked him.

'He was younger than Daniel, David. Can you imagine that?' asked Jimmy, shaking his head. 'Can you picture Daniel, the year before he went to university, already in a war? Bathurst Billy'd joined up, trained, fought, got defeated and captured while Daniel was still studying for his HSC, and now he was telling me what sheila smelled like, as if he'd turn up his nose at the chance of a sniff.

'Bathurst Billy said Vegemite cost four dollars – twice the price of bully beef – because it was "classed as a medicine". But when he heard it was for Townsville Jack, he gave me it for free. He was a lovely little bloke.'

*

Jimmy sketched an altar, drawing pencil marks along a folding ruler and marking corners with a try square. He used full lines and broken lines, measured out in inches, with fractions shown as two half-sized numbers on either side of a bar. Jimmy's plans were clean but complicated, often working over two levels, with exploded details, and arrows like half-smiles. He imagined everything as made up of joists and joints. There were no curves, only angles.

He couldn't remember what else he used to see inside the spirit houses in Thailand. He imagined objects or models. He thought they might have been animals.

'Myer'll know,' he said.

I had no idea Myer had been in Thailand.

Myer was drinking with Solomon in the Club, but when we arrived Solomon went straight to the pokies, because Solomon played the pokies on a Saturday.

'Pincus,' said Jimmy.

'He wants something,' said Myer.

'Remember Thailand?' asked Jimmy.

'No,' said Myer, pushing his beer coaster with the tip of his ring finger.

'The little houses,' said Jimmy.

'No,' said Myer, tapping the table.

'Where the Thais kept their ghosts,' said Jimmy.

'No,' said Myer, shaking his jowls.

'Like in the Thai Dee,' said Jimmy.

'She's got a nice arse,' said Myer. 'She'd look good in glasses. Or out of them.'

Myer pushed his spectacles off his nose and balanced them on his forehead.

'Come on, Pincus,' said Jimmy, 'don't mess me about.'

'I spent the war in Changi, Jimmy,' said Myer. 'I was in the concert party. We didn't have to go on the line.'

Jimmy smiled tightly.

'You worked next to me, Pincus,' he said, 'up to your waist in water.'

'I sang songs and told jokes,' said Myer. 'I cheered the men up. I was a comedian. I used to have an act with Cowboy Miller. We did a song called "Changi Races", dressed up like boongs with lampshade hats on. Everyone laughed. Funny? They thought they'd wet themselves, but it turned out to be the monsoon.'

'I dug ulcers out of your leg,' said Jimmy, 'with a spoon. I nursed you when you thought you were dying.'

Myer laughed.

'The only time I nearly died was on stage,' he said.

Jimmy sighed.

'I need to know what was inside the spirit houses,' he said. 'I can't remember.'

'I can't help you, Jimmy,' said Myer. 'I was part of the chorus but I sometimes performed solo. Blokes still write to me. I was in Changi, not Thailand. You've got me mixed up with some other good-looking fella.'

'You don't remember,' said Jimmy.

'I can't remember what didn't happen,' said Myer. 'I was a weak man. I shouldn't've been a soldier. I could never've survived on the line.'

'You were strong,' said Jimmy. 'You made it back.'

'There's things I like to talk about,' said Myer. 'The songs we used to sing, like "Changi Races". Oh, that was a good one. Funny? I thought I'd wet myself, but it turned out to be the monsoon. Because it wasn't about horseracing, was it? It was about *frog* racing. Fucking frog racing. Do you remember your mate? What was he called, Queensland Bill or something? He used to be a bookie and he ran a book on the frogs. He called them "the hops", remember? Because they weren't the gallops or the trots.'

'I'd forgotten that,' said Jimmy.

'Lovely bloke,' said Myer. 'I've often wondered what happened to him after the war. Went back to Queensland, I suppose.'

Jimmy shrugged.

'Probably up there now, racing cane toads,' said Myer.

'Could be,' said Jimmy.

'Remember, Jimmy,' said Myer. '"You'll never get off the island!" Funny? I thought I'd wet myself, but it turned out to be the monsoon.'

Both men's attention passed to the silent boxing on TV.

*

We walked back from the Club with a couple of drinks under our belts.

'The Changi Concert Party,' said Jimmy, shaking his head. 'I don't know if there was a troupe of Japs in Cowra doing *The*

Mikado, or an SS entertainment unit singing songs about Churchill in Scotland, but the Aussies and the Poms had these jokers, and what a bloody mixed bunch they were. There was a comedian called Happy Harry whose catchphrase was "You'll never get off the island." That was just about all he ever said, really. There was Bluey, the fella with the ventriloquist's dummy, and a bloke who played sonatas on a gumleaf. He had it all bloody worked out. Other blokes might steal his guitar, or the Japs might smash it, but nobody was ever going to pinch his bloody gumleaf.

'The worst were the poets. Christ, there were some shithouse poets in Changi. They should've been locked up for their bloody poems. And there was a yodelling cowboy. We inflicted a yodelling cowboy on our own men, David.

'It's a funny thing, but I reckon some of those blokes were happy as Harry with the way things turned out. It wasn't as if they were world-class performers. If it weren't for the war, they'd be playing to twenty blind pensioners at the Maitland CWA. In Changi, they had thousands turn up for every show. They were the heroes of the bloody camp. They must've been the only blokes in history who thought, *We're in a war! You beauty! At last, I've got a chance to dress up as Sheila!*'

'What about Myer?' I asked him. 'What did he do?'

'Myer? He was a medical orderly.'

'No, I mean in the concert party.'

'He wasn't in the concert party,' said Jimmy. 'Apart from Happy Harry, there was a string of blokes who only knew one joke: "There was this Irishman, this Englishman, this Scotsman and this Jew . . ." You know the one. But I went to watch them like every other bugger, because they were the only show in town.

'They were always rehearsing their pantomime for Easter or their revue for the King's bloody birthday, but never anything for Christmas because we all knew we'd be home by Christmas.

'And then one day Bathurst Billy had enough of waiting for

Christmas and decided to get back home under his own steam. He disappeared under the wire with a map, a compass, Quilpie and a couple of Poms. The Japs caught them a week later, beat the daylights out of them and threw them into a cell. They stayed there for two months.

'I tried to get to see Bathurst Billy when he was banged up. There were no windows in the building, and you couldn't tell where they were keeping him, but I stood outside, as close as I could, having loud conversations with Townsville Jack, trying to let Bathurst Billy know what was going on – which was, of course, bugger all. We saw the Japanese Gestapo, the Kempetai, arrive in their starched uniforms and polished boots, and I think one day I heard Bathurst Billy screaming, but it might've been a gull, you know. It could've been a seabird.

'They stayed a few days and then they left, still neat and pressed and clean, as if they'd never had a drop of blood under their fingernails. I don't know what they did to them in there. I don't like to think about it. There's some things you can turn away from. It's all right not to look.

'In August 1942 all the officers ranked higher than colonel were taken from Changi to a special officers' camp in Japan, where they could order each other around and salute themselves all day. They left Callaghan in charge of the rest of us, and he was determined to maintain military discipline, to carry on as if we hadn't surrendered to the Japs.

'Callaghan was keen that we should all keep up appearances, like it was the best dressed army that won the war. We all had to shave every day, and keep our hair above the collar. Men who'd managed to hang on to walking shoes had to give them to officers. Other Ranks could either wear boots or go barefoot. If you had a good shirt or pants, you had to pass them up too. Some blokes, the only thing they had left was their spare clothes, and then they didn't even have those.

'A new Jap took over the camps too. We called him "Major General Fuck-You", but I dare say that wasn't an accurate translation from the Japanese.

'Fuck-You asked all the prisoners to sign a document promising they wouldn't try to escape, which was a bloody joke because there was nowhere to escape to anyway. And what type of bloke would see a chance to get away from the Japs but think, *Hang on, I can't jump ship now because I promised I wouldn't?*

'Some blokes reckoned that if we signed it we'd lose the right to army pay, because we'd no longer be doing our duty as soldiers, which was to escape. But no bugger was escaping anyway, and we weren't getting any pay, so it was a pretty bloody academic argument.

'I suppose Callaghan thought if we didn't stand up to the Japs then, we never would. I reckon he saw it as his chance to lead the army into a fight, and he wasn't going to retreat or surrender. It was a battle of wills, and he was going to show the bandy-legged bastards what he was made of – which was one hundred per cent military bullshit, from top to toe. He was all army, Jack Callaghan, and he ordered us all not to sign, so the Japs paraded us outside in the sun, lines and lines of men behaving just the way the army likes them to – all doing the same useless, mindless bloody thing.

'Callaghan didn't know if he was Genghis Khan or Ghandi. He had the troops practising passive resistance against the samurai. The Japs couldn't figure out what to make of it. Why would we surrender in battle, when we had weapons, and suddenly decide to stand up for ourselves now, when we were beaten? We were the most cockeyed bunch of mugs they'd ever seen.

'They pointed their machine guns at us, and the blokes behind them made pistols with their fingers and mimed mowing us down like grass. After a few hours men were pissing and shitting themselves, collapsing and lying in their own vomit.

'Callaghan and Ramsay were called away from the parade ground, but we didn't know why or even that they'd gone. The worst thing was, by this time we'd let ourselves hope that Bathurst Billy and the others had got away with it. It'd been three months and they were still alive and, truth be told, the Japs hadn't turned out to be half the monsters we'd thought they'd be. Then the bastards showed they really did have no mercy. They let the bloody Changi Concert Party play to the blokes collapsing in the heat of the barracks square, with their Jew jokes and music hall songs and jocks in frocks and heels and wigs.

'When the yodelling cowboy climbed onto the barracks roof to give a recital, I looked over at the Jap gunner and whispered, "Shoot me."

'In the end, nobody got shot, although a couple of blokes died standing to attention, and I always wondered what their families would've thought if the army'd let them know how they'd really lost their lives, that they'd drilled themselves to death.

'Callaghan and Fuck-You reached an agreement that Fuck-You would change his request into an order, which meant we were only obeying under duress, and it was all right to have our fingers crossed behind our backs.

'We marched back to our barracks, where we found out that Bathurst Billy and the others had been executed in front of Callaghan and Ramsay.

'Ramsay came to our hut, to talk to Bathurst Billy's mates.

' "He made us all proud," said Ramsay. "He walked into the field with his head held high. They offered him a blindfold, but he turned it down. The Japs let him say a few last words, then he looked the firing party right in their slitty eyes and shouted, 'Shoot straight, you bastards!' and the Nips opened up. They caught him in the head and the heart. He never made a sound, and I reckon he was dead before he hit the ground."

'When the others heard, they clapped and cheered, and shouted, "Vale Bathurst Billy!" Ramsay saluted them and marched out of the hut. I caught up with the sergeant major a few steps away and gripped him by the shoulder.

' "What exactly did Bathurst Billy say before he told them to 'shoot straight'?" I asked.

' "He said he had no regrets," said Ramsay. "He was giving his life for the country he loved and his home town of Bathurst."

'And that's when I knew that everything Ramsay had told us was a lie, and my little mate had died slowly, struggling and screaming, blindfolded and scared.'

BONDI

SATURDAY 28 APRIL 1990

We sat in silence, Jimmy's jaw trembling, until finally I had to speak.

'We forgot to have lunch,' I said.

'We had a liquid lunch,' said Jimmy.

'I can't just have a liquid lunch,' I told him. 'I'm only thirteen.'

'Well then,' said Jimmy, 'what do you want to eat?'

'Fish and chips,' I said. 'A yiddisher fella invented them.'

Jimmy tried to cuff me. I swayed out of his reach.

He had only just fallen into his armchair, so he wasn't happy about pulling himself back up. As he stood, I heard his knees creak.

'Fish and bloody chips,' he said, as if he had never heard of such a badly matched couple.

We had to go halfway to the beach to get to Greco's fish and chip shop, which sat on a side street off Bondi Road, opposite the Regal Hotel, just beyond the point on the horizon where the ocean met the sky. From Greco's you could only see the sky. We walked down the opposite side of Bondi Road, past the shabby unit blocks with Hawaiian names and scribble-tagged walls, until we reached the bus stop, where two tall Japanese boys got off the bus from Bondi Junction.

They were dressed in black wetsuits and carrying surfboards. The tallest smiled excitedly at Jimmy, and asked, 'Could you please say the way to Bondi Beach?'

Jimmy rubbed his chin, then looked up at the clouds. The Japanese surfers followed his eyes.

'First, you'll have to cross the road,' he said.

A garbage truck bellowed down towards the sea. Jimmy motioned them to step out in front of it.

'Quick!' said Jimmy. 'Speedo! Speedo!'

But the surfers held back until it had passed. They trailed Jimmy across the street, to the bus stop near Greco's.

'Now,' said Jimmy, 'you've come a fair bit out of your way, I'm sorry to say. You'll have to take the next bus back to Central Station.'

'But the driver –' protested the taller boy.

'Didn't know anything, mate,' said Jimmy. 'Probably just got off the boat.'

The 380 bus came crying up the hill.

'Quick,' said Jimmy. 'Jump on! Speedo!'

The surfers climbed on board and headed west towards the city.

Greco's walls were decorated with a mosaic of blue and white tiles, which made pictures of the sea god Poseidon, a mud crab, and a Greek flag. We joined a short line and ordered two battered gemfish. Jimmy pointed out a poster of whitewashed villas looking out to the Mediterranean, on the wall behind the counter.

'This shop used to be owned by a Jewish bloke,' he told me. 'A fat fella who came out from the East End. They called him

Alfie the Eel, because they were supposed to eat jellied eels in Stepney, but he didn't sell eels in Australia. You can't get them, and nobody wants them.

'I'll tell you something, though,' said Jimmy, still staring at the poster of the Greek island, 'Alfie was born and bred in London, but he didn't paper his takeaway with pictures of Nelson's Column. A lot of the shops along here used to be Hungarian, or German or Polish Jewish, but you didn't see the Danube or the Rhine or the bloody Baltic Sea on the walls. They used to say the Jews had no loyalty to the places they lived, but they didn't spend all their time dreaming of going back where they came from, unlike every other bugger who stepped off at Circular Quay. All you see in our shops is postcards of the Dome on the Rock, a bloody mosque.

'Everybody loves Israel these days,' said Jimmy, 'but nobody wants to go and live there.'

A Greek sold us our fish and chips in foam boxes with plastic knifes and forks wrapped in paper napkins. Jimmy liked to have pickles with his chips, but they only had vinegar at Greco's. Jimmy squeezed the plastic bottle so it spurted like a hose.

The chips were crunchy, hollower than I remembered. I used to come to Greco's with Dad. When *Shabbes* was out, we'd drive to Bondi and buy a bag of fresh bagels, and stop on the way home to pick up a fish dinner. I didn't understand what had happened to those days, and why I couldn't have them still.

'He's a good bloke, your dad,' said Jimmy. 'I wish he'd come around.'

'He's too embarrassed,' I said.

'It's not him that should be embarrassed,' said Jimmy.

Dad didn't drink but he used to see Jimmy for a frame of snooker on a Sunday, and they'd talk about football and cricket, and me and Daniel, and business and the news. Dad stopped coming to the Club when Mum left him for the Dark Man. He thought everyone would laugh at him, but really they were all sad for him, and would only laugh if they went down to the car park and saw the stupid yellow car he'd bought.

'I lost a son-in-law,' said Jimmy, 'with everything else.'

'Everyone's still here,' I told him. 'You've just got to start talking to each other again.'

He pulled down his cap.

'When's your dad coming to pick you up?' he asked. 'I need to have a word with him about the window frames.'

I wondered if he was joking.

'I'm staying with you,' I told him.

'He might be able to tell me what kind of glue to use,' said Jimmy. 'Your dad knows that kind of thing.' He smiled to himself. 'The boring cunt.'

Jimmy finished his chips and threw the box into the bin.

'Time to go to the Club,' he said.

'We've just been there,' I told him.

Jimmy looked at his watch, which he hadn't put on that morning.

'I'm supposed to be meeting your father,' he said.

'It's Saturday,' I told him.

'Oh, Saturday,' said Jimmy. 'A day of rest for the Jewish people, but business as usual for the mahouts.'

He crossed Bondi Road carefully, looking both ways for elephants.

'They must be Mohammedans or something,' he said.

*

By the time we got back home Jimmy had forgotten about my dad and the mahouts and was back in the story about Townsville Jack.

'Once Bathurst Billy had gone,' said Jimmy, 'I lost interest in everything. I still wanted to live, but not there and not then.

I let my mind go back to evenings with Mei-Li on the blanket on the beach, and I wouldn't talk to the other blokes because they weren't there.

'I didn't work and I didn't eat. I was angry with the army. I thought maybe if Callaghan had let us sign their piece of paper, the Japs might have gone easier on Bathurst Billy. But I wasn't mad enough to die just to spite Callaghan, and you can only live in a dream for so long. One day my beautiful Mei-Li disappeared for me and Townsville Jack came back, as big and ugly as before but a little bit changed inside. Townsville Jack was only ever on the edge of being in the army, and the thing with Bathurst Billy pushed him over. He refused to go on parade, then he refused to be punished. I went along with him because I just didn't care. We were walking through the camp, not doing anything we'd been ordered to do, when I had to dash to the dunnies. On my way back I saw Townsville Jack had walked past Callaghan, dressed in his pressed shorts and shiny shoes, and not bothered to salute him.

' "You!" shouted Callaghan. "Soldier!"

'Townsville Jack didn't look around, because he didn't think he was one.

'Callaghan jogged up to him, still shouting.

' "Step back," he ordered, "and salute me."

'Townsville Jack cocked his head, and looked at Callaghan as if he'd gone berko.

' "Do you know who I am?" asked Callaghan.

' "An Australian prisoner of war," said Townsville Jack.

' "I am the commanding officer of Australian troops in Changi," he said. "You salute the bloody Nips, so you'll salute me."

' "I salute the Nips," said Townsville Jack, "because if I don't, they'll beat my brains out with a bamboo pole."

' "Well, if you don't salute me," said Callaghan, "I'll tear your head off with my bare hands."

'Townsville Jack almost squared up, but left his fists hanging by his sides.

' "I've never seen an officer do anything with his bare hands," he said.

'Callaghan stepped forward – he was always game, I'll give him that – but Sergeant Major Ramsay jumped between them. He told Townsville Jack he was on a charge. Townsville Jack let himself be arrested just to find out what would happen.

'I came too, in case he needed a lawyer, or a cabinet maker. Ramsay and Snowy White escorted Townsville Jack to the orderly room, where Callaghan was already hearing charges against other prisoners who had been caught growing their hair or owning shoes.

'An orderly clerk typed out the charge against him, that "contrary to good order and military discipline, he had refused to salute an officer".

'Callaghan asked Townsville Jack a lot of questions about awareness, like was he aware that he was still subject to military discipline, and was he aware that a soldier salutes the King's Commission, not the bearer of the rank, and was he aware that any problem he might have with any individual officer in the room had no bearing on his responsibility to behave like a soldier?

'Townsville Jack told him he didn't have a problem with any individual officer in the room, but he didn't plan on behaving like a soldier now that he'd surrendered, because there wasn't any soldiering to do any more.

' "Were you conscripted into the army?" Callaghan asked. "Were you coerced? Did you, for instance, fall asleep in a dockside pub and wake to find yourself chained up in the hold of a troopship heading for Singapore?"

'Townsville Jack shook his head.

' "Well, in that case, you signed up for this. When the army says "fight", you fight. When the army says "stop", you stop. There's one big war going on here, Private, not eighty-five thousand little ones. You signed up to serve your country, and that's what you're doing if you obey the orders of your commanding officer."

'"How does this serve my country?" asked Townsville Jack.

'"It maintains the dignity and cohesion of her armed forces," said Callaghan, "enabling them to preserve their fighting strength and capability for the next occasion it is called upon – which, please God, won't be before too long.

'"You may be a prisoner, Private," said Callaghan, "but I am not."

'"So go home, then,' said Townsville Jack. "Go back to your wife."

'Callaghan tapped his pen on the pad on his desk.

'"Do you know why I am not a prisoner?" asked Callaghan. "Because I'm still doing my duty. I'm preparing for the day when we're all going to rise up and kick these Jap bastards off the island. Now, how do you plead to the charge?"

'"Not guilty," said Townsville Jack.

'"Very well," said Callaghan. "The court finds the defendant guilty as charged."

'Townsville Jack shrugged.

'"Do you have anything to say for yourself?" asked Callaghan.

'Townsville Jack shrugged again.

'"I have spoken with the commanding officer of your unit," said Callaghan. "He says you have an exemplary record in combat."

'Each time Townsville Jack shrugged, the movement of his shoulders was smaller.

'"Why are you not billeted with the rest of your unit?" asked Callaghan.

'"You'll have to ask them," said Townsville Jack.

'"Two-shilling fine," said Callaghan. "Dismissed."

'Townsville Jack got a name as a ratbag agitator,' said Jimmy, 'but he never agitated for anything as far as I can remember. He just wanted to be left alone to run his own race.

'Eventually we settled down to life in Changi, because you get used to anything if it goes on long enough. We were bored and hungry and worried for our families. We spent most of our waking time waiting for letters that never came, that banked up in some Jap sorting office in a queue to be censored, so by the time you got a card telling you your brother was still alive, he was probably dead.

'The Japs started paying blokes for working, and paying officers for doing nothing. I scrounged a few tools and the odd bit of wood, and set myself up as a cabinet maker, and every now and then a fella would come in and ask for something you'd never've thought anyone could want in a prison camp, like a sewing box or a footstool.

'Either the concert party got better or even I got used to it, because I started looking forward to their music nights. The yodelling cowboy came down with beri-beri and, when he'd recovered, he'd lost his yodel, which almost restored my faith in God. But Townsville Jack kept me entertained more than any bloody comedian. He had a thousand yarns about larrikins and knockabouts, and blues and sheilas and the time he'd woken up naked in the nick, with a copper's teeth in his knuckle and the smell of copper's wife on his balls.

'"Who was the copper?" I asked.

'"A Townsville jack," said Townsville Jack.

'Christmas came and we were still behind barbed wire. The cooks made the best of it and gave us a baked dinner made of rice and Christmas pudding made of rice. They tasted like rice, but at least they looked a bit different. The Jews in the camp had Chanukah – it's funny, but nobody ever said, "We'll be home by Chanukah" – and Katz turned up to paint them.

'There were about forty Aussie Jews, and one or two others who never declared themselves, but they had that look, you know. I think there were three hundred Pommy Yids, and a few Sephardic Dutch who'd been captured in Java.

'Katz asked me to go along, and I didn't have anything else to do that year. Myer was the usher – I hadn't met him until then – and the service was led by a dentist. It's funny, I don't think I've ever been anywhere there wasn't a Jewish dentist, but I've never met a Jew with good teeth. There were Jewish doctors in Changi too, and a lawyer and an accountant – but those two weren't officers and they died on the line. They're not real jobs, you see. They don't help men stay alive. Be a doctor, David. If the worst happens, a doctor's always got a chance. But there's no point being a lawyer, because you can't argue with God. That's where the Jewish people go wrong. They're always trying to talk Him around.

'I sat with a Pommy gunner called Raphael, who'd been a mathematician before the war. He used to play chess in his head, so he could've been anywhere – in Changi or walking on the Yorkshire Moors. We lit candles made from paraffin, and ate rice latkes, then danced and sang 'Ma'oz Tzur'. I'm not a religious man, but I've had worse nights – although none of them were outside Changi.

'The Japs never interfered with religious services. They never interfered much at all. They were too busy winning the bloody war. We had an idea what was going on because some of our blokes made radios. They hid them in walls and water bottles and called them "canaries" because they sang. The batteries were "birdseed", bad news was "birdshit". There was a lot of birdshit in that first year in Changi. We heard about the Blitz in London and the Siege of Sevastopol, Rommel at Tobruk and the Russians in the Crimea.

'When the news wasn't birdshit, it was bullshit. When you

listened to Allied radio stations, you'd think the world was upside down, that the Japs had been driven back to Singapore from Darwin, and the fact that we'd all been captured was a trick to get behind Jap lines and eat all their bloody rice.

'But rations were very short in the camp by then. Blokes started taking bigger risks for less. There was a craze for committing suicide, and four blokes in one barracks necked themselves in a week. It was against King's Regulations, but the officers couldn't figure out how to punish it.

'My last cabinet-making commission was to make a chess set for Raphael, but I never saw him use it. By that time, he preferred to imagine the board. We might've made a quid here and there, but me and Townsville Jack were losing weight like everybody else. He had a thing for pies: when it rained, he used to make them out of mud, then line them up in a row to bake in the sun.

'So when we heard the Japs were looking for volunteers for a building project, there were blokes fighting to put down their names. They had the idea that it might be a special offer, a once-only thing, and the Nips would never find anything else for us to do, so they'd leave us all in Changi to starve. The IJA were a bit sketchy on details, but they promised there'd be good weather and well-equipped hospitals, light work and plenty of holidays, and every bloody camp would have a concert party.

'There was a rumour that we were going to build a railway through Thailand to Burma, along a route that'd been surveyed by British engineers who'd decided the whole thing was impossible. But there were also rumours that we were going to be traded with Australia for sheep and that Jesus Christ was coming back on a bike.

'It seems funny when you look back on it now, but we thought the men who didn't volunteer were bludgers, shirkers, afraid of hard work. The fit men were burning up to get a place on the line. They held sprint races to decide who would go. You couldn't hold them back. Even the sick begged to be taken along.

'When you're already a prisoner, you don't believe things can get much worse. What else can they take away from you? We never thought they might take our arms and legs.

'Snowy White's understanding of the Japanese mind made him decide to sign up. It was obvious why they didn't set much stay by feeding blokes when we were just prisoners living the life of Riley, growing vegetables and racing frogs and listening to yodelling bloody cowboys, when their own men were fighting and dying in Burma. Why would they waste their resources doing any more than keeping us alive according to their international obligations – Snowy was very well up on the Japs' international obligations – when we were eating rice that could've gone to their soldiers? In Changi we were useless to their war effort. But if we were working, they'd have to feed us, obviously, because nobody could be expected to build a railway on three cups of rice a day. If they didn't keep us fit, they'd just work us to bloody death, and what would be the point of that? You had to look at it from their side. You had to think what you'd do in their position.

'We weren't just navvies, either. We had professional blokes, tradesmen, skilled engineers, everyone you'd need to build a railway, and we came from the country that had given trains to the world (he meant England). We'd be their logistics, their supply line, as important to their infantry as guns and grenades and those bloody silly boots. They'd probably put us on Japanese army rations and they'd certainly give us our Red Cross parcels.

'As usual, our officers had the good oil on the railway work too. The Japs weren't going to work us like slaves and starve us to death because that *didn't make economic sense*. Everyone liked this argument. We were all economists all of a sudden.

'Katz knew he wasn't going to a holiday camp. "It'll be a graveyard," he said. But he was a gloomy bugger and nobody took much notice of him. He was only an artist, and what would they know? But he wanted to go anyway, because he'd had enough of Changi. He'd got camp life down on paper, he reckoned, and now it was time to see something else, to do his duty to the Australian War Memorial.

'The other thing was, there were a few blokes who'd worked on railways and they were keen to get stuck in again. They missed it, you know. They didn't exactly want to build a railway for the Japs, but they wanted to do what they were good at. God knows what they thought they'd be working as: stationmasters or something.

'Me, I didn't trust the Japs – and nor did Callaghan – but I thought things couldn't get worse than Changi. It was just a failure of my imagination, that's all.

'The officers drew up the lists of blokes to go on the line. They wanted volunteers, but they also wanted to keep units together. They reckoned we'd have more chance of surviving that way. There was no shortage of willing blokes for that first draft, but me and Townsville Jack held out until they raised the second force, before we decided it was better the devil you don't know than slowly starving in Singapore.

'We were always putting our names on lists in those days: lists of trades, lists of the sick, even lists of fellas who were after a place on stage. The concert party held auditions at the end of every month, to make sure no talent in the camp had been overlooked, or one of the untalented blokes hadn't developed a talent overnight. The Japs ordered them to keep their strength at forty, so if a new fella came in, somebody else had to leave, and probably join a working party where they'd have to wear blokes' clothes and talk in an ordinary voice.

'Myer fancied himself as a comic, and he wasn't bad. He didn't do Irishman-Scotsman-Englishman-Jew jokes, he invented his own, and they were usually about life in the camps. "What's the difference between a bowl of rice and Christmas dinner?" "Bugger all." That's the one I remember. He probably had some that were better than that.

'One of the comedians had resigned to become a contortionist. He'd got so thin that his body could do things he'd never imagined before. The contortionist knocked out the Indian fakir, who wasn't Indian, which left a place for a comic.

'Five blokes were auditioning: Captain Galbraith, who was the usual army bastard, Myer, Bluey and Little Bluey, and a double act from Launceston that pretended to be one bloke with two heads. The idea was funny, but they didn't really have any jokes.

'Myer worked out all these punchlines like, "Laugh? I thought I'd wet myself, but it turned out to be the monsoon." Galbraith did a bit of Jew-baiting about why are synagogues round, which might have been funny if synagogues were round.

'The judges were split and wanted a couple of days to make their decision. While they were out, Galbraith had Myer's name put on the list for the line. Myer said he was sick, but they told him it would be a good place to recuperate. Then he said he'd recovered, and they told him he could give the sick blokes a hand. Myer said he didn't want to go, but they told him it was an order, and the day before the judges came back with their decision, he was gone.'

Jimmy spat on the ground.

'The judges chose Galbraith anyway,' he said. 'They thought he'd be more popular with the men.'

*

Sometimes, listening to Jimmy's stories got too much for me. All the pain and hunger and disappointment started to seem real, and I had to ask him to stop.

'Stop what?' asked Jimmy. 'We're not bloody doing anything.'

He went to the fridge to fetch a bottle of beer, came back and opened it on the step.

'I'm tired of talking anyway,' he said.

And then he sulked.

I wondered if anyone would make a movie of Jimmy's life, and whether they'd get someone Jewish to play the hero, or if they'd just use Bryan Brown like always. I didn't know who was going to turn out to be the hero anyway, and who was going to die in the end, although I was fairly sure the Japs wouldn't win the war.

'We should get to the gym,' said Jimmy suddenly.

Jimmy had many different ways of saying he was going to the Club, including 'taking a breath of fresh air', 'walking around the block' and 'popping out to see a bloke about a dingo'. It was '*shule*', 'the elephants' graveyard' or 'the Rookwood waiting room', but I'd never heard him call it 'the gym'.

When we reached the Club, Jimmy chatted to the man with the guestbook but didn't sign me in. Instead, we took the elevator to the basement, where the Club's minibus, The Tank, waited to transport members home within a five-kilometre radius of Bondi Junction, at the discretion of Johnny the Head, a Maori with a skull the size of a basketball. The Tank was mainly used by gamblers on pension day, when they'd dropped the train fare back to Redfern into the Queen of the Nile, but Johnny the Head had occasionally driven Jimmy to my grandmother's house after a long lunch, although Jimmy always made him park around the corner.

He was smoking a roll-up in the underground carpark when Jimmy and I climbed into his bus. The cigarette looked the wrong size for his head.

'City of Sydney Police Boys Club,' said Jimmy.

'This isn't a taxi service,' said Johnny the Head. 'You know I can't take you to another club.'

'It's not a bloody RSL,' said Jimmy.

'So why would you want to go?' asked Johnny the Head.

'What do you care?' asked Jimmy.

'Why do you people always answer one question with another?' asked Johnny the Head.

'Why do you?' asked Jimmy.

Johnny the Head drove us across town to Riley Street, near the Domain, arguing with Jimmy about the All Blacks. Jimmy firmly believed rugby union was a soft code and all Coconuts were cannibals. Johnny the Head, who lived in a red brick apartment block two streets from my grandmother's house, thought Jews were weak and comically small, too busy talking to ever get anything done.

Johnny the Head bit into a spongy doughnut, and smeared his mouth with blood-red jam.

'Wipe your face, mate,' said Jimmy. 'You've got missionary on your chin.'

'You people'd be a damn sight better off if you'd listened to the missionaries,' said Johnny the Head.

'You people wouldn't have diabetes if you hadn't eaten them,' said Jimmy.

Johnny the Head let us out at the door of the police boys club. A team of junior gymnasts from Gymea tried to board the minibus. Jimmy encouraged them.

Inside the building, a plaque on the wall above the drinks machine acknowledged Jake Mendoza's contribution to the club. Boys' voices, hardly broken, echoed across the basketball court like crows in a cave. Jimmy led me upstairs to the boxing room, where schoolboys changed into board shorts and singlets, and left their long gym bags crowded around a box of scuffed and crumpled gloves.

Jimmy took a seat facing the boxing ring next to Slow Eddie Finkel on the bench along the wall.

We breathed leather and sweat, while big men bullied bags that hung like fat corpses from a beam.

'Have you seen Yuri before?' asked Slow Eddie. 'He's the same weight as Kid Berg.'

'My cock's the same weight as Kid Berg,' said Solomon, panting from a climb down the staircase and pushing Slow Eddie aside with one buttock.

'What's this? Tush week?' asked Slow Eddie.

'Move up and shut up,' said Solomon.

'What's your business here, you fat-arsed *faygeleh*?' asked Slow Eddie.

'I come,' said Solomon, 'to feel what my faux French faux friend Earnless Cash might call the frisson *sportif* of the presence of a future champion. I am also drawn here by a sense of nostalgia for the winter afternoons when I myself laced up the twelve-ounce gloves and faced a variety of young opponents including one Edward Hyman Finkelstein, known then as "Eddie the Virgin", due to both his unparalleled unpopularity with the fairer sex and the fact that his name appeared to contain the word "hymen". If my memory serves me correctly, I knocked him from one corner to the other using little more than my famously accurate jab and an uncanny grasp of the physical geometry of the square ring.'

'You were twice my weight,' grumbled Slow Eddie.

'You gave away half a stone,' said Solomon. 'Rumour has it that was the last thing you ever gave away.'

A boy with eyes as flat as his nose climbed into the ring, followed by a hawk-faced trainer wearing focus pads on his hands. The trainer asked for a round of uppercuts on the pads. The boy bent his knees, squared his shoulders and bounced his fists off his targets with the rhythm of an avalanche.

'Everything else has changed,' said Solomon, 'but boxing gyms have stayed the same. It's like they were perfect to start with. You can't improve on the ring and the bags, just like you can't invent a new punch. And that smell . . .' – he sucked up perspiration and liniment – 'If you could bottle it, you could sell it.'

'They do,' said Jimmy. 'It's called Fosters.'

'It's the smell of guts and fear,' said Solomon, 'of young men ready to fight.'

'It's just leather and sweat,' said Jimmy. 'You make everything out to be more than what it is.'

'You're a miserable old bastard,' said Solomon, 'did you know that?'

'I thought I was your little ray of sunshine,' said Jimmy.

The walls of the gym were papered with yellowed curling posters advertising fights that were over between fighters who were dead.

'You see him,' said Jimmy, pointing to a picture of a little man peeping out from behind a pair of fat gloves. 'He's still with us. That's Henry Nissen, the best Jewish boxer to come out of Australia.'

'Nissen, *pischen*,' said Solomon. 'He wasn't even the best Jewish boxer called "Nissen".'

'Henry won the national flyweight championship from Harry Hayes in 1970,' Slow Eddie told me. 'Me and Jake were at ringside in Melbourne.'

'His brother Leon held the amateur title,' said Solomon. 'Now *he* could fight.'

'They were identical twins,' said Slow Eddie. 'They boxed the same. It's genetic.'

'The Schiller twins had the same box, and it was certainly genetic with them,' said Solomon.

The boy in the ring wore a Star of David embroidered on his shorts.

'It's a nod to the nineteen-thirties,' said Solomon, 'when

Jewish fighters held titles all over the English-speaking world. Except Australia.'

'There was Jack Kid Berg and Ted Lewis in London,' said Slow Eddie. 'And Slapsie Maxie Rosenbloom and Barney Ross in New York and, of course, Benny Leonard –'

'The greatest fighter who ever lived,' all three old men chanted together.

'Although *Ring* magazine only ranked him as the all-time number eight,' said Slow Eddie.

The boy in the ring threw punches that left holes in the air.

'Boxing went to shit when the *schwartzers* started winning everything,' said Slow Eddie. 'Nobody cared any more.'

'The best negro fighter was Saoul Mamby,' said Solomon, 'whose mother converted to Judaism when he was four years old. Even though he was only a light-heavyweight, he could've beaten Muhammad Ali when he won his world title in 1980.'

'I could've beaten Muhammad Ali by 1980,' said Slow Eddie.

Slow Eddie gave a dawdling imitation of the Ali shuffle, without moving from the bench.

'There was also the *schwartzer* Ronnie "Mazel" Harris,' said Solomon, 'who joined a *shule* after he had been hit by a car.'

Jimmy slapped his thigh.

'What a mensch,' said Slow Eddie. 'He even wore his yarmulke in the ring.'

'And he beat Sugar Ray,' said Solomon.

'Was that Sugar Ray Robinson or Sugar Ray Leonard?' asked Jimmy.

'It was Sugar Ray Seales,' admitted Solomon, 'the lesser known.'

'Wasn't he legally blind?' asked Jimmy, closing his eyes.

'Not at the time,' said Solomon. 'That came several years later.'

'At least the diagnosis did,' said Jimmy.

All around me, I saw hands, some of them moving faster than my eye could follow. There were gloves flying towards fractured mirrors, knuckles sinking into sagging bags, scarred and swollen joints wrapped in grey bandages that covered sailors' swallows tattooed on the muscle above the thumb. They were all working hands, like Jimmy's, not soft gladhands like my Dad's.

The old men turned back to the ring, where the boy threw a jab and a cross, then ducked a pad and came back up with a hook.

'Nice lateral movement,' said Slow Eddie, miming the combination.

'Yuri's the first Australian Jewish professional fighter in two generations,' said Jimmy. 'A Russian kid. All the old yiddisher fight fans come to watch him.'

'Who else turns up apart from you?' I asked.

'No one,' said Solomon.

The trainer towelled the boy down.

'Yuri's not sparring today, fellas,' he called.

The trainer unlaced the boy's gloves, and Jimmy, Slow Eddie and Solomon walked up to the ropes to shake his hand.

'*Zol zion mit mazel,*' said Solomon.

'I'm sorry,' said the boy, 'my English is not very good.'

*

I thought Jimmy and Solomon would stop off at the Club on the way back from the gym, but they both seemed exhausted by watching somebody else exercise. Solomon drove us to the shops on Bondi Road, where Jimmy looked around for a new set of pencils while he took up his war story with a vague, distracted determination.

'Before we left Changi, we collected all the kit we were told to take along,' he said. 'Blankets, mosquito nets, musical instruments, books, a bit of medical gear. We didn't want to carry too many medicines because the Japs'd said there were hospitals already set up for us. We imagined wards and corridors, microscopes and X-ray machines, men in white coats prescribing penicillin.

'Ramsay came to our barracks to say goodbye. He wished us all good luck and told us not to expect any rest camps, because the Japs wouldn't've had time to build them. He said he didn't need to remind us that we should sabotage the bastards at every chance we got, but we didn't have a duty to get ourselves killed doing it. He told us to keep our heads up and our noses clean, to remember we were Australian soldiers and, no matter how bad things might get, to never, ever give up.

'Ramsay had a special word for Townsville Jack.

'"Well," he said, "you're finally getting away from us, you bloody commo. And now you're off to build a railway. Infrastructure for all men to use. There'll be no first- and second-class carriages on the train to Burma, I can guarantee you that. Or on the way up to Siam, if what I hear is right. You'll be as equal as when you were bloody born."

'"I'm not a commo," said Townsville Jack.

'"Oh, you will be," said Ramsay. "You all will be. Or else you'll bloody die."

'We shook hands with the mates we were leaving behind, and exchanged cap badges and postcards, any little things we had, souvenirs of other men's lives. We clasped arms and slapped backs – we never hugged, I remember that – and told each other we'd never get off the island.

'"Laugh?" shouted Myer. "I thought I'd pissed myself, but it turned out to be the monsoon."

'Nobody knew what he was talking about.

'We were taken in trucks to Singapore station. I could've jumped out the back. I could've run. We had to wait for hours on the platform before our train arrived. The boongs just stared at us, the Chinese tried to slip us food. Most of us thought we'd get a troop train, but Snowy White reckoned they'd put us on the regular civilian express, which would get us to Bangkok faster because they wouldn't have to muck around with the schedules.

'The only locomotive in the station was a rice train, a chain of steel rice trucks dragged along behind a steam engine. We guessed the Nips used it to supply their troops, but nobody was much interested in it, because there's nothing about an empty rice train that matters to anyone, unless you're rice.

'Suddenly the Jap guards, who'd been asleep or drinking tea or tormenting the Chinese with sticks, decided it was *tenko* hour, so they counted us a couple of times and started herding us towards the rice train. The carriages had every comfort you'd need, if you happened to be a sack of bloody rice. There were no seats, no benches, no windows, nothing. The Japs crammed us thirty to a truck. There wasn't even space for every man to lie down, let alone room for our cooking gear, so we traded it with a boong for a bag of stinkfish.

'We spent the next four days in that carriage, taking turns to stand, squat and stretch out. Townsville Jack stood like a statue on one side of me, Katz wriggled like a fish on the other, and the sun came down on the roof and walls and turned the carriage into an oven. We cooked from the inside. Sick men shit themselves, everyone dripped sweat like a shower.

' "Laugh?" shouted Myer. "I thought I'd wet myself, but it turned out to be the monsoon."

' "No, mate," said Townsville Jack, "you've wet yourself."

'I craned my neck over the shoulders of men pissing into the wind, to watch Malaya and Thailand go by between the carriage doors. There were water buffalo grazing in the fields, rubber trees laid out in rows like bloody soldiers, peasants gazing at the sun. It might even have been beautiful, but it did bugger all for me.

'We came to the line in rice trucks, cooked like rice, slept in rice sacks at night, and we were buried in rice sacks as coffins. They turned us into rice, David, into grains of men.

'The train stopped every few hours. We drank water from the engine and the guards beat us back with batons and swords, and even the most wide-eyed Jap-happy fools realised there wasn't going to be any rest camp. I've said our officers were all piss and wind, but bugger me if it didn't turn out that the IJA's officers, the *chuis*, didn't know the truth from a rat's turd either.

'Men died on that train. Everywhere I went, men died. It was like our time on earth was ending and we were leaving one by one.

'At a whistlestop in the bush, I climbed out of the carriage and missed the siding, tumbled down an embankment into a ditch. I tried to pull myself up with a fistful of long grass, but the stems snapped and I rolled onto my ankle and cried out. The Japs hadn't noticed I'd gone. If I hadn't moaned, the train would've left without me and somebody eventually would've found me. Maybe the boongs would've sold me to the Japs, but perhaps Chinese guerrillas would've taken me into the jungle. I could've lived off monkeys and snakes, hit the Japs in their bases then disappeared into the night.

'I could've had a war without uniforms, without parades, without military bullshit, with men who couldn't surrender because they knew they'd be murdered. The same men we killed when our war was over.

'But none of that happened. Townsville Jack hauled me onto his big, strong shoulders and carried me to the carriage. He strapped up my ankle with the sleeve of his shirt and gave up his space for me when it was his turn to lie down. So Townsville Jack spent the last two days of the journey to Thailand like a soldier at attention, although that's the last thing he was in the whole bloody world.'

BONDI

SUNDAY 29 APRIL 1990

At two o'clock the next morning, the screaming started. Jimmy was running for cover, jumping into ditches, returning fire. I felt like I was inside his dream. I could see the jungle where he fought; I was frightened with him as he pushed away creepers and leaped over vines. I wondered if he was going to die as he called out for Mei-Li in the night.

He woke me early with eggs for breakfast. They looked up from my plate like tigers' eyes.

'They're good,' said Jimmy. 'Eat. We're moving out this morning.'

'Out where?' I asked.

'Out of the camp,' he said. 'The furphy is we're heading to Siam, but if you believed every bloody furphy we've been told, we'd've been home a dozen times by now. Have you packed your kit?'

'No,' I said. 'I'm not a soldier.'

'Come on,' he said. 'If you don't get a bloody move on, we'll get left behind.'

I stared at him hard. He looked back and laughed.

'Gotcha!' he said.

I'd forgotten Jimmy was a joker, a clown, the grandad who was always trying to tickle me, to pick my pocket, take my watch.

He showed me a new sketch, of a building like a golden church, and ran a blunt fingertip up the rise of the spire.

'The first time I saw a spirit house was outside a coffin maker's workshop in Ban Pong,' said Jimmy. 'We fell out of the train and into a stinking boong camp there, with rats and lice and hairy centipedes. A bloke got bitten and he died. Another bloke just died. The guards let us wander around the town, begging for food. The coffin-maker gave us bowls of congee and cups of cold tea. The next night we marched along the railway line to Kanchanaburi. It was all right to start with. These things always are. You play the "at least" game. "At least I'm not in a rice truck any more" or "At least I'm outside."

'We were tramping in the dark because it was too hot to move during the day. I marched with Townsville Jack. Katz was next to us, but he wasn't really marching, just walking. That bloke couldn't look military if you stuffed him into a shell and fired him out of a cannon. Behind us was Myer, the sad little joker.

'Kanchanaburi was the base camp for the railway, a small town alongside a river. We marched in but we didn't stay. We pushed on in a cloud of sick men's farts, but we were weak and hungry and throwing away gear because everything started to weigh more as we went on, and in the end it was like we had giants on our shoulders. The soles of my boots came away from the uppers and I walked in socks on stones and through streams, and my blisters burst and my feet were shredded, grated.

'The Nips drove us along with sticks, beating us across the haunches like we were cattle. They cracked Townsville Jack around the neck, back and legs to keep him going, but he never showed any sign of stopping and when I couldn't take another step he let me lean on him and he carried my weight to the next camp.

'Blokes would collapse by the side of the track and the Nips would kick them in the head to get them moving again. These fellas'd try to cover themselves, roll up like babies, and the guards would whack them in the small of the back, or wallop them across the knees. Sometimes a mate or a stranger would haul them up and drag them on. Sometimes they'd just lie there until the sick cart rolled down the track, and the medics would either take them or bury them.

'Whenever we stopped, Thai traders swarmed around us. The Japs paid them a bounty for rounding up stragglers, who they liked to pretend were trying to escape. Escape. You can't escape from the jungle in the dark. You can't escape from the jungle at all.'

Jimmy's voice had grown lower, as if it were going to ground. He was still following the lines of the steeple with his finger, tracing the route of the march through the jungle.

'One night we stopped at a *romusha* camp for Asian workers, and there were coolies scattered around, some of them dying, most of them dead. Cholera had been through them, and we were expected to sleep with the corpses or burn them. They were only little fellas to start with, but they'd shrunk like children. The Japs said they were Tamils. I didn't know what a Tamil was – still don't, really. The only thing I can say for sure is they die easily.

'The coolies built the railway. There were hundreds of thousands of them on the line – Tamils, Burmese, Malays and Chinese – chattering like monkeys, dying like roos in a cull. They couldn't organise, didn't know how to look after themselves. They lived in their own shit. There was nothing we could've done to clean the place up, even if we'd've had the strength. I pushed a body aside and maggots wriggled out of its mouth like teeth scampering away from a tongue. After that, I didn't look around. I found a way to focus on whatever was in front of me, and to make sure I was standing behind something big and reassuring, like Townsville Jack.

'The Japs lined us up for cholera vaccinations. Their doctor punched my arm with a needle like he was stabbing me, or branding me *Property of the Imperial Japanese Army*, because that's what I was. Quilpie knew it was a trick, so he kept jumping the back of the line and never got his needle. They breed them tough in Western Queensland, but no bugger ever said they breed them bright.

'By a creek in the jungle we built our own camp. We made huts even the boongs would've abandoned, nests for spiders and scorpions strung together out of bamboo and palm leaves lashed with creepers. While one team put up the cookhouse and stores, the Japs gave the rest of us hammers, picks and buckets and set us to work on the line.

'The railway track followed the river along the cliffs. Thailand from the mountains looked the way I imagined China, with waterfalls, temples and caves. I didn't have a picture of what Thailand might look like because I'd never had to bloody think about it.

'We started work before dawn and finished up before the heat of the afternoon. We had to build a railway into rock, but the Japs had no machinery for us. The idea was to do it by hand.

'"I don't fucking believe it," said Townsville Jack.

'Me and Townsville Jack worked the hammer and tap. I held and turned the drill while he knocked it into the ground with a plumb hammer. When we'd sunk a hole, we scraped out the rock dust, poured in water and planted a stick of dynamite. Once the dynamite blew, other blokes came in to carry away the rubble. Hammering wasn't digging, but it was close. The trick was to let the hammer do the work, said Townsville Jack, and I think he felt he could've landed a worse job, and probably had at some time, in Townsville or thereabouts.

'Two lots of blokes watched us work: our officers and Jap guards. Life upcountry was a big "at least" for the officers, at least at first. They didn't have to work, just draw up the lists of men who were fit to go on the line. Anyone can tell another man to do what they won't do themselves. It's not a talent or a trade, it's a vanity. We looked after the officers. We went out to work to keep them fed and clothed. They were like our children.

'The Japs paid us twenty-five cents a day for working and the officers thirty dollars a month for not working. Even after all the Japs' deductions for rent, rice and rags, the sirs could afford to keep themselves in tobacco and duck eggs. They bought breast-milk from nursing mothers in the villages, and kept stashes of food hidden in the secret compartments of trunks I'd carved for them.

'There was a lot of bullo coming from the officers about us all being in the same boat, but out of the Aussies in F Force who left Changi to build the railway, more than a thousand diggers died, but only three officers. It was safer for an officer on the line than on the battlefield. The best officers came out with the working parties and tried to look after us. The worst complained about giving money to the hospital fund.

'A lot of the guards weren't Japs, they were Koreans. I wouldn't've known a Korean from a Tamil before I left Sydney. It's funny the things you learn, and the places where you learn them. We called the guards after the seven dwarfs, because they all had silly wispy bloody beards and none of them was taller than a chimneysweep. There was Dopey, who was stupid, and Sleepy, who was even stupider. There was Happy, who was always scowling, and Grumpy, who was always smiling, and Bashful, who was the biggest basher of them all. There was Sneezy, who didn't really have anything to do with sneezing, we just needed somebody to be called Sneezy, and then there was Doc, who looked the cleverest because he had a high forehead and thick glasses, but I've met koalas with more brains than that idiot. I've known brighter bloody carp.

'Looking at the guards, you couldn't see how the IJA could possibly have beaten us. But the guards weren't fighting troops. You don't waste good men on minding skeletons. They were the scum of the army: retards, rapists, thieves, hunchbacks – and they were all so bloody short. But you also had the poor, skinny, hopeless blokes who never wanted to join the army in first place, because they didn't like fighting or they were too gentle or too religious or too clever. Every now and then you'd get one of them as your guard, and it'd be almost like dealing with a human being. And you had to realise that the railway wasn't the best billet in the Nip army either. They were dying too, not of beri-beri maybe, and certainly not of bloody starvation, but cholera doesn't know if you're a buck-teethed bandy-legged bastard or a six-foot-four ringer from the bush. It turns your mouth into an arsehole either way. They died out there too, the Japs and the Koreans: not in our numbers but with the same bloody pointlessness. They died guarding prisoners who had Buckley's chance of escape. But then some nights I think, *What if we'd just risen up? What if all us zombies had climbed out of our graves and come at the bastards? What if all down the line the camps had rebelled at the same time?*

'For sure, we'd've lost men – hundreds, maybe thousands of them – but we lost thousands anyway. For sure, we'd've starved in the jungle – most of us – or been captured by natives or eaten by tigers (not that I ever heard of any bugger getting eaten by a tiger), but some of us would have survived. You know how I know that? Because there's always one fella who gets away, who escapes the massacre, who hides under the corpses, who breathes through a reed in the river, who finds a friendly village headman . . . There's always somebody.

'Those poor bastards on the Sandakan death marches, they all died. All but six of them. What could have been worse than that? Why didn't they fight? Why didn't they try to grab the guns off the guards? Slit their throats as they slept? I know, David. Do you understand that resignation is a kind of hope? Can you see that? People talk about the Holocaust. They talk about sheep to the slaughter. They talk and talk and talk, but nobody who hasn't lost their freedom knows what it's like to be a prisoner. Nobody who wasn't there.

'The Japs had a code called bullshit. According to bullshit, we had surrendered when they would have given their lives for the Emperor and died like shattered jewels – if they had been fighting troops, that is, and not bloody prison guards. So, because we had given up, we were less than soldiers, less than men, and that meant they could do anything they liked to us.

'I got bashed on my first day on the line by Happy, because he'd noticed me. The trick was to blend in with the mountain, but now and again you caught their eye and there was nothing you could do but cop it sweet. Happy got it into his head that I was loitering at the drill, and gave me a kick in the pants to help me along. He wasn't too pleased with his first kick, so he booted me again. I lost my footing and landed on my face, but I got up in time to catch another punt in the small of my back.

'I'd been kicked worse in Bondi. I'd been bashed harder at school, but I'd never felt so helpless, so worthless, so bloody surrendered. If I'd fought back, he'd've killed me.

'An officer named Cowley stepped in front of Happy and said, "The man's had enough," so Happy got started on Cowley. The Japs had some funny ideas, although not the sort that'd have you laughing. They thought that if a bloke went down when they whacked him, he was showing disrespect, because in the IJA you took your punishment standing. They thought they could get hit without falling, and we had lost the war without fighting.

'Cowley stayed upright but he lost two teeth and never came out on the line again. The Japs liked to humiliate the officers, but it was tall fellas who copped it the worst, because it made the slopes feel big to bash them. They liked to stop Townsville Jack and slap him in the face, or sweep his legs out from under him while he rested on his hammer, or roll rocks at him from the top of a cliff. They were trying to knock him down like a skittle. But they saved their worst for Bluey, because they could sense he was weaker and he'd be the first to break.

'Some blokes are just unlucky. They latch on to the wrong thing early on and they can't shake it off. Bluey had the dummy called Little Bluey, but he must've robbed a theatre, or inherited it from an uncle, because he was the worst bloody ventriloquist in the world.

'He was a handy fella otherwise – good with tools and engines – but Little Bluey was the thing that set him apart, so Bluey clung to him like shit to a sheep. He spent a year in Changi rehearsing his act, but he couldn't get on the concert party because his lips went ten to a dozen every time he said a word, while Little Bluey's mouth generally stayed as still as a painting.

'Bluey should've been anything but a ventriloquist, but a ventriloquist was the only thing he wanted to be. He reminds me of Arnold Zwaybil, who wanted to be Frank Sinatra but sounded like Donald Duck.

'Before we left Changi somebody'd said we should take a canary, and an officer had the idea of building a radio into Little Bluey. Quilpie, who was a bit of an electronics expert, fitted it up. Little Bluey was a much better dummy after the operation, because you couldn't see Bluey's lips moving when he talked.

There wasn't a lot of radio reception most of the places we went, but then there wasn't much we could've heard that might've helped us either.

'The dummy was the most recognisable thing in the camp. He had orange hair, bright red lips and big bulgy eyes. He looked like the clown at Luna Park. Only an idiot would hide something in Little Bluey, so the only time the Japs ever picked him up was to knock Bluey over the head with him. The guards hated Bluey because he was six foot four. They thought it was some kind of insult to the Japanese, that he was saying, "The reason you're short is that I'm tall. Otherwise, you'd look the right size." So they used to beat him every day, for some bullshit crime like blunting a drill, until he fell onto his knees and they could look him in the eye.

'Because Bluey was so big, he needed more tucker to keep going, but every bugger was starving. The Japs only gave half rations to the sick, so the working men had to share their food with the fellas in hospital.'

'I thought you said there were no hospitals,' I said.

'There was no bloody St Vincent's,' said Jimmy. 'There was no Royal Prince Alfred. A hospital was just another bamboo hut where we put the sick. There was no equipment in the hospitals, no drugs. The only thing they had in common with hospitals was diseases.

'Bluey was in and out of hospital. Sometimes the Japs beat him so hard they broke his bones – and that got easier as his bones got brittler – and the doctor had to strap him up and splint him and send him back onto the line.

'So every single bloody morning Bluey got up and went to work knowing that he was about to cop the beating of his life, in front of his mates in a foreign country for no reason except that his family had always been as lanky as the streetlights at home in Warracknabeal, Victoria. I watched them whale into Bluey one day, while a good officer shouted and screamed and waved his arms around and the Japs acted as if the noise was just a monkey laughing in the jungle.

'Bluey stood up for as long as he could while Happy punched him, then Bashful kicked him in the back and he dropped to his knees, but this time Bluey didn't put his hands up to protect his head, he clapped them together to pray. And while Dopey and Sleepy belted him around the ears, Bluey begged God for help.

'Dopey thumped him on the top of the head, like he was trying to drive him into the ground, while Happy kicked at his chin. Bluey didn't flinch and he kept his eyes closed, so he couldn't anticipate the next hit. His head rocked from side to side, and blood ran from his nose and mouth.

'The sky was different that day, as blue as buggery but filled with long white drifting clouds. And you've got to remember, the blokes were hungry, so hungry we were hallucinating steaks, seeing mirages of potatoes in the trees. Half the men on the line were giggling mad from the pain and exhaustion and sheer bloody endlessness of it all. After a while, even the violence didn't seem real. How could it keep on happening? Why would it? If there was a god, where was He? And God meant a lot to some blokes, especially the country boys. Often, He was half the reason they'd gone to war, to fight godless Orientals and knock a bit of God into them. You can only believe in nothing for so long before you stop believing in yourself. But if you believe God is good and then He *never, ever* does anything to help, no matter how bloody terrible the situation gets, then you have to think maybe it's all bullshit and everything's pointless, and most of the blokes weren't ready to do that just yet.

'Bluey went down and got stretchered off as usual, but a fella named Fredericks, who had a beard like a prophet – but then, we all did – turned to me with eyes like silver coins and said, "It's a miracle. The Lord saved him." As far as I could see, the Lord hadn't saved Bluey from anything, unless the Japs had planned to shoot him or toss him over the cliff, but Freddie was convinced Bluey had only made it through his beating because God had sent an angel to look after him.

'"Did you see the angel?" Freddie asked all the blokes on the hammer and tap. "Did you feel His glow?"

'Suddenly, everyone started shouting, "Praise Jesus!" and falling to their knees like Bluey. Naturally the Japs belted them around too – and they got hit a lot harder, because the guards hadn't had to waste their strength knocking them down in the first place. I stood there and watched a crowd of men crumbling, just giving up and letting their minds fall apart. But while they were being beaten by the Japs, the blokes were singing. They started out all on different songs, but it ended up with the lot of them chanting, "Swing Low Sweet Chariot", because it's a hymn for slaves.'

*

There were no *frummers* out walking on a Sunday morning in my grandmother's street, just a procession of Maoris on their way to church. The broad-faced women wore spotted frocks and bright hats, the men smart shirts and polished shoes.

Johnny the Head stopped to say g'day to Jimmy.

'What's in the pot today?' asked Jimmy.

'Kosher meat,' said Johnny the Head. 'What're you building?'

Jimmy grunted. Johnny the Head strained over the fence to see Jimmy's drawing.

'It looks like a *wharenui* for *Patupairehe*,' he said.

'You look like you should be wallowing in a waterhole,' said Jimmy.

Johnny the Head told me to look after my grandfather, who had a few possums running loose in his loft. 'What I mean,' said Johnny the Head, 'is he's as mad as a meat tray.'

'I'm not the one who dances around with his tongue sticking out,' said Jimmy.

Johnny the Head explained to me that Jimmy had no understanding of Maoritanga and if Johnny the Head showed the same kind of disrespect for traditional Jewish customs, such as pawn-broking and fiddling on roofs, he would be dragged up before the discrimination people.

'Anyway I haven't seen your wife for a while,' he said to Jimmy.

'You've probably eaten her,' said Jimmy.

Johnny the Head belched.

They both laughed, then enjoyed a short argument about the Wallabies.

'So, what else is new?' asked Jimmy. 'Apart from gunpowder, the telephone and the horseless carriage?'

'I hear you people've got a fighter,' said Johnny the Head, 'going up against our boy Hone.'

Johnny the Head raised his fists and danced about a bit.

Jimmy twisted his lips.

'If Hone's got a head like yours, Yuri couldn't miss him with his eyes shut,' he said.

'If Yuri's got a nose like yours, Hone could hit it from Auckland,' said Johnny the Head.

The two men nodded at their own wisdom.

'I've never met a Maori who couldn't fight,' said Johnny the Head. 'Or a Jew that could.'

'Who do you think would win a war?' asked Jimmy. 'Israel or New Zealand?'

'Jewish doctors, yeah,' said Johnny the Head. 'Jewish accountants, yeah. Jewish lawyers, the courts are full of them . . .'

'Defending Maoris,' said Jimmy.

'. . . but boxing's not in your blood,' said Johnny the Head.

Jimmy smiled.

'Tell your boy to bring a machete,' he said. 'He will anyway.'

'The only thing he'll need is a knife and fork,' said Johnny the Head. 'What sauce goes best with Jew?'

Johnny the Head licked his lips.

'Put your tongue away, Johnny the Head,' said Johnny the Head's wife, who had a beard tattooed on her chin. 'Come to church and leave the Jew to build his bird table. He's not hurting anyone.'

'His fighter won't be hurting anyone either,' said Johnny the Head.

Nancy the Beard took Johnny the Head by the wrist and tried to march him off to church, but he was too heavy to drag.

'Are you going to the fight, old man?' asked Johnny the Head.

'Why would I pay to see a Maori have a blue?' asked Jimmy. 'I could go to the Beach Hotel and watch for nothing.'

'All the brothers'll be there,' said Johnny the Head, 'barracking for our boy. While the Jews sit in the box office, counting the takings.'

Jimmy's lips wobbled. He bit down on his dentures and steadied his chin.

'Oh, I'll be there,' said Jimmy. 'We all will. There won't be a Maori in the house. We'll buy up all the seats.'

'Hurry up and get to church,' said Nancy the Beard, 'before they buy that too.'

Johnny the Head shook hands with us both and walked away humming a hymn.

'Now I've got to go to the bloody fights,' said Jimmy.

I waited until he had finished complaining about that before I asked him what had happened with the angel.

*

'Well, six men got taken to hospital, and the rest of us had to work two hours extra to meet our total, our darg, but something changed in the camp after that day. Blokes started to call it "The Miracle of Monday", and the fella who'd first identified the angel, which most people'd thought was just a cloud, started to call himself "Reverend Jebediah" and hold prayer meetings, where men stepped up to the front and told their own stories about the Angel of Siam, who somehow got the name Seraphiel and the head of an eagle.

'Seraphiel was sighted all over the camp – at the cookhouse, in the creek, over the graves of the dead – but mainly he floated over the hospital, keeping an eye on Bluey until he made a full recovery, which took a lot longer than usual because he'd burst both eardrums by not protecting his head.

'Townsville Jack had a knack for predicting the future. He said, "You know what's going to happen next? Seraphiel's going to have a word with the Reverend Jebediah." And he did. The Reverend Jebediah announced at a prayer meeting that Seraphiel had told him the thing to do was surrender ourselves to God and not to man. "Haven't we surrendered enough?" asked Townsville Jack. The Japanese were no longer our masters, said the Reverend Jebediah. We had to serve the angels instead.

'Anybody but another madman could see the Reverend Jebediah was *meshuga*, but he gave the blokes something to hope for, the idea that an angel might come down and save them, that we didn't all have to die.

'After the Reverend Jebediah had passed on the griff that the angels were in charge now, the Japs took him away and broke all his fingers with a plumb hammer. So then the Reverend Jebediah realised that Seraphiel, like the Japs, was in favour of building the railway, because in this way we could get the news of the Lord's word to Burma where the population were godless Mohammedans. So hope became another jailer.

'There were about twenty Seraphielites by then, and they turned into the hardest workers in the camp, because they were doing God's bidding. We started meeting our dargs by midday, but these blokes worked on until they collapsed, then picked themselves up, prayed and started again.

'Once Bluey got back to the line, the guards figured they'd repeat the trick. So they waited until Bluey insulted the Emperor by dropping his hammer, then they knocked his bloody voice out of him.

'Everyone was waiting for Seraphiel to show up and smite them, but Bluey was on his own. Even our officer that day was a Seraphielite, and he didn't intervene in case it stopped Jesus from coming back to earth. Dopey, Sleepy, Bashful and Happy made a circle around Bluey, kicking him like a Sherrin, all of them aiming for his head, until Townsville Jack threw down his hammer and ran at the dwarfs, grabbed Bashful and Happy and pulled them off.

'So they all forgot about Bluey and whaled into Townsville Jack instead. By the time they were finished he was just a lump of meat on the ground. But when the Reverend Jebediah walked up to his body and cried, "A saint walks among us! Saint Jack of Townsville!", he still managed to get up and break the Reverend Jebediah's nose with a right cross made in heaven.

'I'd run out of "at leasts" by then. I couldn't see how things could get any worse. I tried to imagine what I had thought war might be like before I joined up – frightening and tough, maybe, but never this. In 1941 I thought I'd come alive. By 1942 I'd started dying.

'The only thing I had left were memories of women, and there were so few of those. I thought about everything Mei-Li had ever said, every time she had looked at me, the feel of her skin on mine, her breath in my mouth, her shadow in the light of the opium lamp . . . But I kept going back to chances I'd missed to get close to girls, the times I'd been nervous and shy, too frightened to talk. What the hell was I scared of? Did I think I was going to live forever?'

I stopped him with a hand on his arm.

'Can you stick to the war for a bit, please?' I asked.

'This was the bloody war,' said Jimmy.

'What about Townsville Jack?' I asked.

'He was in better shape than me,' said Jimmy. 'He was recovering on the line, working as hard as ever – which is to say, only when the guards were watching – in splints and a sling, with a bandage around his head, when he said, "At least I'm not with my old unit."

'Me and Townsville Jack talked about everything, but I still knew bugger all about him. He told thousands of stories, but he always left out places, dates and names. If you asked him a question he didn't want to answer, he'd just say, "That was Townsville, Jack."

'But that day he started talking about his unit. He said they'd trained in Darwin under one commander and he'd seemed like a fair bloke. There wasn't a lot going on in the camp and sometimes the boys would walk into town – which was a fancy name for a handful of hotels and humpies, and the worst looking women in the world – and start a blue with the boongs or the fishos or the other bloody troops, and the worst that would happen to them was they'd get a couple of days in the lock-up, which they usually needed to dry out anyway. There was discipline, but not the brutal, stupid kind. It was the discipline of mates looking after each other, of knowing when to stop. Once they'd got to Singapore, their commander was sent home and replaced by a retread who looked like a fat king. The troops weren't told why, of course. They were kept in the dark and fed furphies, like the story that the first bloke had been a defeatist, or he was rooting the general's wife.

'But once they'd shipped out to Singapore and got stuck in, Townsville Jack's diggers had done well. Everyone had the same story. We didn't feel like we'd lost a battle, so how could we have lost the war?

'As they retreated to Singapore, a couple of the men lost their nerve under the shelling and ran, but you couldn't call it cowardice, it was more like madness. One bloke thought the bombs were planets dropping out of the sky. You couldn't blame a fella for trying to get out of the way of that.

'But some of the officers were no good, and Townsville Jack's commander couldn't control them. He didn't know them, and he put the bad ones where they could do the most damage. They realised Malaya was a lost cause before anyone else, and they didn't want to die for nothing. But you have to want to die for nothing in a war, because otherwise you just give up fighting and the whole show goes to buggery. So the officers were hiding and disappearing and leading from behind, and skiting that they'd shoot the men who did the same.

'The commander was brave, said Townsville Jack. He'd parade around in front of enemy fire, rallying blokes who couldn't hear him for the noise, ordering corpses to polish their boots. That was the thing about the toothless: they'd survived one world war, so they didn't believe anything could kill them. And they knew the more you tried to save your own life, the likelier you were to die – but the commander couldn't convince his officers of that, and the men laughed at him behind his back, because he spoke like he had airs, like a fella who read books. And the union blokes all hated him because of what he'd done between the wars.

'Townsville Jack said he'd had problems with his unit in the war, but at least he was on his own now. At least, at least, at least.'

Jimmy coughed.

'You didn't hear much about the angel Seraphiel for a while, but the blokes in the camp went through all sorts of other crazes: collecting butterflies, learning Japanese, writing limericks, making tattoos, pressing flowers, keeping invisible pets, just about bloody everything. A lot of fellas took up knitting with bamboo needles, unravelling dead men's clothes and turning them into blankets. For a while a few got into painting, but Katz was the only one who stuck with it, and he gradually gathered all the brushes and paints and pencils and paper from the fellas who gave up or died. And usually the ones who gave up were the ones who died.

'Then the Reverend Jebediah went up a hill to collect some timber and while he was chopping wood he bumped into Seraphiel again, and came back down with the Seven Commandments of Seraphiel carved into his arm in blood.

' "I am the parchment," he said. "I am the tablet of stone."

'This time the Reverend Jebediah found it hard to muster up a decent mob of followers, but eventually he wrangled four apostles, who swore to live according to the laws of the angel Seraphiel, stopped eating rice and started refusing medical treatment, and when the last of them died we fought over his Bible, which was the most popular book in the camp because it contained the word of God and you could sell the pages for cigarette papers.

'Most of us were in one of two factions: blokes who thought the war would be over by *this* Christmas and the fellas who bet on Easter. There was a third group, who thought we'd die there, and they all did. The blokes who survived, you wouldn't've picked them – except the bloody officers, of course. They weren't the strongest men physically. They weren't the pick of the bunch for brains either. But they were the type who could see the good in every situation. They'd be lying bleeding to death, trying to hold their guts together and thinking, *Well, at least it's not raining.*

'At any other time, in any other place, you'd've wanted to push them under a car. But in the camps and on the railway, they were the type you needed to have around to make you see there was still some beauty left in the world.

'It was all bullshit, of course. Every day was bloody awful – especially for a bloke like Bluey – and you were just torturing yourself by going on. But nobody wants to die, even when there's no point in living.

'Every bloke had something he thought would bring him luck. Some men kept their cap badges, others still had their house keys, because they'd need them when they got home. Bluey carried a horseshoe. It must've been the unluckiest horseshoe in the world. Townsville Jack had his tote bag, which he used to rub like the Buddha's belly, and I had my memory of Mei-Li.

'All of us, the godless and the god-fearing, were always looking for a sign. If the guards beat us, we thought they were angry because the war was nearly over. If they laid off us, we thought they were wary because the war was nearly over. If supplies were short, we thought the Allies were strangling the Japs and the war was nearly over. If we had a bit to eat, we thought they were fattening us up because the war was nearly over.

'But the war just dragged on and on.

'I worked in bare feet, bleeding, with insects crawling over my ankles, up my legs, into every scab and crack and hole. I thought I'd get used to flies in my eyes, like the cows or the boongs, but you never do.

'We were eaten by sandflies and lice and bugs that bit or stung or gnawed at you all day and all night. We were meat for them, meat and rice. Mosquitoes stole our blood. We were eaten from the outside, and eaten from the inside too. I could feel the acid boil in my belly, burning through the walls of my stomach. And diseases ate my skin with rashes and sores, left me like I'd been roasted over a spit, like a pilot who'd gone down with his plane. It made me feel ashamed to look that way. My skin was the outside of me, the part that people could see, and it was ugly and disgusting and it stank.

'But it would all have been bearable if the bastards hadn't been so bloody cruel. That's the thing: once you've decided somebody is subhuman, you've got to make sure they end up that way. It was the same on the line in Thailand as in the camps in Poland. Work them to exhaustion, starve them half to death, cover them in filth, don't let them wash, leave their diseases untreated, count them, count them, always bloody count them, and then see if they behave like men.

'The counting was the thing for me, all those numbers, screeched out in bloody Japanese, over and over for hours on end. We were counted every morning, on the marches and in the camps, as soldiers and as prisoners, as if every life mattered, to the Japs and to the army, when, really, none of them did.

'The Jap army didn't even care about the guards. They were cowards and bludgers and bloody Koreans. They were bored and they spent half their time bashing each other. I remember Dopey copping a whack from his *gunso* for sleeping on the job. He woke up to a big heavy slap around the cheeks, then had to stand and take his medicine until the *gunso*'s slapping arm got tired.

'Me and the rest of the boys gave the *gunso* a big cheer, which at first he seemed to like, but then he got the idea that we thought he was on our side, so he came up with a new game. He ordered all the blokes to stand in two rows, facing each other, and throw punches, like the bare-knuckle boxers in the old picturebooks. He didn't speak any English, so he couldn't explain the rules. You just had to learn them by breaking them and having a fist crash into your face. He wanted us to box but we weren't allowed to defend, so every punch had to land. If a bloke didn't connect, a Jap hit him across the back with a cane.

'They set mates on mates, so I was paired with Townsville Jack. Now, Townsville Jack was a handy little fighter. He'd worked a few six rounders at the Old Tin Shed, but he thought it was a mug's game and he wasn't a mug. He was only there to pocket his purse and pad out the other bloke's record.

'He knew every trick to sell a punch. He slapped his fist past his wet palm to make a sound like knuckles on skin. He rolled every time my hand came close, and he slashed me with his long, sharp thumbnail in the soft skin over my eye to make so much blood that even the Japs had to call off the blue.

'We were like dancers taking turns to lead each other, or two tomatoes trying to throw the same fight. We could've been professional wrestlers, the big fella and me. We could've done anything, after the war.

'And now I'm going to watch a yiddisher boy blue a Maori at the Other Club,' said Jimmy, 'without him.'

*

I was nearly fourteen years old, a man under Jewish law, but I didn't look like a man. I had matchstick arms and spindly legs. People were always trying to feed me up. I did push-ups in my bedroom at night – ten sets of ten, then fifty crunches – but my muscles did not seem to be growing like the boys' in the boxing gym.

When I was younger, I'd wanted to be a soldier (or an astronaut, or a Jedi knight) but I didn't have much idea of what they did. I knew they carried guns and drove around in tanks, and fought and killed bad guys, but I imagined their lives as clean, their uniforms smart, their rifles polished. They never ran out of ammo and they never gave up. It was the bad guys who surrendered, because they were cowards and their cause was wrong. Once they were in prison where they belonged, they were treated humanely – better than they deserved – and at the end of the war they went back to their families, thankful to the Allies for sparing their lives and convinced our way of life was better than theirs.

But it was hard to be a soldier in my house because Mum would not let me play with guns. If friends brought around their toy pistols, they had to leave them on the front deck before they came inside. I wasn't even allowed plastic knives or hand grenades, which was unfair since the boy over the road had a pedal-driven armoured car and he was Jewish too. But Mum was a pacifist – except when it came to Israel – and Dad was a pacifist about arguing with Mum, although he did let me play shooting games at Timezone when we went to see James Bond movies on George Street.

I was allowed to watch war films, though, and read war books because they were history. I knew the names and dates of campaigns, and could recognise most World War II uniforms. As I had grown a bit older I had realised war was probably horrible and I would be as useless at fighting as I was at everything else. I was happy there was no national service any more, and I wouldn't be yelled at by a sergeant major and made to crawl on my elbows under barbed wire. I knew I'd never be able to get through an assault course, when I couldn't finish the obstacle race at the school sports carnival.

But I had wondered what it would be like to come under fire and hear bullets whiz past my ear. I thought I would probably run away and hide, or curl up and cry, because I was Jewish and soft. I knew I would not have been able to survive what Jimmy had gone through, and I didn't think I'd want to.

'Would you join the army again?' I asked him.

Jimmy wheezed, and braced himself for a cough.

'No,' he said. 'And that's why I'm telling you this, so you don't either.'

'What if Australia was being invaded?' I asked.

Jimmy swallowed.

'Nobody invades Australia,' he said. 'We invade other countries.'

He turned his head and spat.

'What if the Arabs invaded Israel?' I asked.

'They wouldn't need an old man,' said Jimmy. 'Or a young boy.'

There was blood in his spit.

'But what if I was twenty-one,' I asked, 'and the Arabs invaded Israel?'

He wiped his mouth with the back of his hand.

'The war would be over in the time it took to train you up,' he said.

'What if nobody had joined the army,' I said, 'and the Japs and the Germans had won the war?'

Jimmy shook his head.

'You've got to make a choice,' he said, 'but that doesn't mean there's a right one. I'm not saying I wouldn't fight, I'm saying I wouldn't fight like that. One infantryman here or there makes no difference. One guerrilla is worth a section.'

'You just wanted to be with that girl,' I said.

'Yeah,' said Jimmy, 'I did.'

'They have girls in the army now,' I said.

'Not like that one,' said Jimmy.

I thought he meant they weren't Chinese.

'What if there weren't any guerrillas in the war?' I asked.

'What if you did something useful,' he said, 'like go to the shed and look for my staple gun?'

'How would that be useful?' I asked.

'I haven't bloody got one,' he said, 'so it would keep you out of the way for ten minutes while I finished my drawing.'

*

'As we worked on the railway, everyone around us shrank,' said Jimmy, ruling short, careful lines across the starchy drafting paper, 'until we were all as thin as cornstalks, with mouths as long and stiff as Little Bluey. The skin was pulled so tightly across our bones, it looked like we were always smiling. We were as happy as skulls. Townsville Jack said to me, "Are you laughing at me? Get that stupid smile off your face." "That is my face, you silly bastard," I said. "And what've *you* got to smile about?" '

Jimmy snorted, and coughed out a raspy laugh.

'I don't know,' he said. 'It seemed funny back then.'

'Bluey was fading away. He lost interest in his life: get up, get beaten up, go down, bleed, starve. He copped a bad thrashing from Grumpy – even though he was the kindest natured of all the guards – for not bowing to a Jap. He bowed, of course, you'd be mad not to bow, even Townsville Jack used to bow, but he didn't get low enough. Something must've upset Grumpy that morning. Maybe he found out his wife back in Seoul had run off with the *kimchi* man or something, but he must've known it was hard for a tall bloke like Bluey to get down low, when his knees were so crook from the bashings he could hardly get up again. Grumpy whaled into Bluey like Bluey'd delivered the *kimchi* himself. It looked like he was trying to kick bits off him.

'Bluey's body was twitching on the ground, like a baited cockroach, with Townsville Jack crouched next to him saying, "Stay with us, Bluey. Don't go." When the orderlies took him, Townsville Jack shouted, "Bluey! Hang on, mate! Hang on!"

'Townsville Jack was shaking, his face was purple. He had to take great gulps of air to breathe. He swore and spat and scratched the dirt until his fingers bled.

'Bluey necked himself in the night. We found him swinging from a beam. He'd had to tie his legs up behind his back so that when he swung off the side of his bunk his feet wouldn't touch the ground. He was naked and half-skinned and for all the world he looked like a side of beef hanging from a hook.

'We could have minced him into sausages, a dozen for every man. The Japs did it in New Guinea – they ate their own. But we cut the poor bastard down and put him in two feet of mud, because two feet was as deep as we were allowed to go.

'I carved his memorial cross and burned his name into the bamboo. The Japs let us have a funeral. Grumpy brought flowers to the grave and lit a candle. The bugler played the Last Post, and we buried with the body a name and description of every dwarf who'd ever walloped, whacked or leathered him, and the date and place of the crime.

'The next time I saw Bluey,' said Jimmy, 'he was hanging in the wardrobe at home. But Little Bluey made it back to Changi. He made it back to Warracknabeal. Victoria. They sewed him a blazer and a beret and he used to march on Anzac Day with the rest of the Warracknabeal mob. They've even given him medals because Bluey's got no children, no grandchildren, nobody to wear his ribbons on parade except a piece of fucking wood.'

Jimmy squeezed on a dowel stick until his knuckles trembled.

'In the jungle we slept on a bamboo platform with no mattress,' he said. 'As we starved, our limbs grew as thin as the struts. My shoulderblades and hips sank between the bars. We were packed together like cigarettes in a box. I slept between Katz and Townsville Jack. When Katz rolled, we all rolled.

'Rats ran across our blankets, and lice lived in our clothes. Lice and Rice. Rice and Lice. Little bloody grains of white. The cooks made our meals in a kwali, a cauldron, the way they cook in hell, with a chimney built from oil cans to funnel out the steam.

'We had rice with a pinch of vegetable and maybe a piece of meat fat. When they served it up with maggots, we ate the maggots. The maggots ate the corpses, so what did that make us?

'Sickness was the other killer, but I was lucky. Every time I got sick, I had a sick mate in hospital with me and a fit mate to help us out. I had tropical ulcers with Myer, dysentery with Katz, and half-a-dozen malarias with Townsville Jack.

'Dysentery was the worst of all. It sends you to the dunny fifty times a day. You shit the heart out of your body. If you don't get medication – and all it takes is a couple of tablets – you shit yourself to death. The Japs wouldn't release the tablets. They never explained why.

'I'd just come out of the hospital after a week of the worst, most horrible, most pointless bloody human degradation you could imagine. Katz had to poke my bowels back into my arse with a stick.'

There were tears in Jimmy's eyes.

*

'They wouldn't give us our mail,' said Jimmy. 'I had one letter from the *Zayde* the whole war. He told me about the weather in Sydney, which was hot because it was summer.

'I was worried about my mother.

'"We'll've been posted missing," I said to Townsville Jack. "She won't know if I'm dead or alive."

'He looked me up and down.

'"I don't know if you're dead or alive," said Townsville Jack.

'Later we were given printed postcards that said we were prisoners and we were being treated well. We were told the Japs would make sure they got back to Australia, but mine never did.

'When the wet season came, even the Japs stopped getting mail. You think of hell as fire, but hell is water. The rains fell like the four million soldiers in the IJA all pissing on as at once. At the same time the guards got orders from Tokyo that the railway needed to be finished quicker, so they started the speedo. During the speedo we had no dargs, we just had to work until human beings couldn't work any more, and then keep going. We worked waist-deep in water. It was like the world after the flood. Our two-foot graves filled with water, the soil swelled, and the corpses of our dead mates popped up out of the ground. One morning I saw Bluey floating towards me, rotten and eaten, and I screamed like a woman. That picture has never left me, never.

'Men died faster in the speedo because the work was harder,

the days were longer and the rations were even shorter because floods could cut off a camp for days. The Japs went berko with the bashings, trying to beat us into building faster. Then cholera came down from cholera hill, where the coolies had all died, and it hit Quilpie first. When a bloke's got dysentery his blood turns to water, but when a bloke's got cholera his shit turns to milk. It drained all the moisture out of Quilpie's body. He looked as if he was being sucked into himself. His skin dried and wrinkled like an old man's ball bag. He looked seventy, although he can't have been older than twenty-three. Just before they die, good men take the faces of angels, but with cholera your mouth purses up like an arsehole. Quilpie vomited up his soul and then he passed.

'I saw a hundred other blokes go that way. We couldn't even give them graves because burial spread cholera. Under an overhang on the cliff, we burned the bodies of our mates on a pyre, like an offering to the dancing devil, while it rained all around. Sometimes the wood was too wet to burn and the corpses just lay there, stacked like kindling one on top of the other.

'The huts weren't waterproof. Ours didn't even have a roof. We had to pull a sheet of tenting across the bamboo for cover, but the tent was ripped and rotten. You can sleep naked in the rain, but when you wake it feels as though the rain has been drumming at your skin, washing it away.

'We were all so small and weak. We had to narrow the dunny pits to stop the blokes falling into their own shit and drowning. Not that it made much difference in the monsoon, when the shit floated back to the top and chased us into the river.

'We had bugger all by then. Nothing. It was like living before things were invented, before tools, before clothes. Oh, we had one thing. We had bloody malaria, the lot of us. The first time I got crook with it, I felt like I was dying. By the third or fourth, the fevers passed like moods. I'd be cold and stiff, then hot and shaking, trembling and vomiting. Townsville Jack would towel me down with a piece of old rag, then I'd recover for a few hours and take my turn cooling him, holding a bowl under his chin to catch his guts. We were closer than lovers. We were brothers in sickness. It was the same with Katz.

'At first, malarias were allowed to stay in hospital until the worst of their fevers passed, but when the speedo came in we were forced out onto the line. I broke rocks to make rubble for landfill while I was lying on my back, trembling and puking, and thirsty, so thirsty . . .

'A mosquito bite on my leg turned soft and pussy and grew into a tropical ulcer. I had ulcers all around my ankles and calves, from grazes and cuts that had stayed damp and undressed while I worked, but this one grew from a spot into a dome, and ate its way through my skin towards the bone.

'An Australian surgeon visited the camp once every two weeks. He came up and down the line on his cart with his meat saw – because we were meat – chopping and slicing and planing men away. He was a good man, but he wasn't a saint. He was usually tired and angry, and there wasn't much he could do for anybody because he had to hack them up without anaesthetic then leave them to recover without drugs, so if they didn't die from the shock of the cut, they died from neglect afterwards.

'The guards didn't kill too many blokes, but every death was a murder because every life could've been saved with medicine or food or just a few days' rest, but the Japs literally drove us to our graves, David. They rounded us up and herded us into the mountains to die.

'Townsville Jack carried me to the surgeon to show him my ulcer. I had to wait outside while he sawed off a man's leg at the knee. His scream jumped inside of me. I felt myself screaming for him.

'The surgeon saw me in the operating theatre, which was

a bamboo table with a bucket. In the bucket was the last man's fresh leg, and two others. My mind almost left me then. I didn't want to lose my leg, David. There'd been an old fella in Bondi after the Great War – the *Zayde* knew him – called Peg-Leg Pete, who'd been blown up at Passchendaele. His name wasn't even Peter – I think it was Albert – but they called him "Pete" because it went with Peg-Leg. He sat showing his stump, begging for beer outside the Tea Gardens Hotel. The thing he hadn't got became the thing he was. We used to taunt him, David, when we were children. We used to throw stones at him. God help me, but once I stole his wooden leg and threw it into the ocean. I needed my leg, David. I needed to stay complete.

'The surgeon said my ulcer wasn't gangrenous, that I needed to bathe it then spoon out the infection. The medical orderlies were busy trying to save the previous man, who died. They nearly always died when you cut their leg off. Townsville Jack found some boiled water and cleaned my leg, then he got a spoon – an ordinary teaspoon – and gouged my leg. It was like being eaten alive. All the pain I'd felt until then was nothing. He dug so deep into my leg, the spoon scraped the bone.'

For a moment, Jimmy couldn't talk any more, then he said, 'It stank. The whole thing stank. The thing I remember most about Thailand is the smell of life rotting.'

He went up to pour himself another drink and I saw he was limping.

'I did the same, eventually, for Myer,' said Jimmy, 'and Katz did it for Townsville Jack.'

*

Jimmy's voice ran hoarse. He took a whisky to smooth it out, but the drink made him cough, and his glasses bounced on his nose. He spat into his handkerchief and stuffed the rag back in his pocket.

'I'm tired of the sound of my own voice,' he said. 'You tell me something.'

I didn't know anything. I'd never done anything, apart from eat cat food once.

'I'm just a kid,' I said.

'But what do you think about things?'

Nobody had ever asked me.

'I don't like them,' I said. 'I wish they were back the way they used to be, with Mum and Dad still together and us all living in the same house. I wish Mum and Dad hadn't met other people who don't really like me. I wish they weren't angry with each other, and you weren't mad with Mum, and everybody could just be friends again. And I wish Daniel would come back from France.'

Jimmy nodded and adjusted his spectacles.

'Every time I live somewhere, everyone else moves out,' I said. 'First Daniel went to France, then Mum went to Redfern, now Grandma's gone to Mrs Ethelberger's. Nobody wants to stay with me, but everyone tells me what to do.

'Also,' I said, 'I wish I wasn't Jewish. I don't see what good it does. It just gets me picked on. And I wish my dad did something other people do, like drive buses or build houses, instead of sell glue. And I wish I could fight like your boxer and kick the shit out of people who call me names at school.'

'What do they call you?' asked Jimmy.

'Little Boy Glue,' I said. 'Little Boy Jew, Gluebag, Sticky Fingers, Sticky Dick, Tricky Dicky, Dickhead. I've got so many Dick names that some kids think my real name's Richard, but it's just that Dicky rhymes with Sticky. If they're trying to be friendly, they sometimes call me Rich, but that just ends up as Rich Jew, then Moneybags, then Jewbag and back to Gluebag. Nobody at school calls me David. Even the girls. I fucking hate them all.'

Jimmy furrowed his brow. It looked like a rusty tin roof.

'I thought you'd be happy,' he said, 'what with your rollerboard . . .'

'Skateboard,' I said.

'. . . VDs . . .'

'CDs,' I said.

'. . . and Ita Buttrose Walker.'

'Walkman,' I said.

Jimmy massaged his chin.

'We used to make cricket bats out of fence posts,' he said.

'I know it was worse then,' I said, 'but that doesn't make it any better now. At least your mum and dad stayed together.'

'Everyone did,' said Jimmy. 'It was like pass the parcel in those days. The bloke who pulled the wrapping off the sheila got to keep her. But it didn't mean they were happy. Just trapped.'

I frowned in sympathy with old people, then two of them drove down my grandmother's street in their Volvo.

'It's Maurice and Sylvia,' said Jimmy. 'Quick! Commit harakiri!'

They parked at the kerb.

'We were just in the area,' said Sylvia.

'Surfing, were you?' asked Jimmy.

'And we thought we'd drop by,' said Maurice.

Jimmy invited them into the yard, but not the house.

'I'll get straight to the point,' said Maurice. 'We've found a unit and we'd like you to come and see it.'

'Why?' asked Jimmy. 'Are you moving?'

'It'd be perfect for you and Frida,' said Maurice.

'*This* is perfect for me and Frida,' said Jimmy.

'It's a serviced apartment,' said Maurice, 'independent living with care on call.'

'We already live independently,' said Jimmy.

'We should speak to Frida,' said Sylvia.

'She's out,' said Jimmy.

'On a Sunday?' asked Maurice.

'Why not?' said Jimmy. 'She can do what she likes. She's not in a home.'

Maurice waved a flyer around.

'This isn't a home,' said Maurice.

'No,' said Jimmy, pointing to my grandmother's house. '*This* is.'

Maurice made him look at the leaflet. It showed a smart, suntanned old man sitting across a candlelit table from his smiling, elegant wife, sharing a bottle of red wine over dinner.

'Well, that's me and Frida, isn't it?' said Jimmy.

'It *could* be,' said Maurice.

'Look,' said Sylvia. 'She's happy he's drinking.'

'It can't be Frida, then,' said Jimmy.

'Won't you even come and look at it?' asked Sylvia. 'It's not as if you do anything else.'

'I'm working now,' said Jimmy.

'Of course you are,' said Sylvia.

Jimmy agreed that when Frida came back they would call Maurice and Sylvia and drive out to view the unit. Sylvia reminded him they would be closer to her and Maurice.

'Family's very important to Frida,' said Sylvia. 'I know she wants to be near her brother.'

'He's dead,' said Jimmy.

'Who is, dear?' asked Sylvia.

'Her brother,' said Jimmy. 'Mick.'

I could see he was lost.

'Who do you think that is in front of you?' asked Sylvia.

He raised his thick grey eyebrows. 'That's Maurice, you *yachna*,' he said, recovering quickly. 'Don't you recognise your own husband?'

As their Volvo drove onto Bondi Road, Jimmy turned to me

and said, 'They come here to tell me what to, as if I'm bloody seven years old, never mind seventy. I remember Maurice when he was in nappies. Oh, he's a big man now. He's a *pharmacist*. Well, he should write himself a prescription for waddling.'

'He should write Auntie Sylvia a prescription for ugliness,' I said.

'He should write Mrs Ethelberger a prescription for meddling,' said Jimmy.

'He should write Solomon a prescription for fat,' I said.

'Anyway,' said Jimmy, 'pharmacists don't write prescriptions. They just fill them.'

'He should stick to that,' I said.

'My oath,' said Jimmy, and patted me on the back. 'Maurice wasn't in the war. Too young. Too waddley.' He licked a Tally-Ho. 'Myer used to waddle too,' he said, 'the bow-legged bloody galah. He was always trying to find something to keep hold of, and I could see he wanted to latch on to the Japs. He was full of talk of the Emperor for a while. He tried to learn Japanese, but he didn't have the brains. And the guards he was listening to were usually speaking Korean. I don't know why Myer joined the army or how they let him in. He wasn't a pharmacist in those days. He was a tobacconist, with fingers as brown as a boong. But he was the only one out of all of us who didn't smoke.

'Once he'd got over Japanese, Myer started to speak Hebrew, or something like it. One morning before *tenko* – which was so early there was never anything before it – Myer tore his jap-happy Tarzan nappy in two, clipped a square piece to his head and draped a strip of cloth around his shoulders like a tallith, and wanted to go out to work like that.

' "But you're bollock naked," said Townsville Jack.

' "The Torah says you should cover your *kop*," said Myer, "not your shlong. If I'd lived a religious life then God wouldn't be angry with me and I wouldn't be here."

'Myer didn't know – none of us knew – what was happening to the *frummers* in Europe.

'Townsville Jack made Myer rip a strip off his tallith and wrap it around his *shmekele* like a bandage, and Myer went outside to pray. The Japs didn't seem to mind. They never paid much attention to Myer. He had a habit of making himself so small, he almost disappeared. Even when he was walking around like he was dressed up in dishcloths, the guards more or less left him alone.

'It was something new for the other blokes, and the few that cared asked Myer questions about his religion. Even though he knew next to bugger all, he'd talk to them about his tallith which, he said, had knotted fringes, even though it didn't.

'A couple of blokes made talliths themselves, just to take the piss, and walked around behind Myer spouting gobbledegook, which was pretty much what Myer was doing too.

'Eventually, Woolly, one of the younger blokes – he didn't look young any more, but I could remember when he did – came to our hut and asked if he could convert.

'"You want to join the Japs?" asked Townsville Jack.

'"The Deuce," said Woolly. "The Jewboys, the Jewbags."

'Townsville Jack pointed him to Myer, and Woolly kneeled in front of him. Woolly had seen God in a burning campfire, and God had told him that Judaism was the true religion and Woolly ought to leave the camp quick smart and go and live in Jerusalem with Jesus.

'But Woolly didn't know how to be a Jew. Katz, who'd been sketching Woolly's wide eyes and open mouth, offered to help him convert.

'"First you don't eat pork,' said Katz, "which should be easy enough here. Then you don't mix milk and meat – ditto. Then all you have to do is cut off your foreskin and you're in."

'Woolly went off to think about it, and we didn't reckon we'd see him again, then the silly bastard came back a couple of hours later with blood running down his legs and a slit pink hood in his hand. He'd circumcised himself with a stone, like an Abo. The wound got infected and he died, but Myer buried him under a wooden Star of David.

'The next bloke who came to see Myer was a rat-faced Kiwi medical officer called Sprout, who told us the English were the lost tribe of Israel and the Jews were imposters. He'd got the good oil between the wars from the New Zealand prime minister. The Kiwi was a very boring cunt. Myer listened to him for about an hour. When he'd finished, Myer took off his tallith and gave it to him.

'"All right," he said, "you can be the Jews."

'And that was the end of Myer's religious period.

'Katz still painted secretly, but he'd started drawing openly. He had permission from the Jap commandant to illustrate the surgeon's medical notes and, between Katz and the doctor, they put together a sort of manual of jungle medicine.

'His sketches showed arms and legs, faces and thighs, with huge red tears, like windows blown out by bombs. But he was good at drawing bodies, Katz. He had a feeling for flesh.

'Dopey the dwarf had to check all his drawings to make sure they weren't escape maps.

'One day he brought Katz a clean piece of paper and said, "Make sexo." Katz thought he wanted to root him for a sheet of foolscap.

'Katz shook his head because, even though he was an artist, he wasn't like that.

'"I have wife," said Katz, although he didn't.

'"Yes," said Dopey. "Draw your wife."

'And then Katz understood. Dopey wanted a picture of a white girl. The funny thing was, Katz had done this before. He knew exactly what Dopey was after, and the way things were bound to turn out, but he also knew that men need three things to keep them alive – food, water and the memory of women. Katz had something he could trade with the Japs.

' "One white woman, one egg," said Katz, and Dopey agreed.

'It only took Katz about ten minutes to draw a woman. I watched him, and it was amazing. His pen never left the paper. I don't know who he based his picture on, but I wished I'd met her. She had breasts like bloody hot-air balloons, and big black winking eyes. Anyway, she was a modest girl, with her legs crossed to cover herself, and she was wearing boots because Katz didn't like to draw feet. Dopey came back after an hour, and Katz pretended to still be working on the sketch. Two hours later, Katz brought him the drawing.

' "Sexo!" said Dopey. "Number one!" and gave him a duck egg. We split it three ways.

'The next day Dopey came up to Katz carrying the drawing and pointed his finger between her legs. "No hole," he said. "Number ten!"

' "One hole," said Katz, "two eggs."

'He managed to convince the guard that a dirtier picture should cost him more. I'd never seen anything like it – the bargain or the girl. This time Katz made the guard wait all evening before he handed it over.

' "Your wife?" asked Dopey.

'Katz said it was. Dopey looked happy but he didn't come back for a week, and when he did, he whacked Katz across the face with the butt of his rifle.

' "Number ten!" he shouted. "Number ten!"

'With sign language, bashings and a bit of help from Sprout, who spoke cathouse Japanese, Dopey thought Katz had cheated him. He'd got the griff that a white woman's hairy hole was actually around the back. Katz tried the "back hole, three eggs" trick, but Dopey demanded two free pictures and said he wanted a blonde this time. So Katz did these strange drawings of fair-haired girls glancing over their shoulders, looking a bit surprised, as you bloody would. Dopey was well satisfied with these, and even fed Katz a biscuit to make up for the bruise on his cheek.

'Eventually, it wasn't enough for Dopey to have pictures of women on their own. He wanted to see them with white men with giant shlongs. This was a problem for Katz, as he wasn't sure whether Dopey thought white blokes were built backwards as well. The first of the new-style drawings was a big, imaginative picture, and it was anatomically impossible, but it earned us two eggs.

'It was a while before Dopey realised he'd been doing himself out of a root. He'd had enough of pictures of fair-dinkum Aussies ravishing Katz's inside-out wife. He wanted to see IJA soldiers having a go at her and her blonde friend, who Katz christened "Bucket" after his next-door neighbour's dog. One thing I noticed was that all Katz's blokes, Aussies or Japs, seemed to be Jewish, if you know what I mean.

'I reckon Dopey fell in love with the girl Katz drew. He kept asking Katz to show him a photograph, but Katz told him his only picture of her had been confiscated at Changi. Katz would draw other women for him – my wife, Townsville Jack's sister, Myer's niece – but none of them had the same effect on Dopey. I suppose it was because he always remembered the first time.

'Dopey brought Katz new pens and paper. He even found some paints – God knows where – for him to make coloured pictures. But he changed from wanting one new one a week to one a day, then more than one. Katz didn't have the energy to draw them, so Dopey got him excused from the hammer and tap and had him working full-time on the pin-ups. But no matter how many women he drew, Katz never got more than two eggs a day.'

Jimmy rolled the memory of a duck egg between his thumb and forefinger.

'Katz was keeping us all alive,' he said, 'but his mind started to go. He began to look at living men and see corpses. He used to be able to show a man's character by the line of his lips and the sparkle in his eyes, but suddenly all the eyes he drew were empty. One man working on the line asked Katz to make a portrait of him. All Katz gave him was a picture of a patch of freshly turned mud in the jungle, and the next day the poor fella – Tom Walsh was his name – fell over and died. A couple of the worst types reckoned Katz had done it deliberately, just to see if he could – which showed what kind of thoughts were going on in their brains – or that it was some sort of Jew magic.

'It looked like Katz was going to end up under the mud himself, but Townsville Jack managed to straighten it out by explaining that although the Jews certainly killed our Lord and Saviour, it was the Japs who were responsible for the death of Tom Walsh. That and a kick up the arse sent them on their way.

'We tried to talk to Katz, but he said he was a war artist and his job was to paint what he saw and all he could see was death, death, death, and if he didn't record that basic truth then he was failing in his duty. Then he stopped painting people at all – or jungle or earth or rails – only skies. And his skies were clouded with the spirits of dead soldiers, all holding their heads and screaming.

'So I took his brushes off him, and his pencils and his paper, and I buried them under a tree, and I carried him to the hospital. Dopey couldn't understand the problem and thought he might be able to solve it by kicking Katz to death, so I ran off to get Sprout to interpret. In the end, Dopey managed to rustle up a pen and a few scraps of notebook, stuck them under Katz's nose and said, "Sexo! Sexo!"

'Katz coughed a bit of blood from the kicking, but smiled and started to draw, because drawing always made him smile and because he was out of his tiny mind. Katz scribbled away happily until Dopey came back with an egg, and Katz showed him the picture of a girl who was fatter than an elephant with her legs open wide, and between her thighs she had fangs. Her nipples were spiked like spears, and her tongue was a razor blade, and she split the Japs open and left them bleeding like women.

'Dopey dragged him to his feet and slapped him around the face, but Katz kept on grinning, and as he got slapped his cheeks turned redder and redder, and he looked happier and happier. Doc shouted to Dopey to stop, because he'd never get another sexo picture if Katz was two feet under.

'The Japs left Katz alone after that, until he recovered from whatever had been eating his brain, although one of the guards kept pestering him to draw another sexo with teeth. You can never tell what might be some bloke's fantasy, especially if he's a bloody Nipponese.

'One morning we marched off to the line in the pounding bloody rain piping "Whistle While You Work" to the dwarfs. It was the heaviest fall of the season. It dropped curtains of rain over our eyes so we could hardly see where we were going. We had to keep one hand on the shoulder of the man in front, and our feet sank into the mud every time we took a step. It was like walking in weighted boots, the kind they use to teach horses to jump.

'At the worksite we slipped and slid and bathed in bloody mud. By the end of the day we were all caked in it, then the sun came out and baked it on. We looked like statues made of clay, golems come to life. When we smiled it cracked our faces, and we couldn't stop laughing, because man comes from dirt and to dirt he will return, and death couldn't be any worse than this.

'But when we came back for dinner, the camp had gone – the cookhouse, the hospital, the storehouse, everything. Even the guards' barracks had been washed away. Everything we had left had disappeared. The earth had moved from under it. Eight men in hospital had died.

'We searched the soil for dixies, for anything. All I came up with was a cap badge. A bloody cap badge. Townsville Jack dug up his tote bag, which he buried two feet under each time we moved. We'd saved our stake money, but we'd lost our last certainty: that the place we left in the morning would still be there in the afternoon. We had to march five miles to the next camp, which was already overcrowded. Most of the blokes there had dysentery and, within a week, there was an outbreak of cholera.

'One evening I saw Townsville Jack sitting outside our hut, with his head between his knees and his arms hugging his legs, rocking from side to side.

' "What's the matter with you?" I asked.

' "I don't know," said Townsville Jack. "I'm so hungry I can't think straight. I don't want to be in the army any more. I don't want to be in prison any more. I want steak and onions."

' "Coming up!" I said, and handed him a pint of rice.

'He sniffed the dixie, which smelled of bugger all.

' "Mmmm," he said. "Lovely. How's she cooked?"

' "Well done," I said.

' "Mmmm," he said. "Just how I like it."

'He took a spoonful of rice and smacked his lips.

' "Bloody good beef, this," he said. "You can taste the paddock."

' "I got it sent up from Rockhampton specially," I said, "because I knew it was your birthday."

'And Townsville Jack burst into tears.'

*

'There was sometimes a break in the work when the guards had exhausted themselves beating us and shouting. I remember they called one *yasumi* when the rains were light, and I collapsed where I stood, but Townsville Jack climbed a cliff to take a look at the country. When he reached the top, he found another fella already there, crouched in an overhang, wearing grass on his head.

'"What're you up to, sport?" asked Townsville Jack.

'"Birdwatching," he said.

'"Is that something to do with the radio?" asked Townsville Jack.

'"No," he said. "I'm an ornithologist. I write down the names of birds."

'"What's the point of that?" asked Townsville Jack.

'"Don't you want to be free like a bird?" asked the ornithologist.

'"No," said Townsville Jack. 'I want to be free like a man."

'The funny thing was, there were no birds around there anyway. We'd eaten them all.

'The guards came back with a couple of extra men they'd dragged out of the hospital. One of them was an old soldier, crook with dysentery, hobbling on a stick.

'"It's Snowy White and the Seven Dwarfs!" said Townsville Jack.

'Snowy gave us a wave.

'"I've been waiting the whole war to say that," said Townsville Jack.

'I couldn't sleep that night because of a new pain inside me. I thought I'd felt every bloody hurt there was, but this was something different: it was like an ache in my organs. The surgeon was in camp. He pressed my guts then told me he'd have to remove my gall bladder. Then and there. Tied to the bed with no anaesthetic. I was so frightened, David. I was terrified of the pain. The surgeon cut into me and there are some things your mind doesn't let you remember because if you did you'd never be able to think about anything else, so I couldn't tell you how it feels to have an organ pulled out of your body while you're fully conscious and lashed to a bamboo frame, but even Katz couldn't stay in the room.

'I was back on the line in a few days. It doesn't make any

difference not having a gall bladder. They're like officers. I don't know what they're for. But I never felt as strong again after the operation. Maybe it was my imagination, but it was like I'd started to die. And I was tired of all the pain.

'Katz brought me tucker from the Dutch camp, to help me get my strength back. There were thousands of Dutch on the line, but they were like Tamils to me. I'd never given them any thought. I knew they ate cheese, talked double-dutch and needed a beer to give them a bit of dash, but that was it.

'The Aussies didn't trust them. A lot of the Dutch were boongs, Eurasians, but Katz seemed to get on with them all right and they had better cooks than our lot.

'The food didn't help me though. Katz even gave me some yak meat, but I still got weaker.

' "You've got melancholia," said Townsville Jack. "Don't give up now."

'But I couldn't see where this was going to end any more. The world had forgotten us. The best thing I could hope was the Japs would win the war and take over the world and let us out. I thought I might neck myself, but I knew there was no need. If I waited, the melancholia would kill me on its own.

'And then this bloke Sprout appeared again, with his Japanese oaths and his funny sideways mouth, and he said, "I can help you, Jewboy. You can buy your way back to Changi, if you know the right people."

'I didn't like the fella, didn't want him hanging around while I was dying.

' "Who're the right people?" I asked.

'He grinned like a schoolboy.

' "Me," said Sprout.

'He was a sick joke, a big-noting skeleton with ulcers up to his neck, skiting like he was the king of the Kwai.

' "So why aren't you there now?" I asked.

'"I will be," he said, rubbing his thumb and forefinger. "I'm going to own the fucking place. I just need a bit more *gelt.*"

'Oh, that was it.

'"I don't know you, Jimmy," said Sprout, "but I know what you are. You people've always got the shekels stashed away. Am I right? I'll bet you've got a pound of gold hidden up your arse."

'What an idiot.

'"You're welcome to look," I told him. "You can pick out the nuggets."

'Sprout smiled again, six teeth short of a cemetery.

'"That's the Jewish sense of humour," he said. "Look, Dopey's been asked to recommend men to go back down the line."

'"Dopey?" I said. "What's it got to do with that pervert?"

'"He's the only Jap in the guards," said Sprout. "The rest are Koreans. You blokes don't know bloody anything."

'I knew Sprout was matey with Dopey, and I knew Townsville Jack would kill him if he ran off with our money, and I knew it was over for me if I didn't leave.

'I asked Sprout how much he needed, then collapsed because I was too weak to talk. I sent a message to Katz, who was painting amputations in the operating theatre. He came slowly, because nobody had the energy to waste hurrying any more.

'"Dopey's going to get us all out of here," I told him.

'As I heard myself say it, I knew we were fucked.'

*

Jimmy found an old kitchen shelf to use as the base of his spirit house. On his bench he cut a broken cupboard door into rectangles the size of tombstones, then handed them to me to paint red, like the walls of the spirit house at the Thai Dee.

In 1953 Jimmy had gone for a drink with Katz on Tuesday lunchtime and not returned until Thursday afternoon. When he came back home carrying a bunch of flowers for Grandma, she threw a brass *Shabbes* candlestick at him. It missed his head and flew out into the road, where it was crushed by a car. Jimmy had kept the other candlestick in the pair for thirty-seven years. I watched as he trimmed it down to make an incense burner.

'You've never thrown anything out, have you?' I asked.

'I threw Myer out once,' said Jimmy. 'He was misbehaving with the drinks cabinet.'

Jimmy had papered the living room in my grandmother's house with a roll of flock wallpaper he had bought from the landlord of the Regal Hotel when he'd renovated the pub in 1964. Grandma said it made her home look like a saloon bar, but Jimmy argued it absorbed cigarette smoke and loud noise. He had saved the wallpaper offcuts in a packing case with no handles (although Jimmy stored a small collection of handles in the meat safe, none of them fitted the suitcase) and he measured them up with his folding ruler for the inside walls of the spirit house.

'That'll give them something familiar to look at,' said Jimmy.

I painted the outside walls using a jar of homemade emulsion that dated back to Katz's days as a set decorator in Kings Cross, then Jimmy and I sat and had a mug of tea for smoko, and looked at what we had done.

'This is like watching paint dry,' said Jimmy.

I carried Jimmy's tool bag into the front yard and sat on the ground while he nailed the base of the spirit house to the poles.

'Hammer,' said Jimmy.

I passed him his hammer.

'Nails,' said Jimmy.

I handed up a cluster of nails.

'Spirit level,' said Jimmy.

I laughed.

'Get it?' I said.

'Get what?' asked Jimmy.

'*Spirit* level!'

'Yeah, very good,' he said. 'Now pass the bloody spirit level or I'll brain you.'

I asked Jimmy if I could have a turn with the hammer.

'Be careful,' he said, but I knew what I was doing.

When I took hold of the handle, I imagined myself outside my body, looking on as my hand raised the tool and brought it down smack on the head of the nail, a boy watching a man. I landed square and drove it half a centimetre into the wood. That felt good to me, somehow real. As I admired myself hammering, I lost the angle, and knocked the nail a little to the left. I tried to pull it back straight, and smashed the hammerhead onto my thumb. The impact cracked my thumbnail and crunched the bone, but at first it didn't actually hurt. This was because I had grown tough, coarse, hard. I was a carpenter – a chippie – a manual labourer doing a handjob.

Instinctively, I stuck my thumb in my mouth and sucked it: not like a crying baby, more a snake-bit survivor in the jungle, calmly draining the venom from his wound.

'Let me look at that,' said Jimmy.

Out of my warm, wet, comfortable mouth, my thumb felt like it was clamped in the jaws of a trap. I watched blood run black under the nail. The thumb throbbed, and swelled like finger-puppet, until Jimmy bandaged it up with some gauze he had unravelled in 1974.

'I suppose you'll be after workers' comp now,' said Jimmy.

'I could do with a bottle of Coke,' I said bravely, 'and we haven't had lunch.'

We hurried to the Club. Myer and Katz were quarrelling about great Jewish racing drivers. Solomon was drinking neat whisky.

'Straight spirits?' said Jimmy. 'What's up with you? Wake up feeling like a man, did you?'

'Oh, I woke up feeling like a woman,' said Solomon, leering, and traced the shape of a girl's body in the air. 'Like Greta Torpin – remember her? Big bloody boobs and a *tochis* to match.'

'The wisdom of Solomon,' said Jimmy.

'Don't knock it,' warned Solomon. 'Look at all the money it's made me.'

'Meaning what?'

'Meaning I used my brain and now I don't have to live down there with the *schwartzers* and the *frummers*. You used your hands and where did that get you?'

'My hands got up Greta Torpin's skirt,' Jimmy snapped, 'and the only thing of yours that got up there was your dreams.'

'Not in front of the boy,' said Solomon. 'All I'm saying is it might be time you moved somewhere nicer.'

'I paid for that bloody house,' said Jimmy. 'It's mine.'

'Does that mean you have to live there forever?'

'Who lives forever?' said Jimmy. 'Anyhow, what part of your brain does it take to run a *schmatta* shop on Darlinghurst Road?'

'The business part,' said Solomon. 'The yiddisher *kop*, which was passed down the generations to every one of our people with the notable exception of Isaac "Jimmy" Rubens, who couldn't keep hold of a dollar if it was nailed to his hand like Christ to the cross.'

Solomon grabbed one of Jimmy's hands and turned up the palm, looking for stigmata.

'My son Solomon,' said Solomon, 'who is the lucky recipient of both his father's commercial sense and irresistibility to women, has recently bought, with his lovely wife, a new(ish) and (reasonably) well-appointed unit near the golf club. It's negative geared, so he doesn't even *want* to make money on it. You could rent it from the boy, and let your *shtibele* to the *schwartzers*.'

'They allow Jews into the golf club?' asked Jimmy.

'You don't have to play golf to live near a golf course,' said

Solomon. 'Just be happy to think of other people enjoying themselves on the green – anti-Semites, Nazis and the like."

'Why does everyone want me to bloody move?' asked Jimmy.

'It's for your own good,' said Solomon.

'So what's that to you?' asked Jimmy.

'I'm your mate,' said Solomon.

'Name one thing you've ever done for me,' said Jimmy.

'In 1947,' said Solomon, 'I bought you a gelato.'

The old men seemed restless. They didn't have anything to say.

'I don't know why we come here,' said Jimmy.

'I've been coming here forty-five years,' said Solomon.

'It must be your shout by now,' said Katz.

'He thinks forty-five years is a long time,' said Myer. 'I've been coming here fifty years.'

'You can't count the war,' said Solomon.

'Oh?' said Myer. 'He has a manual. It tells him how many years he can spend in the Club. Perhaps it tells him how many times a man can sleep with his wife.'

'I've only slept with his wife once,' said Jimmy. 'And that was during the war, so it doesn't count.'

'I have never slept with his wife,' said Katz, 'in times of peace.'

'I slept with her on VJ Day,' said Myer. 'Pass me the manual.'

He tugged at Solomon's shirt, tore an imaginary book from his breast pocket, flicked through invisible pages, found a non-existent paragraph and followed it with his finger.

'It's a grey area,' he announced.

'It is now,' said Solomon. 'Bless her.'

Myer wagged his finger at me.

'Put that picture out of your mind *now*, young man,' he said, but I had no idea what they were talking about.

'I'm so hungry,' said Solomon, 'I could eat a whore.'

So we all marched up to the Sunday roast buffet and served

ourselves with the special, which was the same every week of the year: roast leg of lamb with rosemary. I took slices of warm meat in gravy, and a nest of powdery potatoes. Jimmy had lamb and chicken and fish and prawns and pumpkin and cabbage and carrots and cauliflower cheese and brussel sprouts, with potatoes, pasta salad and a Yorkshire pudding. He piled it on his plate like a cake, and iced it with thick brown gravy.

'Now that's what I call a baked dinner,' he said.

'Isn't Frida feeding you?' asked Solomon, whose plate was invisible under a mound of lamb.

'She's not there,' I said.

Jimmy frowned.

'Has she run off with Slow Eddie Finkel?' asked Myer. 'They shouldn't be hard to catch.'

Jimmy puffed like a steam train.

'She's gone to stay with Mrs Ethelberger,' I said.

Jimmy squeezed his hands between his knees, waiting for the attack, but the old men were distracted by a stray thought from Myer.

'I mated Slow Eddie Finkel last week,' he said.

'Your progeny will be the ugliest baby in human history,' said Solomon.

Solomon sucked in his lips and pulled his cheeks into line with his nose, so he looked like a sheep's bum with eyes.

'I never forget a face,' said Jimmy, grinding a phantom cigar between his teeth, 'but in your case I'll be glad to make an exception.'

Solomon noticed the bandage around my thumb.

'If you rub your shlong any harder, it'll come off,' he warned.

'I hit it with a hammer,' I said.

'That'd do it too,' said Solomon.

'Was it a meat hammer?' asked Myer.

'It was a claw hammer,' I said. 'I was banging in a nail.'

'Was it your thumbnail?' asked Myer.

'Let the boy tell his story,' said Solomon. 'We've heard enough about your handjob to last until the second coming.'

'He never had a second coming,' said Katz.

'So, tell us, David,' said Myer, 'which of the incalculable number of broken and neglected utilities in the Rubens household were you attending to when you decided instead to crush your own thumb to avoid your duties and get sent back down the line to recover?'

'I was helping Jimmy make a spirit house,' I said.

'What's that, then?' asked Solomon. 'A place for Old Longpockets to hide his whisky bottles?'

'Drop it,' snarled Jimmy.

'Listen to him,' said Solomon, 'the kosher Clint Eastwood. Go ahead, punk, *oy vey*.'

Katz offered everyone a drink, but Jimmy said, 'I'm going home. I've had better conversations with Witnesses on the doorstep.'

He mimed slamming a door in their faces.

I looked proudly at my bandaged thumb, confident I would soon grow my first scar.

*

I pasted up the wallpaper while Jimmy cut wood for the roof.

'We handed every penny we'd saved over to Sprout,' said Jimmy, 'and he promised Dopey would have us back down the line in a week. It turned out he couldn't get us to Changi, but he could arrange for us to be transferred to a hospital camp. In the hospital camp, he told us, there'd be light work, dry weather and drugs. The other problem was there was only room for two bodies on the boat, so Katz and Myer would have to wait two weeks for the next transport. Myer was already off with the fairies, and Katz didn't care. Two days, two weeks or two years was all the same to him. We'd done our money and he didn't believe in anything any more.

'Me and Townsville Jack were waiting on the banks when the boatman arrived in a barge that looked as old as the countryside, with an eye painted on the side to ward off evil spirits. We were naked except for our loincloths and we had nothing with us, nothing at all except Townsville Jack's empty tote bag. Our faces were covered with beards that grew out in every direction. Our mothers wouldn't've known us. You couldn't tell we were human.

'The boatman picked his way through the shallows with a pole. The barge was already loaded with sick men from even further up the line. Their bodies were stacked three deep, curled into each other. The boatman had a gold tooth, so of course we called him Flash Rat and, as usual, we couldn't've been more wrong. He tried to clear a space, to gently push away the arms and legs and find us a sliver of deck to lie on. He had his son with him, a boy with a smile that made you want to live. The boy gave us water and spoke English. He said, "I think your war is nearly over."

'We asked his father's name.

'"Cha Ron," said the boy.

'"Nice to meet you, Ron," said Townsville Jack, holding out his hand.

'I remember a gentle journey upriver, watching weaverbirds nest in the trees and kingfishers swoop into the water.

'"The ornithologist would've loved this," said Townsville Jack, but the ornithologist was dead.

'I didn't have melancholia any more. I knew the war must've turned against the Japs and we were heading for a safer place.

'We fell asleep and woke up a day later, to see the boatman rolling corpses over the side.

'"More room," said his son. "Less disease."

'But he had searched the bodies for identification, and he gave me everything he'd found. I memorised each man's name and unit, for their families and for the reckoning.

'The boatman fed us duck eggs and rice, and jasmine tea boiled on his motor.

' "Hang on a minute," said Townsville Jack, "we're going the wrong bloody way. This isn't south, it's east."

'He looked around at a river that was almost as narrow as the barge.

' "We're heading for the mountains," he said.

'The boatman spoke through his son.

' "The place you are going to is different from the other camps," he said to Townsville Jack. "These other men may die," he pointed to the rest of his cargo, "but you, you are an officer, so you will survive."

'Townsville Jack nodded.

' "You are an officer," repeated the boatman's son. "Do you understand that?"

' "I'm an officer," said Townsville Jack.

' "They made you the leader because you are so tall," said the boatman.

' "That'd be it," said Townsville Jack.

'We travelled about thirty miles until we reached the end of the river, where the barge was met by two bored Japs in a bullocky. We were the only men to get off. The boatman tried to unload the corpses, but the Japs refused to take them. Me and Townsville Jack were so tired and weak we couldn't even climb into the cart.

'The Japs made chimpanzee noises, but in the end they helped us up.

'We were on the cart for two days. The trail was as rough as the Birdsville Track. I felt every pit and puddle in the place my gall bladder used to be. Finally we reached a sealed road, where a *gunso* and a crew of Koreans picked us up in a truck. I lost track of day and night. We were taken out twice, to shit in a clearing, and fed on rice and dirt. When we finally got within cooee of a cluster of huts, the Japs tossed us out like sacks of rice and left us lying in the middle of the path. We crawled under the shade of a tree and fell asleep. We were woken by a tall man with sunken eyes, wearing patched shorts and shiny shoes and carrying a stick.

' "Are you officers or men?" he asked us.

' "I am an officer," said Townsville Jack, "and this is my batman."

' "Officers' quarters are to the right, sir," he said, offering a salute. "You can make your way there when you're ready."

' "We can't walk," said Townsville Jack.

' "I can help you, sir," he said, "but your batman'll have to wait until there's an MO to carry him."

' "I'll stay with him," said Townsville Jack. "I'm worried he'll try and escape."

' "Oh, there's no escape from here, sir," said the tall man. "We're very well guarded."

' "I was joking," said Townsville Jack.

' "Of course, sir," he said. "I'll send two orderlies."

'He saluted and marched off.

' "Have I gone bloody berko," asked Townsville Jack, "or did that bloke just march?"

'We'd been under the tree for a while when a wiry little fella limped over and looked at us with his head cocked, like a monkey. He had black sunken eyes and small pink hands, and he prodded Townsville Jack on the shoulder, as if he didn't believe he was real.

' "It's you, Pete, isn't it?" said the monkey man. "It's me, Diamond Tom."

'Townsville Jack tried to sit upright.

' "What the bloody hell are you doing here?" he asked.

' "Taking my annual holiday," said Diamond Tom. "What do you fucking think?"

'"Good to see you, mate," said Townsville Jack, and tried to hold out his hand, but his tired arm dropped before it could stretch to Diamond Tom.

'"I heard you say you were an officer," said Diamond Tom.

'"I was promoted in the field," said Townsville Jack.

'"Which field?" asked Diamond Tom.

'"This one here," said Townsville Jack.

'Diamond Tom rolled two cigarettes, one for me and one for Townsville Jack.

'"You'd better watch yourself," said Diamond Tom, "or they'll throw you in the boob."

'"We're already in the boob," said Townsville Jack. "Or haven't you noticed?"

'"No," said Diamond Tom, "*the* boob."

'Townsville Jack shook his head.

'"You're as mad as a maggot, Diamond Tom," he said.

'"If I were you," said Diamond Tom, "I'd get back on my feet and disappear into the bush. There's a couple of good men camped down by the river, pretending to be choleras, living off the fish they catch."

'"If you were me," said Townsville Jack, "you couldn't bloody move."

'I tried to take my weight onto my legs, but the jungle air pressed me back down. I thought, *This is how it must feel to be paralysed, like you're awake but you can't wake up your limbs.*

'"The orderlies are coming," whispered Diamond Tom. "Pretend you're delirious."

'"I *am* bloody delirious," said Townsville Jack.

'The officers' quarters was just another bamboo hut with an attap roof, but at least we didn't have to build it before we could sleep in it. There were two clean-shaven men squatting in the doorway, drinking warm water and smoking hibiscus leaves. They rose and saluted as the orderlies rested Townsville

Jack on a spent palliasse and dumped me on a platform on the floor.

'A tall man visited us in the afternoon with the fella with shiny shoes by his side. He introduced himself as Lieutenant Colonel Duffy to Townsville Jack.

'Duffy might've been fat once, but his body had eaten itself in the jungle. Now he was drawn like the rest of us, but his bones left him wide hips, like an archway. His figure reminded me of an empty bottle. He had lost his front teeth, and the new shape of his mouth made his voice whistle. He had one lazy eyelid that drooped like a curtain over his right eye.

'And he looked like he should be on horseback. Duffy always seemed as though he was riding the length of a column, looking down on his men. He should've worn spurs and carried a crop. He had standards. That was the main thing with Duffy – he was a standard bearer. Like an ancient bloody Roman.

'I could see he was older than the rest of us, but age is just your distance from death, so we were all pretty much equal there. He talked a bit like somebody from another time, but maybe it was another class. There was something . . . womanly about him, a curl of his lip or a swing of his hip, something he hadn't been able to harden. Callaghan didn't have that, but Duffy wasn't worth the wax on Callaghan's moustache tails.

' "What is your name and rank?" he asked Townsville Jack.

' "My name is that with which I was born," said Townsville Jack. "My rank is that which I have earned."

' "He's delirious, sir," said the man with shiny shoes.

' "Thank you, Captain Evans," said Duffy.

'Evans was a different kind of build – thin, of course, but there'd been a time when he'd had so much muscle that he hadn't been able to lose it all. There were one or two men like him, drill sergeants and PT instructors, *meshugannehs* who, when the day's work was over, would try to pump out ten pull-ups on the beams in the hut, until their silly bloody bones cracked. He had sunken eyes but they were still bright, and – incredibly – he bothered to grease back his hair. God knows what he used.

'Duffy squinted at Townsville Jack.

' "Do you need anything?" he asked.

' "Just rest," rasped Townsville Jack.

' "The Japs had you labouring, did they?" asked Duffy. "Well, that's all over now."

' "And lace," said Townsville Jack, "I need lace to make a doily."

'We heard the rumble of a work party limping back to camp, and I waited for the slap of gruel slopped into dixies, but before the cooks served the men, a soldier came into the hut carrying Townsville Jack's meal on a bamboo tray.

' "Rice, sir," he said to Townsville Jack. "I'm afraid your batman will have to mess with the ORs."

'I pulled myself up by the bedpost.

' "Save your strength," said Townsville Jack. "There's enough here for two."

'We ate his rice and it was good – as far as rice goes – but I still managed to drag myself to join line at the kwali. I needed one stick in each hand to walk the distance, but a couple of blokes lent me bony shoulders to lean on. Looking down the row of POWs, I realised me and Townsville Jack were the only men in the camp wearing beards.

'After dinner there was a *tenko*, but it was called by Duffy not the Japs. He counted us easily, which was a relief, but then he started an inspection. A bloody inspection! I couldn't believe it. He marched up to me, standing there balanced on my sticks, and said, "Haircut and shave, soldier."

'I shuffled back to the officers' quarters and fell down next to Townsville Jack on the palliasse.

' "I've just been sent to the barber," I said. "Where the bloody hell are we?"

'"We're back with my old unit," said Townsville Jack, "and we're going to die."

It was the first time I'd heard him talk like that.

'Duffy called in just before the lights-out bugle call.

'"With respect, Captain," he said (he had decided Townsville Jack must be a captain), "this isn't the merchant navy. All the officers in my camp are required to be clean shaven. It's cooler, it's healthier, and it helps show the Japs we haven't lost all self-respect."

'"I've got a skin disease, sir," said Townsville Jack.

'"We all have skin diseases," said Duffy. "That's no excuse for looking like a caveman. I want to see you and your batman trimmed and scrubbed by tomorrow."

'"I am a sheep," said Townsville Jack.

'"Well then, get yourself shorn," said Duffy.

'In the morning a soldier brought a pair of shorts and a shirt for Townsville Jack, but nothing for me. He showed us to the barber, who worked from a stool under a tree. He had a scissors but no comb. I went first. He had to shave me without soap. My cheeks and chin bled, but afterwards I splashed water on my face and felt better.

'He trimmed Townsville Jack's beard like it was a hedge – which it more or less was. When it was cut close enough to make out the line of his jaw, the barber asked, "Do I know you, sir?"

'"Forget it," said Townsville Jack.

'The barber patted Townsville Jack's shoulder and carried on cutting, but he worked more carefully, gently even. When he'd finished, he took a mirror from his pocket and showed it to Townsville Jack.

'"Is that how you remember yourself?" he asked.

'"I don't know who I am, Foley," said Townsville Jack.

'"Keep it that way, eh?" said Foley.

'"What the hell's going on?" I asked Townsville Jack.

'We were on our way back to our hut when Duffy and Evans marched up. Duffy was about to say something officerly to Townsville Jack, when he noticed the features on his clean shaven face. He looked at Townsville Jack closely, and me not at all.

' "It's you," he said to Townsville Jack.

' "Who?" asked Townsville Jack.

' "The wolf in sheep's clothing," said Duffy. "Now get that uniform off."

' "No," said Townsville Jack.

'Duffy was only a bit shorter than Townsville Jack, and his rank added a couple of inches to his height. He stood tall and stared like a snake charmer into Townsville Jack's eyes, but Townsville Jack just wiped his forehead and smiled his country boy smile.

' "You've no right to those," said Duffy, pointing to the makeshift pips on Townsville Jack's epaulettes.

'Townsville Jack pulled them off and handed them to Duffy.

' "Now get to your quarters," said Duffy.

'Townsville Jack didn't move until Evans called three NCOs to stand behind Duffy and puff out their chicken chests.

' "Give me a minute," said Townsville Jack. "I need to pack."

He stuffed an officer's dixie into his white tote bag.

' "I knew it was you," said Evans.

' "Of course you did," said Townsville Jack.

' "The old man will have you on a charge tomorrow," said Evans.

' "Of course he will," said Townsville Jack.

'They stood inches apart, their fists clenched by their sides, staring into each other's eyes.

' "You can keep the shorts," said Evans. "Give me back the shirt."

' "No," said Townsville Jack.

'Evans raised his hands slightly.

'"You're not proving anything," said Evans.

'"I've got nothing to prove," said Townsville Jack.

'The NCOs came closer, but Evans waved them away. In the ORs hut, we took a dead man's bunk and slept together, side by side.

'"Duffy was my CO," said Townsville Jack.

'"Who are you, mate?" I asked him.

'"It doesn't matter who I was," said Townsville Jack. "My father said I'd disgraced the family name, so I thought, *Bugger youse, and to hell with the family name*, and I chose another."

'"Townsville Jack?"

'Townsville Jack shook his big head.

'"I joined up as Peter Fry," he said, "the same name as I used in the nick. Me and the army got on all right to start with. In jail I got used to being bellowed at and bashed, so that didn't worry me. I grew up in the country, so I knew my way around guns, and I liked the army training. I liked being fit. I even liked digging bloody holes. There's not much else to do but dig holes when you've got a year's hard labour in Townsville, so you might as well get good at it.

'"But I never liked Duffy. He thinks he's a born leader, but you've got to earn the kind of respect he thinks he's got coming to him, and Evans is a fucking coward."

'Townsville Jack fell asleep, and I was lulled into dreams of home by his sad, familiar snore.

'We woke up to a bugle call and an NCO patting his cane on the foot of the bunk, calling, "Everybody out!" After another *tenko* by Duffy, Townsville Jack was led away.

'There was an orderly room in Camp Duffy, just like in Changi. They even had a picture of the King on the wall, although it was only a drawing. Duffy told Townsville Jack he was disappointed that one of his own men should come before him like this, having fraudulently obtained camp property and robbed his comrades by sitting around while they had gone out and worked. Obviously, we could've said the same about half the officers on the line, but Townsville Jack didn't make a big thing about that. He didn't want a revolution. He didn't even want anyone to help him. I've never met a bloke like that before or since. He was like a country of his own, "plucky little Belgium" or something.

'He was told he had impersonated an officer and disobeyed a direct order to return his kit.

' "In this camp," Duffy told him, "you are a soldier first and foremost, then you are a prisoner. As a soldier, it is your duty to respect your officers and obey their orders. We *all* have the greatest chance of survival if we retain the discipline of an Australian fighting force. You only have to look at the Tamils, perishing in their own filth: they've got no officers, no hierarchy, no discipline, no ranks, and they die. Do you want to die like a coolie? Is that what you want?"

' "The coolies die because they've got no doctors," said Townsville Jack, "not because they've got no officers."

'Townsville Jack was found guilty. He was always found guilty. I don't think he'd ever beaten a blue in his life. As his punishment he was put on half rations for a week.

' "You must be bloody joking," he said.

' "The prisoner is dismissed," said Duffy.

'I thought I might get hauled up before Duffy too, but it turned out there was no such charge as "impersonating a batman", because there's no point in it.'

BONDI

MONDAY 30 APRIL 1990

Jimmy sent me to school with a note saying I'd been absent for two days because I'd hit my thumb with a hammer. The teacher knew I came from a broken home, and she asked if I had really hit myself or if someone else had done it to me. I was tempted to blame the Dark Man, or even the Woman in White, but I knew I was lucky to get away with the excuse at all.

When I came back to my grandmother's house Jimmy was fitting the walls to the base of the spirit house, as a pair of lorikeets looked down from the telegraph wire.

Barry Dick crossed the road to ask Jimmy if he wanted to put on *teffilin*.

'Not now,' said Jimmy, 'I'm busy.'

'It's a mitzvath to be busy,' said Barry Dick, 'but it's also a mitzvath to put on *teffilin*.'

'Is there anything that isn't a mitzvath?' asked Jimmy.

'Yes, there is,' said Barry Dick. 'Making graven images.'

'There's not a lot of that about any more,' said Jimmy.

'Isn't there?' asked Barry Dick. 'Can I ask what you're doing?'

'I'm building an extension,' said Jimmy.

'Oh,' said Barry Dick, 'that's fine then.'

'Fine, is it?' said Jimmy.

'It should be fine,' said Barry Dick. 'Remember: *Moshiach* is coming.'

'I'll leave some biscuits out,' said Jimmy.

Jimmy's latest drawings showed a tiled sloping roof supported by pillars and decorated with dragons. We looked at his sketches of guttering laced with snowflake jewellery, and Jimmy said he didn't think he had the eye for the fine work any more.

'I could paint them,' I offered.

Jimmy cocked his head, as if he had heard something in the wind. He fossicked in the shed – among the dolls' arms and false teeth, the spectacle frames and watchstraps – until he found a tin of gold paint, left over from one of Daniel's old modelling kits.

'The ORs' quarters were crowded,' said Jimmy as I traced a dragon's tail. 'The air smelled sweet like crushed bedbugs, and rank like shit. We were supposed to be building an airfield in the mountains, and working parties went out every day to try to level the land, but I think everyone knew by then that there was never going to be an airfield, just another burial ground. There was no discipline on either side. We were nowhere, surrounded by malarial forests where tigers and leopards and hog deer lived like bloody dinosaurs. The Japs took bribes to keep healthy men out of the working parties. The sick just died.

'Foley and Diamond Tom were in our hut, talking about dead mates with Townsville Jack, when five men burst in wearing hoods and waving sticks.

'I thought they must have had a concert party here and this was some kind of a rehearsal. But they were moving like bashers, like guards, rolling their shoulders, pushing, puffing themselves out, filling the space in the hut.

' "You!" shouted the leader.

'Diamond Tom turned away but the leader grabbed him by the back of his neck and smashed his face into the side of our bunk, crunching the bridge of his nose against the bamboo.

'Townsville Jack jumped but Foley held him back, and the other hoods swung their clubs and stamped their feet.

'"Stealing tobacco!" shouted their leader.

'While two of his men held Diamond Tom's matchstick arms, the leader dragged his loincloth down to his knees. Diamond Tom's buttocks were already sore with scurvy, and weeping patches of pus.

'"Ten lashes!" said the leader, and pulled a raggedy leather strop from the belt loops of his shorts.

'"You wait a fucking minute there," said Townsville Jack.

'"Stay out of this, Fry," said the leader. "This is Vigilance Committee business."

'"And what the bloody hell is a Vigilance Committee?" asked Townsville Jack.

'"Forget it, Pete," said Diamond Tom. "Let them have their fun."

'As we stood there, the leader thrashed Diamond Tom, while his men kept us back. Pieces of his skin flaked off on the belt. Diamond Tom squirmed and yelled and, in the end, he blacked out.

'Townsville Jack rushed in as if he was going to try to revive him, then sidestepped like Ted Kid Lewis, ducked and lunged at the leader and tore off his hood. He was a pale fella with pissy eyes, red hair and a nose like a block of wood.

'"Evans," said Townsville Jack.

*

'Katz and Myer arrived with the next truck. Myer was disorientated. He thought he was back in Changi and kept rehearsing for the concert party. Katz took a week to recover from the journey, then decided his first job was to paint the scene inside our hut, but Evans ordered him to repair a wall in the officers' quarters.

' "I'm not a soldier," said Katz.

' "We're all soldiers here," said Evans.

'It was just like we were back in Changi.

' "If you're a soldier," said Katz, "why don't you go and kill someone?"

' "I'll fucking kill you if you don't watch it," said Evans.

' "Oh, I've got it," said Katz. "You're a *Japanese* soldier."

' "Leave him," said Townsville Jack to Evans. "He's a mental case. I'll go and fix your wall."

'As he walked off with Evans, Townsville Jack asked, "What's the go with the Vigilance Committee, sport?"

'Evans didn't like Townsville Jack calling him "sport", but at that time he still wanted Townsville Jack as an ally, so he let it pass. Besides, how can you stop a digger saying "sport"? You can hardly cave his head in. That's what we thought at the time, anyway. We still had no idea what men could really do.

' "When Lieutenant Colonel Duffy took command of this camp," said Evans, "he had problems keeping control. The men were . . . you know what the men were like. They had no discipline. They were used to running bloody wild with the boongs in Darwin. They weren't soldiers."

' "They fought like bloody soldiers," said Townsville Jack.

' "They fought like cornered dogs," said Evans.

' "You should try it yourself," said Townsville Jack.

'Evans smiled and sighed.

' "You won't provoke me," he said.

' "The Japs couldn't provoke you," said Townsville Jack.

' "When Lieutenant Colonel Duffy first tried to run an orderly room," said Evans, "to clamp down on the stealing and swearing and the slouching, the men threatened him with a bashing."

'Townsville Jack laughed.

'"You don't understand the army," said Evans. "You never did."

'"I know what I know," said Townsville Jack.

'"You can't keep order without an orderly room," said Evans, "so the old man asked the Japs if he could use one of their guardrooms."

'Townsville Jack couldn't believe it. He could hardly speak.

'"He did it because he's a gentleman," said Evans. "You wouldn't understand that, either. He thought there was a common bond of decency between officers – no matter what the army, no matter what the cause, we all have the same responsibilities to the welfare of our troops. The Japs told him where to go, of course – they couldn't give a blue monkey about our welfare – but they let him build the boob, a bamboo pen where we keep criminals. Don't look at me like that. It's no worse than they do in Changi.

'"But the men didn't like the boob," said Evans, "so they tore it down and went back to their old ways of shirking and cursing and plundering the officers' vegetable garden at night. The old man had to do something to restore order. The men forced him into a position where he had to say, 'If you won't obey my rules, I'll hand you over to the Japs.'

'"I tried to talk him out of it," said Evans. "I told him he'd misjudged the mood of the ORs. They'd think we'd gone Jap-happy, that there was no difference between us and them. But he couldn't see another way. There were men stealing anything that wasn't nailed down. They were stealing from him. They were stealing from the dead.

'"So a few of us formed the Vigilance Committee, a third force between officers and men, to act in the spirit of military law but outside of King's Regulations. We sort things out amongst ourselves, before they ever get to the Japs. It's been the only thing that's kept this camp together."

'"You're a fascist, Evans," said Townsville Jack.

'"You don't even know what that word means," said Evans.

'Evans stopped walking and used his stick to draw a line in the mud.

' "I need you on my side, Fry," he said. "The men look up to you."

'Townsville Jack dug his heel into the dirt and dragged it through the line.

' "Are you with Diamond Tom and the thieves?" asked Evans.

' "I'm not with thieves," said Townsville Jack.

' "So why aren't you with me?" he asked.

' "When the shooting started," said Townsville Jack, "when the shooting *really* started, you disappeared like a rabbit under a hat, *sport*. You'd left your fight on the bloody parade ground. I know it. The men know it."

'Evans smiled with relief.

' "Is that all it is?" he asked. "You think I wasn't there when the bombs were falling? I was there all right, Fry. I was manning the radio."

' "You're not Signals," said Townsville Jack.

' "I went where I was most needed," said Evans. "You know what your trouble is, Fry? You're always trying to second-guess the chain of command. Stick to your job and we'll all be right."

' "Is that so?" asked Townsville Jack. "And what's my job now, exactly?"

' "We need blokes like you," said Evans, "to help keep order here and keep the Japs out."

'Townsville Jack laughed.

' "That's not what blokes like me do," said Townsville Jack. "I know you, Evans. I remember you in training, all spit and bullshit. You love the bloody army."

'Townsville Jack looked around the camp. "This isn't the way I planned to spend my bloody twenties."

' "Do you think I did?" asked Evans.

' "You know what?" said Townsville Jack. "I reckon you did."

'"Then you're a bloody idiot," said Evans.

'"This place has got everything a bloke like you could want," said Townsville Jack. "Everybody's got to follow orders or they get their bloody heads bashed in. Everybody's bloody yelling and shouting all the time, and it's all bloody pointless. We've got a weak man in command, so you can step up and prove yourself. And," Townsville Jack spoke slowly now, pronouncing his words one at a time, "there's no bloody women."

'Evans stiffened and Townsville Jack pretended to flinch.

'"You're a dead man," said Evans.

'"We all are," said Townsville Jack.

*

'We quickly got our stake up from selling Katz's pictures to Duffy's NCOs, and Townsville Jack ended up in the centre of most things that were happening around the camp. Blokes just naturally came and told him things. The Japanese commander wasn't a bad man, they said. He'd work us to death without a second thought, but he wouldn't beat us to death for the hell of it. There were the usual experts in Japanese military psychology among the prisoners – blokes who'd been posties and wharfies in civilian life – and they could tell the commander knew the war was lost, and he and his men were planning their escape.

'It was still hell. We were starving and flooded and beaten, and blokes died the day you met them, before you could even remember their name. And there was a Jap they called "Lucy" – for "Lucifer" – who was a devil with a stick and whip. But most of the other guards were moonshine-brewing drunks who slept through the working parties and would turn a blind eye to buggery for the price of a coconut. But all this made it harder for Duffy. Normally the officers could say they had to keep us in line or else the Japs would come down on us, but the Japs just ignored all his military bullshit and treated us like slaves. The commander wouldn't see him, refused to hear his complaints, so Duffy lost authority that way too.

'The blokes tried to get Townsville Jack to talk to Duffy and warn him about Evans, but Townsville Jack reckoned the truth was murkier than it looked, and Evans was operating with Duffy's understanding if not his agreement, and Townsville Jack didn't care either way anyway.

' "I'll tell you what," he said, "I'll give you six-to-one that when this war ends we'll find out they were in it together."

'Townsville Jack started taking two-flies-climbing-up-a-wall-type bets. It caused trouble from the start. Evans gave him a warning, said there was no drinking, gambling or womanising permitted in the camp.

' "Womanising?" said Townsville Jack. "You're bloody mad."

'So when Townsville Jack got his orders to go and see Duffy, he thought it must be about the bookmaking – "Either that or the womanising" – but the old man just wanted a chat. There was nobody else in his quarters, and Duffy closed the door.

' "Private Fry," he said, "how are you finding life at – to use its semiofficial name – Camp Duffy?"

' "One jail's the same as another," said Townsville Jack.

' "Oh, it's not so much a jail here," said Duffy. "It's like Changi. It's an army camp."

' "It's just run by the wrong army," said Townsville Jack.

' "Exactly," said Duffy. "And, like Changi, it will be ours again soon enough. The tide of the war is turning, Private Fry. We'll all be home by –"

' "Christmas?" said Townsville Jack.

' "Exactly," said Duffy. "All we have to do is survive until then. You've got to understand the importance of leadership. Look at the boongs: all equal, all slaves. Is that the kind of society you want?"

' "I don't want any kind of society," said Townsville Jack.

' "It's a question of leadership," said Duffy. "I know you're a communist, but tell me this: suppose you had an election here and you chose your own leaders. How much respect do you think the Japs would give to a commander elected on a platform of less discipline, fewer orders and a cake with candles on every man's birthday? Just how long do you think your Lenin would last among the samurai, Private?"

'"I never said we should elect leaders," said Townsville Jack.

'"No," said Duffy, "you were just going to step into the gap yourself, like the Bolsheviks, weren't you? With no official authority, no moral authority and no conscience at all. You didn't join the International Brigades, Private Fry. The AIF is a hierarchical organisation. Commands are issued from the top down. This is because experience has shown this is the only way to win battles. If you disregard the chain of command, you are acting against the interests of the army. You are actively aiding the enemy. You are working for the IJA."

'"But we didn't win the battles," said Townsville Jack. "We surrendered."

'That night, Townsville Jack turned over and said to me, "They're not going to get me, you know."

'"Who isn't?" I asked.

'"Anybody," said Townsville Jack.

*

I had forgotten we had tickets to the fights at the Other Club – we seemed to be going out all the time these days – but Jimmy reminded me we had to support our race, even if it meant giving money to the same anti-Semites who had treated a hero so shamefully after the war.

The Other Club was only about a hundred metres from the Club, but was never visited by Jimmy or Sollykatzanmyer, even though it was a much better club than the Club. The Other Club even had a swimming pool. But Solomon had been refused entry to the Other Club in 1951, and the old men believed the bouncer had stopped him because he was a Jew – rather than the fact he was wearing a lei around his neck and singing 'The Banana Boat Song' – so they had spent no money there for the next thirty-nine years, just as they would never buy a Japanese or German car.

They were prepared to make an exception this time only because they knew the Other Club would make a loss on a boxing night, since the fight game was dead and buried and even Jeff Fenech – 'Jeff *Gonif*, more like' – had taken the year off.

Solomon picked us up in his Volvo and drove us to the Other Club.

Jimmy stopped for a cigarette outside the door. Solomon, bored, watched him smoke. They were both wearing hats and coats, like they were in disguise. In the lobby of the Other Club, a trestle table blocked the top of the stairs. A big, tired man with tattooed roses around his neck was taking money and peeling cloakroom tickets out of a book, underneath a poster of six sets of fighters squaring up around a V.

Jimmy tapped the table and wondered out loud if he'd made it himself.

'I know you,' Solomon said to the ticket seller. 'You're the spruiker from Bad Boys.'

The man ignored him and warned Jimmy not to break the table.

'You told me it was free entry,' said Solomon, 'then I had pay ten bucks at the window and five at the door.'

'Do you want to buy a ticket,' asked the tattooed man, 'or make a complaint?'

'I'm a returned serviceman,' said Solomon, 'and you robbed me.'

The big man sold two tickets over Solomon's head.

'You shouldn't've been in a strip club,' he said.

Jimmy read the top line of the poster: '*An Izzy Berger promotion.*'

'Tell Izzy we're here,' said Jimmy.

'He doesn't care,' said the ticket seller.

Six boys with the same broken nose waited behind us.

Solomon threw a fifty-dollar bill onto the table and the tattooed man stood aside.

The fight was held in the memorial hall, and nobody had tried too hard to decorate it like Las Vegas. There were VIP seats on the stage, looking out over the ring, and ordinary chairs scattered around the floor in loose, broken lines. Everybody in the audience looked like a boxer or a boxer's bleached-blonde wife. There were more Aborigines than I'd even seen in one room, which was about twelve.

Men sat in clusters of gym mates, wearing the same awkwardly lettered tracksuits. The trainers smoked and drank beer from the bottle, while their boys sucked orange juice through straws. Two lightweights danced around the ring like jockeys at a ball, ignored by the crowd.

Solomon bought us drinks from a hole in the wall, while Jimmy took a seat next to Johnny the Head.

'Is this your tribe, then?' asked Jimmy, nodding to a row of empty chairs.

'Some of the brothers thought twenty-five dollars was a lot to pay to watch a Jew get beaten,' said Johnny the Head. 'I told them you can't put a price on something like that.'

The ringmaster wore a shabby tuxedo, frayed at the tails. The wing collar of his dinner shirt was buttoned tightly across his throat, making it look as though only his bow-tie fastened his head to his body. He drew out every word as long as a sentence ('laideeeeeeeeeeeeeez and gennnnnnnnnnnelmen') and nobody paid him any attention at all.

'The winner of the next event,' he bellowed, 'will walk away with the most coveted belt in New South Wales, the Heavyweight

Championship of the Sydney Area. In the blue corner, with three wins and only two losses, is –'

Two fat heavyweights with shorts worn high on their bellies squared off across the canvas. They shuffled back and forth, suddenly throwing jabs into space, but whenever they got close enough to punch each other, they bounced off an invisible cushion until they were at opposite ends of the ring. The referee tried to bully them into the middle, but they hardly touched. The bell rang and the fighters rested on stools until the ring girl held up a card marked *2*. I thought it was the score, but it was the number of the round. She turned to face our table and wriggled to make her breasts wobble.

She looked tired and used, with a tight mouth and bored eyes, but it was the first time I'd ever seen a woman walk around in her underwear, except my mum.

'That's her,' said Solomon. 'It's the stripper from Bad Boys. Do you know, she can peel a banana with her –'

'Not in front of the boy,' said Jimmy.

She blew a kiss into the air.

'That was for me,' said Solomon.

'She probably thinks you're some kind of banana,' said Jimmy.

In the second round the heavyweights clashed heads and cuddled.

'Get on with it, you bludgers!' shouted Solomon.

When they came back for the third round, the red fatty rushed at the blue fatty, who looked at him sideways and stuck out his fist. The red fatty ran straight into it, fell onto his back and wouldn't get up.

'You know why nobody watches boxing any more?' said Solomon. 'It's because it's shit.'

The announcer spent five minutes trying to marry the winner to his belt, which looked like my grandmother's Seder plate, then asked him if he had any words for the crowd. The man thanked them for their support, said his opponent had been a tough, experienced fighter, and promised he'd be back here in Marrickville for his next fight.

Lots of nothing happened for a long time. Old boxers climbed into the ring and wandered around, as if they'd got lost on the way to somewhere else. A collection was held for a former State champion with a broken leg, who Jimmy swore he'd seen running on the road the day before. Nobody was watching the ring, but they all turned to look at the door when Mendoza walked in wearing his navy blue suit, followed by a line of short-haired boys in tight T-shirts and heavy jewellery, and took his seat on the stage.

'And now,' roared the announcer, 'it's the event we've all been waiting for, the Bondi Junction fight of the cennnnnnnntury. We've got two local boys squaring up for the Pan-Pacific International Professional Boxing Foundation of Australia and New Zealand Interim Welterweight Championship of the World. From the leafy lanes of Woollahra via the mean streets of Odessa comes Yuri "the Cosssssssssssmonaut" Kogan! And from the beautiful beaches of Bondi via the bloodhouses of South Auckland is Hone "The Headhunter" Harris!'

Yuri jogged out of his dressing-room looking pale and small. The bigger Maori swaggered in from the other end of the hall – I think he must've got changed in the bathroom – with his hands on the shoulders of his trainer.

The fight started quickly. Yuri felt out the Maori with a couple of jabs, then caught him immediately with a straight right.

'Watch his hands!' shouted Johnny the Head to Hone.

'Wash your hands!' shouted Solomon to Yuri. 'You've got Maori all over them.'

Hone tried to hit Yuri, who swayed and ducked and slipped, then realised he didn't have to do any of those things and could make the Maori miss him just by stepping back.

'Look at him!' shouted Johnny the Head. 'He's shitting himself.'

But Yuri wasn't even bothering to hold up his hands.

Hone charged at Yuri, dropped his head and tried to push him against the ropes, but Yuri caught him with two uppercuts and ducked out from under him. I looked around to see that Jimmy was breathing with Yuri and mimicking his punches with his fists.

'Hook him, Yuri!' shouted Jimmy. 'Fucking hook him!'

Yuri smashed into Hone's chin with a left hook and the Maori went down.

The crowd began to leave immediately. Mendoza led them out.

'What a load of bloody rubbish,' said Jimmy.

I thought he'd be happy.

'The Maori couldn't fight,' he said, 'so now we don't know if our boy's got the goods. It was a Mendoza match. I should've known.'

'What a waste of time,' said Solomon.

'A heap of crap,' I agreed.

My head was tingling. My heart was banging. I had loved every second.

SIAM DIARY
1944

I don't know where we are. I don't think this place even has a name – not in English, anyway. The Japanese call it *kassoro*, the airfield, but there is no airfield here and there never will be. I call it Tartarus, the dungeon of Hades, and I cannot understand why they need an airfield out here in the jungle.

As near as I can guess, we're about one hundred miles from the border with French Indochina, so perhaps they hope to fly missions into the north of the colony, or resupply their troops in bases around the delta. We have had no news of an Indochinese campaign since we became captives. We know the Japs marched into Hanoi and the Siamese reclaimed their lost territories, but perhaps they have been beaten back. There could be loyal French troops massed on the Thai border, or even the Red Army.

Our Christian soldiers no longer believe in salvation. We buried another today, a man called White Alf, who had family in Cairns. White Alf had dark skin. His mate, Black Alf, was as pale as an albino. They used to play the harmonica together and sing. After Black Alf died, White Alf lasted two days. We have abandoned our cherished formalities: the service, the prayer, the Last Post. Men volunteered for the burial party so as to plunder the body. They gave Black Alf a timber cross as a marker, but Grimshaw, whose dour name suits his demeanour, tipped the sack of White Alf into a shallow pit, then drove a single stake into the ground above him.

'I hope I got his heart,' I heard him say. 'We wouldn't want him back as a vampire.'

The other men laughed – diggers, gravediggers, the henchmen of Hades – through toothless mouths and bloodless lips. They have to make a joke of this to survive. They must set themselves apart, and act as if a man's life were no more precious than his harmonica, which they traded with the Japs for a jackfruit and beans.

But I cannot become detached from death. Each Australian's passing grieves me as if I he were my blood. It is like losing a child, watching a son and heir perish, and with him my dreams. I despair of this softness in me, the weakness that cleaves me. But it means I have not lost my humanity. The Japs have not stripped me of my soul.

I always was a lonely man. Once I thought it was the artistic sensibility that set me apart, then I believed it was my ambitions. Here, we are all the same – miserable tortured wretches. All the same but me.

Some of the men are coarse and tough, and honest and loyal, and brutal and stupid. If the warder's boot were on the other foot, they would deal with Japanese prisoners the way the IJA treats us, like farm animals or flies, to lose their wings for a passing amusement, or be slaughtered because it is the season to kill.

Others are good men who have shed their compassion because it left them only pain. They struggled to become debased and hardened, and treat everyone but their mates – officers, ORs and enemies – with a bitter, sarcastic disdain. They have embraced their hopelessness and no longer remember a time when they were free. Their only liberty comes through choosing the attitude they take to their slavery, and pitting themselves against their own kind.

I heard of a man removing the photograph of a comrade's wife from the pocket of his corpse and selling it to the Japs to abuse and ridicule. She does not matter because she is distant, and safe, and he has no further call on the living because he is dead, and safe.

It seems to me that those who love life the most are frequently the first to perish, while others survive as shadows who have long forgotten that there is any good reason to be human.

I wish it were easier to divide the thieves from the rest, but the thieves are not in a group, they are in a place where men fall. It is not an easy thing to snatch food from the mouth of a starving man, a fellow who was once perhaps your friend. What little we have in our stores is disappearing before it can be rationed out. The rice has always been taken by the cooks, now it is also taken from them. When two sets of hands have already dipped into the supplies, there's little left for the working men, and they view their reduced rations as yet more proof that systems have broken down, leadership is illegitimate and it's every man for himself. They compare our performance in the field with our running of the camp and, on both counts, they see cowardice where there should be cunning, frailty where there should be strength.

The law is enforced by vigilantes. They are not the worst of men, but no one can ignore the pleasure they take in inflicting punishment on their pitiful comrades.

From Changi to the railway to this, the last camp, the only thing that has kept us alive – we unlucky few who live – has been our organisation, our dictatorship, our communism. Without it, we are dying, even here where the work is lighter, the guards uninterested and the weakest long dead. Our society has collapsed, and the men look for scapegoats rather than solutions. We are a Jacobite mob, the baying crowd at our own guillotine.

The thieves take licence to behave as they do because they have lost their faith. Anarchy is destroying us, and the answer to anarchy is order. Surely they can see that.

There must be a way to save us all.

BONDI

TUESDAY 1 MAY 1990

Jimmy and I worked undisturbed while the lorikeets danced like acrobats on the wire. By late afternoon our spirit house looked like a temple.

'Six o'clock?' said Jimmy. 'Is that the time? Iron a shirt, you scruffy bugger. We're off to see your girlfriend.'

We were almost late for the Thai Dee because I couldn't find the iron. Then I couldn't put up the ironing board. Then I couldn't make the iron work because I didn't know you had to fill it with water.

Dee was sitting behind the counter, under the picture of the King of Thailand, filling in a crossword and ignoring Sollykatzanmyer. When I came in, she grinned and cried, 'Hot chip boy!'

I blushed because she had remembered me, even though she hadn't remembered my hot chips last time. She adjusted my shirt collar at the table, because I had ironed one tip pointing upwards and the other aiming down.

'Could we have the menu, please, darling?' asked Solomon.

'Get your own,' said Dee. 'You know where they are.'

Solomon sighed.

'Thailand,' he said, 'is often referred to as "the Land of Smiles".'

'Auburn,' said Dee, 'is sometimes known as "the Place of Fuck Off".'

Solomon waddled back from the counter with the menu.

'You're looking tired, Ernie,' he said to Katz.

'I've been sleepwalking,' said Katz, who was carrying a pocketbook *Macbeth*.

'Really?' asked Solomon. He turned to me. 'Ernie Katz,' he said, 'is a somnambulist. Human history – of which Katz is a self-styled student – is rife with examples of famous people who were also somnambulists, including Lady Macbeth. Ernie Katz, on the other hand, is known for his somnambulism but nothing else. His is a tidy life, entirely uncluttered by achievements.'

Katz fished Solomon's handkerchief out of his jacket pocket.

'Philosophers interpret the world,' said Solomon. 'The point is to change it. That is a quote from Charlie Marx, once a great hero of Ernie Katz, now widely regarded as the biggest single cause of human misery since Arnold Zwaybil first pushed his stool to a piano and began banging the keys like they were five-bob whores he'd picked up in the Patton.'

Katz blew his nose on Solomon's handkerchief.

'Nominally,' said Solomon, 'Ernie Katz adhered to Marx's credo, but in actual fact he resolved to change the world as little as possible while interpreting it ad nauseam, the word "nausea" stemming from the feeling experienced in one's guts when one is forced to listen to a political diatribe delivered by Ernie Katz, the workers' champion who refuses to do a day's work.'

Katz carefully folded Solomon's handkerchief and put it back in his pocket.

'It is as if Katz has taken a pledge to leave the world exactly as he found it, and not litter it with children, grandchildren, works of art or anything else, apart from a small billboard that used to sit in the window of the New York Restaurant on Kellett Street, advertising *Today's special: lamb chops (2) and chips*. There was something of a flourish to the tail of the *2*, as I remember, a hint of artistic promise that was never to be fulfilled, because Ernie Katz was lazier than a lizard, and even his somnambulism is notable only for the fact it offers a unique glimpse of Katz doing two things at the same time: to wit, walking and sleeping.'

'Leave him alone,' said Jimmy. 'None of us sleeps soundly.'

Dee told Sollykatzanmyer what they were going to eat.

'And the handsome young man will have hot chips,' she said, tickling the back of my neck. 'In his dreams.'

'That's not all he'll have in his dreams,' said Myer.

'We all wake up screaming in the night,' said Jimmy.

'*Nisht*,' said Myer. 'Forget it.'

'Why do we still pretend?' asked Jimmy.

'Have a drink,' said Solomon. 'You're turning into a *faygeleh*.'

'I can feel his hand creeping up my leg,' said Myer.

'That's not his hand,' said Solomon.

As was customary, Solomon made a fuss over the prawn crackers.

'A prawn is not kosher,' said Solomon. 'It has neither fins nor scales. It is a bottom feeder, a *faygeleh*.'

'A tribe of cannibals could feed off your bottom for a week,' said Myer.

'His mind is always on my tush,' said Solomon, taking the cracker and biting into the cloud. 'According to the sages, it is permissible to eat *traife* to save oneself from starving. I have a hunger for Dee that I know will never be sated.'

He licked the curves of the cracker with his long grey tongue.

'You think she'd taste like prawns?' asked Katz.

'She'd taste like tinned fish,' I said.

The old men stopped talking and stared at me. Jimmy blushed. Even Solomon's ruby cheeks turned redder. Katz, who had been about to take a drink, snorted beer down the twin channels of his mighty nose.

'Where did you get that idea?' he asked.

'Modern girl,' I said.

'What's Jimmy being saying to you?' asked Katz.

I munched a prawn cracker.

'I need another beer,' said Katz.

'Self-service,' said Dee, throwing her hand towards the fridge. Her fingernails were painted red, like her lips. She fetched the entrees from the kitchen while Katz collected Singha beers.

A pile of flyers on the cash desk caught his eye.

'Look at this,' he said.

Solomon grabbed a leaflet.

'*Arnold Zwaybil*,' he read. '*In concert.* "In concert" with who?'

'It's at the bloody Club,' said Myer, reading from the back.

'We ought to picket,' said Katz.

Dee swayed over with a plate of curry puffs.

'Do you like him?' she asked. 'He's a famous singer.'

'Arnold Zwaybil,' said Solomon in the tone he generally saved for 'Ernie Katz', 'is known as the Eastern Suburbs Frank Sinatra. He did not earn his title by singing, dancing, acting or even bedding *shiksas* of every race and nation. No, he was given the guernsey by the *gunsel* Jake Mendoza, on account of his being the cousin of Jake's lovely wife, the long-suffering Deborah, who chose to inflict some of her pain on the rest of us by insisting her husband promote Arnold as a lounge singer, when he displayed as much talent for crooning as Pincus Myer shows for the curious new Olympic sport of synchronised swimming. And yet this disgrace to the musically gifted race that gave the world not only Allan Sherman and Herb Alpert but also Bette Midler and Neil Diamond found no difficulty in securing concert space anywhere in New South Wales, since his promoter typically offered clubs the choice of either booking his artiste or burning down. Similarly, customers were permitted to leave the building while Arnold Zwaybil was playing, but only if they were prepared to do so on their knees, which can be a difficult manoeuvre for a punter with shattered kneecaps.

'Yet even these innovative techniques failed to build Arnold a following beyond – or, indeed, within – his immediate family, and he eventually disappeared from the public eye along with Jake's other unfortunate protégés, Giuseppe Milano, "the Western Suburbs' Frank Sinatra"; Alf Cockburn, "the Sinatra of Sydney's South"; Col Tanner, "the Aussie Tony Bennett"; and Freddy Freed, "the Dover Heights Dean Martin".

'And there he would've rightly remained, buried under radiograms, eight-track cassettes and a mountain of cheesecloth shirts in what Trotsky called "the dustbin of history", were it not for an inexplicable nostalgia that grips the community once a year, and which sees the Arnold Zwaybil Show resurrected in all its former glory – which is none – and tour the Hakoah Club, the RSL, Rose Bay Bowling Club, Woollahra Golf Club and, to the mystification of its regular clientele, the Coogee Bay Hotel.'

Dee nodded.

'They gave me tickets,' she said. 'Do you want them?'

'If I forget he's shithouse,' said Solomon, 'may my right hand whither and my tongue cleave to my palate – which is what seems to have happened to Arnold.'

'Do you want tickets?' asked Dee, showing the old men a fan of passes. 'If you don't go, I will.'

'I'll take them,' said Myer.

He reached out, but Dee jerked her hand away.

'Say "please",' she said.

'I don't want these seats for myself,' said Myer. 'It's for the Jewish people. As long as we can pack the hall with our own kind, the goyim will not bear witness to the depth of our humiliation.'

Dee tossed the tickets onto the table. Myer swept them into his lap.

'So,' said Solomon to Jimmy, 'I hear Frida has gone to visit the divine Mrs Ethelberger. And taken her suitcase. Is it true she left because you wouldn't fix the wardrobe?'

'I've got other things to do,' said Jimmy.

'Like building the ghost house?' asked Solomon.

'Like keeping your big fat *faygeleh* nose out of my business.'

Solomon's eyes widened, and he pretended to be hurt.

'Current thinking has it,' said Solomon, 'that ghosts are what they call a "low priority" for housing, on account of the fact they're dead. Frida, on the other hand, an aged pensioner and returned serviceman's wife, would be somewhere near the top of the list for a comfortable home, ranked above all but recently released paedophiles and retired serial killers.

'For this reason,' said Solomon, 'the majority of sane individuals who intend to stay married would undertake the necessary repairs to their own fibro palace before constructing a similarly unfashionable residence for pixies, fairies and so forth.'

'It's not for fucking pixies,' said Jimmy.

'I knew it!' said Solomon. 'It's just for fairies! He's a *faygeleh*!'

'*Nisht!*' said Myer. 'Jimmy's building a spirit house so that they'll come back.'

'Who will?' asked Solomon, looking around in case they had already arrived.

'All the dead ones,' said Myer.

Solomon turned his head and nodded slowly, as if he were counting idiots with his forehead.

'It'd want to be a big place,' he said.

Jimmy taunted a fishcake with his fork.

'I'm building it to make them leave me in peace,' said Jimmy. 'It's for Moishe and Billy and Bluey and Townsville Jack.'

Solomon stared at him.

'Has anyone here got any marbles?' he asked.

The men pretended to search their pockets. Jimmy shook his head.

'Don't you ever think about Moishe?' he asked Solomon.

'Moishe?' said Solomon. 'I don't even think about Myer.'

Myer looked pained.

'Would it kill you to be serious for once?' Jimmy asked Solomon.

Solomon relaxed into his chair, as if he were about to light a cigar. He made a steeple of his fingers and peered through the gap at Jimmy.

'Jimmy Rubens,' said Solomon, 'is a serious man. He is a serious drinker, and he is seriously ill. He hasn't spoken about the war for *forty-five fucking years* and he wants to raise it now, at the dinner table, on our sacred Tuesday night – and, as far as I can tell, he's not even fucking pissed. This raises the sixty-four-dollar fucking question, "What exactly does Jimmy Rubens have to say that is suddenly so fucking urgent?"'

Solomon smiled thinly, his eyes angry, and bowed towards Jimmy.

'I've been having dreams,' said Jimmy.

'You've come off your meds?' asked Solomon.

'What if I have?' asked Jimmy.

'You should go back on them.'

Jimmy ground his dentures.

'Because you don't think I can face the world without pills?' he said.

'Because I don't know why you'd want to,' said Solomon.

Jimmy coughed.

'*Gey gezunt*,' said Solomon.

'What about you?' asked Jimmy. 'Do you take them?'

'I don't need to,' said Solomon.

'Why? Because you're a fat cunt?'

Solomon patted his belly with satisfaction.

'Because I haven't see the things you've seen, Jimmy.'

'You saw enough,' said Jimmy.

'But I don't see it any more,' said Solomon.

Jimmy took off his glasses and focused on nothing.

'What can you see, Jimmy?' asked Katz.

'I see their shadows,' said Jimmy, 'and hear their footsteps.'

Dee laid the main dishes on the table, spicy and steaming. I smelled chilli, ginger and basil, and imagined Jimmy's first days in Singapore.

'They're here because they want something from me,' said Jimmy.

'They want you to go back on your meds,' said Solomon.

Katz pushed a bottle of beer towards Jimmy.

'Drink them home,' he said.

'That doesn't work any more,' said Jimmy.

Jimmy rose and drifted across the restaurant to the spirit house. He seemed light and vague, like steam on the wind. For a moment I could hardly make out his outline, then he came back into focus, kneeling at the altar in a jasmine cloud. He coughed hard. His shoulders trembled. He wheezed and he blew, pulled a grey rag from his pants and wiped it across his lips.

I watched him poke his finger into the spirit house and lift out the figures of an elephant and a horse. He carried them carefully to the table.

'Remember these, Pincus?' he said to Myer.

'Yes,' said Myer.

Jimmy smiled.

'You *do* remember,' he said.

'They were here last week,' said Myer.

Jimmy slammed the animals onto the table.

'You can't just deny it,' said Jimmy. 'You can't pretend it didn't happen.'

'He can do whatever he likes,' said Katz.

Katz balanced the elephant on the rim of his plate.

'There were elephants in Thailand,' said Jimmy.

'You see elephants everywhere,' said Myer. 'You've got elephantitis.'

'There's no such thing as elephantitis,' said Katz. 'It's elephantiasis.'

'A man with elephantitis can grow *beytsim* as big as his head,' said Solomon.

'That's rice balls,' I said.

'What on earth have you been telling him?' asked Katz, walking the horse around the table.

'Everything,' said Jimmy. 'The whole kit and caboodle – whatever the hell a caboodle is.'

Katz made the horse drink from a saucer of chilli sauce.

'You think that's good for the boy?' he asked.

'It's good for me,' said Jimmy, coughing.

'You're obviously the picture of health,' said Solomon.

'It's made me realise there's some things I've got to do,' said Jimmy.

'Like build a house on sticks?' asked Solomon.

'Yes, like build a fucking house on sticks,' said Jimmy. 'Don't you see? Their bodies are still in Thailand, or . . . somewhere else.'

'A digger is buried where he falls,' said Solomon.

'They hate it there,' said Jimmy. 'They want to be here.'

'My experience of dead people,' said Solomon, 'is they don't care whether they're in Kanchanaburi or Kangaroo fucking Island. The living, on the other hand, *just cannot leave the fucking dead alone*. It's you who wants them back, Jimmy. You're stirring their bones. You're not letting them rest.'

Jimmy set his jaw.

'I'm doing this for them,' he said.

'You're doing this for you,' said Solomon. 'And you're not even thinking about what it's doing to Frida. Or Myer. Or the boy.'

'What about me?' asked Katz.

'Nobody gives a fuck about you,' said Solomon, which meant he loved him more than anyone else in the world.

Jimmy snatched the horse and elephant from Katz.

'We just sit here,' said Jimmy, 'or in the Club, or wherever, talking like we worked the machines together at Willie Frankel's *schmatta* factory then retired with a gold watch. We never talk about the ones who aren't here, or why.'

'It's you who won't march on Anzac Day,' said Solomon.

'Anzac Day's what brings them back, you fucking idiot,' said Jimmy. 'They want to be remembered as people, not as soldiers. The army was just a moment in their lives, and the worst bloody moment at that. They want to be remembered for how they lived, not the way they died. So yeah, I've built them a house. What the fuck have you ever done for them?'

'I sat *shiva*,' said Solomon.

'You sat on your arse for what you believed in,' said Jimmy, 'Katz marched on his legs, and I'm making a house with my hands.'

Jimmy stood and turned to go.

'And you're paying the bill with your money,' said Myer.

Jimmy threw twenty dollars over his shoulder. It floated to the table and landed in the sauce.

'Look after the living,' Solomon shouted after him, 'and the dead'll take care of themselves.'

*

'After Townsville Jack thrashed the Vigilance Committee,' said Jimmy, weaving across the pavement on Gray Street, 'Duffy turned up at our hut.

'Katz was sitting on his palliasse, writing his diary in tiny little letters on cigarette papers that could've been put to better use making a smoke, when Duffy surprised him with a "Good evening". It'd been a while since Katz'd heard anyone say that.

'"I hear we have another artist in the camp," said Duffy.

'"Do I know him?" asked Katz.

'"I myself dabble in watercolours," said Duffy, "but I make no great claims for my talent, and I have certainly never won the Archibald prize for portraiture."

'"Portraiture isn't the measure of a painter," said Katz.

'"I'd like to offer you a commission," said Duffy.

'Katz thought he wanted him to make a pin-up.

'"I'd like you to paint me," said Duffy.

'"Paint you what?" asked Katz.

'"Paint my portrait," said Duffy, "at this moment in my career, in command of this camp."

'"I'm sorry," said Katz, "I'm here to record the war for the Australian War Memorial."

'"I'll give you one duck egg for each sitting," said Duffy.

'"It's a done deal," said Katz, folding away his diary.

'Duffy must've sat for Katz half-a-dozen times,' said Jimmy, 'and he talked while Katz painted, to give Katz a better idea of the man he was, so that his true personality would shine through in the portrait, like the Mona Lisa. He told Katz he knew he wasn't loved. He wasn't there to be loved. He wasn't our mother, he was our commander, and it was his duty to command. Some men were followers, others leaders. He had always been a leader, in the Great War and in business and in the Old Guard. He had volunteered to take command of the force because the man before him wasn't a leader. He was a whinger. He complained to the general staff that the strategy in Singapore was suicidal and he was leading his men to their deaths, so the staff pulled him out, shipped him home and put in Duffy instead, because Duffy did what he was told, and if he was told to defend Singapore then he would defend Singapore.

'Orders were decisions. They might be right, they might be wrong, but once they were made, they had to be carried out. Duffy took orders from the top and gave them to the bottom. If his predecessor had done the same, the troops would be better trained, and better behaved in captivity. "They couldn't even drill properly, when I got them," said Duffy.

'"What's the use of drill here?" asked Katz.

'"You have the artistic temperament," said Duffy. "You wouldn't understand."

'The officer Duffy had replaced had treated the other ranks like mates. "He was as bad as a socialist," said Duffy. Duffy had learned you didn't get results from being liked, you got them from being respected. Good men gave respect where it was due, but the worst types – the thugs and thieves who wouldn't listen to appeals for honesty and order – would only honour a man they feared. And if they didn't fear Duffy's justice, they'd better damn well fear the Japs', because that's what they were going to get if that's what it took to save the rest of them.'

*

The lights were on in my grandmother's house when we came home. The warm air smelled of lamb casserole and brewed tea. Grandma was sitting on the lounge, watching TV. She nodded to Jimmy and opened her arms to me.

'You look so skinny,' she said.

Jimmy sat next to her.

'How was Mrs Ethelberger?' he asked.

'Crazy about cats,' said Grandma.

'Is that why you came back?' asked Jimmy.

'No,' said Grandma. 'I was worried you'd starve the boy.'

Grandma took Jimmy's hand. He closed his eyes.

BONDI

WEDNESDAY 2 MAY 1990

While Jimmy smoked his first roll-up of the morning, Grandma came to inspect the spirit house. She walked around it bent over with her hands behind her back and looked inside.

'What is the *mishegas*?' she finally asked.

'It's a house for the spirits of the dead,' said Jimmy.

He looked at his work boots.

'I know that sounds odd,' he said.

Grandma nodded and stroked her chin.

'These spirits,' she said, 'are they Australian?'

'You know who they are,' said Jimmy.

'Moishe?' she asked.

Jimmy coughed hard.

Grandma squinted to see the spirit house more clearly.

'It looks like a Turkish brothel,' she said. 'Why would my brother want to live here?'

Jimmy bent his elbows and balled his fists.

'It's the way they look in Thailand,' he said.

'You think they'd want death to be like Thailand?' she asked.

Jimmy snorted and coughed.

'So what kind of spirit house do *you* think Moishe *ava ashalom* would've wanted?' he asked.

'A house like this one,' said Grandma, waving towards their cottage. 'He'd like to live with us.'

Barry Dick came out of the *frummers'* place, smoking a cigarette, with his shirt tails outside his trousers.

He wished Grandma *shalom* and asked, 'How do you like your extension, Mrs R?'

'You're an idiot,' said Grandma.

'She means "an Hassidic",' said Jimmy.

'Your father was a fool too,' said Grandma, 'but at least he didn't dress like one. What's the matter with you?'

Barry Dick nodded and smiled, because God had told him to be patient with old people. He patted the spirit house.

'I've been to Thailand,' said Barry Dick to Jimmy. 'I know what this is. Let me ask you something: if I were a Buddhist priest –'

'You were once, weren't you?' asked Jimmy.

'I was *briefly* a novice monk,' admitted Barry Dick. 'But if I were a Buddhist priest, and you were a Buddhist, what do you think I would say to you if I saw a Sukkot hut in your yard?'

'You'd probably ask me for a bowl of rice,' said Jimmy.

'I might say,' said Barry Dick, 'that I didn't feel it was appropriate for a Buddhist family to build a Jewish structure, especially in a Buddhist area so close to the Buddhist school and the Buddhist temple.'

'What Buddhist temple?' asked Jimmy.

'The one I would attend if I were a Buddhist.'

'If you were *still* a Buddhist,' said Jimmy.

'This is an analogy, Mr Rubens,' said Barry Dick.

'If you were still a Buddhist,' sighed Jimmy, 'and I was a

Buddhist, and you found me building a Sukkot hut, you'd probably have the sense to keep *schtum* about it, because you'd know I'd remember you when you were Jewish, and when you were a Hare Krishna, and when you used to stand on Town Hall steps selling *Green Left Review*. All right?'

Barry Dick smiled, like the 'Smile' stickers he used to hand out when he danced with his tambourine outside Woolworths, and Jimmy convinced him it would be mitzvath to drive me to school.

When I came home Jimmy had taken down the spirit house and stacked up the parts in the shed.

'I had everything wrong,' he said. 'Frida's right. We have to start again.'

*

We began to build another spirit house, this time from fibro and tin. The outside walls were cream, like my grandmother's house, but the inside was still papered with the flock wallpaper. Jimmy covered the floors with squares of material left over from when he'd carpeted his living room in 1971.

As Jimmy fell into the rhythm of his work, he started to remember again.

'Diamond Tom was a pathological thief,' he said. 'He stole Evans's bloody belt and sold it to one of the mental cases, who wore it across his shoulders like a bandolier. Two hours later, the Vigilance Committee rushed into our hut, waving their clubs around and shouting.

'"Innocent men, move to the side!" said Evans.

'Townsville Jack didn't move.

'"Private Fry," said Evans, "stand down before I knock you down."

'Townsville Jack gave him a friendly smile, then smashed him in the face with the right cross that had floored the angel

Seraphiel's representative on earth – the same right cross he had never used in the boxing ring in case it spoiled his unbroken record of losses. Evans tottered, tripped, and fell over his own feet.

'Two others ran at Townsville Jack, and he knocked them both down, the first with a left hook, the second with a kick they don't teach in any boxing gym.

'Diamond Tom grabbed Evans's stick, and I took another from one of the fallen men. We tested their drive in the air, like cricketers at a crease.

' "I don't care what you do in the rest of the camp," Townsville Jack told the Vigilance Committee, "but stay out of my fucking hut."

'The Vigilance Committee backed out the doorway.

' "Thanks, Pete," said Diamond Tom, and Townsville Jack knocked him out as well.

'The next day Townsville Jack went to Duffy and asked if we could be moved to another hut. Duffy said there were no free bunks but, if we wanted, we could build a place for ourselves. He might've been joking but Townsville Jack took him at his word and staked out a bit of flat ground between the cookhouse and the creek.

'We all went out to fetch timber from the hills. Townsville Jack was excited about digging the foundations.

' "You don't need to dig foundations for an attap hut," I told him.

'But Townsville Jack had an idea for a new design of hut. He had Katz draw up the plans while I cut the timber. It had four bunks, separated by partitions, and the highest roof in the camp. There were two shuttered windows and a front deck, and a barbecue pit around the back. It looked like a boong's dream of a Swiss chalet, and the Japs took a bung to look the other way.

'"I always wanted a place like this," said Townsville Jack, and he hung a sign over the door that read *SCKAJ*.

'We lived in SCKAJ like a little family. Those were the best days in prison. The railway was finished and Camp Duffy was flooded with sick men from up the line. Any intelligent person could see that you can't starve men into skeletons and expect them to build a railway. Stupid people couldn't see that, so the railway got built. Most of the new blokes died, but we were more or less immune to death by then. Unless it was a close mate, it didn't really bother us. I suppose we'd started to think of life as something that ended at twenty-four years of age.

'Snowy White came down from upcountry. He liked Camp Duffy, thought it was an insult the way the Japs made our officers work on the line, said it showed they didn't take us seriously and told us some more about the Geneva Convention, which I was starting to think he must've had a hand in drawing up himself.

'"Look at the *chuis*," said Townsville Jack. "They just sit around and get fat. Figuratively speaking," he added, since there wasn't a white officer in Thailand who weighed more than nine stone.

'"Just because the *chuis* live better than us doesn't mean we'd live better if there were no *chuis*," said Snowy White.

'"They take the best of everything," said Townsville Jack.

'"You'd do the same if you were them," said Snowy White.

'"But I'm not them," said Townsville Jack.

'"So how can you judge them?" asked Snowy White.

'Snowy White was the first of the new arrivals to join the Vigilance Committee when problems started up again. The boys from the line wouldn't give up their kit to the *chuis*. Most of the enlisted men wouldn't salute. If there had ever been any difference between Duffy and the Vigilance Committee, it disappeared. Evans and his men took off their hoods and started wearing special "VC" armbands, until the Japs confiscated them.

'None of it really touched our hut, though. We sat around talking about cakes and pies and potatoes, while Katz painted and I carved, Myer made jokes and Townsville Jack cracked his knuckles. We told each other about the women we'd had and the women we'd wanted, and the things they hadn't let us do to them. Me, Katz and Myer talked about growing up, but Townsville Jack never said a word about anything that had happened before he left home. It was as if he'd always been a man, as if he'd fallen fully formed from a tree, although he once said he had a brother in Victoria.

'Some nights, we sang songs. Townsville Jack had a voice in those big strong lungs. He liked show tunes and music hall, and every now and then he'd whistle "Changi Races". He was humming that melody when he came back from the river and told me, "I've found a champion frog."

'"Bonza," I said. "Let's eat it now."

'"But it's a racing frog," said Townsville Jack.

'He put his hand down his jap-happy and pulled it out.

'"Do you see?" he said. "He's got the same markings as Rivette."

'"Bash him on the head," I said, "and toss him in the kwali."

'"But we could make our fortune," said Townsville Jack.

'"We've been down this path before," I told him.

'"But last time we were beaten by insider knowledge," said Townsville Jack. "This time, we've got the knowledge. This frog'd beat any other frog in the camp."

'"There are no other frogs in the camp," I said.

'"I could find some more," said Townsville Jack.

'Townsville Jack called his new frog 'Can Nearly', after Keneally, and because, he said, "She can nearly jump as high as this roof." I should have flattened Can Nearly with my mallet then and there. I should've put a stop to all the bullshit before it started.

'Townsville Jack was right: he found four more frogs in the mangroves. I was right too: we should've made frog curry.

'The frog races started up again, in a clearing in the jungle where Townsville Jack marked up the track to "regulation size". We had a problem because no bugger had a shirt to stretch across the poles, so we had to build barriers from attap, like every bloody thing else.

'This time, though, Townsville Jack made up a story about each frog, so blokes could back something that appealed to them. The frog called "Ginger Meggs" was a mischievous little battler. "Les Darcy" was the toughest frog ever to jump in the ring, and he didn't want anything to do with the bloody war. "Phar Lap" was the people's frog. "The Don" was a hopper who could only be beaten by a bouncer.

'Can Nearly didn't appear in any events until one of the other animals was stolen and eaten by Diamond Tom.

'There was nothing else to do in Camp Duffy, so frog racing became very popular very quickly, but it caused a lot of trouble that nobody had expected.

'A decent fella named O'Connor had a soft spot (in his head) for Phar Lap. He had a couple of wins on the frog – or maybe another frog that Townsville Jack had decided was Phar Lap after the first Phar Lap had escaped – but he always put all his winnings on the next race. He borrowed his stake from the camp shylock at thirty per cent interest, but when the shylock came to collect his debt, O'Connor pushed him out of his hut.

'The shylock turned to Evans to get his money back, even though it was against the camp rules to loan money at interest. He hired the Vigilance Committee to sort O'Connor out, and they bashed him senseless for two shillings, which was the exact amount O'Connor owed the shylock. It wasn't the money, it was the principle of the thing.

'The O'Connor episode made Evans's boys look like the thugs they were, and some gamblers formed an Anti-Vigilance Committee Committee, and picked off a couple of individual VCs after dark. Soon there were fights every night. Worse than that, blokes were backing frogs instead of buying food, and selling their jap-happies to the locals just to raise a stake. And if there was one thing that got Duffy's goat, it was seeing soldiers walking around naked.

'Three times Evans warned Townsville Jack to stop, but Townsville Jack was convinced he was making his fortune again, even though all the money in the camp wouldn't've bought a bicycle in Australia.

' "You're causing chaos," said Evans.

'Townsville Jack laughed, because the chaos had nothing much to do with frog racing.

'Townsville Jack announced that the biggest race of the season would be the Miracle Mile. The track was only fifteen foot long, he explained, but that was a mile "in frog terms".

'Every man in Camp Duffy wanted a punt on the Miracle Mile. On the night of the race there was nobody in the mess because nobody had contributed to the mess fund. There was nothing to eat in the entire bloody camp. Townsville Jack had warned the punters that a new, untested frog named Can Nearly was joining the field, but by now the blokes had realised that a frog is a frog is a frog, and you might as well just pick one you like and stick with him, because they all hop the same way.

'There must've been a hundred blokes at the clearing. We had stewards carrying torches to light up the field. Townsville Jack strummed a mandolin and sang "Duffy's Races". We were just about to put the frogs under starter's orders when Evans walked out from between the trees and barked, "You will close down this race meeting immediately, Fry."

' "I will not," said Townsville Jack. "Why should I?"

' "Because that's an order," said Evans.

' "That's no reason to do anything here," said Townsville Jack.

' "It's the *only* reason to do anything here," said Evans.

'Townsville Jack scratched the back of his neck.

' "But you're standing in the members' stand," said Townsville Jack, "and you're not a member."

' "Don't talk gibberish, Fry," said Evans. "Pack up your side-show and leave."

' "I'm not going to do that, sport," said Townsville Jack, and he pushed Evans aside.

Evans leapt at him and took a swing, but Townsville Jack slipped the punch. He jabbed Evans in the ribs, not so much to hurt him as to show him he was open to a body shot. Evans dropped his elbows and exposed his chin. Townsville Jack flicked him on the jaw.

'The men jeered and cheered, enjoying the show. If they weren't going to watch a race, at least they'd get to see a fight. A fella they called Blue Alf, a redhead who used to help out Townsville Jack, started running a book. Shorty Burns backed Townsville Jack's experience against Evans's fitness; Snowy White put his money on the *chui*.

'But Evans wasn't going to fight.

' "Clear up and piss off," he said, "or I'll put you on a charge."

'Now the men realised they were witnessing a terrible injustice. Every hour of every day, these blokes lived through the filthiest horrors the Japs could devise, and they couldn't do a bloody thing about it. But this time they had a chance to stand up and be counted, and to a man they all lined up behind Townsville Jack.

'I stood at the beginning of the track with a bucket of frogs in my hand, looking Townsville Jack in the eye, and I could see into his thoughts. He'd always known this was the way it would end. His destiny was to be St Jack of Townsville no matter how many priests he punched. He was going to be St Jack the Martyr.

'I saw him waver, and I saw him decide.

'"We're holding this race," said Townsville Jack.

'One of the Japs, a guard with a droopy eye like Duffy's, had followed the noise to the clearing. It wasn't against Jap laws to hold a frog race – they didn't have rules for things like that – so Droopy just watched from the members' stand as Evans tried to close it down.

'And Evans saw that if he tried again to stop the race, his men would rip the flesh off his bones. But he saw everything else too. He knew the outcome, the same as Townsville Jack.

'"Don't do this," said Evans.

'"Why not?" asked Townsville Jack. "To save you?"

'Evans stepped back from the crowd and turned on his heel and marched towards the officers' quarters.

'Townsville Jack's starting pistol was a clap and stamp; the stewards released the frogs and the winner was Can Nearly by a neck, although Can Nearly didn't actually have a neck. Whoever caught the rest of the field got to keep them and eat them, because everybody knew there wasn't going to be another frog race.

'Townsville Jack kissed Can Nearly. He didn't turn into a prince, but Townsville Jack said he already was a prince, the prince of frogs. He paid out the winners and counted his take from the losers, and passed the money to me, along with his tote bag.

'"Here," he said, "it's yours."

'After the race Townsville Jack went to the river to wash, and they came for him while he was naked: four officers rushed him at once. Evans wasn't with them. Townsville Jack knocked down the first while another dived for his legs.

'Somebody shouted there was a blue on, and I ran down to the banks with a bamboo stick in my hand, but by the time I got there it was all over red rover. If they'd been bashing him, I would've jumped in, but they were just holding him, telling him to calm down.

'They threw Townsville Jack into the boob, and the men stayed up all night, mumbling and cursing and threatening to break him out, but he was still there in the morning when the officers marched Townsville Jack to the orderly room.

'They gave him a court martial and Duffy sat in judgement. They told him he was entitled to representation, but Townsville Jack said he could defend himself, and it sounded like he'd break their necks if they came near him.

'Three of the charges were gambling, assault and incitement to mutiny, but there were at least a dozen more. Townsville Jack's defence was the mutiny had grown without his knowledge; he hadn't asked for it and he hadn't wanted it. He'd been trying to stage an entertainment, like a concert party, and he'd intended the profits would go to the hospital fund. And he hadn't assaulted anyone. He'd defended himself when he was attacked.

'"You cannot be 'attacked' by your superior officer," said Duffy.

'"I could if he had a bit of go in him," said Townsville Jack.

'It was a proper trial with witnesses and evidence: a betting slip, an IOU, even a crushed frog, and in the end Duffy found against Townsville Jack.

'"You've paid no attention to any of the sanctions in this camp," said Duffy, "formal or informal. Worst of all, your insubordination was witnessed by a soldier of the Imperial Japanese Army, who must now realise how far military discipline has crumbled in this camp. For that reason above any other, you've left me no choice but to hand you over to the IJA for punishment."

'"Hand me over?" said Townsville Jack. "Do you really think it's your rabble that's keeping me here?"

'They handcuffed him and sent him to the camp commandant. Lord knows where they got the handcuffs. Probably Duffy carried them all the way from Changi, like Bluey carted Little Bluey and Townsville Jack hauled his white tote bag.

'The Japs gave Townsville Jack his choice of punishment. He could either be crucified or take a beating with pickaxe handles. I guessed he would pick crucifixion, but that's because I didn't really know Townsville Jack.

'"I'll take the sticks," he said.'

BONDI

THURSDAY 3 MAY 1990

Mum was holding one of her imaginary conversations on the phone.

'He's good,' she said. 'I'll tell him you asked.'

'I hate him and I wish he was dead,' I said.

'He says the same about you,' said Mum. 'He hadn't realised what an essential part of our little family you were until you were gone.'

'I'm not a part of *his* family,' I said.

'Yes, that's what he says,' said Mum, 'so now it's time for you to come home.'

'But I don't want to come home,' I said.

'Last week you were begging me,' said Mum.

'Jimmy needs me here,' I said.

'I think you've confused yourself with a bottle of whisky,' said Mum. 'Oh, goodbye, darling.'

'Goodbye,' I said.

'Not you,' said Mum. 'Christian. Why the hell do you want to stay with Jimmy now? I've spent all week trying to persuade Christian to have you back.'

'We're doing a project,' I said.

'You're building a doll's house,' said Mum. 'I heard.'

'It's not a doll's house.'

'You were never interested in my doll's house,' said Mum.

'It's a ghost house,' I said.

'Do you know,' said Mum, 'I often wish I'd had a daughter.'

I made a squealing noise, like a girl.

'If you want to stay, then stay,' said Mum. 'But if you don't go to school, I'll have you thrown into an orphanage.'

'They don't have them any more,' I said.

'In Romania,' said Mum.

She asked me if I had spoken to my dad, but she knew he wouldn't phone my grandmother's house.

'You could call him yourself,' said Mum. 'I'm sure he's worried about you.'

'He never worries about me,' I said.

My dad was a good person, but all he thought about was the Woman in White and how to keep her giggling in bed. He hadn't even given me my pocket money for a month. I checked Jimmy wasn't around and dialled the number that used to be my number but was now her number. My dad answered, and said, 'I'm worried about you, David.'

It was like he had been talking to Mum, but I knew he hadn't because he hadn't said a word to her since the day she left him.

'Why don't you come and stay with us?' asked Dad.

'Because you said I couldn't, and now I don't want to.'

At least Dad didn't pretend the Woman in White was missing me, but he did ask me to meet him for lunch.

'It's a school day,' I said, in case he'd forgotten I went to school.

He said he'd bring a letter for my teacher – she was getting a lot of them these days – and we could eat sandwiches in the park. I suggested he should take me to a restaurant instead.

I had a worse than usual morning at school. Two fat kids chased me around the basketball court, calling out, 'Gluebag the Jewbag!' They planned to dunk me through the hoop because I had killed Jesus. I wanted to stand and fight them to the death, but I ran away instead, pretending it was a game. It made me ashamed of myself, and angry at my dad for not having bashed me when I was younger so I would know how to defend myself against bullies now.

Dad arrived at the school gates in his yellow Toyota Camry, wearing a cream shirt with a flapping collar and a wide blue tie. Dad's business was called Blue's Glue, so he always wore blue ties to work, and usually blue pants too. When I was younger I had begged Dad to buy me a blue tie, but now I owned one and I thought it was stupid.

When I was little, Dad had been a hero to me, although I knew he had never been to war. He told fantastic jokes and could kick a football so high it almost vanished into the sun. He wore fat gold rings on his fingers and a smiling gold watch on his wrist, but he usually had sauce on his shirt cuffs, and he was never quite shaved. I thought he must be a millionaire. He drove easily, and never swore at other cars.

But when he met the Woman in White, his clothes became smarter and his cheeks smoother. He was more serious and grown-up. She had changed everything about him except his stupid car.

We ate at Avram the Israeli's Café, which was owned and managed by Dad's friend Colin from Scotland. I had a steak, so I would grow strong enough to stand up to the fat kids. Dad ordered a chicken schnitzel but didn't really eat it.

Dad asked about everyone except Mum, then told me the Woman in White would make a very good mother.

Oh God.

'She's not pregnant, is she?' I asked.

Dad laughed, as if he'd never had sex with her.

'A mother to you, I mean,' he said. 'Why don't you come and live with us?'

First nobody wanted me, now everyone did.

'It's not fair of your mum to dump you at Jimmy's,' said Dad.

'I like it there,' I said. 'They treat me like a grown-up.'

'He hasn't got you drinking, has he?' asked Dad.

'No,' I said, 'but he talks to me.'

Dad put an arm around my shoulder.

'I thought we always had great talks,' he said.

'That was before,' I said. 'Now you just tell me that *she* told me to wash behind my ears.'

'Well, you should,' said Dad.

'Why?'

'Because otherwise potatoes will grow there.'

'Then I'd be a freak,' I said, 'and I could make my fortune.'

'You might be able to get tax breaks as a primary producer,' Dad admitted.

'I wish she'd just leave me alone,' I said. 'She's not my mum.'

'If you saw her more often, she'd be more relaxed,' said Dad. 'Think about it, anyway.'

He dropped me back at school in the yellow Camry. I made him let me out in a side street, so the fat kids wouldn't see the car.

*

Jimmy had half-built the new spirit house by the time I got home. It followed exactly the original shape of my grandmother's two-bedroom weatherboard cottage.

'I thought Townsville Jack could share with Bluey,' Jimmy told her, 'and Bathurst Billy could bunk with Moishe.'

Grandma shook her head and went back inside.

'Pass me the mallet,' said Jimmy, and he started to talk.

'The commandant asked Duffy to officially hand over Townsville Jack to IJA discipline, and Duffy marched him, still handcuffed, across the piece of mud the Japs called a parade ground. Duffy bowed to the Jap and passed Townsville Jack to the enemy. Before he left him, he squeezed his arm, like he was on his side.

'We all thought they'd beat Townsville Jack in the guard house, but the *gunso* decided to take him to the worksite. They made a little ceremony out of it, a bit of a *yasumi*. They picked ten Koreans and had them stomping around like sumo, slapping their sticks in their hands, working themselves into a rage.

'I wanted to do something to help, but there was nothing, nothing. I threw down my pick and ran up to him, tried to pass him a hibiscus cigarette, but his hands were locked behind his back by Duffy's cuffs. He couldn't take the cigarette and he couldn't protect his big beautiful head. They ordered him down on his knees. When he didn't move, the *gunso* kicked him in the arse and sent him sprawling.

'The guards lunged at him. They dissolved into a scrum, and then a mob. It was like a riot aimed at one man. And all of them bashed him around the head. All of them.

'When Townsville Jack collapsed, they re-formed into two lines, a gauntlet, and the *gunso* picked him up and threw him in. Our blokes were vomiting. Some of them were crying. Townsville Jack was silent, but his eyes were screaming, his knees were trembling. He tried to run, but the guards tripped him and kicked him and set on him when he was down, laughing like imbeciles. They were fighting each other to get to him, to land another stick on his skull.

'After the third run, Townsville Jack was bleeding from his ears, nose, mouth, eyes, and everyone was calling for the guards to stop. Duffy was shouting, "For God's sake, he's had enough!", but they didn't let up.

'It took three of them to pull the big man to his feet for the fourth round, and straightaway he dropped face-down into the dirt. So they stamped on him and thwacked him and pounded him and bashed him, like they were trying to crush him to a powder, as if they were grinding rice.

'One bloke hit the back of Townsville Jack's head so hard that he broke his club, and he wandered off, giggling, to find another.'

Jimmy couldn't speak any more.

I brought him a bottle of beer from the kitchen. He popped off the cap on the base of the spirit house.

'Nobody slept that night,' said Jimmy. 'The men stayed awake talking about making a noose out of vine, marching to the officers' quarters, dragging out Duffy and hanging the bastard. They were going to get Evans, too, and the whole Vigilance Committee, give them a proper, military-style send-off and dump them in one big bush grave. The angriest of them wanted to rise up against the Japs too, and die fighting at last. Even Myer had the madness in his eyes. He sat at the end of his palliasse, weaving a rope.

'Duffy called *tenko* early. The men lined up with sharpened stakes hidden in their jap-happies. I had a cane, and I held it in my hand, like a guard. Duffy's cheeks were grey and his eyes were red, but he stood straight and tall as he walked up to each of us in turn and read our tight faces. My hand twitched at my stick. Duffy stopped and examined me like a doctor looking at a patient. When I didn't swing the cane, he moved on.

'When he had accounted for every man, Duffy announced that the morning would be a *yasumi*, given by the Japs to allow us time to prepare for a concert party, the first they'd ever let us hold in the camp. As we were dismissed, some men booed, but ten minutes later they were sewing frocks from blankets and making breasts out of coconut shells.

'The work was light for a couple of days, and the men composed songs about Duffy and Evans, setting the lyrics to music-hall tunes. They called them traitors, fascists and worse.

'I didn't go to the show, but the other blokes told me I'd missed a good night. They'd sung and danced and dressed up as sheilas for the *chuis*, accused them of collaboration and cowardice, and even made it rhyme. The *chuis* had laughed at all the jokes and applauded at the end.

'"What a bunch of fools they are," said Blue Alf, but nobody talked about justice again.

'Later on the Japs ordered us to make a trench like a moat halfway around the camp,' said Jimmy, 'and the furphy was we were digging our own graves. As soon as the Allies set foot in Singapore, the Japs were going to massacre all the POWs. It took a long, long time to finish that hole. Not many blokes gave it their best effort. At night, me and Katz sneaked out and filled it back in.

'There was no canary in Camp Duffy, but we got the griff from Thai traders. The Japs were on the retreat everywhere, they said. There wasn't long to go. We just needed to hold out another few weeks, maybe a couple of months.

'I knew I was going to survive. Everyone who lived through it knew they'd be the ones to make it, but I suppose the ones that died thought they would too. If you knew you were going to be slowly starved and tortured to death over three stinking years, you'd just neck yourself, wouldn't you? So you've got to pretend you're special.

'Townsville Jack knew he was going to survive. He had a destiny. He was going to change the world, reorder it to suit Townsville Jack. But first he was going to root every sheila in Victoria, starting with Bluey's sister in Warracknabeal. Katz made a picture of her for him and I pinned it to the ceiling over his bunk, but Townsville Jack didn't open his eyes. He never saw her there.

'Evans put me on a working party, doing nothing, just wasting another breath of life. I came back early with a live frog in my jap-happy. I was going to push it into Townsville Jack's hands and see if the feel of it woke him up. Then I was going to eat it. I thought I had it clutched tight, but the little bastard wriggled away. You can't do anything with frogs, really. They're a mug's game, if ever there was one.

'There was a furphy going around that the Allies had developed a doomsday bomb. If you dropped just one of them from a plane, it could wipe out a whole city. And they'd done it to Japs, they'd kicked a town into touch, burned everyone.

'Then one day we stopped bowing to the guards and they released our Red Cross parcels. They gave up their guns but still stood sentry with sticks like the ones they'd used on Townsville Jack.

'Eventually the guards disappeared into the jungle, but they were rounded up again by big white Queenslanders. They couldn't believe we were part of the 8th Division. They thought anyone who wasn't in Changi must be dead. They fed us bully beef and beer and we were as sick as dogs. They brought medical supplies and we gave Townsville Jack a shot of morphine, and he slept with a smile.

'I sat by Townsville Jack's side, like I'd done so many times, feeding him, nursing him, changing his dressings, wiping his arse, telling him the stories the Queenslanders had told me, about the ways the world had changed. I said how a mob of the boys had got into a few of the guards and given them a bit of a bashing, but nothing too clever. In the end, they didn't so much want to get revenge on them as just forget them.

'Sometimes Townsville Jack made a noise, and I thought he might understand me, but his jaw was broken in four places and they'd driven his teeth into his tongue.

'"We've made it," I said to Townsville Jack, but I knew he hadn't.

'I felt crook about myself after that, so I went for a smoko, bludged a drink off a Queenslander, then came back to the hut.

'I told Townsville Jack I'd heard Dopey and Sprout had been killed in a landslide on the line, but he had no last words.

'He lived his life like every one of his words was his last.'

*

'I try to understand what happened,' said Jimmy, 'but some blokes are just dogs. They're bloody mongrels and that's all there is to it. There was no reason to kill Townsville Jack, no reason to batter Bluey, no reason to take my mates away from me.

'If it's wasn't for Townsville Jack, I wouldn't be around now. The strongest and best man died, David. The cleverest and most cunning men died. But me and Myer and Katz survived, the last of the Mohicans.

'With Townsville Jack gone, I got the melancholia again. I buried him then took his bunk. I lay where he used to lie, and tried to die like he did. For two days. I didn't eat or drink. I spoke to Myer, but Katz tells me Myer had already gone back to Changi. I listened to Evans tell me he was sorry, and Duffy explain that things hadn't happened the way I thought they'd happened, but it was all a dream. They had both shipped out.

'Diamond Tom broke into the orderly room and stole the evidence from Townsville Jack's trial. We burned the betting slip and the IOU in the Japs' incense burner, and left the bones of the frog under the bunk where Townsville Jack had stored his stable. Katz slashed his portrait of Duffy to pieces and burned the scraps.

'Me and Katz were the last to leave Camp Duffy. We travelled to Singapore the slow way, by truck, by boat and then by jeep. The driver was a good fella, but he could see how we'd been treated and he couldn't understand why we weren't looking for revenge.

'"What could we do for revenge?" Katz asked him. "Strip the guards of everything, inject them with cholera and beri-beri and tie them up outside in the rain, naked in their own shit? We could find every man's best mate, who'd saved his life over and over again, and starve and torture him to death, or we could just turn our backs on the bastards and walk away. Because if we broke one Jap's nose or even his neck, that would be like saying that's all Townsville Jack was worth, or Bluey or Bathurst Billy."'

I couldn't understand. It didn't seem right. If it were me, I'd have shot them all.

'It's like the Jews and the Germans,' said Jimmy. 'What could we ever possibly do to pay them back? After the war, there were Jewish partisans who wanted to poison the German water supply. They might've murdered hundreds of thousands of them, but six million? How could they ever kill six million Germans?

'When I think about how I spent those years of my life – three years of my twenties without women – I tell myself we might not've fought back but we never collaborated either. We sabotaged the bastards and their railway every chance we got. We laid weak beams, hid termites in the timber, siphoned and stole and stalled, but you know what? It made no bloody difference at all. They got their railway finished, and finished on time, and it was a damn good railway and it ran supplies to their troops in Burma until they lost the fighting, and then it carried their retreating men home. What could be worse than that? We died so our enemies might live. That's the way I think sometimes. Other times I'm just glad to be alive, that I lived to see my children and my grandchildren, that you've got my face – you poor buggers – and my name. Because there's so many that didn't have that.

'At the end of the war MacArthur made every last bastard of the IJA into a POW,' said Jimmy. 'So you'd think they'd riot behind the barbed wire, wouldn't you, and fight the Yanks to their deaths? Or at least cut their own guts out, like they expected us to do. There were five and a half million Japs in the IJA at the end of the war, and you know how many committed harakiri? A few hundred, mostly officers. More of our blokes necked themselves on the bloody line, when you count the fellas who just gave up. Not only did the Japs jack in the war, they jacked in the whole idea of fighting – scrapped their army, navy, air force, the bloody lot.

'But I don't hate the Japs and Koreans, not even the bastards who killed Townsville Jack. Some of them were mongrels, some of them weren't, but they were all soldiers in an army, and they were following orders just like us. There's only one fella I hate, and that's Lieutenant Colonel William Randall Duffy, the Nazi cunt. If I met him now, I'd fucking kill him with my bare hands, even though I know he's already dead.'

Jimmy closed his strong old cabinet-maker's fingers around a soft ghostly throat and squeezed.

'The jeep took us to Changi,' he said, 'and when me and Katz knew we didn't have to keep going, we just collapsed. Our bodies shut down. I was laid up in hospital for two weeks before I had the strength to ask a coolie to take me to the new headquarters of the All Chinese Union of Rickshaw Men. He told me there was no union any more. He'd been there, this fella, on the fringes of it. He knew them all, and what had happened to them, but he'd kept his head down and run from the shooting. He wasn't proud of it but he had children to feed, and sometimes that counts for more than anything.

'He told me Chinese Frank and the rest of the union had been interned by the British when we went up to Malaya. Chinese Frank offered his men to fight alongside the army, but the authorities didn't trust them. They didn't want a commo dog snapping at their arse while the Japs were biting at their head.

'But every man's got his own reasons to go to war, and in the end it doesn't matter a damn providing he's trying to kill the same blokes as you, and the Poms finally realised the commos would make the best fighters against the Japs because they had the most to lose. They weren't going to survive any occupation. When the Nips had almost reached the Straits, they gave Chinese Frank and the others a bit of training in sabotage and guerrilla warfare, and sent them off to defend the undefendable. They let them have arms – at last – and uniforms, and the commos called themselves the Malayan People's Anti-Japanese Army, almost as long a name as the All Chinese Union of Rickshaw Men.

'By the time the guerrillas were released into the city, it was running with streams of fire; burning oil had been carried by the river into the quays. There were men cooked in their sampans, corpses clogging the drains like they'd been turned to shit before they died.

'Chinese Frank and the rickshaw men fought the Japs in the streets. Long after we'd surrendered, they were sniping from the roofs of shophouses and throwing homemade bombs from trees. There were only a few hundred of them, and tens of thousands of us, and they watched us from windows and bushes as we paraded into Changi and thought, *What the hell are they doing?*

'The first thing the Japs did was screen the Chinese for commos and collaborators. They rounded up the men, took them to the Happy World amusement park, left them for three days without food, surrounded by troops, and marched them past hooded traitors – maybe they were police, maybe they were criminals – who denounced them. Some of them were tortured. Most of the MPAJA were in the jungles by then, but Chinese Frank got caught behind the lines, and he was taken down to Changi Beach, shot, bayoneted and drowned.

'So it was true that we'd saved Singapore from a Nanking,' said Jimmy, 'because in Nanking they killed everyone. In Singapore they only murdered the best. When we surrendered we saved the lives of the cowards and the collaborators, the Jap-happys and the boongs, and made sure our allies were tortured to death.

'The rickshaw man said he couldn't help me with Chinese Frank, but he could take me to see Mei-Li, who was running a noodle shop with Lim. I didn't know . . . I couldn't . . . My hands started to shake. I couldn't speak, there was all this . . . a feeling in my mouth, I . . . I knew it wasn't . . . I could hardly believe she was still alive, but I was terrified of what she would think of me. I was ashamed of my body, with all its scars and sores. I was as thin as noodles. I just couldn't get fat again. And I couldn't control my bladder, couldn't sleep in the dark. I shook with the shits, woke up vomiting in the morning. I didn't want anyone who knew me to see me. I didn't think anyone who knew me would want me.

'And it wasn't just my body, it was my brain. I couldn't make sense of what had happened, couldn't learn the lesson, couldn't force it to be worth something. It seemed to me that in the camps I'd stopped being a man. I'd let other people do whatever they wanted to me. I'd stood by while they murdered my friends. I'd bowed to their murderers. I'd called them "sir". I'd let my soul be raped. Not just by the Japs, but by the army too. I'd surrendered the minute I'd put on a uniform.

'I thought Mei-Li would hate me, because Chinese Frank had fought and died. So I didn't go and see her that day. I went back to my hospital bed, full of new kind of pain. Two days later I had my new uniform cleaned, and the nurses bathed me, and I greased back my hair and polished my boots, and I got another rickshaw man to take me to the noodle stand. All the rickshaw men knew the place, and I realised right away it had nothing to do with their noodles. I was surprised to see they even sold noodles.

'I saw Mei-Li wearing a long, dark smock, with her hair tied back. She looked older and more beautiful, like the years had given her the strength they'd taken away from me. My heart, David, my heart, it . . . it . . .

'I walked up to her slowly. She saw my uniform and turned away.

' "It's me," I said. "The Australian soldier."

'My eyes, David, I was crying . . .

'She looked back at me and asked, "Which Australian soldier?"

'She could speak English now. I held out my hand. She stepped back.

' "No," she said. "There are Chinese watching."

'She didn't used to care about that in the war. My knees trembled and gave way. I had to sit on the pavement beside her. Mei-Li gave me a bowl of noodles and charged me for them.

' "Can you use chopsticks?" she asked.

'I could barely use a knife and fork any more. I talked up at her while she served her customers.

' "I'm sorry about your brother," I said.

' "I have no brother," she told me.

'She looked at me hard.

' "I remember your name," she said. "You were Billy."

' "No, no," I said, "Billy was my little mate."

' "No," said Mei-Li, "Billy was a tall man. Maybe an American."

' "I'm Jimmy," I said, "from Sydney."

' "Ah," she said, "you knew Frank."

' "Your brother," I said.

' "He was not my brother," said Mei-Li. "He was a comrade. I know you. You visited the union with your friend. You didn't give us weapons, so many comrades had to fight with bird rifles and died. And now you are back. Why? To enforce British rule?"

'"I couldn't give a fuck who rules Singapore," I told her.

'"Do you have a weapon?" asked Mei-Li. "Give me your weapon."

'I stood to try to hold her. She picked up a knife. The other rickshaw men gathered around silently and watched until I sat back down with my noodles.

'I stayed there all afternoon, all evening, all week, watching Mei-Li as she made food for the rickshaw men and taxi drivers. I bought a sleeping mat and rolled it out on the pavement at night, and I ate noodles four times a day, waiting for Mei-Li to talk to me. She said "Go away", "Leave me alone" or "You're worse than a dog", and asked if I had mates with guns. The rickshaw men made friends with me, they called me "Noodles" and we sometimes played fan-tan to pass the time.

'"The noodle stall was a commo front, a place to hand over money and information. At first nobody would come because of the Australian soldier, so I sold my uniform and bought a blue vest and Chinese pants, and a hat like a lampshade, and I became a part of the street. One day I started helping Mei-Li with the noodles.

'"Thank you, Noodles," she said, but that night she asked a couple of thugs to move me along.

'"I am sorry, Jimmy Noodles," she said. "We have had a long war, and now another is coming. I think you were a kind soldier, but there were many soldiers then. And what we need isn't kindness, it's guns. If you do not have them, go now."

'I tried to kiss her but the thugs dragged me away. That night I found Chun Lau's, where Townsville Jack had met his whores, and started smoking the pipe. It was weeks later that Katz came for me. He'd been upcountry with the War Graves

Commission. I woke up on the floor, with Chun Lau shaking my shoulder.

'"Noodles," he said. "Noodles, Noodles."

'He pressed a bowl of warm Chinese tea to my lips. I drank, then slid back, breathing hard.'

'He picked me up and pointed me to the back exit.

'"This way, hurry," he said.

'He thought Katz was the military police, but Katz took me back to hospital and, in the end, it was Katz who told me it was time to take the boat home to Sydney.

'The day we left Singapore I was waiting for the boat in a sailors' bar at the quay when I got talking to a planter from Ipoh. He said he was surprised to see a healthy soldier like me – because I was fit then, at last, and strong – going back to Australia when they'd soon be needing me to take on the commos. He asked what I'd done in the war and I told him I'd been in Changi.

'"Well, I'd think you'd want to catch the next one," he said, "since you sat out the last one."

'The commos launched their insurgency a couple of years later, and diggers went back to Malaya to kill the only blokes who had been on our side all through the war, but I'd come home by then, to find the *Zayde* had died. My mother didn't recognise me. I thought it was because I was so damaged, but after she buried the *Zayde* she couldn't see anybody. It was as if he'd been her eyes.

'I frightened her, and I'd waited months to come back to her. I was drinking and yelling and punching holes in walls. Everyone was angry with me, and my sisters told me to leave. When I first saw your grandmother again, I was living in a unit in the Cross with Katz. To me, being with him was like being alone, because I was so used to his body, his smell. There's no part of Katz I haven't seen, no inch of his skin I haven't touched. We've got the same stories.

'The unit was owned by Jake Mendoza. Katz lived there rent-free, but every now and then he'd come home to find Jake in his bed with a showgirl or two, and – if it was Ernie Katz's lucky day – Mendoza might move over and make a space for him.

'I slept on the lounge. I didn't care where I lived, as long as it had a roof to keep out the rain. There was a bathroom down the corridor, but that was full of showgirls half the night too.

'It was good for us, living in the unit. It brought us back into the world slowly. In Kings Cross nobody minded much what you did, if you were mad or if you were drunk, and me and Katz were mad and drunk a lot of the time.

'We worked around Mendoza's club. Katz was painting signs and the backdrops for the shows. I was trying to rent space for a workshop, but doing odd carpentry jobs for Mendoza while I waited for something to come up. The bastard never paid us, but we drank for free and there were plenty of women.

'I met up with Moishe again, and he took me home to meet his sister. I asked her if she'd come dancing with me, and a year later we were married.

'We had children right away. I hoped for boys. I wanted to name them after Townsville Jack and Bathurst Billy, but she gave me three girls.'

'Four,' I said.

'But now there's only three,' he said.

I shook my head.

'What happened to the fourth?' I asked.

He turned his face away from me.

'She's dead,' said Jimmy.

'Did she throw herself out of a window?' I asked. 'Or take poison?'

Jimmy spat.

'Are you going to build a room in the spirit house for her?' I asked.

He ignored me.

'Then you could board it up,' I said.

He glowered.

'That would be a grown-up thing to do,' I said, and I knew it was.

BONDI

SATURDAY 5 MAY 1990

We glued matchsticks together to create a raffia suite for the lounge, and laid sticky-back plastic as lino in the kitchen and bathroom. Jimmy cut a bathtub from a pill bottle. We tried to coax a toilet from another medicine container, but the proportions were wrong. If the bath was the width of one spirit, then four of them could've fitted on the dunny seat.

Although we couldn't install working taps, we did manage to plumb in a shower. When the shower filled with water, it drained through a network of twisted drinking straws like the one that led from the guttering to the gate.

'Katz went commo after the war,' said Jimmy. 'He knew a wharfie who raised money for the Malayan Communist Party. He told us Mei-Li was killed in the emergency that the government wouldn't call a war because that would frighten off the planters' insurance companies. When I heard she'd died it was like a train rushing through my heart. I couldn't speak. Because I'd never given up the Mei-Li I'd had before the fighting, never replaced her with the Mei-Li I'd met when the war was over.

In my memory they were two women, and I'd always love the first one because she had helped me survive the camps. And if I hadn't been able to save her from the commos or the fascists – or the diggers or the Poms – then that was my fault, not hers.

'I was in this club once – this fucking club here – and there were young blokes – young in 1960, they're probably dead now; I hope they're fucking dead – back from Malaya, passing around photographs of dead guerrillas. They called them "CTs", communist terrorists. There was one Chinese corpse with long black hair, still beautiful, although her cheeks were puffy with death, wearing British MPAJA khakis, next to a British-supplied Sten gun, and her killers had ripped open her shirt and torn a breast out of her bra. This young fella boy said, "Come here, digger, and take a look. This'll put lead in your pencil."

'But it wasn't Mei-Li,' said Jimmy. 'At least it wasn't Mei-Li.

'In war some people just disappear forever. They vanish from the place they lived, they even vanish from its memory. But Mei-Li is still there for me, like a bamboo fire on a cold night.'

He swallowed.

'I didn't want to talk to anyone about the war,' said Jimmy. 'The Japs had me locked up for nearly four years, and I wasn't going to give them another minute of my life. Frida never asked questions. It wasn't a crime to have secrets in those days. Women weren't supposed to understand things. They were told the best thing for us would be to forget what'd happened and start again.

'I sometimes worried that people would think I didn't speak because I was ashamed, and I *was* ashamed. I was ashamed not to be Superman, not to be God, not to be able to rise above it and save everyone. In the end, I suppose, I was ashamed not to be Townsville Jack. But what did he accomplish in the end? Five-eights of bugger all.

'He wouldn't take orders from anyone who was less of a man than he was, he wouldn't pretend, he wouldn't play along, and so he died. Townsville Jack couldn't give in to Duffy because Duffy was all smoke and mirrors, but the whole bloody thing is smoke and mirrors. Townsville Jack would be alive if he'd kept his head down, if he'd kept it bloody bowed. But he died for what? A fucking racing frog? Where's the sense in that?'

Sweat puddled the underarms of his short-sleeved shirt.

'I'm as dry as the bloody Todd River,' said Jimmy, wiping his brow with his wrist, so I went to put on long pants for the Club.

Sollykatzanmyer were glowering at each other across the table. Katz read from the latest edition of *Newsletter*, which had a report on the RSL Bowling Club's recent victory against the Probus Club of Avalon.

'There's some good sorts in the Probus Club,' said Katz.

'The wood is a slightly asymmetric ball,' said Myer.

'In that way it reminds us of Greta Torpin's jugs of old,' said Solomon.

'My balls were slightly asymmetric when the blonde *shiksa* gave me a handjob after the AJEX Anzac Day march in 1951,' said Myer.

The old men noticed us as Jimmy ordered drinks at the bar.

'Here he is,' said Solomon, 'Jimmy Rubens, builder to the dead.'

Jimmy sat down.

'How's the ghost train going?' asked Solomon.

'It's a spirit house,' said Jimmy.

'Anything I could do to help?'

'You could stay out of our way,' said Jimmy.

'Don't you need any pictures?' asked Katz.

'Pictures would be good,' I said.

'I'd have to see the house first,' said Katz, 'so I'd know what size to make them.'

Katz seemed to be serious, but I could never tell with the old men. Even Jimmy didn't look certain.

'What're they going to wear?' asked Solomon.

'Who?' asked Jimmy.

'The ghosts.'

'White fucking sheets,' said Jimmy. 'How should I know?'

'Clothes maketh the ghost,' said Solomon.

Jimmy scowled.

'What the bloody hell does that mean?' he asked.

It meant that two drinks later we all climbed into Solomon's Volvo and drove four blocks back to my grandmother's house.

'*Schwartzers* everywhere,' cursed Solomon, as if his steering problems were caused by veering around crowds of Maoris in the road.

'You'd think you'd moved to Crown Heights,' said Jimmy, 'never mind Dover Heights.'

My grandmother had found her deckchair and was sitting out front, staring at the spirit house.

'Good afternoon, Mrs Rubens. Still as pretty as ever,' said Solomon, kissing her forehead with his fat wet lips.

'What are you doing here?' she asked. 'I thought I told you never to come back.'

'That was 1953, Mrs R,' said Solomon. 'You've forgiven me since then.'

'Drunken bum,' she muttered.

'You've done a good job, mate,' said Katz to me, patting the roof of the spirit house. To Jimmy, he said, 'I've seen better. Can't pretend I haven't.'

Solomon studied the master bedroom.

'Where are your wardrobes?' he asked.

I was still working on them. I showed him our drawing and

he made a note of the measurements on a pad he carried, with a pencil and tape measure in case somebody should suddenly need to be fitted for a pair of pants.

Grandma stayed outside while we men drifted through her bead curtain towards the drinks cabinet.

'What's it to be, fellas?' Jimmy asked.

'Whisky,' we chorused.

Mine came in a seven-ounce glass, topped with ice and drowned in water. The others drained their drinks like vodka, and settled down to a short game of insulting each other.

Katz read from the label on the whisky bottle.

'*Johnnie Walker Black*,' he said. 'This is going in my diary.'

Solomon grabbed his chance.

'Ernie Katz,' he said, 'is a diarist, like Samuel Pepys, although a more appropriate comparison might be Charles Pooter, the fictitious author of *Diary of a Nobody*, since Katz, indisputably, is a nobody, and not to be confused with any of the more important Katzes in art history, such as the genuine artists Shemuel Katz, whose courtroom sketches of Adolph Eichmann's trial in Jerusalem brought him world attention; Emmanuel Mane-Katz, who was famous for his depictions of Hassidic life; or even Mickey Katz, the master of the klezmer clarinet and author of the classic Yiddish parody song "How Much is that Pickle in the Window".

'Certainly his diaries would do much to dispel any confusion about his identity, and separate him from the more productive Katzes – or Katzen – of this world. Indeed, one has to wonder what Katz, who generally speaking goes nowhere and does nothing, finds to write in his diary: *Went to club, bludged a drink, ducked my shout, slunk off home*.'

Katz tapped his fingers on the table.

'The Diary of Solomon Solomons would, of course, be voraciously devoured by the public,' he said, 'just as Solomon himself has voraciously devoured everything set in front of him – or to the side of him, or behind him – for the last seventy years. A typical entry might simply read *got fatter*.'

While Solomon and Katz together composed an imaginary day in the life of Myer, Jimmy and I sneaked out the door.

*

Grandma was out shopping when I unscrewed her mezuzah from the doorjamb, prised open the case and pulled out the scroll. I folded it and rolled it tightly, so it would fit into the tiny glass tube I'd made from an old thermometer, and I mounted it on the spirit house frame.

The spirit house now had a timber extension, and decking made from lollypop sticks that Jimmy had salvaged from every Paddle Pop Daniel and I had ever eaten at my grandmother's house.

When Grandma came back with meat, fish and matzo meal, she asked, 'What do you need that for?'

Jimmy looked away.

'It took you ten years to build one for Deborah Who Lives in Israel,' said Grandma. 'Why do they get one now?'

Jimmy shrugged, hunched, and pressed his lips together.

'Did they put a man on Mars?' asked Grandma. 'Was it on the news and I missed it?'

Jimmy coughed and it sounded like woodwork, as if he'd planed strips from his throat and sawn through his larynx with a lathe. Then Grandma went to put the shopping away and Jimmy drifted back to 1946.

'While I was in Asia, I wasn't thinking about what'd happened to me,' he said, 'but coming back to Australia was like coming back to the camps. I saw dead men's faces on the country platforms at Central Station, corpses drinking coffee in milk bars.

'I didn't have much to do with the ex-prisoners' organisations, but I was happy to see my old mates again. I was the best man at Myer's wedding to Mrs Myer. There were one or two others, from Changi and the line, who'd meet in hotels, and we'd share a steak and talk about the concert party and the bloody Seraphielites, and the way Professor Scaly and Croaker Keneally gyped Townsville Jack at the frog races, but they fell away or moved away or died, and the only ones I kept in touch with were the Yidden.

'We all got our back pay and it was more money than most of the blokes had seen in their lives. A lot frittered it away on horses or stupid business ideas, or bought land at the back of Bourke and hid from the world.

'I got a letter from Bargo, which was a surprise, as I didn't think he'd made it out of Changi. He asked to meet at the services club in the city, and I supposed he wanted to hear how Quilpie had died.

'I didn't recognise him in the taproom, all dressed up like Jacky in a three-piece suit and a red bow tie. He didn't mention Quilpie. He told me he was concerned for me, Jimmy Rubens, and worried that I hadn't made any plans for the future.

'He said there was no time to take a *yasumi*. He was calling a *tenko* of all the poor fellas who hadn't provided themselves with life insurance, because life insurance was *ichi bun* and it was time we all went on *speedo* and bought ourselves a policy quick smart.

'"You think I should insure my life *now*?" I said. "When nobody's trying kill me?"

'"I know what you've been through," said Bargo. "We've all been through the same, Jimmy Rubens. We think we've survived everything the world's got to throw at us, we reckon we're invulnerable, but can I let you into a secret, old mate? We're not. You know, I read in the paper the other day about a bloke who lived through the bombing of Singapore, Changi, the railway, the hell ships, the coalmines in Japan and even the bloody atom bomb in

Hiroshima, then went under a bus on George Street in the rush hour, leaving behind a young wife and three children and five hundred pounds' debt."

'"Where did you read that?" I asked.

'"The *Sydney Morning Herald*," said Bargo, "the paper of record. Now, that man's family would've had no worries about the future if he'd only thought to provide himself with life insurance."

'"I might've known the fella," I said. "Can you remember his name?"

'"It was a common one," said Bargo, "Macgregor, or something Scottish like that."

'"I think I knew him," I said. "Lovely bloke. They used to call him 'Jock'."

'"Just think about Jock's widow," said Bargo. "She lost a good man and her children lost a father, but they also lost their future. And the tragedy is, that final misfortune need never have happened if only Jock had shown some foresight and made sensible provision for them in the form of life insurance.

'"Do you have children, Jimmy?" he asked. "Do you have a wife? Or a brother or sister who relies on you? Do you look after an old friend from the camps? Somebody like Jock, who might've lost his way? Because a lot of us don't do it easy, eh, and you've got to have been through it to understand it.

'"Men are often reluctant to provide themselves with life insurance," said Bargo, "unless it is provided by somebody they trust. I'm sure you wouldn't buy life insurance from somebody you don't trust, Jimmy Rubens, not after all we've been through. But there's one company former prisoners can trust, and that's the Former Prisoners' Trust. It's made up of former prisoners like you and me, which is why I personally provide myself with insurance from the Former Prisoners' Trust."

'The cunt,' said Jimmy, and spat.

'Then Bargo said to me, "May I ask you, Jimmy, have you yet provided yourself and your dependants with life insurance?"

'He hadn't even bothered the head on his beer.

'"Yes," I said, "I have."

'"Well," said Bargo, "that's probably a step in the right direction. But have you provided yourself with *enough* life insurance?"

'"I hope so," I said.

'"I hope so too," said Bargo, "particularly after everything we've been through. It would be a catastrophe to leave our dependants – whoever they may be – short; we who realise we owe our lives to mateship, and to other people providing for us. I know somebody who can help you calculate your real life insurance needs, old friend, and give you the peace of mind you need to walk across George Street, or any other street, at any time of the day or night."

'He gave me a card and whispered, "He's one of us."

'"I went to put the card in my wallet, but I couldn't find it in my jacket. I patted myself down, quickly and hard, like I was being searched by a guard.

'"Jesus, Bargo," I said. "I've been robbed. In the services club! What sort of a bloke would pull a low stunt like that?"

'"Are you sure?" asked Bargo.

'"As sure as the *gunso* calls *tenko* after the bugle," I said. "As sure as the *chuis* get the best parts of the yak. The fella I bumped into at the door must've been a dipper."

'So Bargo bought me a beer and a whisky.

'"Old mate," I said, "I lost track of the time. I've got to get home to my wife and three kids." (Your Auntie Stella hadn't been born yet.) "Is there any chance you could sub me the cab fare?"

'Bargo gave me ten bob and I crossed the road and drank myself slit-eyed in a hotel full of Chinese. When Bargo's ten bob was finished, I pulled my wallet out of my pants and spent ten bob more.

'Bargo'd found me through Callaghan, who was trying to pressure the government to pay us our subsistence allowance. Callaghan ran a charity called the Society of Soldiers, because to him the important thing'd always been that we were soldiers, not prisoners, and as soldiers we should've been entitled to three-shillings-a-day allowance to feed ourselves off base. A lot of the blokes really needed the money by then, because they'd bought worthless insurance policies that only paid out if they died in an accident, and paid annual contributions to the Ex-POWs' Benefit Fund, which turned to out to benefit only one ex-POW, a low bastard coward of a captain.

'The last time I ever wore my uniform was for the coach trip to Canberra, where we stood to attention outside Parliament House while a bugler played Reveille, and Callaghan presented our petition to the deputy assistant junior undersecretary for lost causes.

'The government didn't want to hear our case. They weren't interested in an old man's war. They were already fighting young men's wars in Malaya and the East Indies, and gearing up for Korea. After he'd handed over a list of our names, Callaghan marched down the ranks, inspecting us.

'*He bloody loves this*, I thought, and that's when I got out for good.

'After that final little *tenko* we went around Canberra having a bit of a drink, and I was stuck talking to Snowy White, who was a shrunken old man by then, but he could see the government's point.

'"I mean, we weren't actually helping the war effort," said Snowy White. "If anything, we were helping the Japanese war effort."

'So I picked him up and threw him through a shop window.'

BONDI

SATURDAY 12 MAY 1990

We worked all week on the spirit house, before and after school. We didn't stop for a smoko or go to the Club. Jimmy called it our *speedo* period.

The work was difficult and delicate. We put in a chimney, although we didn't bother to run a flue down to the fireplace. We built a coal bunker out the back. From the skeletons of pipe-cleaners I made coathangers and an antenna. With a jeweller's loupe held to his eye, Jimmy cut fine detail into the furniture. The biggest problem was making the washing machine – which meant we had to extend the plumbing – and the oven. The television grew out of a matchbox, with a screen made from plastic left over from the windowpanes.

'What I don't understand,' said Grandma, 'is why there needs to be an empty room.'

'It's for Elijah,' said Jimmy.

'I know who it's for,' said Grandma.

Jimmy dropped his eyes as Solomon's Volvo screeched around the corner and into the street.

'You're still alive!' the tailor shouted, hugging Jimmy and letting ash from his cigar fall on his shoulders. 'Thank God!'

'We thought you'd had a stroke at least!' said Myer.

'I was going to organise a memorial service,' said Katz, 'with Arnold Zwaybil on the organ.'

'Haven't you got anything else to think about?' asked Jimmy, but I could see he was pleased.

'I've brought these,' said the tailor, handing him a parcel as wide as a cigarette packet and as long as a domino box.

'Cigars?' asked Jimmy.

Jimmy opened the box with difficulty. His fingers, so steady when he worked with wood, trembled at the simple challenge.

'*Schmatta*,' he said, pulling out a tiny brown jacket and pants.

'Don't you recognise them?' asked Solomon. 'It's what Moishe used to wear. I cut it for him myself. And this,' he showed him, 'a shirt for Bathurst Billy.'

It was white and collarless, and detailed down to the buttons.

'And what, *lieber Gott,* is this?' asked Jimmy, shaking a white leather capsule out of the carton.

'It's a tote bag,' said Solomon, 'for Townsville Jack.'

The suit was the right size for the wardrobe I had made, and the shirt would fold up and rest in the drawer of the dresser.

'I was up all night,' said Solomon.

'You shouldn't drink so much,' said Grandma.

'Those are the first clothes I've made in ten years.'

'Rags and cabbage,' said Katz. 'But this is art.'

Into Jimmy's hand he dropped two tiny pictures.

'I painted them myself,' he said.

The first was a sepia miniature of a young man in military uniform. 'Moishe,' said Katz.

The other was a portrait of a jockey on horseback.

'It's Phar Lap with Jim Pike,' said Katz. 'After Stuart Reid. I thought Townsville Jack would like it.'

Jimmy put on his loupe and examined the picture. A rigid man in red silks rode a chestnut gelding under a pale blue sky.

'How did you get it so small?' asked Jimmy.

'Well,' said Katz, 'first I painted it ordinary sized, then I zapped it with a shrinking ray from the planet Zog.'

Myer hovered around uselessly.

'And what have you brought, Pink-tush?' Jimmy asked him.

'Good sense and good wishes,' said Myer.

'Well then,' said Jimmy, 'goodbye.'

The old men trouped back into the Volvo. Solomon blew the Reveille on his car horn as he pulled away. Barry Dick drew back his curtain and stared.

'What the hell did they mean by all that?' Jimmy asked me.

I looked at the brown suit Solomon had made for Grandma's brother, Moishe known as Mick.

'Uncle Mick died after the war, didn't he?' I asked.

'That's the end of the story,' said Jimmy. 'The last chapter. When I first got back to Australia I used to find it hard to be in company. I couldn't talk to people and, when I did, I'd suddenly go into Japanese or Malay. It was hardest to be around women, because I still felt ugly and deformed, but the worst thing was I wasn't comfortable with Moishe, and we'd grown up together, been best mates. We should've grown old together.

'We used to have a little party every Saturday night: me, Katz and Myer and Moishe. I had to ask Moishe, but I knew it hurt him to be with us, because Moishe thought he should've gone to Singapore. He'd only got out of it because he'd walked out of training. He reckoned he should've been captured and thrown into the camps. He felt he'd deserted his mates, even though he'd fought the Japs all through the war. He got it into his head that Billy had died instead of him.

'There was a huge gap between us. Moishe came back a hero, I was . . . I don't know . . . People thought about it differently then. They were glad we'd returned, but everyone knew we'd surrendered, and most people didn't believe we'd been starved and tortured and made into slaves. They thought it was an excuse for not escaping. First we hadn't fought, then we hadn't escaped. But Moishe, he had a chest full of medals, and a rank he never even mentioned. He thought the medals weren't rightly his. When he was in his cups, he used to try to give them to me.

'Moishe grew darker and darker. When he first came back he got a job at a bank, but he left one morning without saying a word, and came home to stare at the walls. He stared and stared, and then he started to talk to them. One night, when we'd been drinking in Bondi, he went swimming in the ocean. He left his clothes folded on the beach and he didn't swim back. They never found a body and we never gave him a funeral. He's listed missing, and God knows there were enough missing men in our generation.

'I know why Frida married me,' said Jimmy, 'even though she knew I was a drunk. She wanted to keep something of Moishe, and the last piece of Moishe she had left was me.'

*

I was told to put on my smart pants, because we were going out. We walked to the Club, where two men were unloading amplifiers from the back of a truck. The stacks were marked *AZ*.

'Do you know what that stands for?' asked Jimmy.

'It's the chemical symbol for nitrogen,' I said.

'It stands for "Absolute Zero",' said Jimmy, 'which is English for "Arnold Zwaybil".'

Myer was sitting with his Arnold Zwaybil tickets in front of him on the table, but Sollykatzanjimmy were united in their determination not to go to the concert with him.

'He's setting up upstairs,' Myer told them.

'I've never been upstairs in my life,' said Solomon.

'No sheila would let you in,' said Myer.

'They wouldn't let him in downstairs either,' said Katz.

At five o'clock the Ladies' Auxiliary held a chook lotto. Myer won a size-sixteen frozen chicken but donated it back to the Club.

'They've got chickens in the bar and a turkey in the concert hall,' said Jimmy.

Katz pointed to a small thin man directing the road crew at the bottom of the stairs.

'It's Izzy Berger!' he said.

The man turned around. Katz waved. Izzy Berger looked at his spats, as if he'd been recognised by his shoes. He was wearing a pork-pie hat, even though hats were prohibited by one of the six hundred and thirteen bylaws and regulations of the Club, along with stubbies, thongs, singlets, work boots and motorcycle gang colours.

Berger stared warily at Sollykatzanmyer, who shouted and waved like schoolboys at the back of a bus.

'Izzy Berger!' cried Katz. 'The Jewish Brian Epstein! The kosher Allen Klein!'

Berger walked towards him, frowning.

'G'day, Ernie,' said Berger, nodding gravely. 'G'day, Jimmy.'

'Don't tell me you're looking after Arnold Zwaybil, the singing table,' said Katz.

Berger sighed.

'I am an artists' manager,' said Berger. 'I have a roster of clients.'

'I have clients too,' said Katz. 'Meet Solomon Solomons, the fattest man alive, and Pincus Myer, the world's worst liar. Maybe you could work them into a double act.'

'I don't do freaks,' said Berger.

He seemed to want to walk away.

'I heard you don't do anything,' said Jimmy. 'I heard Mendoza broke a guitar over your head and made you eat an LP.'

'That's ancient history,' said Berger. 'They don't even make LPs any more.'

Izzy Berger held his big, heavy mobile phone in his hand, willing it to ring.

'Can I get you a drink?' asked Katz. 'I'll pay for it out of my own pocket, then double the price, add a bit extra for service, and take it out of your advance.'

Berger shook his head.

'You've been talking to Lucky Jack Gold,' he said. 'What can I say? "Lucky" by name, *putz* by nature. If it wasn't for me, nobody would've heard of that bloke.'

'So whose fault is it that nobody's heard of Arnold Zwaybil?' asked Jimmy.

'He's one of the most popular entertainers in the Jewish community,' said Berger.

'I wouldn't walk up one flight of stairs to see him,' said Solomon.

'He couldn't walk up one flight of stairs,' said Myer.

'It would be too much for the stairs,' said Katz.

'Very funny,' said Izzy Berger. 'I'd hire you all as clowns if you weren't so fucking ugly. Now, are you going to let me get on with my job, or do I have to pay a bloke to knock you?'

Izzy Berger went to tell someone where to put the lights, while Sollykatzanmyer sang 'Strangers in the Night' like dogs howling at the moon.

The old men drank steadily, pausing occasionally to think of something that was better before the war, such as the taste of tomatoes, the cut of a man's cloth, the tramline to Bondi and the behaviour of the younger generation. They were particularly unimpressed with skateboarding.

'Why are you wearing that shirt?' Jimmy asked Solomon suddenly.

'To cover my chest,' said Solomon.

'It's your best shirt,' said Jimmy.

It was purple and silk, like the lining of a coffin.

'Mrs Solomons put it out for me,' said Solomon.

'Are you sure she didn't put it out for the garbos?' asked Myer.

'This is a lovely piece of cloth,' said Solomon, stroking his sleeve with his thumb.

'A man'd be proud to be buried in it,' said Myer.

'Dracula, for instance,' said Katz.

Solomon bared his fangs.

'What I wonder,' said Jimmy, 'is why Mrs Solomons of Dover Heights, formerly Rita Heller of Newtown, chose such a marvellous blouse . . .'

'A chemise . . .' said Katz.

'. . . such a wonderful chemise,' said Jimmy, 'for her beloved husband to wear on a bog-standard night out at the club with his three best mates and a thirteen-year-old boy?'

'Knowing Mrs Solomons as I do,' said Myer, 'and, believe me, I do know her – she was like a sister to me during the long nights in 1940 when Solomon was away on military training – I would guess that particular chemise goes with one of the evening dresses in her own extensive wardrobe, which was furnished with no expense expended by her husband's contacts at the haute couture end of the rag trade, such as Kippax Street Bernie and Knock-Off Norman Schama.'

Solomon sighed.

'Mrs Solomons will be joining us this evening,' he announced, 'for drinks and dinner.'

'As will Mrs Myer,' said Myer. 'I will send a car for her presently.'

'Mrs Rubens,' said Jimmy in an odd voice, 'is also disposed to honour us with her presence.'

I was confused. As the old men laughed, their wives walked into the bar.

Grandma was wearing her best purple dress and a silver tiara. Mrs Solomons had dyed her hair blue and painted her lips purple, and Mrs Myer, who I had never seen before, wore a purple sash and looked a bit like the Queen.

'Oh my,' said Solomon. 'It's Diana Rosenberg and the Chicken Supremes.'

'Sit down, love,' said Jimmy to Grandma.

'I'm not one of your two-pot floozies,' she told him.

The women insisted on going straight upstairs, where they perched on a line of foldaway chairs that Jimmy had made in 1967. Their husbands squeezed between them, leaving me next to Katz. A comedian came on stage to warm up the crowd, but I was the only one who laughed, since most of the audience hadn't turned on their hearing aids.

There was an interval for Sollykatzanmyer to rush to the bar, then the house lights dimmed and a beam like a searchlight found a figure even smaller than Izzy Berger, with a stoop that might've been a hunch, wearing a white suit and fedora.

A dumpy woman with a light beard clapped furiously as the light led the man to his piano stool.

'It's Zelda Zwaybil,' hissed Myer, 'the Eastern Suburbs' Ava Gardner.'

'Good evening, ladies and gentlemen,' said Arnold Zwaybil nasally, 'and welcome to an evening of laughter and tears.'

He bashed his thick fingers on the keyboard.

'Fly me to the moon . . .' he sang.

'Gladly!' shouted Solomon.

Arnold Zwaybil smiled and waved to the crowd. The Rolex on his wrist was almost as big as his face. He put his heart into the songs, but he didn't seem to understand the words. He sang 'I Only Have Eyes For You' as if the important point was that he didn't have ears, and dedicated 'New York, New York' to the New York Restaurant in Kings Cross.

The audience talked over 'I Left My Heart In San Francisco' ('Where'd you leave your voice?' shouted Solomon) and 'Leaving on a Jet Plane' ('Go!' called Solomon. 'Go!').

When he crooned 'These Foolish Things', Grandma and the wives sang 'Old Man River' to drown him out.

He sang 'Sail On', which was a hit for Lucky Jack Gold and not Frank Sinatra but, said Katz, Izzy Berger made him perform the song at every gig, so Izzy could take a small royalty.

The crowd was gossiping and kvetching, and sharing food they had smuggled in, when a deep voice from the folds of the velvet stage curtains said, 'Of all the gin joints in all the towns in all the world, she walks into mine,' and Arnold Zwaybil looked up from his piano.

'Play it once, Arnold, for old time's sake,' begged a young woman's voice.

'I don't know what you mean,' said Arnold Zwaybil to the air.

'Play it, Arnold,' she said. 'Play "As Time Goes By".'

Even Solomon was silent as Arnold Zwaybil persuaded the tune out of his piano. Even Katz sang along with chorus. Myer's wife hummed a harmony that lifted the song out of Arnold Zwaybil's hands, and Mrs Solomon joined in too. Suddenly the whole room was singing.

After 'As Time Goes By', Arnold Zwaybil played 'Come Dance With Me', and Grandma stuck an elbow in my face and a knee into my thigh as she pushed past me to the end of the row, with Jimmy's hand in hers.

At the front of the concert hall, just below the stage, Grandma and Jimmy danced together, first lightly then tightly, as Arnold Zwaybil sang 'A Nightingale Sang In Berkeley Square'. Solly, Myer, Mrs S and Mrs M all joined them. Only Katz and I stayed on our seats, and Katz, for all his clenched teeth and hard swallowing, couldn't hold back his tears.

BONDI

TUESDAY 15 MAY 1990

'Where the hell has he put my sewing machine?' asked Grandma, searching her kitchen cupboards. 'He's a bloody *meshuganneh* on wheels. What does he want with a sewing machine?'

I knew where it was, but I didn't want to say.

'God forbid he'd ever sew anything,' said Grandma, looking under the dining table.

Jimmy had gone to see the doctor to get his test results. I was supposed to meet him after school but had come back to change out of my uniform, so the women would notice me on Darlinghurst Road.

'He's probably buried it,' said Grandma.

I looked at myself in the mirror over the mantelpiece and pulled down the brim of my baseball cap, to make me look older.

'It's in the shed,' I admitted. 'We've, uh, stripped it for parts.'

'Parts? What parts of a sewing machine does he want? He's a bloody klezmermaniac.'

'We used the needles for towel rails,' I said, and hurried to the front door.

*

I found Jimmy at Kings Cross Station, next to a busker with one leg who played a guitar with one string. Blackfellas crowded out the entrance, laughing, swearing and drinking wine from a box.

Jimmy pointed to the window of the apartment he used to share with Katz.

'They weren't bad days,' he said.

I told him Grandma had taken back her sewing machine and ripped out the towel rails.

He didn't seem to know what I meant.

Jimmy showed me some of the places that were important in the old men's stories – the building that used to be the Patton Club, another that was once Aphrodite's, and the New York Restaurant where Katz had painted the sign *Today's special: lamb chops (2) and chips.*

'We had a beer or two on Kellett Street,' said Jimmy, 'and a few jars on the strip. Maybe I was drinking to forget the bloody camps, but there was more to it than that. I wanted to fill my head with new memories, to cram out my nightmares. I had a year of fucking and falling over.' He laughed. 'Another year like that and I'd've been done for.'

He stopped.

'The last few weeks,' he said, 'I've felt like I've been having that time again: what with going to the fights, remembering the war, taking Frida to a show, seeing Mendoza and that *gonif* Izzy Berger . . . We've even had the cops around. It's like living through a bloody second childhood.'

He shook his head.

We stopped outside Solomon Solomons & Sons, Continental Tailors. Jimmy pointed out Solomon's son Solomon, a tape measure around his neck like a tallith, big and broad where his father was just fat, and I could almost see the tank of a man that Solomon used to be.

Jimmy gave money to beggars and ducked around spruikers, to find Katz blowing into a hot coffee at Vitto's. Katz said he'd been going through his old things and had some stuff to show me, if I wanted to come up to his room and see his etchings. While Jimmy kept his appointment with Manny the Spoons, Katz carried his coffee back to his unit, where a sketch of a rickshaw rested on top of his diary on the writing desk.

He showed me pictures of a toothless old Chinaman and a sampan at sunset.

'They're all I've got left of Singapore,' he said, 'and everything from the camps is at the War Memorial in Canberra. I hid those sketches under the cholera patients and buried them in their graves. After the war I went back with the war graves recovery parties to dig them up. Half of them had been eaten by cockroaches. Everyone's a bloody art critic.'

I told him Jimmy had said he wouldn't be alive without Katz.

'I did some things I'm not proud of,' said Katz, 'but I'm not ashamed of them either. I paid my way, I helped my mates. But when I was a boy in Balmain, I used to work for Jake Mendoza, sketching naked women to sell in the playground. That's how Mendoza got started, you know, selling pictures of women. It was a few years before he moved up to selling actual women.

'I didn't mind Jake in those days, and I needed him, just like I needed Townsville Jack and Jimmy in Changi. He looked after me, or rather he organised us Jewboys to look after ourselves. But the things he did with women were wrong – trading them like drawings . . .

'I often wonder if Mendoza would have ended up the way he did if he hadn't had my pictures to sell. I look around the Cross and see all the heroin skeletons and dull-eyed corpse girls, and I wonder if, on some level, it's all my fucking fault. But that's stupid, isn't it? If it hadn't've been Jake, it would've been someone else. The King of the Cross might've been Gozo Joe Stone.'

Katz got up to walk around, his hands clasped behind his back like a teacher pacing a classroom.

'It wasn't that I had a problem drawing girls, even for the Japs, it's just that I knew how it would grow, from girls in swimsuits to women with one man, two men, three men. That's how pornography works: it starts with the smile and it grows into . . . well, you know.'

'Actually,' I said, 'I'm only thirteen.'

'She starts off on her feet and ends up on her knees,' said Katz. 'Then on her back, with her legs pulled over her head. It's like war. First there's the shooting, then the bombing, then the burning, then the slow, slow torture of the prisoners . . .'

Katz turned his eyes to his window, to the traffic on Darlinghurst Road.

'Would you like a cup of coffee?' he asked suddenly. 'We could get another cappuccino from Vitto's.'

The doorbell rang. Jimmy climbed upstairs clutching an envelope.

'I need more tests,' he said. 'That's all they ever say. It's a con, a bloody pyramid scheme.'

We arrived home to find Grandma putting away the Singer.

'Have you been sewing all day?' asked Jimmy.

'Of course not,' said Grandma. 'Slow Eddie Finkel had his way with me all morning, then Arnold Zwaybil came calling in the afternoon.'

'As long as you haven't been wasting electricity,' said Jimmy.

Grandma folded her hands in her lap.

'What did the doctor say?' she asked.

'The usual,' said Jimmy. '"Hava Nagila".'

'Did he give you something?'

'I had an envelope,' said Jimmy, 'but I must've left it on the train.'

Grandma yawned.

'You'd lose your hat if it wasn't glued on,' she said.

Jimmy touched his bare head.

'I must've left that too,' he said.

[Sckaj, 133 Silver Street, Bondi. 17-05-90. 11:00 am.]

Mr Rubens, I'm Daniel Spiegeleier, from the *Australian Jewish Times*.

G'day, Danny. Can I get you a drink? There's grog in the shed.

Would I be able to have a water?

Why not, Danny. Live dangerously, eh? I don't go much on water myself. The cockies need it more than us.

Yeah, but I'm sober.

I'd hope so, mate. It's eleven o'clock in the morning.

No, sober as in AA. I don't drink.

How does that work, then?

Well, instead of drinking beer, I do something else.

I can't interest you in a whisky?

Believe me, I'm interested, but you know how it is: one's too many and a hundred's not enough.

Like sheilas.

I suppose so. But I'm not a sex addict.

You mean you're a *faygeleh*?

No, I . . .

Just kidding, Danny. I'll get you a water, mate: it's a man's drink, and don't let any bugger tell you different. The *Jewish Times*, eh? My Frida loves your paper, especially the death notices. Do you write those yourself?

No, actually, I'm the editor. Those are advertisements.

So how can I help you, Danny? I've got nothing to advertise.

I don't sell the ads, I write stories.

And you want to write one about me?

I think what you're doing is very interesting.

It's no bugger's business but mine.

A lot of people in the community are talking about it.

What are they saying?

Well, they think you're building a Sukkot hut on a stick. In May. And they don't know why.

Haven't they got anything else to think about?

Would you like to explain it to our readers?

I don't reckon so. I don't stickybeak in their yards, and I reckon they'd be a damn sight more interesting than mine.

May I ask if you're a war veteran?

I'm a returned serviceman. That's what they used to call it.

How do you feel about the recent desecration of the Anzac in the memorial gardens?

They ought to find the bastard that did it and string him up.

Do you think that society recognises the sacrifices made by men like you?

I don't . . . I didn't intend to make a sacrifice.

But you did, didn't you?

I did what?

You sacrificed your youth.

I was twenty when I joined up. There was no such thing as youth when I was young. I was a man.

That's my point.

What's your point?
That people like you have often been forgotten.
People like me?
I'm told you were a prisoner of war.
Every soldier is a prisoner of war, Danny.
That's very poetic.
Thank you. Whisky is my muse.
It must've been hard.
Hard?
To be a prisoner.
'Hard'? You think it must've been 'hard'?
I'm just trying to . . .
That's your insight? That it was 'hard'?
I didn't mean . . .
It's the easiest thing in the world to be a prisoner, Danny. You just have to surrender.
Do you think people know enough about what men like you went through?
Yes.
Yes?
Yes.
But there are children at school who've never even heard of Changi.
And there are pensioners in Carlingford who've never heard of the Dalai Lama. What does it matter?
Perhaps if they knew more about it, they wouldn't vandalise memorials.
You think memorials matter? Do you want them to build a statue to every man that died?
I suppose it wouldn't bring them back.
You don't need to bring them back. They're here.
In our hearts and minds?
In our wardrobes and baths.

I'm sorry, I don't follow you.
Don't worry, Danny, you'll find someone else to follow.
This house you've built: is it true it's a monument to Thai-Australian friendship, and the bonds formed between people like Weary Dunlop and the river trader Boon Pong during the construction of the Burma Railway?
You can say it's that, if you like.
So why is there a mezuzah on the door?
You tell me.
Perhaps it's a specific bond formed between Jewish Australians and Thais like Boon Pong.
That'd be it.
Did you actually know Boon Pong during the war?
No.
But you worked on the Burma Railway?
Yes.
Did you know Weary Dunlop?
No.
Were there many Jewish POWs working on the railway?
Some. Most of them'd be dead now, but.
Might you be the last one?
I might be, but I'm not.
Have you ever told your story?
I've told it to my grandson.
Would you like to tell it to our readers?
I don't think so.
But it's an important story.
It's a private story.
I see your home is called 'Sckaj'. Is that a Yugoslav word?
It sounds like a plum brandy or something, doesn't it?
Is it?
It might be. I don't speak Yugoslav.
Okay, well, nice to meet you, Mr Rubens, and sorry to have

wasted your time. Before you go, can I ask you a question?
All you've done is ask me questions, and now you're asking me if you can ask them.
In your time as a prisoner, did you ever cross paths with a man they called 'Townsville Jack'?
[Silence.]
Mr Rubens?
[Silence.]
Mr Rubens, I'm sorry . . .
[Sobs.]
He was my uncle, my father's brother. He passed away before I was born. Did you know him?
He said he had a brother in Victoria.
That's right. In Warrnambool. The family bred horses.
Come into my house, Danny. This is your home. And I'll tell you about a giant of a man whose footsteps shook the earth.

*

Grandma put down the receiver when Jimmy and Spiegeleier walked into the living room, so I guessed she'd been on the phone to Mum. We went together to the front step, where she shelled peas into a bowl, her knees spread to make a cod's mouth of her skirt.

'Are you all right?' Grandma asked, rubbing my hair. 'He hasn't been driving you mad?'

I told her I liked his stories.

'I don't even know them,' said Grandma. 'There're bits that I can put together myself, when he screams for his bloody Chinese girl, or I look at his scars. He sometimes used to let something slip to Moishe, and Moishe'd tell me about a beating or a torture or some other terrible thing, but that was in the early days. It ended when Moishe left us.

'He's my husband,' said Grandma, 'but I don't really know

him. I knew him before he went to war. When he came back, he was a different man. Nobody knows him now except those *schnorrers* in the club.'

She smiled and kissed me.

[Sckaj, 133 Silver Street, Bondi. 17-05-90. 1:00 pm.]
So tell me, Mr Spiegeleier, who was my mate? Who were his family? And who the fuck are you?
My name is Daniel Spiegeleier. It means 'fried eggs' in German. For years I called myself 'Danny Eggs'.
Are you sure I can't tempt you with a drink, Mr Spiegeleier?
You've already tempted me, but I can't give in.
You've got an iron will, mate. It's a family trait. Although not necessarily in this area.
I know my uncle was a drinker. It was part of his shame.
God calls last drinks before you know it, son, and there's no bolting back to the bottle-o once you're dead.
As I explained, I have a problem.
Yes, you're a *faygeleh*. But these days that isn't seen as a problem. It's sheilas who have the problem, trying to find a husband in a city full of *faygelem*.
Do you want me to tell you about my uncle, Mr Rubens?
I'm sorry, son. I'm an old man, and I'm frightened. I've lived

my life this long without the story. I don't know how I'll live with it.

My father couldn't live with it in the end. He thought it was his shame that he stood by and let it happen.

As Marx said, 'Men make their own history but not in the circumstances of their own choosing.' And that's not Groucho.

So why did you do that funny thing with your eyebrows?

It's a habit, Mr Spiegeleier, like all your twitches and tics.

I've got post-traumatic stress.

It must be a tough life, being a journalist.

You learn to tell a story. That's all I can say for it.

So tell me. Go on. It's time.

My grandfather, Zachariah Spiegeleier, called himself 'Bill'. I don't know why he chose that name, because he never paid a bill in his life. At school the kids'd called him 'Fried Eggs' and in time it got shortened to 'Fried'. When he was a young bloke he became a bookie with a spot in the ring in Randwick. He couldn't fit his real name on the tote bag, so he used Fry. William Fry.

Horseracing was as bent as buggery. It was no place for a Jewish boy, although there were a few of them around. They were supposed to have a head for numbers, an eye for figures. There was a syndicate on the track, a kind of loose alliance of Jews and Irish. I don't know there was much love lost between the O'Reillys and the Cohens, the muscle and the brains, but my grandfather said it held together for a good few years, until a family from Surry Hills decided to take over.

They said they'd work with the Paddies but not the Yids, on account of the death of Jesus, which they saw as a hit on one of their own. And the Micks had problems with the Jesus thing too. They swooped onto the track in the morning – when the bookies were making deals with the stablehands and trainers – wearing crucifixes and waving razors and clubs. My grandfather

had his throat cut by an Irish standover merchant they called St Peter, after his medallion. According to him, when St Peter sliced through his neck he said, 'This one's for our Lord and Saviour.' But my grandfather was prone to exaggeration and drama.
He should've been a journalist.
If there's drama in the *Australian Jewish Times*, it's passed me by.
I meant a proper journalist.
With respect, Mr Rubens, you don't know my history.
So get on with it. That's what we're here for. But you've been talking for ten minutes and your uncle hasn't even been born yet.
The Jews tried to organise against the Paddies and the Surry Hills mob, but they didn't have the numbers or the stomach for a fight. Most of them faded into SP betting or illegal casinos, but Bill Fry left Sydney and went to ground in Warrnambool. His scar made him look like he was easy to cut but hard to kill, and he was worried that some fellas around the place would take it as challenge. That's how I remember my grandfather, as a big old man with a pink ridge around his neck. As a boy, I used to worry his head would fall off. He always said, 'If it hasn't happened by now, it never will.'

He used to tell me St Peter had cut him like a *shochet* butchers a cow. He lost a lot of blood, more than he thought he had in his body, and when he didn't die, my grandad turned to God. It often happens like that. He became religious, although there wasn't much he could do about it in Warrnambool. The nearest *shule* was in Geelong. He dropped 'Fry' – which had become a dangerous name to carry in sporting circles anyway – and reverted to Spiegeleier, although he still went by 'Bill'.

He settled down with my grandmother, a schoolteacher, and they had two girls and, I always thought, one boy – my dad, Stan.

Bill was a wonderful grandad, really, full of long stories and little kindnesses, but he couldn't stand straight at the pisser. He always had a rort running, a con going. He was bookie from his cap to his boots, even though in Warrnambool he ran a horse stud.

I used to go down there for the summer, and he'd try to teach me about life. He told me the most important thing in the world was family, and I thought he meant my dad. I never knew Dad had a brother.

Bill grew angrier as he grew older. His religion didn't seem to comfort him any more. He just sat on his deck, smoking cigars and raging at the sunset over the paddock. He died when I was twelve, a month before my bar mitzvah.

Dad had to organise the funeral. He tried to track people down. He got a couple of the old yiddisher bookies together, to compare the scars they'd earned from the Surry Hills mob, and found a cousin of Bill's, Harold, who hadn't seen him since 1938. I was with Harold at the wake when he asked Dad what had happened to Joshua. It was the first time I'd heard his name. Dad told Harold Joshua had disappeared.

'What do you mean "disappeared"?' asked Harold.

I'll always remember the way he said that word, as if he thought Dad had thrown Joshua into the garbage and had him buried in the dump. It's funny, though: I knew straightaway they were talking about my uncle.

Dad told me the story that day. I suppose he was too sad about Bill to keep it a secret any more and, with Bill dead, the secret didn't matter anyway.

His older brother grew up in the tack shed and on the track. He loved him and looked up to him, but he could never keep up with him. Joshua wasn't a nice yiddisher boy. He was a throwback to something else, a tinker from the old country, always in trouble.

He spent a year in a boys' home, the only Jew. People said that was what made him hard, but Dad said he wasn't hard, just tough. He was a man around the hotels of Warrnambool, and fought in the tent when Jeremiah Cain's World Famous Boxing Troupe came to town. He even went off with them for a season, from Horsham to Mildura.

Joshua worked as a bookie's runner and a cockatoo, then started his own SP business out of the Station Hotel. He got into trouble with the local Irish like his dad, and he hopped freight trains all the way to Sydney to try to join up with Phil the Jew. But by the time Joshua arrived in the Cross, Phil the Jew had retired, and Jake Mendoza was still a petty crook fencing car radios, so Joshua tried to make something out of his boxing. He fought at the Sydney Stadium, at the bottom of the card with the beginners and bums. He had a talent for feints and evasions, and a chin that could keep him on his feet if the other bloke got through his guard, but he didn't have much patience for the discipline, so he settled into losing to pad the other fella's record.

My dad went up to see him fight once. He was calling himself Vic Brown for some reason. He was up against a fat baker, and he put on a proper show because he knew Stan was in the crowd. They went toe to toe for six rounds. Joshua lost, but the crowd threw coins into the ring and cheered for both of them.

He told me about that fight.

I think it was his last.

Yeah, he said that.

He went the distance for his brother.

In his story, it was a sheila.

There was a woman too. Dad said there was always a woman. After the fight, Joshua took Dad drinking with his mates. It was like a circus, Dad said. There were strongmen and wrestlers and spivs dressed like ringmasters, and even a dwarf.

Joshua followed the sun north to Brisbane, where he met the *shiksa*. That's all she was ever called. No one knew her name – or even her religion, except that she wasn't Jewish. She was supposed to be beautiful, but that's just what people assumed, because of Joshua being a ladies' man. They said she was bad, but Dad didn't know in what way. Maybe she was the madam of a brothel, or maybe she was the barmaid at the pub. Anyway, Joshua moved in with her.

Bill Spiegeleier sat *shiva* for a year, in a *shule* in his own head, and told Dad and his sisters never to speak to Joshua again.

They did, of course, but not often, and always from a distance. They heard Jack's girl died of influenza, and Jack went back on the swag. A drifter in the Station Hotel told them Joshua had got into a fight in Brandon and ended up in jail in Townsville, and they'd only let him out when he promised to join the army. He sent a letter to Dad from Singapore, saying the goyim all called him 'Townsville Jack'.

We never knew he'd enlisted as Fry, let alone Peter. I'd never have thought of it.

It would've been the name he used in court. He would've made it up on the spot.

He named himself after his father, and the bloke who cut him.

You might be reading too much into it.

My dad loved Joshua, but when he disappeared he never tried to look for him. He'd just let it lie, to protect his mother, he said. But as he grew older his childhood became real again, and he wanted to be with his brother. He remembered Joshua rubbing his face up against the head of his horse, riding bareback through the paddock, firing shotguns at tin cans.

Just before he died, Dad would wait in the drive of his house for Joshua to saddle up and take him out riding. He wrote him long letters to an address overseas, and waited by the mailbox to get a postcard back.

And that's it. That's all I know.

Thanks, mate. Are you sure I can't get you a drink?

I'm fine. Honestly.

You won't mind if I have one myself.

Look, I'll take an orange cordial.
L'chaim.
L'chaim.
Your uncle preferred something stronger.
He sounds like a stronger man than me.
He was a fucking army.

*

The story was printed in the paper on Friday morning. By lunchtime there was a policewoman in my grandmother's street, trying to move along all the old people who had come to look at our spirit house, and some others who had stopped by to find out what all the old people were looking at. Barry Dick and the *frummers* walked up and down the line offering the men the chance to put on *teffilin*.

I didn't recognise most of the crowd, although they all looked pretty much the same, with tremendous eyebrows and pursed, puzzled lips.

'It's like the line-up for an Arnold Zwaybil concert,' said Jimmy.

Daniel Spiegeleier interviewed people about why they were there, for a story about the enormous influence of the *Australian Jewish Times* in Bondi Junction and the Waverley area. Several readers had misunderstood the story, or only looked at the picture. One thought there was supposed to be a spirit house outside every Jewish home in the street. Another tried to put money in the roof. Two Maoris believed they had joined a bus queue.

Spiegeleier passed Jimmy an envelope, which he opened slowly. Inside was a fragile grey photograph of a tall, smiling boy with deep-set eyes, holding his big hands under his chin like a boxer, and a smaller picture of the boy grown into a man, wearing a uniform and crouched by a mortar.

'Yes,' said Jimmy. 'That's him.'

BONDI

SUNDAY 20 MAY 1990

I woke before dawn when I heard Jimmy pissing and spitting in the bathroom, his cough echoing around the walls. He knocked softly on my door, and I pushed my penknife inside my pillowcase and hid my present under the bed. I pulled on a hooded top and followed Jimmy outside, where he stood watching the sun rise over the spirit house.

He waited at attention, his bent old back pulled straight like a flagpole, the palms of his hands flat against the pockets of his pants. He wore two medals over his heart, and the light winked on the polished metal as the sun climbed past.

We ate breakfast on the deck while Grandma slept: cream-cheese bagels, orange juice and eggs on toast from a café in Bondi Road. Jimmy wrapped a red ribbon around the house, with a bow tied across the front door like rose petals, or a wreath.

I recognised the ribbon from a box of chocolates Mum had bought my grandparents for their ruby wedding anniversary.

'I knew it'd come good one day,' said Jimmy.

Grandma came out of the bedroom dressed in her best purple

frock. She put on the kettle and sang a sad song in the kitchen. Jimmy shuffled and watched his feet, as if he were afraid to look at her, but Grandma smiled and passed him a small neatly packaged parcel.

Jimmy unwrapped a tiny red cheongsam with a golden bow across one shoulder.

'For Mei-Li,' said Grandma. 'Something modest to wear in that house full of men.'

Jimmy laid the cheongsam on the sleeping mat in the timber extension of the spirit house, and kissed his wife on the lips.

The *frummers* always woke up early, to make sure they fitted enough God into their day. Barry Dick and two bearded Americans crossed the road carrying trays of cakes and bags of *teffilin*. They stopped at the gate to mutter a *broche*, and mumbled another at the door.

'You can put the tucker on the dining table,' said Jimmy, directing them through the bead curtain, 'and the *teffilin* in the fridge.'

Grandma dusted the mantelpiece and plumped up the cushions, pulled back the curtains and opened the blinds. She took all the bottles out of the drinks cabinet and arranged them like chess pieces on the shelf below.

Myer and Solomon turned up at 10 am in the Volvo. Solomon was wearing his hair slicked back and his Dracula shirt.

'Where's the booze?' he asked. 'I'm as dry as a camel.'

'I thought in the war you'd learned how to get a camel wet,' said Myer.

'That was no camel,' said Solomon, 'that was your wife.'

They rolled towards the drinks table, pushing and pinching each other. Grandma had poured whisky into a decanter. I gave them each a glass. They closed their eyes, threw back their heads and drank. Solomon shook his face. His jowls quaked.

Myer pulled Jimmy's sleeve.

'Here,' he whispered.

Jimmy opened his palm to a tiny pair of spectacles.

'Moishe needed them after the war,' he said. 'I found his prescription in the vaults.'

Jimmy held them to the light, as if to see it through Moishe's eyes.

'Moishe always stood his round,' said Myer. 'He was a mensch.'

All the men had a drink for Moishe then another for Mick, even though they were the same person.

'I wonder what he would've been,' said Jimmy, 'who he would've been.'

'A bank manager,' said Solomon, 'a family man. Respectable. Grandchildren.'

They stood quietly for a moment, until I said to Jimmy, 'I've got something too.'

I showed him a carving I'd made from a clothes peg.

'Gottle of gear,' I said, 'gottle of gear.'

'Have you gone berko?' asked Jimmy.

'It's Little Bluey,' I said, 'for Bluey.'

I thought it looked like a doll, anyway.

'Bluey . . .' said Jimmy. 'He'd've been anything but a ventriloquist.'

'He couldn't throw his voice,' said Myer.

'He fell at the first hurdle,' agreed Jimmy.

'We'd all've been different people without the war,' said Solomon. 'Except Katz.'

Sylvia and Maurice parked their Volvo behind Solomon's car. Maurice carried a cake into the house.

'It's from David Jones,' said Sylvia.

'Welsh fella?' asked Jimmy.

The *frummers* squinted at the cake, in case it wasn't kosher. I grabbed a slice and stuffed it into my mouth before anyone could tell me we had to say a prayer first.

We all stood on the front deck.

'So this is it,' said Maurice, tapping the spirit house.

'This is what?' asked Jimmy.

'Whatever it is,' said Maurice.

'Yes,' said Jimmy, 'it is.'

Maurice nodded his head three times.

'We think it's absolutely wonderful you've done this,' said Sylvia.

Jimmy grinned and folded his arms.

'We just think it might've been better if you'd built your haunted house in the backyard, rather than the front,' said Maurice.

'Or in the shed,' said Sylvia.

They asked if Jimmy had found the time to talk to Frida about the unit. He said it was the next thing on his list.

The neighbours filed into my grandmother's house. Johnny the Head brought a case of beer. Nancy the Beard had baked a pavlova.

Katz walked up from the railway station in drainpipe trousers, a white shirt and a bootlace tie. He looked like a good cowboy come for a gunfight with mean Barry Dick, but the two men just shook hands and talked about painting and whether or not *Hashem* approved of pictures of the world.

Katz was carrying *Darkness at Noon*.

'This is the first party he's been to since the Communist Party,' said Solomon, snatching the book and opening it upside down.

'Ernie Katz,' said Solomon, 'is a disillusioned idealist. This means he is . . . This means . . . Katz is . . . I don't know . . .' Solomon shook his head. 'He's just a cunt, really.'

Solomon suddenly grabbed Katz and hugged him. Katz fought him off with a wriggle and a push.

A Rolls Royce with the number plate 'Big One' pulled up at

the electrical substation. The chauffeur lumbered out and opened the back door to Jake Mendoza and a much younger woman with legs as brown as Dee Why sand. She took Mendoza's arm as they walked around my grandmother's house and into the backyard.

'It's the King of the Crossword,' whispered Solomon.

'Who the hell asked him?' asked Jimmy.

'I am here in my capacity as a community leader,' said Mendoza.

Jimmy glowered, but I handed him a beer.

'Let bygones be bygones, eh?' said Mendoza. 'On this auspicious occasion. Although I've got no idea what kind of fucking occasion it's supposed to be.'

A canary yellow Camry parked at the gate. Dad stepped out.

'I asked him too,' I told Jimmy.

Dad lingered at the fence. Jimmy hurried over to shake his hand.

'You don't mind me coming?' asked Dad.

'It's a free country,' said Jimmy. 'Thanks to the efforts of men like Katz, who painted us fighting for it.'

I stood between Jimmy and Dad. They each put a hand on my shoulder and talked over my head.

'I've missed our games of snooker,' said Dad.

'You always did miss,' said Jimmy.

'Somebody had to give an old man a chance,' said Dad.

Barry Dick balanced his siddur on the roof of the spirit house and recited a blessing. When he was finished, the Maoris chorused 'Amen'.

Faces turned to Jimmy, who turned too, because he thought they were looking at something behind him.

'Speech!' cried Solomon, and clapped.

Trapped, Jimmy took his place behind the spirit house.

'I don't know what to say,' said Jimmy.

'Brilliant!' said Myer. 'Churchillian!'

'I built this house for me,' said Jimmy, 'but I suppose all of us have got memories we need to . . . put away. Some of us are returned men . . .'

Mendoza beamed.

'. . . and we lived through things we'd rather forget, in Egypt, in Libya, in Singapore, in Malaya and in Liverpool.'

Mendoza nodded.

'But there's things you can't just put out of your mind – mates that you promised you'd remember forever, because if you didn't then nobody else would and they'd die without mourners and walk the earth like . . . ghosts. It takes more than just a burial to lay a soul to rest. And I mean the souls of the people who are left behind.

'There's blokes here who went to war with me. Ernie . . .'

He held out his hand to Katz, who joined him by the spirit house.

'. . . Pincus . . .'

Myer came to Jimmy's side.

'During the worst times,' said Jimmy, 'there's only two things that keep you going – your mates and your sense of humour. Pincus here was the funniest man in Changi . . .'

Myer flushed.

'. . . he was the mainstay of the famous Changi Concert Party, and the only one who didn't have to dress up as a sheila to get a laugh. No Aussie who did time in Changi will ever forget the clown prince of Selarang. For three and half years he had us all in stitches that even Weary Dunlop couldn't've sewn up.

'Laugh?' said Jimmy, 'I thought I'd wet myself. But it turned out to be just the monsoon. Give us a turn, Pincus Myer!'

Myer looked at the ground.

'Anyone could've been a hit in Changi,' he said. 'We had a *captive audience*.'

Everyone laughed.

'There's a song we used to sing in Changi,' said Myer. 'It was written about a mate of Jimmy's who was a real . . . sportsman. He can't be with us today, because age didn't weary him.

'Nor,' said Myer, sounding his words one at a time, 'did the years condemn. I'm not much of a singer, so I'm going to ask Jimmy and Ernie to help me out here.'

Myer sang softly as if it were a hymn, '"I went to Changi races, it was on the twelfth of June . . ."'

Katz joined in with a voice that seemed too big and bassy for his skinny body, '"Nineteen hundred and forty two on a summer's afternoon . . ."'

Jimmy clapped time softly to their song, and bowed his head when the audience applauded.

'I can't go yet,' Jimmy whispered to me.

'Go where?' I asked.

'I'm waiting for Dominique,' he said.

Dee from the Thai Dee floated through the gates, wearing a cheongsam like the one Frida had sewn for Mei-Li. She looked even more beautiful outside the restaurant, and the *frummers* stared at her even though she wasn't kosher.

Dee stroked the roof of the spirit house.

'Did you make this yourself?' she asked Jimmy.

'The boy did a lot of the work,' he said.

'Oh!' squealed Mei-Li, and she clapped.

And the old men were right. It did make my weenie get bigger.

Dee picked up the elephant Jimmy had stolen from the restaurant.

'There are no elephants in this country,' she said.

'No,' said Jimmy, 'I don't suppose there are.'

She dropped the animal into her purse, then touched the mane of the stolen horse.

'Could they keep that?' asked Jimmy. 'Please?'

'Your friend liked horses?' she asked.

'More than anything,' said Jimmy.

Dee cut the ribbon and declared the house open.

The Maoris danced a haka and stuck out their tongues at Grandma, who stuck out her tongue back. The *frummers* sang 'Hava Nagila', and Sollykatzanmyer danced like Cossacks.

While Mendoza's bodyguard escorted Mendoza to the bathroom, Myer rested a hand on the blonde girl's brown legs.

'How about a kiss for an old soldier?' he asked.

'How about you piss off,' she said.

'So I suppose a handjob's out of the question.'

'Seventy-five dollars,' said the girl.

'Jesus,' said Myer. 'It's gone up since 1951.'

'Hang on,' said Solomon. 'Did you *pay* for your handjob on the AJEX march?'

'I may have given her a cab fare home,' admitted Myer.

'Where did she live?' asked Solomon.

'Wollongong,' he said, 'judging by the size of the fare.'

They drank like soldiers. Even Grandma had a glass of sherry and lemonade, and Dad sipped at a Drambuie.

'I've never seen anyone drink that before,' said Jimmy. 'I don't even know what it is.'

The old men huddled together.

'We should've done this before,' said Katz. 'For the others.'

'I do it every night,' said Jimmy. 'I drink with them.'

Myer rubbed his eyes.

'I do too,' he said. 'I always have.'

Katz took Jimmy's elbow.

'The war shaped our lives,' he said. 'Without it, you'd never've met Townsville Jack. You'd never have known Mei-Li. Some of the shit was worth it in the end.'

Jimmy smiled.

'No, it wasn't,' he said.

Katz nodded.

'You left this at my flat,' he said.

Jimmy took the doctor's letter and put it in his back pocket.

Dad came over and asked if Jimmy wanted to play a frame next Sunday.

'If I'm not there,' said Jimmy, 'start without me.'

I took a swallow of Dad's Drambuie. It tasted like the label.

'Oh my *Hashem*,' said Dad. 'It's your mother.'

Mum came out of a taxi wearing a long-sleeved dress, so she wouldn't look like a slut who'd run off with a Christian. She ran to Grandma and gave her a hug that squeezed the colour out of her face.

Jimmy turned his back to her.

'Dad . . .' said Mum.

I always found it strange when Mum called Jimmy 'Dad'.

'Please . . .' said Mum.

Katz steered Jimmy around and prodded him towards her.

Mum jumped on Jimmy and wrapped him in her arms. He pushed her back, but it was only to look at her, to stroke her long hair before he kissed her. He held her until his arms tired, then passed her back to Grandma.

When Mum saw Dad she walked slowly towards him. I wanted to follow her, to grab them both and pull them together and make us a family again, but they passed without looking or speaking. Mum went to the bathroom, and when she came back Dad had gone.

Mum took me home at eight o'clock, so I wasn't there for the end. I heard later that Solomon was sent to Kemeny's to fetch two more bottles of whisky, and the Maoris brought rum and children. Jimmy carried out his deckchair, and he sat smiling, waving away guests when they blocked his view of the spirit house.

'Now the ghosts are rested,' said Grandma to Jimmy, 'we can do all the things we said we'd do. We can go and see Deborah in Israel, and you can paint the back wall.'

'Israel hasn't got a back wall,' said Jimmy.

'Every day I thank God I married a comedian,' said Grandma.

'I have had a perfectly wonderful evening,' said Jimmy, 'but this wasn't it.'

And he nodded off in his chair.

By nightfall the old men were asleep, with Solomon stretched out drunk on the pavement – just like when he'd been banned from my grandmother's house in 1953.

At dawn Katz shook Jimmy by the shoulders.

'How does a man get a cup of tea around here?' he asked.

'How would he know?' said Solomon. 'Ask a man.'

Katz pursed his lips by Jimmy's ear and whistled the Reveille. Jimmy did not stir. Katz felt his pulse, listened for his heart, thumped his chest and called an ambulance. The ambos covered Jimmy with a sheet when they carried him away.

BOTANY CEMETERY

WEDNESDAY 23 MAY 1990

At the funeral, Grandma walked among the tombstones, leaving pebbles behind. Mum left the service early to help prepare the food with Deborah Who Lives in Israel, who'd flown in from Haifa that morning. Solomon – suddenly 'Uncle Solly' – drove me to my grandmother's house. Katz and Myer sat in the back seat of the Volvo, passing a pewter hipflask between them.

Katz gave me a thick hardback book with a red leather cover.

'My diaries,' he said.

I looked blindly at yellow pages filled with tiny letters.

'There're stories about Jimmy,' he said. 'Memories for you to keep.'

At the house, Solomon and Myer pressed gifts into Grandma's hands: a tiny brown cardigan, a small pair of reading glasses, work boots and a cap. Katz gave her a thumbnail portrait.

'Groucho Marx,' he said.

Grandma shielded her eyes and turned her head, then lashed out, knocking the presents aside, crying that she wanted Jimmy there with her, not away with the ghosts. But we gathered up the things and took them to the spirit house, where we made space for the clothes in the wardrobe in Mei-Li's room.

We all knew where Jimmy wanted to be.

SYDNEY DIARY

APRIL 1949

I have been painting for four months, but the canvas is as empty as my soul. I cannot sketch what I see in my mind, all the terror and humiliation, the hunger and hopelessness, the pointless screaming deaths. I had hoped that my facility (I can barely call it a skill, still less a talent) for art (No! Illustration!) would return within days or weeks, but I am coming to understand it has gone forever, an unspoken part of the bargain, the price I paid to survive. How can I paint with the blood of soldiers, with brushes made from their lashes and dipped in a palette of bone?

Every night I dream the same dream. I wake up in cotton sheets (and that is the cruellest part of all, the nightmare begins with an awakening) to a servant bringing breakfast on a tray. I struggle to recall how I came to employ staff. Did I paint a portrait that captured the spirit of a man (and I know which man, I know who I would have chosen) with such poetry that I won prizes, acclaim, fortune?

I look into the face of a butler, and I recognise a comrade from the war.

'You survived,' I say.

He laughs.

'We all did,' he says. 'The others are out there waiting for you. There's Foley, O'Connor, Grimshaw, Evans and Trent, the tall one they called Shorty and the thief Diamond Tom. There's White Alf and Black Alf –'

'But he died,' I protest. 'I watched them bury him.'

'The stake missed his heart,' says the butler, 'and the soil was rich with corpse meat. He ate it to survive. Now his breath stinks of the grave, and nothing, neither man nor demon, will ever conquer him.

'Come,' beckons the butler, and he leads me from my bed, through my studio, into the parlour, where a tall man sits with his back to me, and my heart cries out with happiness as he turns his head.

'Even you,' I say.

'*Even* me?' he asks. 'Wouldn't I always have been the hardest to kill? How could you ever believe I wouldn't survive?'

'But how?' I ask.

'I hid in the reeds. They put me in a basket and floated me down the river.'

'And the others?' I ask. 'White Alf and Black Alf and Foley . . .'

'Oh, they're dead,' he says.

'But the butler told me . . .'

But when I look back, the butler has gone, and the tall man has turned to bone, and his carpals and metacarpals are shattered, his femurs and radials, his pelvis and wrists, his fingers and toes are all broken into pieces, his death's-head caved in from every side.

That is how I start my day. I take breakfast alone, then return to my studio, in a gown, half-dressed, or naked. I try to paint, but when I raise my brush to the easel, a cankered hand grabs me from the grave and drags my wrist down to my waist, to hang limp and wilted, to mock my pretentions at redemption.

There have been reunions, where old friends grasp each other by the arms with wonder at the muscle that has returned, and see faces they have known only as skulls given flesh, as if a sculptor has applied a skin of clay to a wire frame. They drink beer from the bottle and sing the old songs from the camps, whose lyrics bear nuances only they will ever understand. They have a comradeship born in hell. I know because I have been told.

But I am not permitted in a ballroom or a bar with the men I loved and still love. I will always be alone, never to share my memories of butterflies and hibiscus, waterfalls and the Buddha caves, spirit houses and the very best of men.

Occasionally I receive mail from a survivor of the camps. One envelope contained a bullet and nothing else. I weighed the shell in my palm, balanced it between my thumb and forefinger, and slipped it into my service revolver. I poured myself a finger of whisky, pointed the gun at my temples and squeezed the trigger. In this, as in so many other matters, the Japanese knew best.

But the round was not live. It was not a weapon, it was a warning or a wish, a hope and a promise. I hardly eat, I barely drink water. I do not exercise or socialise or go out in the light. In my refrigerator I store only cooked rice. I ration myself to a pint a day. I eat from a dixie, boil tea in a billy, and I have buried my paintings in graves. The perfumed flesh of women holds no allure for me. I cannot remember why I was ever drawn to something so trivial.

I have sent back my medals. Each one of them weighs more than a man and when I wear them I cannot stand. I have renounced my rank and turned my back on my religion.

I take my first whisky as the sun goes down, and I force myself to think of all those men I failed.

Buddhists believe there are eight echelons of hell, and on the upper levels exist the hungry ghosts, who died violently before their time, or were orphan souls who had no children. The hungry ghosts come looking for the living at night. They have huge stomachs, necks like wire and tiny mouths like the lips of choleras. They can never get enough food to keep them from starving, and when they eat, it turns to ashes in their mouths.

The ghosts swirl around me. I drink and I drink and I drink until they are gone. Then I take myself to bed, and the dream begins again. I wake up in cotton sheets to a servant bringing breakfast on a tray.

For me, there are no trails to cut through the jungle, no loaded boats or cache of live grenades. For me, there is no way of escape.

Lieutenant Colonel William Randall Duffy

REDFERN

SATURDAY 26 MAY 1990

Katz's diaries began on Christmas Day in 1953 when Jimmy didn't come home because he heard Mei-Li was dead.

ACKNOWLEDGMENTS

Thanks to my agent, Deborah Callaghan, as always (except at the launch of my last book, when I forgot to thank her). Thanks to my publisher, Tom Gilliatt, for all the great suggestions he made, and the stupid ones he didn't (ie 'Why don't we put Jimmy in the SAS?'). Thanks to Catherine Day and Julia Stiles, my editors at Pan Macmillan. Thanks to Judith Whelan, my editor at *Good Weekend*, for encouraging and indulging my interest in the Second World War. Thanks to Claire and Ben and Sara, for putting up with me at home (especially when I wasn't drinking).

NOTE ON THE AUTHOR

Mark Dapin was born in Leeds and moved to Australia in the late 1980s. He has been editor in chief of ACP's men's magazines, and a hugely popular newspaper columnist. He has degrees in Social Policy, Art History and Journalism. His first novel, *King of the Cross*, won the Ned Kelly award. *Spirit House* is his second novel. He lives in Sydney with his partner and two children.